THE CATSITTERS

THE CATSITTERS

A NOVEL

JAMES WOLCOTT

HarperCollins*Publishers*

For Laura

HarperCollins books may be purchased for educational, business, or sales promotional use. For information, please write: Special Markets Department, HarperCollins Publishers Inc., 10 East 53rd Street, New York, NY 10022.

FIRST EDITION

Designed by The Book Design Group

Printed on acid-free paper

Library of Congress Cataloging-in-Publication Data
Wolcott, James.
    The catsitters: a novel by James Wolcott.
        p.   cm.
    ISBN 0-06-019414-6
    1. Man-woman relationships—Fiction. 2. Bachelors—Fiction. I. Title.
PS3573.O4575 C38 2001
813'.6—dc21   00-050635

01 02 03 04 ❖/RRD 10 9 8 7 6 5 4 3 2 1

ACKNOWLEDGMENTS

THE AUTHOR wishes to thank the following people for not trying to talk him out of writing this novel and making its publication possible: Sarah Gilbert, for providing the original kick-start and bolt of enthusiasm; Graydon Carter and Aimee Bell, for their tremendous support and assistance under the crisp banner of *Vanity Fair*; John Scanlon, for his hospitality at his country house in the Irish midlands, the best writer's retreat anyone could hope for; his agent, Elyse Cheney, and editor, David Hirshey, for their swashbuckling professionalism; and the top-notch proofreaders and copy editors of HarperCollins. The advice Darlene dispenses comes from a variety of sources, including manuals on sales techniques, studies of proximics in personal relations, and David Reynolds's guides to constructive living. (The "pocketbook test" should be credited to radio personality Barry Farber.)

The author also wishes to honor the memory of Gully, the most defiant and devoted of cats.

1

AT FIRST I THOUGHT IT WAS A HUMAN CRY. As the elevator stuttered open at my floor, I heard a baby wailing behind a neighbor's door, like a tiny captive. Then I realized the sound was coming from inside my apartment, growing louder and more plaintive the closer I got. I set my travel bag down on the faded patch of carpet where the welcome mat used to be before it got stolen. When I unlocked the door, she was sitting waiting for me, her green cat eyes glaring and her ears cocked. Holding the pose just long enough to make her point, Slinky returned her ears to their normal upright position and padded toward me, uttering a cry that expressed confusion, distress, and annoyance all at once. *Where have you been?* She had always been a vocal animal, but this was a note of rebuke I hadn't heard before, backed up with an impressive amount of body language for such a small animal. She paused at my feet, hunching her shoulders and looking up at me as if to lodge a formal complaint.

"I missed you, too," I said, bending to pet her. She ducked under my hand after a couple of head rubs and turned tail, heading for the kitchen. I followed, wanting to see how she had done on her breakfast.

Slinky's water bowl was dry, which was nothing unusual. She often expressed her displeasure when I was absent for a few days by smacking its rim with her paw, knocking it over and spilling water everywhere. I had learned to take the precaution of placing a pan in the sink beneath the dripping faucet, creating a temporary watering hole just in case. But her food dish was also empty, and the kitchen counter was covered with black pawprints, like a mambo diagram in a dance lesson. Fish-shaped crunchy bits were scattered all over the counter and floor where the cat had torn a fist-sized hole into the side of the catfood box. My girlfriend Nicole was supposed to catsit while I was visiting my family in Maryland, but the evidence was that Slinky had fended for herself the entire weekend. I swept the fish-shaped kibble into the palm of my hand, tossing it into the trash can. As Slinky wove between my legs, doing narrow figure-eights, I opened a can of soft food and refilled her water bowl. "Don't eat too fast," I said, stroking her back. Her black fur was matted, salted with dandruff. She looked like a Halloween cat down on her luck.

While Slinky ate, I checked the bathroom for other signs of mischief. I had gotten off lightly this time. A shredded roll of toilet paper lay on the floor in a perforated heap, but she hadn't knocked my shaving products, shampoos, and medicine bottles into the sink, as she had over the Christmas holiday. I cleaned her litter box, laying down a thin spread of baking soda below the fresh litter. I then checked the bedroom, opening the closet doors and checking for fabric holes. Under stress, Slinky sometimes became wool-eater.

The only casualty was the toe of a sock she must have pulled out of the hamper. It was one of my good socks, too, from a pair Nicole had given me for Christmas. I went through the rest of the apartment, doing damage assessment and minor tidying up. It wasn't that warm in the apartment, but after fifteen minutes I was sweating like a busboy, not so much from exertion as from anxiety building a base camp in my stomach. I took off my jacket and aired myself out a little, then grabbed a Coke from the refrigerator and sat down to figure out what might have happened. Maybe there was a problem with the duplicate keys I had made for Nicole, or maybe she had misplaced them. But why hadn't she left a message on my machine letting me know? Nothing's ever easy in New York. There's always a hitch.

It was early April, the Monday after Easter. The living-room blinds were jammed at the top of the window frame, where they refused to budge after I had yanked too hard on the cord a few months earlier. I had planned to get them fixed, but I tend to let things slide until they reach the crisis stage. I opened the window a slice to let in a breeze, then retreated to the far end of the sofa, away from the afternoon sunlight, which was beginning to beat. From where I sat I could see the stone bell tower of St. Teresa's, the bell itself as black as an old tarred cannon in the village square. Birds lined the turret, flapping their wings as they settled on the ledge. The layers of white droppings on the ledge looked like cake icing. The red light on my answering machine, which blinked when I had messages, was a solid dot. I picked up the phone, dialed Nicole's office, and got her assistant, Ty, who always spoke to me as if I were clogging the information highway.

"Nicole Price's office," Ty said.

"Hi, it's Johnny Downs. Nicole in?"

"Not at present." He was more curt than usual, speaking in very distinct syllables.

"Do you know when she's expected back?"

"She's at a clients' lunch, and I believe there may be an in-house conference afterward, but I wouldn't want to go on record with that."

In case there might be a congressional investigation later.

"Well, could you tell her I called?"

"Will do."

"Tell her she can call me after work, if that's more conven—"

"I have a messenger standing here waiting. I'll leave word you called."

I pictured Ty signing for a package with a lightning hand as I dialed Nicole's home number and left a brief message on her machine, just to cover all the bases. In the kitchen, Slinky bent over her water dish, swinging her bottom as if lining up a putt. The hair pressing against my neck began to stick. Ever since high school, my hair has gone sticky whenever I've started to worry, something I excel at. From the outside I look like a fairly cheerful, hearty sort, one of those husky types who help cushion things for all the pointy neurotics out there, but inside I always seem to have some disaster cooking. My mother says that when I was seven I had a panic attack in the planetarium, convinced that the moon was on a collision course with earth, and had to be helped to the lobby. In high school, the swim coach had to fish me out of the diving pool after my muscles seized up and I found myself sinking to the bottom looking up at everybody standing at the edge of the pool staring down (an image that still recurs in my dreams). Since college, overnight hair loss and sudden heart attack on the racquetball court have alternated as my biggest fear, even though I have a loyal head of hair and haven't played racquetball since college. Probably this time, as with the other times, there was no real cause for concern, but the more I mulled, the more bits of recent Nicole dialogue and behavior began to float to the surface, mental clips stuck in my memory like scrapbook photos pasted at an off angle. For instance, the laughing kiss Nicole gave me the night before I left for Maryland, a kiss so high-spirited it bordered on hysteria, although admittedly her happy meter was always turned up higher than mine.

Times like these, you need to consult an expert. My experience has been that when it comes to understanding women, other men are useless. They don't look, they don't listen, they don't *think* about women except in immediate payoff terms. I used to think European men had the answers until I actually met some of these fluffheads. Tending bar at private parties, I'd listen to them hold forth as they made the art of seduction sound like a class in wine appreciation. Every woman they wooed seemed to be a reflection of themselves, with breasts; they wanted to melt into their own arms. No, to get a good read on a woman you have to go to another woman, a female-professional. Every man, if he's fortunate, has a woman friend he can call for a quick scouting report on a romantic prospect, or post-mortem analysis when it all goes kaput. The friend I depended on for guidance and moral support was Darlene Ryder, formerly of Athens, Georgia, currently of Decatur, Georgia. Born in the South but spending her teenage years in New Jersey before moving back, Darlene blended a Southern belle's feminine wiles with a Northerner's no-nonsense direct aim. Even her accent would change, depending on the tack she was taking or the time of year. In the summer, I tended to get the Southern Darlene; in the winter, the Northern.

The downside of dealing with Darlene was that, like a lot of people whose brain is on speed dial, she could get testy when I couldn't keep pace with her thought process. She hated having to explain the obvious, expecting me to get everything the first time, whereas I tend to circle around a subject until I can make a comfortable decision. Darlene dealt in dead certainties and quick conclusions, which also made her more judgmental about people than I tend to be. We hadn't chatted much in recent months because, without specifying why, she seemed to have a bug up her nose about Nicole. When I sent her a snapshot of Nicole sitting in a coffee-shop booth—Darlene also does photoanalysis of people—her sole comment was "She guards her mouth, but I can see why you might find her attractive," a backhanded compliment if I ever heard one. What made her attitude puzzling was that in many ways she and Nicole were so alike, down to their glossy cheekbones, compact figures, and teasing eyes. But maybe that was the problem. Darlene herself said women could get jealous about men they didn't want, and Darlene didn't want me, not in that way. Perhaps she sensed competition in the confidante department. Whatever the reason, I was careful to underplay my feelings for Nicole when talking to Darlene, letting a lot of sentences trail off into nothing. Her negativity toward Nicole made me gun-shy about calling now.

For dinner, I made myself bachelor spaghetti with meat sauce from a jar. I sprinkled parmesan cheese on the tablecloth for Slinky, who took a running leap from the living room and landed on my shoulder, careening to the table, where she licked the cheese until there was a wet spot on the cloth. I watched TV on mute, surfing with the remote control until I came across one of my own commercials, the sixty-second one for Acorn Beer where, in a cathedral-lit bar, I play a pool hustler who sinks every shot until he burps and skids his cue stick, sending the ball dribbling sideways. "Oh, dear," an English announcer intones in a worldly, amused voice. "Next time try a better-behaved beer. Acorn. Deep-dark, yet eminently discreet. Acorn—the beer that doesn't sneak up on you." Watching the ad, I realized that it would take a giant shoehorn to squeeze me back into those crotch-hugging jeans though, I had to admit, my left dimple looked cute in the one millisecond close-up they gave me. (A close-up that was cut from the thirty-second version.) We shot the ad a year ago in a studio in Astoria, Queens, otherwise stocked with discarded soap-opera sets. Practicing pool shots with a nonchalance I hoped would be noticed, I struck up a flirtation with a crew member named Angie who stood with her legs parted like a rodeo girl in tight jeans, one hip outthrust. We rode back to Manhattan in a customized van, jostled up against each other. One thing led to another, and it all finally led to nothing.

With my thumb, I switched off the TV. Since it was still light outside, I decided to take a walk rather than just sit around and let the spaghetti settle. I put on a baseball jacket and gave my hair a quick fingercomb at the bathroom mirror. Instead of wandering the streets like a French poet, I headed across town to visit the new park in the West Village.

It was still under construction but open to the public. There was already a line at the water fountain, where a man with no visible muscles wearing a muscle T-shirt was filling his canteen. Bulldozers and portable toilets, which looked as if they had come under small-arms fire, anchored the corner of the unfinished section. I sat on one of the new benches painted a vibrant green. Opposite me was an older woman in a wide-brimmed hat, her head wrapped in a white scarf. She was smoking a cigarette as if committing each puff to memory. "I hope the smoke doesn't bother you," she said, shooing away a whitish strand.

"Oh, no," I said. "Besides, the wind's blowing the other way."

"During the day it's impossible to have a quiet smoke with all the noise and drilling."

"When are they supposed to have the whole thing finished?"

"Soon. They're dedicating the park to Edna St. Vincent Millay and putting up a statue of her. She lived in the Village, not far from here. Are you familiar with her poetry?"

"Not really. Didn't she have a lot of lovers?"

"Men worshiped her in a way men no longer worship women."

She sounded as if she knew whereof she spoke. A man pushing a shopping cart loaded with assorted old shoes passed between us. The scarved woman finished her cigarette, tapping the stub against the bench before tucking it in a tiny litter bag at her side. She stood, saying good-bye with a silent head bow. The line at the water fountain had thinned to nothing.

I hadn't visited the park on a whim. The one etched-in-stone item on Nicole's schedule was the nightly broadcast of *Bristol Junction*, an English soap opera about the rude, quarreling, yet inseparable patrons of a family-owned pub in the rundown north of England, where the wallpaper looked like brown, faded vaudeville posters. An Anglophile of sorts (her ad job often took her to London), she never missed the show, which was carried by some obscure public TV station on channel 74. I had a hard time making out a lot of the actors' mumbling, but I enjoyed watching them go at each other without apologizing for their characters' aggression or trying to gain our sympathy later by showing their soft, tender chicken parts. Under their rough exterior was a rough core. We arranged our nights together around *Bristol Junction*.

We'd order in dinner and watch the latest episode, adding our own running commentary. "Let's hit the sheets," Nicole would often say afterward, her wrists wrapped around my neck. "Let's burn a hole in them," I would say, trying to make my eyes match my tone.

When I walked home after one of these evenings (I seldom spent the night during the workweek), the air itself seemed more alive, personally mine. Sometimes I would stop and call her from a pay phone, just to let her know I was still thinking about her.

I sat on the bench, watching the little yellow rooms of the surrounding buildings come to dollhouse life as dusk became darker. A few minutes after seven, I hoisted myself off the bench. Since Nicole hadn't called, I thought I might accidentally-on-purpose check on her apartment to see if she was home. On the way I stopped to buy a newspaper so that I would have something to tuck under my arm to give my stroll that casual look.

Either I had mistimed how long it took to walk across Tenth Street or they had lengthened the blocks while I was out of town, because I didn't reach the building across from Nicole's until almost 7:25. I could see the TV light jumping on her ceiling. She was home. I headed for one of the two pay phones on the corner. I dropped a quarter into the slot and heard it ping. First I called my number to see if there had been any phone messages from Nicole. Nothing. Then I dialed Nicole's number. Her machine answered. During the outgoing message, I lifted my head. Her apartment had gone dark. An anonymous voice on the phone said, *"Leave a message after the beep and Miss Price will return your call at her earliest convenience."* Across the street a night doorman in Nicole's building bustled forward and straight-armed the door. Out stepped Nicole.

She was wearing jeans, which meant she had been home from work long enough to change. Her hair was mussed, perhaps from just having pulled the sweater she was wearing over her head. Alongside her appeared a tall man who reminded me of a ship mast. The crown of my head began to tingle. He wore straight jeans and an untucked striped shirt over a T-shirt for that alternative-rocker effect. His hair was black and duded back, with a hint of sideburns. They began to walk together, she slightly ahead of him, then he drawing up even. Although they were across the street, with moving cars in between, they were drawing parallel to the phone booth, close enough to spot me. As a moving van passed, they turned in the other direction, downtown.

I abandoned the pay phone to get a better view, following at a distance. Since they weren't holding hands or showing any overt signs of affection, I told myself that he might be a friend or a coworker paying a social call. Even at an angle, I could see air space between their bodies, an invisible wall. Nicole turned her head as she talked, but he kept his fixed forward, like a driver concentrating on the road. They looked like two people taking an ordinary stroll.

Obeying the DON'T WALK sign, a rare bit of behavior in Manhattan, they waited as traffic blurred before them, standing side by side. Slim Jim, as I had dubbed him in my mind, inclined his head slightly and said something. Whatever it was struck a chord. Nicole hopped in front of him, flung her arms around his neck, and kissed him. This wasn't a friendly-coworker or old-boyfriend kiss. It came from a deep pool of eyes-closed emotion. His hands ran up and down her sides as they kissed. Laughing when they looked and realized the light had changed, they separated and crossed the street.

I stood there a moment as everyone and everything else kept moving, feeling not so much angry and betrayed as embarrassed, singled-out—the victim of a practical joke. I wanted to wipe off whatever foolish look I had on my face, then realized that no one was paying attention to me. I was just another guy on the sidewalk. I wondered where these new sweethearts were heading. Not to his place: she wasn't carrying an overnight bag or even a purse. I began to trail them, speeding up before the traffic changed. They crossed the street in front of the multiplex, holding hands and swinging their arms like Jack and Jill going up the hill. If they were deliberately trying to taunt me, they couldn't have done a better job. Then their hands parted as they climbed the steps of a bistro called French Topping, his hand now guiding the small of her back. It was one of the classier bistros in the Village, with wooden tables, ceiling fans, hanging plants, and actual exchange-student French waitresses who smoked on the sidewalk during their breaks. From across the street, I could see them seat themselves near the window. A waitress brought menus. He held his up to his face like a book. She lay hers flat on the table and swung her head from side to side, as if overwhelmed by all the choices. Without looking at each other, they stretched their hands across the table until their fingers found each other, and interlaced. Only a week earlier we had held hands like that, across a different table.

Half-hiding behind a spray-painted van, I watched as their beers arrived in frosty mugs. It was like seeing a movie being screened only for me. I studied their eye contact. I watched each of them take thoughtful sips as the other one spoke. I watched both of them laugh at one of his witticisms. He was one of those understated humorists, you could tell by the almost invisible ventriloquist movement of his lips. He had probably spent a lot of practice time in front of the mirror perfecting his wry twinkle. They must have had quite a weekend together if she wasn't even able to drag herself out of bed to catch a cab and feed my cat, which would have taken all of forty minutes, tops.

I started to edge away from the van, trying to disengage. I felt like a certified fool, yet I couldn't bring myself to avert my eyes. It was a revelation, watching her like this. With another man, Nicole seemed to shine even more, to turn up the wattage. She looked like a promising starlet, a glamorous prize waiting to be captured and corrupted by the right wrong man. Or a promising student about to bewitch a married professor. Maybe she was radiating with the private joy of having dumped me and found someone new. As she leaned forward, her date reached over with his finger and playfully beeped her on the nose. That was something I often did, too. Didn't she ever get tired of having her nose beeped?

Their hands uncoupled as their salads arrived in wooden bowls. They spread their napkins across their laps and began taking preliminary pokes at their food with their forks. They were big forks, capable of spearing a head of lettuce.

Normally, I would have taken that as my cue to beat a stealthy retreat. Afterward, I would try to be big about it, offhand. I would pretend to be busy the next time we talked, acting blasé about our relationship and giving her an easy out. I'd let her think we were cutting each other loose. When people asked about us, I would shrug a just-one-of-those-things shrugs, implying something about sad quirks of fate and things that weren't meant to be. That was how I had done it in the past, although this was the first time I had ever actually caught a girlfriend cheating on me in open field. With the others, not that there were that many, the evidence had been more circumstantial: a matchbook with a phone number scribbled inside, a date canceled at the last minute for some flimsy reason ("A strap just broke on my favorite pair of shoes"—that may have been the all-time winner). Feeling as if a sword were entering my chest, I knew that this was different. This was more than a setback. This was a kind of verdict. Everything I had been or done in my life had led me to this moment, this humiliation. Fate had decided to put on a little show.

I started to drift down the sidewalk, letting myself be drawn into the current of foot traffic. I've always been someone who avoided confrontation, perhaps because I grew up in a household where confrontation was the chief indoor sport. But then I replayed their kiss on the sidewalk, a kiss that seemed to cut me right out of existence, and a thought flared in my mind: Why should I be the only person whose night is ruined?

Exactly, I heard Darlene say.

Why should she think she got away with something?

She shouldn't.

I crossed the street, feeling strength spreading across my shoulders and through my arms. I unsnapped the top button of my baseball jacket. I walked up the steps of the bistro, taking care not to trip and spoil my entrance, strode inside, and loomed in front of their table. And believe me, I can loom. A waitress appeared before me. Her lips moved, so I presume she spoke. I ignored her. She was just a bit player. Nicole glanced at the waitress, then shifted her eyes to what the waitress was looking at: me, looming. Nicole wiped a trace of something from her lips with her napkin and said, "Oh—*hi*." It was a statement with a tiny question mark attached. She smiled on reflex, like the ad person she was, but everything around the eyes and cheekbones went. It was like seeing a window remain intact as the rest of the building collapsed. Her date, facing away from me, continued chewing. The couple at the table behind them stared.

"Isn't this cozy?" I said. "Well, enjoy your meal and try not to choke." Then, before she could reply, I turned my back to her and left. Someone giggled behind me, a nervous laugh that didn't seem to belong to Nicole. Even her nervous laugh had more melody to it. I walked down the steps, where the Village spread out before me like a wide vista.

2

"*Now* WHAT HAVE YOU DONE?" Darlene said.

"What makes you think I've done something? Maybe I just missed talking to you. It's been a while."

"I can tell by the tone of your voice that this isn't a social call. The only time you pop your head out of the soil anymore is to pick my brain about some dimwit you're dating. It never occurs to you that I might have a life."

"It sounds like you're eating."

"I took a break on the term paper I'm doing for my suburban anthropology class and made myself a healthy late-night snack. I don't load up on candy bars, like some people."

"It sounds like fresh lettuce, real crunchy."

Darlene let that last remark sit.

"Well, I can see I've gotten you at an awkward time," I said. "Something happened to me tonight that I wanted to get your take on, but it can wait, I guess. I'll just call another time." I paused, letting the gravity of my words sink in. After her own pause, Darlene said:

"As God is my waitress, that may be the most insincere routine I've ever heard you do. How can you live with yourself?"

"It's not easy."

"I believe it. Well, if whatever you have to say is that all-fired urgent, I'll set aside the rest of my sandwich to listen to your latest exploit, but it'd better be good, not like some of the anecdotes you've told me in the past that didn't pan out."

"Actually, I think I handled this particular encounter pretty well."

"Maybe so, but you sound a little shaky. Give me a moment to get situated."

I pictured Darlene dragging the phone over to the couch, digging her heels into the cushions, and bringing her bare knees under her chin as she sipped club soda through a straw. She and I had sofas about the same size. Hers was hot-rod red, mine was basic brown. Once she was settled, Darlene said:

"Okay, spill."

"Nicole—"

"I *knew* it," Darlene said. "It was only a matter of time before she revealed her true self."

"You don't even know what she's done! I haven't told you anything yet!"

"Sorry. Go ahead."

"Nicole was supposed to catsit for me over Easter weekend."

"What happened to your regular catsitter?"

"Slinky bit her on the wrist, not hard enough to draw blood, but enough to give her a scare."

"That cat runs on pure spite."

"Anyway, when I got home this afternoon, Slinky hadn't been fed and she'd torn a hole in the box of cat nibbles. She was otherwise okay, but suppose I'd stayed an extra day? So I called Nicole's office and got her awful assistant, then left a message on her answering machine at home that she didn't return. Instead of staying home and stewing I decided . . ."

To my surprise and gratification, Darlene didn't snort, or moan, or pretend to tip over sideways while I delivered a chronology of the evening's events, as she often did when I recounted a fiasco. She understood that this fiasco was different from the rest. She made little verbal nods over the phone as I took her from point to point, from the hand-holding to the kiss on the sidewalk, even laughing with me rather than at me when I told her how I stormed the bistro. "And after I said, 'Isn't this cozy,' real sarcastic-like, I walked out and came straight home."

"And called me first-off, I hope."

"Normally, I would have. But you never seemed that enthused about Nicole, so after I got home, I—"

"No, no, no, no, no!" Darlene wailed. "Don't tell me you called her! God, I wish you hadn't done that. You make a slam-bang impression and then blow it by not leaving well enough alone. Why didn't you call me first, Johnny? I could have coached you on the next course of action. This is what happens when we don't stay in touch."

"I was going to add some choice comments about her behavior, but I never got the chance. She didn't answer the phone."

"You didn't leave some gruff message on her machine, did you?"

"Her machine didn't pick up. I guess—"

Darlene said: "Here's what probably happened. Nicole turned off the answering machine as soon as she got home because she brought the new guy back with her to spend the night and didn't want to risk getting an angry call from you. She probably turned off the ringer, too, as an additional protection. She needs time to soft-pedal what happened at the bistro. She may have told him you're a jealous ex who won't leave her alone, which makes her sound irresistible and might bring out the protector in him. Or maybe she admitted you were a boyfriend she hadn't gotten around to getting rid of. I can just hear her now. 'I feel so bad—I should have told him earlier, this is a rotten way for him to find out. But things between you and me just moved so fast.' It's harder to sell that soft line of bullshit if the phone's ringing off the hook."

"Come to think of it, Nicole sometimes unplugged her phone when I was there. She said she was receiving prank calls."

"Prank calls, my ass. What was Nicole wearing tonight?"

"Why, is it important?"

"What a woman wears is *always* important."

"Jeans, a yellow sweater, sandals . . ."

"An expensive sweater?"

"No, one I bought her for Valentine's Day. I mean it's nice, but— oh, that's just great. After having sex with some other guy, she puts on the sweater I gave her for Valentine's Day. And to think I almost bought her lingerie."

"A man should never buy a woman who isn't his wife lingerie, but that's a whole separate issue. Could you tell if she was wearing makeup?"

"No."

"No, meaning she wasn't wearing makeup, or no, you couldn't tell?"

"No, she wasn't wearing makeup. I got a good look when we made eye contact."

"Now we're cooking," Darlene said.

"We are?"

"Change your phone message tonight. Make it cheerier. And screen all your calls. Do not, I repeat, do not answer the phone. When she calls, don't return the call until you've conferred with me, no matter how happy you are to hear her voice."

"How do you know she'll call?"

"Because you caught her looking like crap. You caught her out in public in bumming-around clothes feeding her face. Pride dictates that she give you a classier kissoff. She'll want to giftwrap your behind before she officially dumps it. Remember, she's a junior ad executive, younger than you and more ambitious. You, I don't know what you are. Still and all, she won't want you blabbing that you dumped her after catching her chowing down a meal with some dude. The balance shifted when you took her by surprise. Her female ego will want to shift it back in her favor. Oh, she'll call. And when she does, we'll be ready. Until then, make no attempt to contact her. Don't call, don't write, don't go anywhere near her apartment or the building where she works. Got it?"

"Okay, okay."

"'Okay, okay' doesn't carry a lot of conviction."

"It's just— I don't get it. Everything seemed fine when I left. We even made love the night before, something we hadn't done in a while. If anything, she was friskier than usual."

"Jesus, Johnny, I just ate half a sandwich. The last thing my system needs is the image of you in the throes of ecstasy. Yuck! When are you going to learn?—sex means nothing."

"What we had was more than sex. Seeing her with him tonight really tore through me. Maybe I overreacted—maybe it was just a one-time thing with them. I don't know if I'm up for psychological warfare."

"If you want her back, you can't be your usual wobbly self. Keep in mind that she's probably in bed with this guy as we speak. Maybe they're making love, maybe she's pretending to be asleep, but I guarantee you that whatever's happening, she's awake and thinking of you. What we don't know is what she's thinking. From the photographs you sent me, she struck me as cold inside, self-centered. She'd have to be, to leave your evil cat unattended while she traipsed around with some bozo."

"Everybody's self-centered."

"You're not. I can barely get you to *think* about your own best interests, much less *do* anything about them. I wouldn't be on my high horse about Nicole if I didn't know that she was different from the other women who have dumped you or changed their identities and moved out of state. Hell, you haven't sounded so enamored with anyone since you met *me*, the joy of your existence. It made me nervous, hearing you go on and on about her—Nicole this, Nicole that—because I could sense disaster dead-ahead. You've never been willing to do what needs to be done to keep a woman, Johnny. You're like most men, oblivious. But if you're willing to be coached, we can at least win a draw with Nicole, unless, of course, you have a better plan."

"No," I said, rubbing my eye.

"Listen, I know I've been ragging you, but you handled it like a pro tonight. A lot of men would have teed off on the other guy and gone alpha-male, overreacting. You treated him like a bit player, and that's going to impress Nicole."

"Really? I thought women wanted men fighting over them."

"Not as much as we want the full focus of your attention, which is what you gave her. Now get some sleep. We can talk tomorrow. Who knows, maybe you can even ask me about my life."

"I know, you and I have some catching up to do. I think I'll take a bubble bath before I go to bed, though."

"You and your bubble baths. You're worse than Zsa Zsa Gabor."

"They help me unwind. Are you working anymore tonight?"

"No, I think I'm going to pack it in, too."

"Hey, I almost forgot: I'm up for a TV commercial where I play an exterminator who accidentally bug-bombs the wrong house."

"That sounds like something you'd do."

"I know, it's like they wrote it with me in mind. Good night, Darlene."

"'Night, Johnny."

I went into the bathroom and filled the tub with hot water, pouring in bubble bath and swirling my hand in the water. I didn't want the bubbles ganging up at one end. Then I went into the kitchen to check on the status of Slinky's water bowl and to grab a late snack. The phone rang.

"Hello?"

"'Hello,' my ass," Darlene said. "Didn't I tell you not to answer the phone? And what's that you're eating?"

"A celery stick."

"Don't lie to me, I can hear the candy wrapper rattling! Suppose it'd been Nicole who called. Suppose she heard you eating a candy bar while running your bathwater."

"I guess that wouldn't make me look very debonair."

"Johnny, you're in a category all your own. Change your machine message tonight, before you forget. Next time, it could be her."

"I'd better go check on my bathwater."

3

DARLENE AND I MET WHEN I WAS A GUEST at a theater festival hosted at the University of Georgia in Athens. I was appearing in the zillionth revival of Saroyan's *The Time of Your Life* and taking part in seminar panels and class discussions devoted to the actual working life of an actor. Our faculty hosts nodded politely at our war stories, but kept alluding to "the commercial theater" as if it were a honky-tonk in the bad part of town. One professor, who had spent his sabbatical studying the repertory system in Sweden (and had the slide show to prove it), kept scratching his eyebrow as if he were about to say something acerbic, and another felt compelled to state for the record that he considered musical comedy "a bastardized form." No one was *personally* rude or unpleasant. This wasn't New York, where people regard it their civic duty to line up and cast their vote on what type of idiot they think you are. Everyone involved understood that the panel discussions were an earnest charade, a sort of jury duty performed in order to justify the cocktail party afterward. I've never heard the word "refreshments" said so often and with such love.

During one of these punch-bowl gatherings, a couple of grad students in the drama department invited me to a weekend party at the house of Caroline Dupree. She apparently was some local legend who was pals with members of R.E.M., the B-52's, and Love Tractor, her big sunshiny head the inspiration for a series of Pop murals painted on the sides of derelict sheds and garages. Her house was on the outskirts of Athens, a three-story that looked as if it had barely survived a recent haunting. From the bottom of the bumpy, rolling lawn, the front porch seemed to buckle. Moving under the porch were round shadows that I hoped belonged to rabbits or well-fed cats. By the time I arrived, the natives were already half-naked from the humidity, head-bobbing to music blasting from stereos on every floor in a multilayered cake of sound. Psychedelic candles dripped on small tables heaped with voodoo trinkets. Plastered on the walls were scribbled-on posters of defunct TV shows and disbanded bands. The central hub of the party was the dining-room table, which offered an all-you-can-ingest buffet. I saw more coke snorted, pot smoked, and pills popped that night than I had in all my years in New York. A non-druggie myself, I wandered through the party with the customary beer in my hand, trying to make conversation with some of the cuter orgy-gals. I was making decent headway with Cyrinda (every woman I met seemed to have a groupie's name), who was wearing a semitransparent black shirt over a semi-transparent black bra that revealed not one but two nipple rings, but otherwise didn't seem that scary. "Gotta light?" she asked, raising a cigarette.

I patted my pockets apologetically and shrugged. She shrugged in return and wandered off, leaving me feeling I had flunked some sort of test. After a few minutes of resuming my role as an interested onlook-er, I instigated a conversation with an acting student I recognized from one of the panel discussions. She had the unruly thatch of hair and a far-sighted squint made for comedy; you could easily imagine her in clown makeup. She asked for the names of some good acting teachers in New York, providing me with an opportunity to wow her with some inside dope. I was about to launch into my Uta Hagen story when she asked me for directions to the bathroom. "I need to pee," she said, clarifying the situation. Not knowing the layout of the house, I gestured to the general area where I thought a bathroom might be, and drifted out to the front porch. The porch railings were lined with beer and soda cans interspersed with mosquito candles whose flames wiggled in the breeze. I could see a hearse parked on the front lawn at a reckless angle, as if it had been abandoned after a stick-up. A young woman with a serious crop of hair was sitting hunched on the hood of the hearse, watching a small fire burn out beyond the railroad tracks. A mosquito candle burned on the hood behind her, casting a fitful light on the arch of her girlish back.

I ambled down the hill, pausing alongside the hearse, as if it were a natural stopping point. Across the railroad tracks at the bottom of the hill, three or four children playing Indian were chanting and hurling batteries into the bonfire to see if they would explode. The railroad tracks shone like a silver ruler in the moonlight. The woman on the hearse wasn't watching the fire. She was scanning the low sky. She wasn't as young as she appeared from the back, but she was still young, the cheekbone nearest to me bearing a beauty mark. Around her neck were a pair of thick, hefty binoculars that looked like they had been used at the Berlin Wall.

"Tracking drug smugglers?" I said.

"Darlin'," she said, cocking her head back toward the house, "the druggies are all up *there*, battling the moths on the back porch."

"Are those night goggles?"

"Yeah. They're not mine. I borrowed them to see if they actually live up to their reputation, but so far all I'm getting is eye strain."

"Are you a bird-watcher?"

"I occasionally bird, but these weren't made for that. We're getting close to takeoff time, so if you wouldn't mind . . ."

"Okay, see you later."

"You don't have to leave, just be quiet for a bit. I need to hear. Sit on the hood if you like. Don't knock over the candle."

I eased myself on the hood and propped my feet on the front fender, taking off my jacket and draping it across my lap.

"I'm Johnny Downs," I said.

"Darlene." We shook hands. "Darlene Ryder."

"We're not scanning for UFOs, are we?"

She gently shushed me. We sat for a few minutes in radio silence, the bonfire cracking in front of us and the party raging behind.

"Hear that?" she whispered.

"Hear what?"

"That."

I listened harder and could hear a flurry of high-pitched chirps somewhere overhead.

"Here they come. Right on schedule."

Above the trees, in an erratic pipeline, poured a contingent of oddly thrown boomerangs. It was a stream of bats. Growing up in Maryland, I had occasionally seen one or two flicking under the lights of the golf course at night, but this was an entire flock, a long tail winging toward us twenty or thirty feet high. Darlene aimed her night goggles at the sky, focusing with her right thumb.

"Wow."

As the bats approached, Darlene whipped the strap from around her head and handed me the goggles. I aimed them at the sky slightly ahead of their flight pattern and saw bats like tiny green dials darting against a green Martian haze. When I handed the goggles back to Darlene, our hands brushed. She hopped off the hearse and twisted backward, tracking the flock as they flew over the party house and into the dark mass of trees behind. A burst of light from the bonfire flames gave me a good look at the back half of a firm little figure, bare legs, and a nuzzable neck.

"They're heading to Cody's Swamp, where all the bugs are," Darlene said. "It's dinner time for them. Well, that was a good ob."

"Ob?"

"Observation."

"Oh. You do this every night?"

"When it's clear. I'm building a bat sanctuary in my backyard so that I can do a more close-up study. I'm not telling my neighbor because I know it would just make her hair spring out. Could you see anything in the goggles?"

"Just a bunch of herky-jerky specks."

"There's an old Indian trick of sitting in the dark with your eyes closed for twenty minutes. Then, when you open them, it's like you have night vision. I tried it once, but got impatient and couldn't keep my eyes shut long enough, but maybe it'd work for you."

"I don't know, I might fall asleep. You want to head back to the party?"

Out of the darkness a voice called: "Hey, Batwoman!"

"Hey, Josh!"

"Were they out in force tonight?"

"The whole squadron."

"Seen Caroline yet?"

"No, I heard she got pulled over for speeding and sassed the trooper, so they've got her locked up until her sister posts bail."

"Who's watching the house?"

"Doug."

"Man, this place'll be cinders by morning. You staying?"

"No, I'm peeling out," Darlene said.

"Well, catch y'all later."

As we descended the hill, the bonfire smoldering ahead, Darlene asked, "Would you like to grab something to eat? My car's parked down near the ditch."

"Sure, but I'm treating. I insist."

"Whoa, a gentleman," she said, waving her hands like Jimmy Stewart whirling into the vortex in *Vertigo*.

"Are gentlemen that scarce around here?"

"Gentlemen, no—men offering to pay, yes. Too many of the men around here are bisexuals, and bisexuals are natural moochers, if you ask me. They're always trying to borrow money to pay for their amorphous lifestyle."

"What about the Athens women? Are they all bi?"

"Most of them don't know *what* they are. Do enough drugs and everything turns into Jell-O until one wiggly shape's as good as another. That's my theory."

It was dark as we approached Darlene's car, a Honda Civic with a Day-Glo University of Georgia decal in the window. Climbing in, I knocked my knee on a flashlight magnetized to the dashboard. After storing her night goggles under the seat, Darlene turned on the overhead light and checked her face in the mirror, dabbing at her auburn curls. Her eyes were an inky blue, her eyebrows a rich chocolate-brown. "Are you buckled up?" she said. "I don't want you flying through the windshield if I have to make a sudden stop. I thought we might take a spin by the Waffle House, unless you have something fancier in mind, moneybags."

"No, the Waffle House sounds fine."

We eased away from the ditch and on to a proper road. Darlene was a good driver, though she hit the curves hard. We wheeled into the Waffle House just as a man picking his teeth was exiting through the front door, followed by his wife, who was carrying her pocketbook in both arms, a mysterious habit some middle-aged women seem to have adopted from who knows where. Inside, Darlene greeted the counter waitress by her first name and headed toward a booth, not breaking stride until she slid into her side of the booth and plucked a menu from the holder in one smooth motion.

After we ordered, Darlene told me some stuff about herself and I told her some stuff about me. She drummed the tabletop with her fingers, not impatiently or nervously but as if she had a nice rhythm going in her head. Her smile seemed to travel across her face before reaching her lips. Leaning forward and giving me her eyes, Darlene said:

"Do you have a girlfriend? Don't get your hopes up—I'm not coming on to you."

"You're not?"

"No. You couldn't handle this much dynamite."

"Don't be too sure of that. I've dated some real divas. Anyway, no, I'm not currently seeing anyone."

"I figured as much. Before I went out to the hearse, I saw you inside the house, and you were scanning the room the way men do when they're on the make. Your eyes got that bullet stare. It's a hard look—not hostile necessarily, but hard." Darlene imitated it for me.

"God, you make me look like a hired killer."

"Well, I'm exaggerating some, but you were definitely checking out the available selections, so I figured either you didn't have a girlfriend or you were looking for a little side-action. From that suede jacket I could tell you weren't a local."

I described the young woman with the see-through outfit, and Darlene nodded.

"If you'd hung around long enough, she might have succumbed, but you would have had a ragdoll on your hands. These druggies turn rubbery real fast."

"Well, while she was still conscious, she clicked off on me like *that.* This other one, too. It's been happening a lot lately. Guess I'm going through a lull."

"How long's this 'lull' been?"

"Six or seven months, since my last relationship ended. We just sort of stopped calling each other. Meeting women is usually no problem for me, it's getting past the early hurdles. I seem to trip up midway through."

"Where do you meet all these women?"

"I'm what's known as an actor-slash-bartender."

Darlene and I swung our legs to the side of the booth as a tired busboy mopped the floor. Darlene said:

"So the problem isn't lack of opportunity. I wish I could watch you in action, see what you're doing wrong. It's probably something easily fixable. How long will you be around?"

"There's a local production I have to attend tomorrow night, along with a party afterward at some theater professor's house. It's the final bash."

Darlene said: "Here's what we'll do. Take me to the party as your date. I won't hang at your side, I'll mingle and keep you under discreet ob. You chat up a few of the female guests and I'll study your 'technique' and see why you keep whiffing out."

"It'll make me self-conscious, being watched like that."

"You're an actor, you should be used to it! Besides, these parties are always swarming, it's not as if you're under a spotlight."

"All right. Would you like to see the play first?"

"No, I get antsy sitting in a theater. It never moves fast enough for me. Some actors take forever just crossing the stage to answer the damn phone. Let's meet outside afterward and I'll drive us over."

"Why are you offering to do all this for me?"

"Are you kidding? It'll be fun. There's nothing more interesting than people-watching, and the best place to watch people is at a party. If anybody ever wrote a decent book on the psychodramatics of parties, they could *clean up*. Besides, you seem like an okay guy. You didn't make fun of my interest in bats, like most people do, or change the subject to something involving you, the way most *men* do. And I admire the fact that you wore a nice jacket to the party and put it back on before we walked in. That was very gentlemanly of you."

"Actually, I put it back on to cover my sweat stains."

"Oh, gross!" Darlene cried, tossing a crumpled napkin at me. We talked a while longer, her eyes darting out the window to the parking lot every now and then, making sure no one was messing with her car.

4

THE PLAY PERFORMED BY the graduate theater department was a minor Philip Barry drawing-room comedy that no amount of furniture polish could restore. The lead actress made a gaspingly beautiful entrance in a shimmery gown that flowed like liquid diamonds, but like the rest of the cast, she spoke as if she were christening a ship. Two hours of enunciation is wearing. I applauded hard at the end, though, to show that I wasn't some New York snob.

Darlene was standing in front of her Civic, wearing a black cocktail dress, a small black pocketbook hanging off one shoulder. She was wearing sheer stockings, which I have a weakness for. I twirled a finger in the air to let her know her outfit was a winner. "Did you have to wait long?" I said.

"A few minutes. Do you think this skirt is too short?"

"I love questions like that. Maybe we should skip the party and take a drive somewhere."

"You wish. Come on, lover boy, let's go. We want to get to the party relatively early to scope out the place. It's always important to know where the bathrooms are, and if there are any side doors for a discreet exit. Also, this professor's wife is probably the hostess, and hostesses always appreciate it when guests arrive before the main crush and help get the party started. Are my shoes okay?"

"Oh, yeah. Sex-y."

"Get in the car."

Darlene drove to a tree-lined street in what seemed like an ideal neighborhood to raise freckled kids. Behind the windows we passed, families were watching TV together and not tearing each other limb from limb. When we arrived at the right address, we remained in the car to take a close look at the house, like bank robbers scoping out a savings and loan. We were early. Ours was only the third car on the curb. Behind a table set up in the living room, a student bartender was fiddling with his bow tie, trying to get it even. Darlene said:

"First, we introduce ourselves to the hostess and compliment her on how everything looks. Be specific, don't just say something nice for the sake of saying it. Volunteer to help carry a bowl or something. They'll be floored at a Yankee showing good manners."

"I'm not really a Yankee, Darlene. I was raised in Maryland, which technically is below the Mason-Dixon Line."

"It's also above Washington, D.C., which is everybody's cut-off point down here. After we get our drinks, you pay me a lot of attention while we chat. We don't want to look as if we're casing the place. Once more guests arrive, I'll excuse myself and leave you to your own devices. When you mingle, be sure to pay attention to the faculty wives. Most of these women get all dressed up for these things and find themselves stranded because their pretentious husbands are either engaged in shoptalk with other men or are chatting up with students in the hope of 'mentoring' them into the sack. So introduce yourself and say something nice about their outfits without getting too flirty. Some of these women are hot to trot and you do not want to get them ignited, especially after they've had a couple of cocktails."

"So why even—?"

"Because it'll make them feel it was worth it making the effort they made to look good tonight, and a smart man wants to please every woman, not just the ones he's angling to ask out. Also, the unattached women will have their interest piqued—they'll be watching a stranger being gracious to women they take for granted and wondering why you haven't made a beeline for them. Too many men make the mistake of indulging the sexual arrogance of younger women."

"That's often been my downfall."

"Be sure not to eat anything that might spill. Somebody sees you wiping off mayonnaise, the party's pretty much over for you."

"I can eat without getting stuff on me."

"Do I have too much lipstick on?" Darlene said, checking herself in the rearview mirror.

"No."

"Okay—let's go."

We put on our party faces and introduced ourselves to the hostess, Margaret Lilyfield, a trim, attractive woman with long, bare arms that must have looked lyrical when they were raised above her head. "My husband should be along shortly," she said. "You must have rushed straight from the play."

"There wasn't a whole lot of traffic," I said. Darlene gave me an invisible nudge. "The house looks beautiful. I love the flower arrangements."

"They're from my garden."

"I should have known."

When our hostess took leave to greet new arrivals, Darlene said: "'I love the flower arrangements.' You sounded almost gay."

"Well, those things happen."

"That woman who just walked in—she's a TA in the psych department, just separated from her husband. I'll introduce you, then let you get acquainted."

The teaching assistant was wearing a V-necked black dress, high heels, and dangly earrings. Her hair was cut in this dynamic, asymmetrical way that must have been a radical departure from whatever hairstyle she had before, judging from the compliments she was getting from other guests. When women reenter active duty on the dating circuit, they put a lot more into it than men do. She and Darlene exchanged flapping handwaves and after saying their hellos Darlene drew her over to introduce us. Her name was Paula, a good, full-bodied name for a woman. Darlene explained that I was visiting from New York, and Paula's eyes fastened on me with interest. Being a visitor from New York made me fresh, out-of-state produce, not part of the local gossip mill. I fetched Paula and myself a couple of gin-and-tonics while she and Darlene chatted. When I handed Paula her drink, Darlene said, "I should say hello to Professor Briar. Can I trust you two alone?"

"Of course," I said with a worldly manner. "So," I said when we were alone, "Darlene tells me you're in the psych department."

"Are you two friends?" she asked.

"Only just met, actually. I've met some wonderful people on this trip."

"I'm doing my Ph.D. on Gestalt therapy as improvisational theater," Paula said. "You'd probably find the topic trey boring."

"Not at all. But I thought Gestalt therapy fizzled out in the seventies."

"It did, but the use of the 'hot seat' has mutated into every part of our culture."

The party grew and swirled around us. Paula asked me what my impressions were of the Philip Barry play, and I ventured a few opinions on the problems with period revivals. This led to a story about a drawing-room comedy I had acted in where I had to wear an ascot that poofed up when I sat down. Paula laughed, so I related another story at my own expense about being bothered by a bee in the middle of a big speech during a summer stock production of . . .

No sooner had I reached the punch line when Darlene suddenly appeared and said in a somewhat wifely voice, "Johnny, may I see you in the kitchen? Sorry, Paula, we won't be but a minute."

I followed Darlene into the kitchen, passing a student helper carrying out reinforcements of onion dip. The swinging door closed behind him. Darlene waited a beat and kicked me in the shin.

"Yow!"

"You're lucky I aimed for the shins. What are you doing out there?"

"I was telling her some theater stories. She seemed to find them amusing."

"'Seemed' is right! She was dying on her feet! I was afraid she was going to keel over!"

"I think you're exaggerating."

"How would you know? You weren't even making eye contact! It's like somebody stuck a quarter in you and you started doing your greatest hits. And I'll tell you something that seems to have escaped your notice: While you were waving your arms around like a bandleader, regaling her with your wit, *she was standing there with an empty glass.*"

"I'll draw her out about herself when we get back out there."

"It's too late for that. You've tortured that poor woman enough for one evening. Let's find someone else, only this time *no* anecdotes and *no* imitating a windmill."

"I guess this is what they call 'constructive criticism.'"

Darlene's shoe tapped against the kitchen floor. "Here's what you do. Stand in the doorway and see if any woman is standing with an empty or near-empty glass in her hand. Then go up to her, I don't care how attractive or unattractive or not-your-type you think she is, and say, 'I couldn't help notice you seem to be running low. Could I refresh that for you?'"

"Suppose she says no?"

"She won't. No woman wants to stand around with an empty glass, it makes her feel like a wallflower. Whatever happens, introduce yourself, ask her a question about herself, and then put a lock on it and *listen*. If I see you need rescuing, I'll pop in."

I went to the bar and asked for a Coke, turned, and did a quick recon of the room. Most of the guests were gathered in bunches, but standing by the piano was an oval-faced woman with pre-Raphaelite hair, dressed in a dark gown. In her hands was an almost empty glass. She was listening to a shorter woman whose body language was a geometric model of tension points. I set my Coke on the bar and ventured toward them. As I approached, the woman with the pre-Raphaelite hair lifted her head and presented a neutral smile, as if trying to decipher whether I was someone familiar or a possible pest. The other woman simply squinted at me.

"I hope you won't find me forward, but I couldn't help noticing your glass was empty. Would you like me to refill it for you?"

"Are you part of the help?"

"'No, I'm just a roving angel making my earthly rounds,'" I said, reciting a line from the Philip Barry play. To the other woman, I said, "How about you? How are you holding out?"

"I'm holding out fine."

From her sulky tone I realized she wouldn't stay long after I returned. She'd finish her drink, poison the atmosphere for a few minutes, then make a curt exit. Which is more or less what happened. I refrained from making any remarks about her once she was gone. Instead, I questioned the woman with the pre-Raphaelite hair about herself. Her name was Penelope, Penny for short. Although she looked like a concert pianist, her vocation was theatrical design; she had designed the sets for tonight's production. She wasn't interested in talking shop, however. Circling around a sore spot, she finally told me she had just had a fight with her boyfriend, who refused to attend the party. I denounced him as an unfeeling cad and agreed with everything she said about him until she reversed course and began mentioning his good points, which I also agreed with, showing I could see all sides of a situation. I rested my arm on the piano behind her, providing a bar of support as she asked me questions about myself that I converted into follow-up questions about her. I kept calling her by her full name. "You can call me Penny," she said with a modest air.

"I know, but 'Penelope' has a flow to it that seems to suit your personality."

"I have a sister named Pandora. You can imagine the teasing she got in high school. 'Pandora's box,' and so on."

"Did it traumatize her?"

"No, our parents taught us to rise above."

Darlene, standing in the kitchen doorway, flashed me the OK sign. I returned my attention to Penelope, who was tapping her tiny straw into her drink. Although I was scheduled to return to New York the following afternoon, I phoned my catsitter and arranged to stay in Athens another few days, spending part of the time with Penny and the rest of it with Darlene, who drove me around and showed me her favorite bat spots. One night we went to the 40 Watt Club and danced like fools. Those were the days that sealed our friendship.

5

IN THE DAYS THAT FOLLOWED my run-in with Nicole, it took
all of my willpower not to cruise past her building to see if her apartment light was on. The immediate radius of her apartment building I
designated as Nicole Territory, off-limits by order of Darlene. I took a
different route to reach the restaurant where I worked four days a week
as assistant beverage manager and lunch-shift bartender so that I could
circumvent her subway stop. After my shift, the hours lay like bricks.
Girlfriendless again, I only had myself to keep me occupied. I tried to
keep myself distracted, but I was so antsy that I couldn't pay attention
to what was supposed to be distracting me. When I tried to read, my
mind bounced off the page like a fly off a windowscreen. I couldn't
watch TV without changing channels blinking-fast. I plugged in my
jukebox and played the same Roy Orbison single until my next-door
neighbor pounded on the wall. I thought that if I threw myself into the
deep end of self-pity, all the hurt I was feeling would be over with
faster.

Playing fetch with Slinky, tossing a catnip mouse which she chased
and returned as if it were a fresh kill, I found one of Nicole's butterfly
barrettes, blue with gold trim. She had worn it the night we went to the
ballet at Lincoln Center. A snowstorm the night before had made walking tricky, so we held hands crossing the streets, taking tiny steps on
the gray ice. After the ballet Nicole peeled off a glove and slipped her

hand into mine. I had left my own gloves at home. We walked along the wall at Central Park South, past the Plaza Hotel and the carriage horses, their breath blowing baby ghosts of vapor into the cold black air. Winter-wonderland conditions released Nicole from her work obsession, reminding her of her childhood in New Hampshire, where her parents, now divorced, ran an inn. She once showed me a picture of herself in a snowsuit, beaming at the camera with her mittened hands stiff at her sides, as if she were imitating a penguin. Her beaming face seemed to welcome anything the world might show. As we were walking along the stone wall, one of the coachmen rang sleigh bells and Nicole turned and kissed me as if I had been the one who made the whole evening happen, from snowfall to sleigh bells. The cold sprung tears from my eyes, giving the street lights a Van Gogh ripple. That night was the first we spent together, a night that extended into an entire weekend. I put the barrette into the drawer of the telephone stand for safekeeping.

Devoid of action, my apartment seemed like a stage set in which all the inessential props had been cleared, leaving the telephone, the answering machine, and the sofa. My nerves spiked each time the phone rang, thinking it might be Nicole. After two rings, my answering machine (an old clunker whose sharp, complicated clicks sounded like a sequence of karate moves), would pick up and play the new greeting Darlene had me record: "Hi, this is Johnny Downs . . . lay it on me after the beep." I monitored the incoming messages through the puny speaker.

My agent, Marjorie, called to relay the news that I didn't get the exterminator ad. She tried to console me by saying, "They opted for someone nerdy."

My former roommate and best friend Tom Gleason also left a message. "Downs. Do you have a fresh shirt I could borrow? I'm tending bar tonight and all my whites are in the hamper."

Darlene preached patience: "She's going to call, I can feel it. She doesn't want to appear too eager. When she phones, she's going to sound as if she's trying to sneak a pitch past one of her clients. Breezy, carefree, swiveling in her chair . . . like she's doing you a favor. She'd like nothing more than to draw a line through your name on her Things To Do list. How are you holding up, pardner?"

As I began to mention my upset stomach, there was a call-waiting click on the line.

"Don't answer that!" Darlene said. "Hang up—I bet it's her."

I hung up. The machine kicked into its karate act. I fiddled with the speaker control and heard Gleason say:

"Downs. I know you're home because you never go anywhere. Don't make me have to tend bar tonight in a yellow shirt. You know yellow makes me look pasty. This is a bar that draws serious babe traffic, and I'm counting on you to bail me out. By the way, I'm reading an old paperback I bought on the street by this former FBI agent who infiltrated the Black Panthers in the sixties. It's pretty wild. Maybe I could loan it to you when you drop off the shirt. I've marked the really cool parts."

I relayed Gleason's problem to Darlene, who said:

"You can't go. I forbid it."

"You forbid it? Who made you queen?"

"I know you. You'll take Gleason a white shirt, visit him at the bar later for a free beer, start dropping little hints, and end up spilling the whole story. You do not want him knowing you've been dumped again. He'll start telling you how to handle women. If he knew how to handle women, he wouldn't be living in squalor."

"You've never even seen his apartment."

"I did, too. It came to me in a dream. I'm going away with Clete for the weekend, but keep me posted if anything happens."

"Clete?" In the four years I had known Darlene, she had mentioned a multitude of names, all of whom for one reason or another had failed to qualify for marriage finals, but this candidate was new to me.

"We started seeing each other around the time you and I were out of touch because you and what's-her-name were in your own little orbit. This will be our first romantic weekend together, so I'm a little nervous."

"You, nervous?"

"I have to restrain myself with men I'm interested in, try not to overwhelm them. You wouldn't believe how sweet and feminine I can be with a potential fiancé. I wear little pleated skirts and everything. Men *love* pleated skirts, especially when you twirl."

"Aside from that cocktail dress, I've never seen you in anything other than hiking shorts."

"I have great legs, admit it."

"I would never deny it. Where are you going?"

"A little island resort off the Carolinas with a beautiful golf course. Clete thinks he's going to shoot a few rounds of golf, ha ha. He's even bringing his good set of clubs. I've got news: The only putting he's going to be doing is into my little hole. 'I've got your hole-in-one, honey, right here. I'll show you exactly which club to use.'"

"Darlene, what's gotten into you? I've never heard you talk this way before."

"Nothing's gotten into me—yet. But I feel a trembling urge coming on."

"Okay, I'm hanging up. Send me a postcard, assuming the two of you don't destroy the island with your lovemaking. And good luck."

"I don't need luck; luck is for losers. But thanks for the thought."

6

BUZZY'S IS A SMALL STEAK HOUSE in the West Village catering mostly to locals. Tourists tend to like their steak houses bigger, noisier, and more midtown. Buzzy's bar is dark and cozy, an interim spot for diners waiting for their table to be cleared or a companion to arrive. The dedicated drinkers go next door to Slannery's Ale House, where there's sawdust on the floor, a dartboard, TVs at each end of the bar, and NYU students high-fiving each other every time there's a touchdown or three-point shot or something equally monumental. Most of our lunch crowd consists of business professionals who ration their booze intake, not wanting to waltz back to the office with that mad-prophet stare some midday drinkers get. So even on busy days I don't have that many drinks to mix, the downside being I don't make much in the way of tips. It's like operating a barbershop in the slow part of town.

After my shift, I ate lunch at the beverage manager's desk in the back office, whose one window, facing a dry cleaner's duct, was permanent-ly taped over. A rotating fan on top of a filing cabinet fluttered the faded memos on the bulletin boards. I was leafing through the latest issue of *Beverage Technology Today,* a suprisingly thick magazine for such a limited subscriber base, when Lyle, the day manager, entered the office.

"Does Dave know you're eating at his desk?" he asked.

"He gave me his express permission. After all, I am the assistant beverage manager, and with that title comes certain . . ."

"Personally, I don't give a squat, I just don't want to catch shit from Dave if something on his desk gets messed up."

A lean man with a leathery tan, Lyle looked like a relief pitcher who couldn't get the big outs. He slid sideways into the chair at his metal desk, which was twice the size of Dave's. Pulling open the top drawer of his desk with a vehemence that suggested he thought someone or something was hiding there, he removed a stapler; punching with the heel of his hand, he stapled a set of pages from his in-box. He tapped the pages of some other papers on his desk to even them up, and stapled those together. He slid both sets of documents into his out-box and returned the stapler to its drawer. Then he leaned back in his chair, taking a breather after all this activity.

"You look tired, Downs. You were dragging behind the bar today."

"Rough night's sleep."

"I thought maybe you were hungover. All that partying."

"Yeah, all that partying I do."

"At least you can take a nap later. I'm stuck here all afternoon."

"A mother's work is never done."

"Downs, I need to place a call," Lyle said, gripping his phone. "If you don't mind."

"No, I don't mind," I said, turning over a page in *Beverage Technology Today* to a spread on silver-plated nozzles in a new sports bar in Denver.

"It's a personal call," Lyle said, straightening his arm and gripping the phone as if intending to hold it hostage. I took a final sip of soda, formally closing the copy of *Beverage Technology Today* and putting it back where I'd found it. I returned to the bar to leave a note for the night bartender regarding a fountain pen a customer had lost. Afternoon sun slanted through the front windows, plunging the dining room into knife-edged shadow. Two of the newer waitresses sat across a table with their heads slightly bowed, folding napkins in a cone of light. They looked like seamstresses in a Dutch painting. Each folded napkin was added to a growing stack at their sides. I thought they were in their own world until the one with her back to the light looked up at me and smiled. She patted her hand a few inches from her mouth, pretending to yawn, and went back to her folding.

7

IT HAD BEEN A RAINY, overcast spring, null and gray, then one day everything burst into lush green, as if nature had exploded from a giant flowerpot. During my off hours I sat in the new park, people-watching and skimming the casting pages of *New York Stage*, circling audition possibilities. There weren't many to circle. Most of the commercial work had shifted to the West Coast, and the theater was in one of its limbo phases. One night I found a couple of telephone messages waiting for me when I got home. The first was from Gleason, the second from Nicole. I saved them and called Darlene.

"Dial my number," I told her, "and when you hear the outgoing message, hit 232. You'll be able to hear her message."

"Hi, Johnny, it's Nicole. I've been tied up in sales conferences for what seems like forever. Have you been watching *Bristol Junction*? I can't believe Darla went off for the weekend with that architect! He's obviously married from the way he keeps scratching his ring finger. Oh, well, give me a call when you're around. Bye-ee."

"So what do you think?"

"Well, she sounds cocky, but her voice cracks in a couple spots. She couldn't really carry off that 'bye-ee.' By the way, is that her usual good-bye?"

"No. She usually says 'See-ya!'"

"Her confidence is a little shaky—she sounds as if she'd like to talk to you, but doesn't want to seem too eager. What's *Bristol Junction?*"

"This British soap opera about these lowlifes who hang out at a pub by the train station."

"Tape some episodes for me. It sounds wonderful."

"Never mind that, what do we do now?"

"Nothing. She expects you to pounce on the phone once you've gotten her message. She thinks you won't be able to resist hearing her gurgling voice. Don't call her back, and I bet you'll start getting hang-up calls tomorrow night. Why don't you get Caller ID so you can make sure it's her?"

"Isn't there something more proactive we can do?"

"In this case, waiting *is* a form of action. So few people can wait anymore—everyone's so impatient—that a person who can wait has reserve strength denied to all those impulsive types. Hang in there, bub. Now if you'll forgive me, I've got books to hit. I intend to get my degree despite your love life."

I was once camped out on Darlene's sofa as she worked on a term paper, her reading glasses perched on her nose as she rifled through three or four books on the Formica table, a set of highlighter pens spread out at her side like workman's tools. She used four different highlighter colors, each corresponding to the degree of importance of the passage. Darlene studied as if she were a general bending over a map, establishing lines of attack. Once she was in "the zone," studywise, she was like Zorro with those highlighters, zip, zip, zip. After an hour or so she snapped her books shut and we went for a drive to visit a friend of hers who sold vintage gas-station signs, which he had nailed to his front porch.

As Darlene predicted, the hang-up calls began the next evening. There were two of them, within a half hour of each other.

"You keep telling me you're an actor," Darlene said. "Let's see what kind of an actor you really are. Those hang-up calls were obviously from her. We don't want her getting too discouraged, so wait out the weekend and phone her at the office Monday afternoon. Speak to her assistant and say, 'Please tell Nicole that I'll be home tonight between

six and eight. Will she receive the message this afternoon? Thank you.'
If he tries to put you through directly to Nicole, insist on leaving a
message. It keeps you aloof and builds up a sense of anticipation. She'll
probably call in the second hour, so as not to seem too eager."

"And when she calls?"

"Keep it crisp. Didn't you once tell me she keeps an egg timer on her
desk?"

"So that she doesn't let callers drone on too long. She likes to tell this
story about how after one tedious phone call in the office, she cried
aloud, 'Don't people realize my time is *short* and *precious?*'"

"Exactly. So no chitchat. Tell her it's important that you meet in person to discuss your relationship. She won't refuse—she's intrigued
now. Once she agrees, thank her for calling and make it sound as if
you're entering her into your diary. In fact, do that in your notebook.
Let her hear the scratch. She won't be expecting anything that busi-
nesslike from you."

"Where should we meet? There was this place she liked, the Green
Hornet."

"Your apartment. You want to be able to stage-manage every move
and detail. This is going to be the last best shot you'll have to read her
face and body and voice, to see if there's any feeling left. You don't want
this to be a pseudo date with drinking and chuckling at each other's
remarks and all that crap. You want this meeting to be definitive. You
man, she woman."

"I just think a restaurant would be more amenable."

"You can go out to a restaurant afterward if things click."

The next day, after some deep breathing and silent rehearsal in my
head, I phoned Nicole's office and left word with Ty, who for once didn't
give me the flick. As Darlene predicted, Nicole phoned a little after seven.

"My, aren't we mysterious?" she murmured when I picked up the
phone.

"Not at all."

"I've been feeling awful about the way things happened."

"Me too."

"I've had trouble sleeping," she said.

Since Nicole had always been an instant snoozer, able to block out
the world the second her eyes closed in bed, this was an admission of
vulnerability she knew I would understand. It seemed all the more inti-

mate for being expressed as a plain statement of fact. Hearing her voice, not filtered through an answering machine but fresh in my ear, her words clicking like dominoes, I felt there was nothing wrong between us that couldn't be fixed with the right words and deeds. I was tempted to tell her that I hadn't been able to sleep either, that there was nothing I wanted more than to have her head resting on my shoulder again as I stroked her hair. Since Darlene's plans had brought us this far, however, I decided not to gum things up and stuck to the script. As a woman, Darlene was able to put herself in Nicole's brain module and anticipate her moves in a way that I wasn't.

"You're not going to trap me in your apartment and try anything funny, are you?" Nicole said with wee too much jauntiness.

"Of course not. I just think we need to talk one on one, without distractions."

"We could order in, if we get hungry. Or go out, whatever."

I took this as a good sign, an indication that Nicole wanted to de-escalate the crisis, maybe make a new start.

"Should I bring anything over to drink?"

Another good sign.

"No, no, I'll handle things. See you then."

After I hung up, I stretched out my legs and stroked Slinky, who had been loyally sitting at my side. I speed-dialed Darlene.

"She walked right into the net!" she exulted. "I wish you'd taped the call. God, I'd love to hear it. How did she sound?"

"Up, except when she confessed she's been having trouble sleeping. Darlene, I'm not sure I can handle this. I really wanted to hash it out with her just now without playing any head games. Why can't I just be honest with her?"

"Please, Johnny, you of all people. If everyone was honest and direct and truly knew what they wanted, we wouldn't need actors, or movies, or novels, or any other form of make-believe. We could just fill out questionnaires to find the proper mate. Intrigue taps depths of response you didn't know were there. Which woman would make a greater impression on you, a woman who tells you exactly what she's looking for in a relationship the first time you meet, or someone who asks you to light her cigarette, and as the cigarette is lit, touches you with a tap on the inside of your wrist without saying a word? From what you told me, Nicole wasn't exactly subtle in the way she picked you up."

"Nobody picked anybody up," I said. "It was a mutual attraction."

Nicole and I met at a product launch for Vivace skincare. I was in the TV ad, playing a dermatologist in a white lab coat; Nicole, I discovered later, was handling the print account. She was entertaining clients and I saw that her glass was dry. Remembering my lesson from the party Darlene and I had attended in Athens, I offered to fetch her a refill, which had the nice side effect of making the two men flirting with her look like inconsiderate logs. We hit it off immediately and left the party together, sharing a taxi downtown. Mine was the first stop. Before I got out, she wrote her phone number on my hand with a pen she borrowed from the cabbie. Darlene said:

"Well, whoever made the first move, I bet she ran tests on you that you weren't even aware of. As I recall, she broke a number of dates with you."

"Just a couple."

"And you didn't call her on it, did you?"

"No. She had good excuses."

"Right. Excuses with penises attached."

"Are you implying she was cheating on me all along?"

"Are you sure she wasn't? Listen, did she apologize at all just now?"

"She said she felt awful about the way things had happened."

"Typical. She didn't say 'I feel awful about what happened,' she said 'I feel awful about the *way* things happened.' In other words, she isn't sorry about what she did, she's sorry she got caught. She's like a celebrity, more concerned with bad publicity than the actual act. Nicole only cares about your feelings insofar as they create embarrassment or complications for her."

"Maybe. But taken out of context, anyone's words can sound cold."

"Well, maybe if you had taped the call, I would have been able to hear her warm, womanly tones," Darlene said in a slightly sing-song voice.

"I can see we've reached an impasse," I said. "Listen, I'm running late. I promised to meet Gleason for a drink uptown."

"Okay, but remember what I said about not spilling the beans about you and Nicole. He'll just gloat and give you contrary male advice based on his own dicking around. He strikes me as one of those guys who secretly wants to be a pimp."

"Well, he does better with women than I do."

"What kind of women?" Darlene said. "The kind you fish off the floor at closing time? The kind who write to inmates on death row? He's never going to change, and he's got just enough going for him to be a bad example to others. That's what makes him dangerous."

"He speaks kindly of you."

"No, he doesn't. And tell him I didn't appreciate the remarks he made about my meager breasts when I last visited. They may be small, but they're peppy."

8

A VOLCANIC STEAM CLOUD from a hot-dog wagon obscured my view of Gleason standing at the front door of Yancy's, the bar where we'd agreed to meet. Slumped against the wall with his arms crossed, he was wearing a green plaid shirt over a pair of husky jeans and work-boots, not that he ever did any work requiring boots. At his feet was a striped bag of laundry.

As I crossed the sidewalk, Gleason pointed to a brown patch I might want to avoid. I sidestepped it in one snappy move.

"Gleason."

"Downs."

"You got your hair cut. It looks good combed back."

"Don't try to sweet-talk me," Gleason said. "You're one of the few guys I know near my size, and you couldn't loan me an emergency shirt? Thanks to you, I had to wear a yellow one with a brown vest and listen to Burger King jokes all night. 'Oh, bartender, do fries come with this drink?'—'No, but my fist comes with your face.'"

"Did you actually say that?"

"Numerous times, under my breath. You could have at least called me back."

"I've been busy working."

"Liar," Gleason said, lifting his laundry bag with the dignity of an American laborer.

"If you don't mind my asking, is that clean or dirty laundry?"

"Clean laundry. I wouldn't bring dirty laundry into a bar. You know me better than that. I should warn you, though—this place is kind of a pit. It used to be a leather bar."

Gleason and I stepped into the cool dark. It was like entering a mine shaft, or an abandoned railroad car. Whatever the bar had been before, there was now a defeated odor of old men and mopped floors. The arrow on an unlit neon beer sign was broken at the tip. The plastic covering on the cigarette machine had yellowed. The jukebox, older than mine, was dark, its electrical plug jammed into the change-return holder. In the corner was an old-fashioned telephone booth with a folding door and compact seat. There was only one patron, an old woman with a venerable bra strap showing. Her pocketbook was planted on the bar, where she could keep an eye on it.

I was wondering why Gleason had invited me here until I saw the bartender emerge from a trapdoor carrying a case of beer. She had a pile of curly red hair knotted with gold twine and long arms which brought out the arch of her shoulder blades as she bent to store the beer in the cooler. On one shoulder was a tattoo of an eagle clutching lightning in its claws. Gleason and I sat side by side at the bar. The stools wobbled, their legs missing a rubber tip or two. The bartender wiped her hands on a rag and slid a bowl of potato chips between us.

"She must want us to share," Gleason said.

"What would you 'gentlemen' like to order?"

"I'll have a Motown in a frosty mug," Gleason said, "and my little friend here would like Squirrel Ale on tap."

"I only have it in a bottle."

"Close enough."

The bartender brought us our beers and unfolded a newspaper that had been left on the bar. She turned the pages with undisguised apathy. Gleason withdrew a small vial out of the pocket of his lumberjack shirt and tapped a pill into his palm. "For my blood pressure," he said. "It's amazing how much stress a person can be under even when you hardly do much of anything all day. But of course I don't need to tell *you* that."

"I do things."

"If you insist. Guess who I ran into the other day? Beth Grimshaw. Remember her from our body attunement class? She was the one whose entire system was blocked, a complete bag of cement. She's now the head of the children's theater department at this college in Connecticut. They tour the local schools, put on puppet shows, and perform updated fairy tales, turning the Big Bad Wolf into an investment banker, that kind of thing. She says there's nothing as satisfying as the laughter of children." He shuddered with horror.

"Those tots are the theatergoers of tomorrow," I said, as if quoting an adage.

"I've got news for you, there is no tomorrow. I'll tell you where the real action is, Downs: senior theater. All those old folks stuck in nursing homes and sunset communities, starved for entertainment, a true captive audience. That's what Hal Spurley is up to, pioneering the Arizona-Florida circuit, doing one-act plays and excerpts. If we were smart, we'd get in on this growth industry. There are even grants available, so you know good money's being wasted."

"I studied with Spurley when he was at A.R.T.," the bartender said. "He hates playing those senior centers, finds them depressing. He says they're like romper rooms for old people, the pastel colors and recreational activities reflecting a refusal to face death."

"He's just bitter because the geezers booed his Beckett monologue," Gleason said.

"You two working?"

Bracing both hands around his glass, Gleason said:

"I've been working on something I'm writing about the last days of Hemingway, right up to the climactic moment where he kills himself. He's surrounded by his four wives, who form a kind of tribunal and Greek chorus as he phases in and out of the past. To poke fun at Hemingway's obsession with androgyny, I may have the most tomboy wife double as F. Scott Fitzgerald. It's a bit tricky, but if you don't take creative risks, what's the point? Downs here has done a number of commercials. Have you seen the one for Reiser's Bakery? He plays the cake guy."

"You two have roughly the same build, you must be up for a lot of the same parts."

"The competition between us is intense," Gleason said. "Downs and I roomed together when we first came to New York, and often auditioned for the same roles. Whoever got the part, it helped pay the rent, so we never let ego interfere with paying the bills, though sometimes he would break down and cry when he had his heart set on a part. Now he has only his cat to keep him company. So what do you do when you're not paying the rent? I heard you were a makeup artist."

"What's in the laundry bag?"

"Laundry."

"I thought maybe you were shipping out to sea."

"I couldn't bear to be away from women that long. Nor they me."

"Yeah, right. Listen, could you guys fend for yourselves while I grab a smoke?"

"Could you bring us fresh chips first?" Gleason said. "These have lost their snap."

"Sure. You can plug in the jukebox, too, if you want."

"I have a jukebox in my apartment," I contributed.

"Downs here is a big Carpenters fan. He has all their singles. He considers Karen Carpenter a *saint.*"

"She suffered as much for her art as any of those authentic blues singers you're always going on about."

"Boys, boys," the bartender said. "I didn't mean to trigger a debate."

"Don't mind my friend, he's just touchy about his sissy musical tastes. What about Estelle over there?" Gleason said, meaning the lady at the end of the bar.

"She's harmless. I'll be right outside if she starts bugging out. I'm Kate, by the way."

"Tom, Tom Gleason. And this is John Downs."

Kate lifted the hinged shelf by the bar, carrying a pack of Kools and a lighter. She left the front door open, leaning against the outside wall. Gleason and I watched her in the reflection made by the mirror above the bar, admiring her smoking technique.

"So what do you think?" Gleason said.

"I thought you were dating Gwen."

"It never hurts to have a new one theoretically lined up, just in case," Gleason said before taking a slow, killer sip of beer.

"She does seem nice," I said. "The bartender, I mean."

"She's being much nicer this time around. Notice how she leapt into our conversation about senior centers and teased me about the laundry bag. Now she's putting on this little show for us."

"What makes you think it's for our benefit?"

"Downs, you're so naive. That woman is butt-proud. Observe."

In the mirror Kate waved to a passerby and then shooed away smoke.

"How could I be so wrong," I said, "now that I see how much bootie she puts into a simple wave?"

"I'm telling you, she's sending out signals. I came on too strong when I first met her, but with you here as my funny little sidekick she's being a lot friendlier."

"Maybe it's me she likes."

"Well, anything's possible."

At the other end of the bar, the old woman's eyes began to water, as if some memory were surfacing. She slapped the bar as if telling whatever it was to go away, and then gripped her glass, girding herself to take a sip.

"Hang in there, sis," Gleason called.

She smiled our way, as if we had shown her a kindness.

"Incidentally," I said, "I appreciate the honor of sitting next to such a powerful presence in the American theater. Thanks a lot. Here you are, doing a monologue on the last days of Hemingway while I'm appearing in ads for local bakeries. I thought you were working on a play about the last days of James Dickey."

"Hemingway, Dickey, same diff. And that bakery ad was nothing to be ashamed of. You're being awfully touchy today. Girlfriend problems?"

"Nothing major."

"Weren't you and that ad babe going to Coconut Grove for some romantic getaway?"

"We had to postpone because of an ad project she's working on."

"Didn't she postpone this once already? Maybe she's stalling because she's seeing someone else. But what am I saying? Why would any woman look elsewhere when she has *you*?"

"Exactly. Darlene says hi, by the way."

"How is Miss Piss?"

"She said you attracted the kind of women who write to inmates on death row. I think she still resents your comment about her meager breasts."

"I didn't say they were meager, I said they were scrawny. There's a difference. And I wouldn't have said that if she hadn't accused me of trying to cop a drunken feel at your apartment. 'Why should I want to scrounge around for your scrawny breasts?' I said. Maybe I was out of line, but she was the one walking around with her blouse half-unbuttoned, wearing a training bra. Tell me, what is the hold this hell-cat has on you, anyway? She's one smart cookie, I'll give her that, but I've never met a snottier bitch, and I've dated some pretty bitter divorcées. Is she *that* good in bed?"

"I wouldn't know. We're just friends."

"I just think that if you're going to be pussy-whipped, there should be some actual pussy involved."

I took a bite of potato chip. In the mirror, Kate savored the last of her cigarette. Lowering his voice, Gleason said, "I've been thinking about coloring my hair. Some gray is beginning to creep through."

"Color it yourself, or have someone do it for you?"

"Christ, Downs, can you picture me buying a hair-dye kit and sticking my head in the sink? That's something *you* would do. No, I'd hire a professional. I just don't want to end up looking like Rex Reed."

Kate flicked her cigarette butt onto the sidewalk and closed the door behind her, making the room dark again and ten degrees cooler. To thank us for letting her grab a smoke, she offered the next round on the house.

"In that case," Gleason said, "I'd like Glenlivet on the rocks. And another Squirrel for my friend."

"Actually, I'd prefer a Coke."

"Bring Junior a soft drink, then," Gleason said. "I hope you don't mind, but we were watching you in the mirror while you smoked. You really know how to lean against a door. Downs here was transfixed."

Kate not only laughed but blushed, something you seldom see a bartender do.

9

"READY?"

"Ready."

I was sitting on the sofa, pen in hand, notebook flipped open on my knee. Slinky groomed herself on the small rug, gnawing and licking between her flexed claws, zeroing in on the problem areas.

"Write this stuff down and study it before you go to sleep," Darlene said. "Let it seep into your unconscious, assuming you have one."

"Aren't we witty this morning?"

"Just trying to lighten things up a bit. Now, down to business. Do you have any old scripts lying around? Leave one open on the arm of the sofa, another on the floor, and a ledger or two from the restaurant on the desk. We want to create a picture of busy clutter. Make her think this meeting is keeping you from other activities—that not only can you live without her, but that's what you've been doing. Turn the lights up to show that your living room is your office and this isn't going to be some cozy *tête-à-tête*.

"When she walks through the door, see if she makes eye contact. If she does, we can play this scene soft. It means she wants to reestablish relations on some level. If she doesn't, it could mean she's afraid, or angry, or about to lie. Once she sits down, don't you so much as offer her a drink of water. If she wants something to drink, let her go get it, and you remain standing. You don't want her staring at the back of your head when she returns from the kitchen."

"Why not?"

"I can't really explain. I just know that I came out of the bathroom once and when I saw the back of my boyfriend's head, I wanted to give it a whap. And face it, Johnny, your head's a pretty juicy target. Once she's situated on the sofa, let her do the talking. Don't interrupt or interpret or make faces. After every answer look into her eyes for several beats. She's probably never gotten silence from you before and it will freak—her—*out*. Don't let the silence become too heavy, as if you're sitting in judgment. But don't try to lighten it, either, by bringing up any of the good times you two had. It'll only make you sound weak. Above all, don't show interest in the other man. He's a side issue. Keep the focus on her. What are you planning to wear?"

"I thought—"

"Don't wear a white shirt, it'll cast a glare. Try that blue one that matches your eyes. Do you have a small tape recorder?"

"I use one to memorize lines."

"Does it have a built-in mike or one that can be placed somewhere?"

"It has an extension with a little bow clip that you can attach to your shirt or something. I hope you're not asking me to hide a mike somewhere and tape Nicole. Forget it, Darlene. I'm not giving her the Nixon treatment."

"This isn't about her. A taped account will enable you to hear any mistakes you make, and could clear up ambiguities later. She may drop hints that you won't hear in the midst of all the emotion. We're not going to blackmail her, bub, just use it as backup in case there's something we need to have clarified."

"It still sounds finky."

"At least think about it. Another thing. She may get crafty and try to change the venue at the last minute. If she insists on meeting at a restaurant, cancel the meeting. Be strict. Believe me, it'll give her a thrill. When the meeting's over, escort her out with your hand on the small of her back. You writing all this down? I don't hear your pen scratching."

"I can remember this."

"Don't lose heart. Listen, you may find out tomorrow that she wants nothing more than to put things right. She may realize she's got herself a real man. Or, in your case, a reasonable facsimile. Don't worry about spooking her by giving her the big stare. She's tougher than you think, probably tougher than you are. Remember, she cheated on you, which makes you the chump. That's why we have to rig the odds in our favor. Who knows, she may melt and spend the rest of the night telling you how sorry she is, rocking back and forth with her legs wrapped around your waist and her hands around your neck. I had a boyfriend who used to claim there was nothing hotter than make-up sex, except maybe hotel sex."

"Yeah, and if you can combine the two—whammo."

"The point is, the world is full of couples who got together after a breakup. The breakup turned out to be just a bump in the road. Even if that doesn't happen, you'll come out ahead in her estimation. For now, scale her down in your mind and tell yourself you're trying to help her. That'll emerge naturally in your tone when you talk to her. Nicole will respect that, and she'll remember it. When a woman remembers a man in the right ways, it can draw her back, especially if the men she meets afterward come up short. She'll think, 'Here's yet another guy trying to jam his hand down my blouse, and there was Johnny, really trying to get through to me.' Whatever you do, don't crack any jokes. Let her see a serious side she hasn't seen before."

I spent the next afternoon "warming the space," to use an acting phrase. I spread a copy of an old script over the arm of the sofa and attached a pen to the front cover, as if I had been making notations moments before Nicole arrived. I cleared the bathroom of investment magazines and removed Nicole's red toothbrush from the holder above the sink. I bought some flowers and was arranging them in a blue vase when the phone rang.

"Johnny, it's Nicole." Other phones rang in the background.

"Hi," I said, too cheerfully for my own ears.

"I was thinking. Maybe we could meet at Simply Delish for dinner. It's usually quiet there, and desserts are free on Friday."

"I think it's best we meet here, without distractions."

After a pause Nicole said, "Okay, I just thought— Sorry, someone just stepped into my office. See you at six-thirty."

"I knew she'd try something!" Darlene said when I called. "She's tricky, but not tricky-tricky, like us. I just had a brilliant idea. Did any of your exes leave behind any lipstick?"

"There may be some in the medicine cabinet."

"Go get a pack of cigarettes. Apply some of the lipstick to your mouth, make it real red and pouty, and take a couple of puffs on three or four cigarettes. Then crumble them up in an ashtray by the sofa. She'll see the lipstick traces and smell the smoke and think you had another girlfriend over earlier. Isn't that inspired?"

"Darlene, I'm not going to put on lipstick and smoke cigarettes like some drag queen. Are you nuts?"

"Come on, Johnny, you're an actor, it's not as if you haven't worn lipstick before. You know what your problem is? False pride."

"I'm beginning to think my problem is you. Let me go, I have to go iron my blue shirt."

No opening night ever had me as keyed up as this meeting did. I scattered more scripts and trade papers in the living room and then, thinking they might look too strategically placed, messed them up a bit. It was sprinkling outside, a dinky rain that the Weather Channel said would intensify overnight. When I heard the downstairs buzzer, I put on a pair of scholastic reading glasses I hadn't worn in years. The elevator door opened, and I heard tentative footsteps. I waited for the buzzer. When it buzzed, I counted to three and opened the door. There was Nicole, holding an umbrella in each hand. I couldn't embrace her without getting poked or impaled, which perhaps was the idea, so I simply stood aside and gave her entrance room. Her coat was spattered with raindrops and her bangs were licked against her baby forehead, what I thought of as the Nicoledome. Her hair was straw blonde, with strands of gold.

"I brought back your Channel 13 umbrella, in case you needed it," Nicole said, glancing past my shoulder.

"Thanks." It was strange, greeting without kissing. Only a few weeks ago we had been sleeping together, and now we were going through these formal maneuvers in separate bubbles of personal space. She removed her coat, revealing a black dress cut sharp to show off her figure without baring much skin, and jazzy shoes with ankle straps. I led her into the living room, guiding her with a phantom hold on her elbow, my hand an inch or so from actual contact. I lifted a *Playbill* off the sofa to make space for her to sit, then turned the chair to face her. This she didn't expect. She assumed we would sit side by side, as we always did.

"I didn't know you wore glasses," she said, tucking her purse tightly at her side.

"When I'm reading scripts."

"They look handsome on you."

"Thanks."

"Do you have an ashtray?"

"In the kitchen." I remained standing. She rose to fetch it. I shifted my body so that she wouldn't see my back when she returned. She carried the ashtray into the living room and sat down, her face lowered. I sat down, pinching my pants above the knees to loosen them a little.

Before, I had only seen Nicole smoke after dinner or right before bed. Tonight, she smoked as if to polish off a pack, her free hand rubbing her cheek like a man acknowledging the need to shave. It was a gesture that said she had been doing some reflecting. I inched forward in the chair, letting her make the first vocal move. She tilted her head and brushed her hand through her hair, sighing.

"I wish I hadn't worn these shoes out in this rain," she said. "I just bought them, I'd hate to have them ruined. I got them on sale and can't return them."

If I hadn't been prepped, I would have responded with something chatty. Instead, her shoe comment dropped into a silent well. After a long pause, I said: "Nicole, I'd like to know what you think happened between us."

She tapped the cigarette against the ashtray. ". . . Sorry, I guess this isn't a time for small talk. Well, since you ask . . . since you put it that way . . . you know, this may be the first time I've seen you without a soda in your hand."

I let that pass, too.

"Well," she continued, "I guess I've been frustrated for some time by the direction or maybe nondirection of our relationship—'stymied' might be a better word. I felt, I guess, that you weren't putting a lot of effort or energy into moving things forward, that as a couple we had slipped into autopilot. We had a set routine, which was partly my fault, I suppose. You'd talk up a storm on the phone about doing this or that, then we'd end up doing the usual thing, which got to be kind of flat after a while. I guess I'm not being very articulate."

She wasn't. Nicole's conversation usually wasn't cotton-packed with fuzzy phrases like "I guess," "I suppose," "kind of." It was as if she had turned down her dial to energy saver. Nicole stubbed out her cigarette and lit another, fanning out the match. When she lifted her head, I made certain her eyes met mine. Her pupils were so dilated, they were almost all black, revealing an involvement, an investment in the moment, that belied all the vague, verbal shrugs she was giving me. I glanced away before we found ourselves in a staring contest, and adopted a guidance-counselor's voice to gently coax to the surface whatever she was withholding.

"Why didn't you talk to me, if you felt that way? Did you think I wouldn't listen?"

"I don't know. I was probably annoyed at you for not noticing or sensing what was wrong. Maybe I thought you wouldn't care."

"Why would you think that?"

"Men seem to want everything centered around them, for their convenience. They don't want to hear there are problems, and I tend to shy away from showdowns. Like that English guy I was living with when I first moved to New York, who lost his job and let things slide until I was completely supporting us—I was relieved when he started dating my friend Tabby and moved in with her, because it got me off the hook of having to confront him. Of course, I haven't spoken to the little traitor since. Tabby, I mean. It wasn't the *first* time she made a grab for one of my boyfriends."

"So you thought if you kept quiet, things would change of their own accord?"

"Are you talking about you and me, or me and that English guy?"

"You and me." *Why would I care about that deadbeat?*

"You were fun to be around at first, but I didn't sense things moving forward. I felt a certain inertia settling in, and I didn't get the sense you wanted to budge from your routine. Maybe I was wrong. Are you sure you don't want to eat?"

"I think we should finish our talk here first."

"Okay, Mr. District Attorney!"

"This isn't a cross exam," I said, but seeing Nicole's smile, started to smile myself. Suddenly, the phone rang, twice as loud as usual, startling me so much that my shoulders jumped. Slinky, who had been hiding under the sofa, dashed into the bedroom.

"I'll get it," I said, raising a palm to freeze things where they were. An absurd gesture, I realized, since it was hardly likely Nicole was going to dive for my phone. The voice in the receiver said:

"Say 'Hi, Suzanne' with some expression."

"Hey, Suzanne!"

"How's it going?" Darlene said in a loud furtive whisper. "Don't say anything to tip her off."

"Funny you should ask. Things have been frantic lately."

"Pretend I just sent you a present."

"And by the way, thanks for the Easter basket, though you know I'm not allowed to have all that chocolate."

"I know, it gives you the runs."

I threw back my head to have a good chuckle. ". . . Listen, kid, I have company—can I ring you back?"

"As soon as Sweet Cheeks leaves the apartment. Pretend I'm keeping you on the phone."

I said a series of good-byes, bending lower and lower toward the receiver, as if getting off the phone in sections. I hung up the phone and returned to my chair. Nicole was sitting up straighter, her face raised. Her expression was a wary mixture of irritation, curiosity, and bafflement. Her cigarette jutted straight up, like a toy smokestack.

"Pardon the interruption," I said.

Nicole shrugged. I clasped my hands to begin where we left off, but then couldn't remember where we left off. Nicole stared at me. I stared back and scratched my ear. "So, this new guy—is it serious?"

As soon as the words were out of my mouth, I knew I'd made a mistake. Darlene had cautioned me not to show interest in the other man, but her phone call had thrown me off script, so technically it was her fault. Setting her face in neutral, Nicole said: "I don't know. Maybe. We met in a movie line a few months ago. The one you didn't want to see because it was three hours long and sounded 'too arty.' Malcolm and his friend asked me and my friend Josie—you met Josie—to sit with them, and somehow he got my work number and one thing led to another. You know, I never promised exclusivity when we started dating, and I didn't ask it of you. We started out as free agents."

"I realize that. But once we got involved, I assumed . . ." Hearing myself sound defensive, I let my voice trail off.

"What I did was shitty, I'm not denying that," Nicole said. "I don't get off on hurting people."

To emphasize the import of what I was about to say, I removed my glasses and attempted to tuck them into my front pocket, forgetting that my blue shirt didn't have a front pocket, just a yacht insignia. Making an instant save, I slid the glasses down my chest until they reached my stomach, where I cupped them in both hands. I leaned forward and tried to sound fatherly.

"So how should we proceed, Nicole? What do you think we ought to do?"

"About what?"

"About us. You and me."

"Stop seeing each other, I guess," Nicole said, just like that.

I blinked, as if I had been hit with a two-by-four. Thinking that she would at least take a moment of deliberation, or at least a meaningful pause, I was unprepared for the promptness of her reply. I blinked again and said: "Then I won't detain you."

I stood and returned the chair to its original position. Nicole remained seated, as if anticipating an argument from me, a final plea, then saw that I was on my feet, drawing the meeting to a close. She looked as if she had been slapped, then deleted the emotion from her face. She poked out her cigarette and stood, brushing stray ashes from her dress. I followed her down the hall as she went for her coat. As I held it out for her, she plunged her arms into its sleeves with an abstract air, as if I were the coat-check person. I handed her her umbrella. She thanked me with a silent nod and turned to leave. I wanted to reach out and turn her around but it was too late, she was already in motion. As I opened the door, she smacked her forehead without actually making contact, suddenly reminded of something. She unclasped her pocketbook and handed me the set of keys to my apartment I had given her. I pocketed them without a word.

"Sorry I couldn't get in Sunday to feed Slinky," she said. "But I left her a lot on Saturday to tide her over, so I figured she'd be fine."

"You made it in that weekend?"

"Oh, sure. I said I would, didn't I? I know how you worry about that cat. If anything happened to her, you'd spring a leak. Remember the time you thought she'd run away?"

I didn't need to be reminded of that particular farce. We gravitated toward the elevator. I pressed the DOWN button and waited, wanting a formal leave-taking that would allow me one last look at Nicole. I knew she didn't expect me to wait with her, which put me at a momentary advantage. We stood without speaking as a neighbor ran a roaring vacuum cleaner in the apartment behind us.

When the elevator arrived, Nicole turned and gave me a surprise kiss on the cheek.

"I have something of yours," I said. I handed her the butterfly barrette, the one she had worn the night we went to the ballet. She nodded as I placed it in her palm. She entered the empty elevator, wedging herself into a far corner and slipping the barrette into her coat pocket. The overhead lighting shadowed her face. The door remained open. She had forgotten to press the first-floor button. Almost in slow motion, she leaned forward and extended her arm.

The elevator door closed, its small grated window framing half her face.

I went into the bedroom and looked out the window at the wet sidewalk below. The shiny dome of a black umbrella passed beneath bony-fingered branches and out of frame. An identical umbrella followed. Either one of them could have been Nicole's. Then the sidewalk was bare. I went to turn off some lights in the living room.

10

"DARLENE, WHAT WAS THAT LITTLE STUNT?"

"It wasn't a stunt, it was a carefully crafted adjunct operation."

"Well, whatever it was—"

"I wanted to make Nicole jealous by letting her think word had already gotten out that you might be available and that other women were ready to pounce. I picked the name Suzanne, because it oozes sexual confidence. Now Nicole won't be able to do a fake sigh and say to herself or anyone stuck listening to her, 'Poor Johnny—he must feel so alone.'"

"We should have discussed this ahead of time. I don't like surprises."

"Too bad. I wanted the surprise in your voice to sound genuine when you picked up the phone. If you had sat there with your mental meter running, knowing I was about to call, it might have sounded too slick when you picked up the phone. Tell me what she said, tell me what she wore."

I told her.

"So she came in strutting it high and tight, did she? I knew she would, to compensate for how she was dressed the night you caught her."

"Her biggest concern seemed to be how rain might affect her new shoes."

"New shoes? She really wanted to dance on your dick. Did she make eye contact?"

"Not at the outset, but when we sat down she mentioned my glasses."

"What were her exact words? I wish you had taped this meeting."

"Well, I didn't. Her exact words were 'They look handsome on you.'"

Darlene snorted. "What a bitch! Complimenting your glasses! She didn't say, 'You look handsome in them,' she said, 'They look handsome on you,' as if your head was a place to model eyewear. She's so awful, I'm beginning to develop a sneaky admiration for her. She's like me, if I were blonde and evil."

"You are evil. And maybe she *was* complimenting me and you're misinterpreting."

"Listen, Johnny, every woman knows the difference between being told, 'You look good in that dress,' and being told, 'That dress looks good on you.' The latter makes you return the dress to the hanger. Nicole understands these distinctions, even if you don't. Did she explain herself in any way?"

"She said things had gotten stale between us. She didn't use the word, but that's what she meant. I thought she *liked* the pattern we were in. It was her idea to unwind after work watching that silly soap opera and ordering takeout. She told me more than once she was able to relax around me. I guess I relaxed her to the point where she was bored out of her skull."

"Don't be so hard on yourself. If she thought it was hopeless between you two, she could have shown enough class to break up with you first before moving on to the next victim. Her cheating isn't your fault. So, I take it, Miss Run Around didn't have a change of heart and leave open the possibility of you two getting together again?"

"No, she closed the lid on that coffin. To her credit, she didn't try to sugarcoat it. When I asked her what we should do, she said point-blank we should stop seeing each other."

"In her mind, she had already cut the cord. I didn't want to say anything before, but when you told me that she was extra frisky the last time you made love, it rang a bell. I've often felt a rush of exhilaration when I knew I was about to end a relationship. The spirit of freedom just seems to overtake my hips, and there's the poor guy thinking he's throwing *me* a hot one."

"Great, that's *so* nice to hear." I went to work on my forehead with the palm of my hand. "So what was the *point* of having this meeting if I didn't have a shot at getting her back?" I said.

"You had a shot, but it was just a slim one."

"Maybe I lost what slim chance I had when you called and planted the notion I was already dating someone else. We were just beginnning to relax when you threw that curveball at me."

"Oh, like that phone call would reverse her decision. Nicole is incredibly competitive with men and women alike. Plus she's got that blonde arrogance. If she wanted to make a go of it with you, she wouldn't let some unknown voice on the phone stop her. In fact, it'd have made her more eager to prove herself. She would have sounded you out about 'Suzanne,' maybe flirted just to see if you were still susceptible. And you would have been, wouldn't you? You'd have melted like a toy soldier."

"Well, she didn't come on to me, so the point is moot."

"How did the meeting end?"

I described waiting with Nicole at the elevator. Darlene said:

"Did she mention the new boyfriend?"

"Yeah, I made the mistake of asking about him. His name's Malcolm, they met in a movie line when she and a friend and he and a friend started chatting and then sat together in the theater. He somehow got her work number and one thing led to another."

"If her lies carried compound interest, we could all get rich. First of all, how did he happen to get her work number unless she gave it to him or made a point of mentioning her company? Second, 'one thing led to another' is a classic cop-out—one thing doesn't lead to another unless the two people want them to. If Nicole had any desire to be faithful to you, she wouldn't have allowed herself to get picked up in a movie line by a stranger. She would have made it evident that her friend might be available, but not her, she already had someone."

I stood, my legs aching from that special fatigue that comes with failure. The scripts and trade papers I had carefully spread about looked stupid to me now, a sham anyone could see through. Darlene said:

"Try to look past this moment and further down the line. Nicole may be out with her new boyfriend right now, wearing her laughing face, but I'm telling you, she didn't reckon on the way you handled her tonight, and it's going to eat at her, especially since you didn't flirt with her when she came in looking tasty, or plead with her when she said you should stop seeing each other. 'Then I won't detain you' is a little stiff and awkward, but it shows some dignity. The next time a new guy disappoints her, *which he inevitably will,* you're going to float back into her mind, and she's going to remember how mature you were tonight. Giving her back the barrette was also a master stroke—we didn't even discuss that option. Don't beat up on yourself."

"The irony is, she told me as we were waiting that she actually did come and feed Slinky once that weekend. If I hadn't overreacted when I got home, thinking she had been hungry the whole time, maybe Nicki and this new guy would have fizzled out on their own without me knowing. It might not have prevented our breakup, but it might have spared seeing the two of them kiss."

"Well, there's a saying: Never reject what reality brings you. Besides, she probably spent all of five minutes with the cat before rushing back to lover boy. It's not as if she did you any great favor. In fact, she might have done the opposite."

"What do you mean?"

"The two of them might have come over together, fed the cat, and taken a quick spin in your bed. Doing it in someone else's bed really boosts the forbidden factor. I'm not saying they *did*, just don't be surprised if you find anything mysterious lying around, like male underwear two sizes too small."

"Forgive me for not falling on the floor with laughter. Why are you making her out to be such a slut? This is somebody I care about."

"I don't think she's a slut, just a user. She uses people, then tosses them aside like a child bored with a toy. When you weren't fun anymore, she went to find a new rattle. The important thing is, whatever she thought she was getting away with—whatever dirty thrill she had at your expense—now makes her feel a little dirty inside. She'll try to ignore it, but what happened tonight is going to shadow her for a long time to come."

"What a consolation."

"Here's your consolation. Two weeks ago you caught Nicole cheating on you with some yo-yo, yucking it up on the street. Now picture her when the elevator door closed. Was that the look of a woman enjoying the last laugh?"

"No," I said, "it wasn't."

"See? Whatever else, you've earned her respect. Continue to be that person, and the women you meet from now on will pick up on that assurance. Now go take a bubble bath and try not to drown yourself in the tub."

I've always been a slow rebounder when it comes to breakups, but this was the first time I felt someone had pulled the plug on me. I went through the motions, blanked out inside. I would see my hand on the doorknob and stare at it as if it belonged to someone else, an alien impostor. After work, I'd walk to the park and kill an hour or so listening to sports-talk radio on earphones. During spring training the baseball announcers sounded bright and cheerful, as if they'd had a fine breakfast and gotten a nice tan, but now, only a couple of weeks into the season with both the Yanks and the Mets bumbling along, the mood had already turned bitter. Even the young fans sounded like old coots, as if every mouth had the same set of rusty hinges. Then I'd switch to WBAI, to find out what was happening on their planet. Late at night I began having choking attacks, dry sobs that sometimes turned into crying jags that fed on themselves and left me feeling lighter in the morning, as if my body had turned into pajamas. Unable to sleep at night, even after a warm bath, I exiled myself to the sofa, where I slept like a soldier on a cot, waking up with the left side of my body aching and my arm stiff. Excited by my change of venue, Slinky sped across the top of the sofa along an invisible ramp that took her past the windowsill, onto the kitchen counter, and looped back into the living room, a route she raced several times an evening. In the morning, she batted at my arm as it hung over the side of the sofa. It was as if she were happy to have me all to herself again.

A few days later a small box arrived via UPS, mailed from Hilton Head, South Carolina, where presumably Darlene and Clete had spent or were spending part of their jaunt. Packed in old newsprint was an Art Deco silver cigarette lighter with a perfumed note from "Suzanne" saying, "To my favorite flame." I cocked the lighter with my thumb. The flame flicked an inch high. Since Darlene knew I didn't smoke, she must have intended the gift as a little pick-me-up. After flicking a few more flames, I set the lighter on the night table beside the ashtray full of Nicole's lipstick-stained cigarette butts that I kept meaning to throw out, but hadn't.

11

AFTER TWO WEEKS of Darlene-prescribed self-pity, with some extra days tacked on for insurance, I picked up my lucky sports jacket from the cleaners and went on a round robin of auditions. Although I do the occasional commercial, I work mostly in theater. This time I didn't limit myself to my usual niche, the beefy character parts (side-kick, henchman, comic foil) that often have more flash and impact than the lead roles. I auditioned for roles I didn't want and couldn't get, standing on stage after stage with script pages wilting in my hands. I even tried out for a new play about methadone patients who meet every day at McDonald's for lunch. There we were, trained actors practicing nodding out and groggily picking at our faces. These strikeouts didn't matter. The purpose was to get moving again, get myself seen, my name bandied around. The alternative was spending every spare hour in my shrinking apartment, which had become a holding pen.

Absorbing blows to the ego that might have broken a prouder man, I landed a small part in a non-Equity showcase production of Bradford Willy's *An Oasis for Fools*, a drama set in a symbolic neon bar on the outskirts of nowhere, where it's always night and the cicadas never clam up. I was cast as the bar's resident cynic, Matthew Prouty, a sip-per of fine bourbon who perches on his stool and mocks everyone's paltry aspirations. According to the play's director, who fancied him-self a deep interpreter, my character was a stand-in for critics of

Willy's earlier work, petty destroyers who can't create, jealous eunuchs who can't . . . , and so on. At the end of the play I get my come-uppance and am exposed as a man Unable To Love, destined to die alone and unmourned. I'm told this by the town barber, who never did like my nasty mug. Until that reversal, it's not a bad part. Cynics always get the best lines, even if the playwright is taking a principled stand against cynicism, something playwrights feel obliged to do.

The initial read-through was held in the director's many-windowed loft in TriBeCa, which he shared with a painter who seemed to paint with both hands, judging by the slap-happy canvases on display. Set on a table in front of a couch long enough to seat a small choir were two bottles of red wine, stacks of plastic cups, and a pile of grapes for nib-bling. The actor playing the town barber embraced the director and, upon being introduced to me, seated himself at the distant end of the couch, presumably to establish his character's opposition to mine from the outset, unless he just wanted more space. Soon the other actors arrived and filled up the couch. As always, I was interested to see who would show up last, the last arrival at the first reading invariably being the actor who considers him- or herself the star of the piece. After some time-killing nibbling of grapes from those seated, the actor playing Dwayne, the male lead, entered the room like the team's leading scor-er, dropping into a separate chair and lighting a cigarette without ask-ing permission. Like so many studly young actors, he sat low in the chair, sticking his legs out for that Calvin Klein effect.

The director explained the genesis of the play and its production his-tory, including its tragic New York debut in 1947. Although the play closed after only twenty performances, it achieved a footnote in the-atrical history for presenting the stage debut of Slide Yarrow in the role of Dwayne, the soulful drifter. Yarrow went on to became a movie sensation in two films before driving his convertible off a cliff in Santa Barbara and dying forever young at the age of twenty-three. After his death a legend sprung up about the production of *An Oasis for Fools*, the rehearsal stills showing Yarrow standing apart with a beer in his hand, looking like a torn-T-shirt Apollo.

Using his hands expressively, the director provided his own capsule interpretations of the characters and said that after close reading, he found the theme of the play to be charity. "The play progresses from faith to hope to charity. Charity not only to others, but to ourselves—

perhaps to ourselves most of all. After all, we can't forgive others until we have truly forgiven ourselves. The play asks, 'Where is God's charity? How can He let us suffer? How can a just God permit suffering?'" Having no immediate answers to offer, the director brought his commentary to a cliffhanging stop. After some of us refilled our plastic cups, we began reading the play aloud, without emphasis. As we read, the director sat poised in a leather chair, leaning forward as if listening with his entire head.

The director found his legs once we began rehearsing in a reconverted but still rundown movie theater near Westbeth. I was sitting on my character's bar stool, minding everyone's business and destroying their dreams, when I heard my name called. The director was bracing his elbows on the orchestra railing and steepling his fingers under his nose. He had a Band-Aid on his bald head, the result of a recent shaving accident.

"Downs, I'm a tad uncomfortable with some of the choices you're making," he said. "Would you like my notes now or later?"

"Now is fine. Fire away."

The other actors assumed an at-ease position.

"Prouty is a man with a false front. I see him—you—as someone who wears a linen suit, bets on races, and considers himself a high roller, but is stewing inside, steeped in self-loathing, a man who has soiled himself. You're giving me the sporty facade but not the shitty underwear. You're a little too plush in Prouty's skin, if that makes any sense."

I nodded just enough not to seem like a yes-man.

"Also, I feel as if you're giving me what Strasberg used to call adverbial acting, as if in the script it said, '"Blah, blah, blah," he said sneeringly,' or '"Blah, blah, blah, blah, blah," he said hopefully.' Try to guard against putting too many end-twists on the lines."

I nodded again, putting a little more into it this time.

"Fine. Good. I love everything else so far, so don't feel I'm picking on you. From where we stopped, then. And Annabeth, sweetheart, try not to curl your fingers so daintily around the straw when you sip. This isn't a soda shop."

Annabeth, who parted her hair in the middle like a traditional folksinger, nodded as if submitting to Mother Superior. Annabeth played Cerrisse, a woman of mysterious means and intent who swanks into this dump as if she's come from a society event. The script calls for her to enter the bar with "an insouciant, though languorous stride." Long and thin, Annabeth looked elegant in repose, like a fashion drawing, but when she moved, it was a case of mind over matter. She couldn't walk across stage without camel-clomping, lowering herself on the bar stool as if it might skid out from under her.

"I'm sorry," Annabeth said. "I lost my place."

"Pick up from 'Is there anything to do in this town, except suffocate?'"

The director was now somewhere in the tiny, dusty balcony. During rehearsal he kept moving around the theater as he offered pointers. It was like trying to pin down a sniper. He gave Annabeth so much fuss that at one point I deliberately flubbed a line reading so that he could pick on me instead. The only other person on stage was the ghostly bartender, Cal, who cleaned glasses as we spoke as if under hypnosis. After rehearsal, Annabeth slung her pocketbook over her shoulder and left the theater with the brisk determination of someone crossing a train platform.

Two days later, the director gathered us into a group onstage.

"Annabeth, as some of you may have heard, has decided to divorce herself from the production. She felt the role wasn't quite right for her, and I'm afraid I came to the same conclusion. In any event, some of you may know Claudia Prentiss who, I'm pleased to say, has agreed to assume the role of Cerrisse." As if on cue, a crack of light appeared at the lobby door and our new Cerrisse entered the theater, her legs slicing down the aisle.

At first glance, Claudia Prentiss appeared to be a woman in raven disguise, or a raven in woman disguise—black dress, black hair, black heels, black stockings, black pocketbook, all of it polished with crisp dollar bills. She carried her head high, her long hair snapping behind her. The director grazed her cheek in greeting. Claudia gave a royal nod to the rest of us. Compared to her, we looked haphazard, underdressed, and ready for the discount bin.

"You must be Prouty," she said, addressing me.

"Yes, ma'am."

She measured me up and down, then asked the director: "Is there any ventilation in this place? It smells sooty."

"I'll have Mitch talk to the building superintendent."

Claudia climbed the little staircase and joined us onstage. "Is that my stool?"

"Ready and waiting," the director said jovially.

"I can't sit on that in this dress. That seat is filthy."

She waited as the director tried to scare up someone and something to clean her bar stool. This took a few minutes, after the first washrag looked like something out of Charles Dickens and the second wasn't much better. After another momentary delay, involving an industrial fan blowing too loud, we began to rehearse. Claudia read from the script, which was heavily notated in small pointy handwriting. Her line readings were nothing special, but her body took up the slack and then some. When she sat on the bar stool, she settled into it as if it were contoured seating. As she leaned forward, she arched her back in a physical purr. Later in the scene, when Cerrisse has downed her second drink and gotten a little dreamy, she dangled one shoe from her toe, as if toying with us.

After her introduction to the cast, it became an unspoken contest between her and Kenny, the actor playing Dwayne the Soulful Drifter, as to who could show up last at rehearsal and be top poodle. As the director pretended to be holding a stopwatch in his hand, some in the cast wagered on which one would keep us waiting longer. Claudia was usually the winner, but on one occasion she and Kenny entered from different doors at the same time, in a virtual dead heat, and the rest of us broke into applause. Kenny looked bewildered. Claudia took a bow.

12

DARLENE CALLED FROM her mother's house in Athens, Georgia, where she was minding things while her mother was on a Caribbean cruise with a gentleman friend. "When's this so-called play open?" she asked. "If you hear something weird, it's just me shucking corn."

I told her the date.

"Will there be a cast party?"

"There may be one on the set after the show. We already have a bar built on the stage, so it's just a matter of stocking real booze and snacks."

"I was thinking, wouldn't it be nice to have the party at your place?"

"I haven't thrown a party since my humiliating thirteenth birthday, when my mother insisted we all play—"

"It's time you did. Host skills are essential in creating the image of a man at ease with himself and his home. Who usually gets invited to these things?"

"The cast and crew, their current sweeties, other actors."

"But if you're holding it in your apartment, you could invite outsiders, too, right?"

"You mean Nicole?"

"Better than that. Does Nicole have a girlfriend that you got along with?"

"I met her friend Pavia a couple of times."

"Here's what you do. Pop an invite to Pavia. She'll be sure to mention it to Nicole. Pavia may even wonder if you're putting out a feeler to her now that you and Nicole are no longer a couple. Even if not, it'll annoy Nicole no end that you're throwing a party she hasn't been invited to so soon after your breakup. Then, a couple of days after you've sent Pavia the invitation, send Nicole one. By the time she gets her invitation, she'll *want* to come to the party."

"You think so?"

"I know so. Never discount female pride. The moment she gets the card she'll be on the phone with Pavia, bee-essing, 'Mine just arrived today—it must have gotten stuck in the mail.' This doesn't guarantee she'll show, but if she does, she'll see you being the center of attention and realize she could have been at your side on opening night rather than just one of the guests. Don't write anything cute on her invitation. Treat her as just another name on the list."

"But, Darlene, if she walks through the door with a date, I'll cave."

"If she walks through that door, it'll be with Pavia. They'll team up to compare notes later. God, Johnny, you know nothing about women."

"That's why I rely on you. My only concern is that Gleason thinks Nicole and I are still a couple, so if she—"

"Do you have to invite him?"

"He's my best friend."

"Friendship's overrated, but let's not argue about that now. You have your notebook handy? Here's what you're going to need. I may fax you some follow-up suggestions. I also want to fax some photos of myself I just took. Don't get excited, they're not nudies. I need your male input about the current state of my hair. Clete likes it long, but the humidity's wreaking havoc with it. I look like a blown mattress."

"Well, it should give the guys at the fax place a laugh."

"Maybe I'll fax them some of the pictures I took of you in Athens in your swim trunks."

"Don't you dare."

"But they're so cute. Do you have a store nearby where you can get inflatable palm trees and animals for decorations? Goofy props always get a party going. Remember that one I took you to where everyone had to wear grass skirts? That was fun."

"I'm not having everyone wear hula outfits, Darlene. Besides, I'm not sure I can do all this—tend bar, rehearse a play, and throw a party at the same time. Why can't you come north and be my official party organizer? That way you could see the play, too."

"Wish I could, butter-butt, but it's important that you do this on your own. Just be sure to get lots of photos taken. Take some of the apartment before the guests arrive so I can see how the decorations look and then have someone shoot the guests once the party's in full swing. I want to study them and see if there're any future fiancées for you to pursue."

"By 'fiancées,' I assume, you mean 'girlfriends.'"

"No, I mean 'fiancées.' Frankly, I think it's time you thought about getting married. No offense, Johnny, but as a single man, you're getting moldy. You've picked up so many bad bachelor habits over the years that they've formed a bathtub ring around you that women can see. When you were younger, even up to just a few years ago, you could get away with being a likable fun guy. That won't cut it anymore. At your age, women suspect that if you haven't gotten married or at least engaged, there may be something wrong with you, some hidden defect or deep resistance. You have to start packaging yourself as marriage material. This party is the first step."

"Maybe I don't want to get married."

"Life isn't all about what you want. As a woman, I'm telling you that you need to be taken seriously as a man, and the only way for that to happen is for you to package yourself as a potential husband. All your life you've done what you wanted, and where are you? What do you have to look forward to?"

"You make me sound like a bowling ball headed for the gutter."

"If you have such a blazing future, how come Nicole blew you off so easily? I'll tell you why. She knew you weren't in the game for keeps. Since I've known you, Johnny, women have dumped you at a faster and faster rate. You've gone from being dumped by Katrina after three years to being dumped by Nicole after barely six months. It's as if the women you meet come equipped with the latest computer chip, enabling them to process the same information about you at faster speeds. After the next upgrade, women will be rejecting you before you say hello. Women don't need to compare notes on you. You're in the collective databank."

"This may come as news to you, Darlene, but not every woman wants to be a wife. Nicole often said she didn't know if she ever wanted to get married."

"And you *believed* her? Where have you been for the last two thousand years? She was testing your attitude toward marriage, and whatever you said clearly landed in the loss column. If you really want to know how women regard matrimony, go to a newsstand and take a look at the bridal magazines. They're the biggest, fattest magazines in the country, packed with nothing but articles on weddings, engagement parties, honeymoon planning, the perfect wedding dress, etc. They're dreambooks, Johnny. There's nothing comparable in the male world."

"I just don't feel like settling down. Even the phrase makes me—"

"Makes you what? Jesus, Johnny, if you were any more settled, you'd reach a complete stop."

"You've never acted like you were all that hot to get married."

"I'm younger than you are, and never you mind. It's *your* misguided life we're talking about for now. Forget possible fiancées for a moment—do you want to impress the woman who broke your heart or not? Don't you at least want to impress this Claudia you've been drooling over?"

"Well, when you put it that way . . ."

After I jotted down the rest of Darlene's to-do list, which included buying six-packs of Evian-water sprays so that the guests could freshen themselves ("that's what all the models do"), Darlene said: "If you know any nice women at work, see if they can help with the party. Women love to be asked for advice. And another thing. If any women at the party smoke, here's an opportunity for you to casually whip out that spiffy lighter I sent you. When whoever she is takes out a cigarette, don't immediately flick the flame under it, like most men do. Steady her wrist with one hand as you flick the lighter with the other, and make eye contact as your heads converge. Make it seem conspiratorial. When you click the lighter shut, take in her whole face. Practice this at home so you can do it in one smooth sequence. It's guaranteed to wow any woman."

"I thought I was supposed to pursue nice girls."

"Nice girls smoke, too, you know. You think nice girls don't pick up nervous habits living in New York?"

"I'm just concerned about other people complaining about the smoke."

"Fuck 'em, it's your apartment. One more thing. *The host never sits.* I don't care how tired you are after the play, you stand the entire party, even if it means leaning propped up against a wall. The most important people in the room always stand."

As opening night and the cast party approached, I pushed myself on five to six hours' sleep. Whipping out the old charge card, I bought ashtrays, glasses, plates, utensils, and strings of twinkly lights, installed a six-foot inflatable palm tree, and made a major haul at the liquor store. I priced caterers, arranged to have silver balloons delivered, and, failing to recruit any volunteers, hired a couple of day waiters from the restaurant to serve drinks and pass around finger food. At night I attended rehearsals that had entered the rocky phase (rehearsals always enter a rocky phase, which sometimes becomes permanent). Jealous of the attention Claudia commanded, not to mention her ability to make the director wring his hands whenever she voiced her disfavor, Kenny began massaging his stomach muscles as he emoted, slowing things to a crawl. As Kenny's jeans became tighter, he dispensed with a belt, his top button occasionally popping open, revealing a few zipper-teeth. After we had gathered onstage one evening, the director said:

"People, I apologize for not addressing this earlier, but I didn't know quite how things were going to evolve. I ask that you put your egos aside for the moment. It's the issue of accents. We simply have no uniformity whatsoever with our Southern accents. You sound like the same species in different stages of development. Downs, your accent is fine."

"I've spent a lot of time in the South."

"Excellent. Whatever. But the rest of you—Foster, you're fine too—the rest of you either have to bring your accents up to snuff or we'll have to do the play without accents, which would make no sense. I'm not asking for deep immersion in dialect here, just enough twang so that we recognize we're in the South, for God's sake." Moving from the general to the particular, he began to address Claudia, who cut him off at the pass.

"According to the text, Cerrisse left town as a teenager and traveled the world, so it makes more sense for her *not* to have an accent, given the company she's been keeping all these years. She only lets traces of it surface when she's with Dwayne, as the person she was peeks out from the person she is."

"That clarifies some things for me, though I do wonder if the audience will understand why it suddenly surfaces. They may not trace its connection to Dwayne. And speaking of Dwayne . . ."

Before the director could finish, Kenny explained: "I'm letting the accent find its own level. I don't want it to be fully formed too early and take on a life of its own. I'm still massaging it."

"Among other things," Claudia said.

"What do you mean?"

"I'm just wondering if you can rub your stomach and pat your head at the same time, because you sure have mastered the first one."

"That's off-topic," the director said. "We're discussing accents."

"I'll have it nailed by performance," Kenny said.

"When are you planning to have your lines 'nailed'?" Claudia said.

"I know my lines."

"Oh, please."

"I know them internally, as words. It's just . . ."

"Then why am I stranded up here listening to your pregnant pauses? Maybe the dead spots mean nothing to you, but I might as well be waiting for a bus in the time it takes you to rummage around for what you're supposed to say. It makes me, if I may quote our director, *a tad uncomfortable.*"

A nervous laugh shot out of me like a sneeze.

"What's so funny, Downs?" Claudia said.

"I, uh, just couldn't picture you waiting for a bus."

"For your information, I've ridden the bus many a time. Don't patronize me. You took a legitimate point and trivialized it with your laughter. I've taken the subway, too, for your information."

"Hey, it's Kenny you're mad at, remember?"

"Well," the director said, clapping his hands together a mite merrily, "I think it's healthy we're getting all this out of our systems rather than letting it sit and fester. Shall we resume? Let's pick up from the line 'The leaves have turned to rust.' And, Kenny, before we begin, I do think Claudia has a point, though she expressed it somewhat savagely. You do tend to hoard your lines. Let the horse out of the barn."

Being compared to a steed seemed to placate Kenny, who nodded as the rest of us shuffled to our proper places.

13

EVERYONE IN THE CAST AND CREW seemed surprised and pleased to receive their party invitations. Claudia fanned herself with hers, her bracelet sliding down her wrist. I didn't receive an RSVP from either Nicole or Pavia, something Darlene told me not to over-analyze.

I loaded my freezer with bottles of vodka. This was a trick I learned from my grandfather, who had been a bootlegger's errand boy back in the old days. Take an empty quart carton of milk, cut off the top, and fill with water. Then insert the bottle into the water and stick in the freezer. After the water freezes, cut away the carton, and voilà, a bottle of vodka in a block of ice. Plant two of these babies on the bar, and you have yourself the beginnings of a certified blast. My last trip was to the florist, where I picked up a pile of gladioli. I told Darlene I could get flowers cheaper at the Korean deli, but she insisted I go to a real florist, saying that any future fiancées at the party would spot the difference. Then I took Polaroids of the flower arrangements, the decorations, and the table setting, as Darlene had asked.

On opening night I arrived at the theater at six and changed into costume. We had to do our own makeup. I could hear the audience straggling in and greeting each other as old familiars. One of the actors sat on a folding chair, praying. Another squeezed a rubber ball in his hand. I steadied myself as I always did before a performance, by counting my breaths from ninety-nine down to one, as if each number represented a descending step, then repeating the sequence, counting upward. I didn't see Claudia backstage, but word was she had made a grand arrival in a black town car. She may have wanted to keep to herself so that she could concentrate and make her entrance as clean as a cannon shot.

Making himself useless backstage, the director, who looked as if he had just given a pint of blood, passed me a couple of notes, which I glanced at without reading. The stage manager said, "Ten minutes . . ." Kenny shadowboxed against the wall, then stopped and bowed his head, shaking out his hands and hopping in place. The Genuflect Theater didn't have a proscenium curtain, so the stage was kept dark before the play began. "Five minutes . . ." I took my spot on the stool, joined by the actor playing the other customer. Cal the Bartender assumed his start position, gripping the business end of a bourbon bottle. The audience quieted.

An Oasis for Fools begins with me, another customer, and the bartender frozen like statues on the darkened stage under a blue neon sign. The blue light made us look like the living dead. We held the pose. I could hear the audience forcing a last cough out of their throats before they concentrated. I closed my eyes and licked the inside of my mouth in front of my teeth. A spotlight began to glow. I always love the moment the light becomes warm. It coated one side of me as Cal poured fake bourbon from the bottle, and the other customer, a town councilman named Seth, said, ". . . I heard he accused Cal here of serving his drink in a dirty glass. He said there was lipstick along the rim. He said he didn't want to be drinking from the same glass as one of Cal's whores."

After a thoughtful sip, I shrugged and said:

"Hell, I'll bet he's tasted lipstick on the rim before."

The audience laughed, grateful for an off-color joke so early in the proceedings. As the bartender nodded, the two of us exchanged local news for a while, indirectly establishing the play's locale, a town stranded at the edge of a dismal swamp. Just as Prouty is about to spring the punchline of a hoary anecdote about the local pastor, Cerrisse makes her entrance, her heels clicking across the floor like dimes. You could feel the audience's collective neck rise an inch when she mounted the bar stool and crossed her legs. Claudia was wearing perfume, something she hadn't done in rehearsal, a scent that suggested afternoon adultery in a French hotel. She set her pocketbook on the bar and ordered a drink. In character, I looked her over good. She acknowledged my interest, raising one hand to her face and briefly toying with the nub of her earlobe with her little finger. Since the left side of her face was away from the audience, this little bit of business wasn't meant for them, it was meant for me. It was this finger, she seemed to be saying, that dabbed the perfume.

"Mind if I wait?" Cerrisse said.

"We'd mind if you didn't."

"How gallant. My car is outside, in need of a mechanic. It's making the sorriest little sound."

"I could call Dwayne at the Esso station," the councilman said. "He can make any engine purr."

"He can make a lot of things purr," I said, with enough innuendo to grow hair.

After some time-killing banter in which the councilman and I try to amuse this beautiful stranger and get to her to confide where she's been hiding herself all our lives, Dwayne appears at the bar door, wiping his hands with a greasy rag. His arms are streaked with oil but his T-shirt is white as innocence. She swivels on her bar stool. He looks at her. She looks at him. He steps inside, penis first. Then Cerrisse rises from the bar stool and kisses Dwayne on the corner of his mouth, triumphantly, a kiss that seems as much Judas's betrayal as a come-on. Dwayne says, "Hello, sis. Been a while . . ." Then the lights dimmed as if time itself was irising out. In the darkness the rest of us slipped into the wings, as members of the audience took the opportunity to cough and rustle in their seats. After a pause, the lights rose on Dwayne and Cerrisse, whose reunion consumes the rest of act one. I watched from the wings. The cords in Claudia's neck showed how hard she was working not only to challenge Dwayne, but to chip some marble off of Kenny. The scene builds to an incestuous kiss, a real mouth-masher, after which Cerrisse asks, "Now what do we do?" They freeze into place locked in embrace. End of act one.

The lights dimmed and the audience applauded. It didn't sound like mercy applause, which can be more humiliating than honest indifference. I could tell from the decibel level in the lobby that the audience was planning to return. They don't always do. Sometimes they go out for a smoke and drift down the sidewalk, never to return. Backstage, the bartender and I observed a minute of ritual silence before the beginning of act two.

The stage became a lake of blue light . . .

At the end of the second act the stage went totally dark and the audience began to applaud, tentatively at first, then with mounting confidence that the play was truly over and nothing else was about to be sprung on them. We took a quick bow under the stage brights, ignoring the patrons running for dear life up the aisles. At the second bow, there was a pocket outburst of applause to which I paid no mind, already thinking ahead to the party. The cast broke ranks, kissed each other madly on the cheeks, and went backstage to change. I stuffed my linen suit into a paper bag and rushed in full makeup to catch a cab to check on the party preparations.

At home, I found two of the waiters sitting on my sofa, eating crackers in front of the TV. They looked utterly at one with themselves and their surroundings.

"Hey, get it in gear, guys."

"Nobody's here yet," said the one with the mustache. The other one switched off the TV and plugged in the twinkly lights around the nonworking fireplace. I asked about my cat. "She's around here somewhere," the second waiter said.

"She's been skulking around," said the one with the mustache. He had positioned the vodka bottles encased in blocks of ice as bookends on the bar.

"I'll be in the bathroom," I said. "Just make sure the cat doesn't make a break for it when the guests arrive."

"The bathroom smells nice."

"Thanks."

I had arranged fresh flowers in the bathroom and set a bowl of potpourri on the back of the toilet. I washed off my makeup and dabbed on some deodorant before whipping on a clean shirt. The door buzzed. "Press the second button!" I called, tucking in a shirttail.

The first guest was a peppy type with short red hair and Peter Pan leggings, a crisp white T-shirt knotted at the midriff over her black leotard. Her energy traveled upward from her heels to the crown of her head. She had the rubber-band snap of a professional dancer. Already my party was paying dividends.

"Sorry I'm late," she said.

"Actually, you're the first to arrive."

"Oh, good. Nancy from Buzzy's said you wanted someone to shoot the party, so here I am, locked and loaded." Strapped over one shoulder was a camera bag that I had assumed was a clunky purse.

"I didn't expect anything quite this gung-ho. What I need is for you to take Polaroids of the guests once the party gets into full swing. I have a camera ready."

"I can do that, but it's sort of like taking pictures at a children's party."

"Well, it'll be mostly theater people here tonight and, believe me, some of them are real babies. Our female lead is a *total* brat, not that I mean that as a criticism."

"For some reason, you don't remind me of other actors I've met," she said.

"Thanks, I think." The buzzer buzzed. The photographer stepped back and spread her hands to encompass a broader concept of what could be done.

"We could keep that corner as clear as possible and pose people against that wall next to the floor lamp," she said. "Steer them there singly or in a group. I can use either the Polaroid or the Nikon I brought, but that way you get a bare backdrop. If I bop around shooting casuals you're going to get eyes closed, people with their mouths open eating and drinking, and a lot of background clutter. I have an ulterior motive, just so you know. I'm branching out into doing actors' headshots, I intend to have my own studio soon, and this would give me an opportunity to introduce myself and give out my business card. Did you ever see Andy Warhol's celebrity Polaroids?"

"No, were they good?"

"They have a real seventies' look, but the man had an eye. The silver balloons you have here remind me of him. By the way, I'm Annette, Annette Bennett."

We shook hands, and her hand softened in mine, as if our introduction were passing from the formal into the personal.

"John Downs," I said.

"Good to meet you, John. It looks like you actually went to some trouble for this party. Most ones I go to these days, it's like being back in college. Chips and pretzels with a stereo playing too loud and lights too dim and the room too hot and this feeling of I've-been-here-before because, you know, you have. Stand over against the wall so I can take your picture."

I put up token resistance as Annette hooked the flash attachment to her camera and fired off a waste shot at the ceiling to make sure the flash worked. While I stood before the wall, trying to decide whether to put my hands in my pockets or not, Annette said: "So how did the play go tonight?"

"Pretty well, actually."

"You sound surprised."

"Well, you never know if a play's going to work until you're in front of an audience. I've been in things that crackled in rehearsal and then just pancaked on stage. And vice versa."

"Were you happy with your performance?"

"Kinda-sorta. I'll let you in on a trade secret. The first night, you're acting defensively. You don't want to make any mistakes—miss your cues, muff a line, drop a prop, pull a Dan Quayle. I had an errorless performance, so in that sense I'm satisfied. But I won't really feel I'm on stride for another performance or so. It's a short run, so I'll be peaking right about the time we're closing shop."

"Look at me and pretend you're peaking."

Annette tipped camera sideways for a vertical shot as I made the face of an actor hitting a Shakespearean high note. The flash went off. Then she told me to dip my head, and the flash went off again.

"Thank you," she said. I had never had a photographer say "thank you" before. She said it gently, cradling the camera as if it now held something precious. It was a good way to get your subjects on your side. I said:

"Can I get you something to drink before—?"

"I don't drink while I'm working but I'll take a mineral water. I love the inflatable alligator on your bed! Was that your idea?"

"No, that was my party planner's. She also suggested the palm trees. Took me all night to blow them up."

"They have devices that do that, you know. You didn't need to do all that puffing."

"Well, it builds lung power, I suppose. I could be the next John Coltrane."

"I had a boyfriend in college whose roommate kept an inflatable doll in his dorm room. He said it was just a joke, but after a while it gave me the creeps."

"Well, you have to trust your radar."

At the bar I poured Annette a mineral water and popped in a slice of lemon. The buzzer was busy. Come-hithery jazz from the compact sound system laid down a night-blue carpet of sound as guests made their way warily down the hall. The director came toward me with both hands extended palms-down, a Fellinilike greeting that directors ought to stop imitating. Nearly everyone headed for the bar. Drinks safely in hand, the guests were guided by Annette over to the apartment's one well-lit corner, where she took a quick mugshot or two before releasing them into the general population. I nursed a long-necked bottle of upstate beer, making every swig look thirst-quenching.

"Is she here yet?" the lighting person asked.

"Who?"

"Our star."

"Which one?"

"The one that can act."

"We're running short of limes," said one of the help.

I was rooting for limes in the kitchen when Tom Gleason arrived. He laid his head on the back of my shoulder and said, "Thank you, Tonto."

"For what?"

"Her." He motioned to Annette, who was posing against the wall a depraved-looking couple I had never seen before. "I love jockey-sized women," Gleason said, rocking back and forth, holding invisible reins. I checked both sides of Gleason and peered around him.

"Funny," I said, "I don't see Gwen anywhere about."

"Gwen loathes the theater, she finds it 'artificial,' so I did the decent thing and spared her. I tried to entice that bartender we met, but she wasn't buying. So where's your honey?"

"Nicole? In St. Louis on a presentation. She's flying in tonight, so she may be able to make it later."

"She seems to be out of town a lot."

"The nature of her job, I'm afraid."

"By the way, good job tonight, man. That outfit was so you. You looked like an alcoholic Australian journalist, if that isn't triply redundant. There were aspects of your performance that seemed modeled on me."

"I was hoping you'd notice. What'd you think of the play?"

Imitating one of Dwayne's monologues, Gleason slid his hand under his Hawaiian shirt and began rubbing his stomach, musing in a faraway voice, "And behind every door, there's a room, and inside every room, there's a closet, and that's where you'll find me, in the room with the closet, with my thumb up my ass."

"Stop that. Kenny's around here somewhere."

"I'm sure he is. Did you catch that little stunt he pulled at the call? After all you lovebirds bowed, he let go of Claudia's hand and took a step forward and gave his own wave to his buddies in the crowd, sort of like the salute a runner gives at second base after he's doubled in the go-ahead run." Doffing an invisible cap, Gleason imitated it for me.

"How did Claudia take it?"

"She looked none too pleased."

"What did you think of her performance?"

"I didn't think she was terrible, considering Kenny. She has that classy quality of looking cool yet on-call. But answer me this, pal: Why was the second act so long? It was twice as long as act one."

"Well, it was originally a three-act play. They dropped an intermission and ran the last two together."

"That's what I figured. Well, some compassionate soul should have done some cutting, because we were sitting there dying, waiting for the damned thing to end. Of course, you were probably too deep in-character to notice."

"You know me, I'm in my own world up there. Help yourself to more food. The vodka seems to be going fast."

"I'll stick to scotch, thanks. I don't want to turn against everybody. Vodka sometimes has that effect on me."

Host duties kept me hopping, which, I found, I enjoyed. I made introductions, congratulated my fellow cast members, freshened drinks, issued the occasional instruction to the help. As the host, I had more liberty to touch and tap the female guests in neutral areas—the upper arms and back—without seeming lechy. I may not have been the lead in the play, but I was the hub of the party. As I was slicing limes during an emergency lime shortage, I noticed that some of the guests were developing damp foreheads. Evidently, the living-room air conditioner was too small to cool the apartment with this many people in it, and for some reason the guests were gun-shy about picking up the

Evian sprays. When I finished with the limes, I dragged an electric fan out of the closet, only to discover the grill was covered with cat hair. I was cleaning the grill with a paper towel just as the door opened to let in new guests. With my luck, Nicole would make an entrance with a date at the very moment I was mopping away cat hair. I ditched the paper towels and angled the fan to blow diagonally across the room. A neighbor I barely knew and didn't remember inviting planted herself in front of it.

"We're nearly out of ice," said the restaurant helper who had bothered me before. He gave me a lot of raised chin after I handed him a twenty and told him to pick up some bags of ice from the deli on the corner. I was hoping to impress Annette with my quick and forceful manner in handling the situation, but she was too busy cornering actors to notice. Behind her, guests unbuttoned buttons and fanned themselves with their hands, moving their bodies to the music. The radio was off and my jukebox was going full blast, the grainy 45s skipping every time someone leaned against the machine. A few couples danced to an old Supremes number. Shrieks of laughter speared up from different parts of the room. A bottle clunked and rolled across the floor as my next-door neighbor and her latest boyfriend made out against the wall, her knee forcibly parting the other's jeaned legs. Balloons were being batted back and forth in an impromptu balloon competition. One woman sprayed her face with a can of Evian, luxuriating in the mist. "Spray me," said her date, offering his face. Then, amid all the commotion, came a sudden, almost imperceptible yet noticeable noise drop. It was as if everyone simultaneously developed split-screen vision, carrying on with what they were doing while watching something else. Even one of the makeout women cracked an eyelid.

"Well, well, well," someone said. "Her Ladyship has arrived."

14

CLAUDIA STOOD IN THE HALLWAY, creating her own radius. She had changed into a black dress even tighter than the one she wore on stage, her hair brushed to a brilliant finish. She had also changed shoes, putting on high heels that muscularized her assassin legs. Draped around her shoulders was a coat decorated with bull's-eyes and arrows. "Can I hang this up?" she said, spotting me amid the gawkers.

"Not only you can, but you may."

I held the back of her coat as she eased out of it.

"It's a beautiful coat," I said. "What fragrance were you wearing tonight onstage?"

"Vertigo. Did you like it? I thought it was something Cerrisse would wear."

I hung up the coat behind a protective layer of sports jackets.

"Oh, look at the kitty."

At the bottom of the closet, ready to spring from her favorite blanket, was Slinky, a threatening communique issuing from her throat. Claudia said: "Why are you cowering? Are you afraid of us?"

"She's shy, like me."

"You don't strike me as the shy type," Claudia said, touching her bare collar bone as she shifted her gaze from the cat to me.

"I mask it with, you know, something or other. I can't think of a pretentious enough word. Would you like a drink?"

"Not now. But I'm dying for a smoke. Would you mind?"

"Be my guest."

Claudia drew a slim pack out of her handbag and tapped out a cigarette. Reaching into my pocket for the lighter Darlene had given me, I said, "Allow me." I lit her cigarette with my hand lightly cupping her wrist. Our eyes met above the flame. Claudia blew a pile of smoke to the ceiling as I pocketed the lighter.

"I thought things went well tonight, aside from the lighting glitch," I said. "You were great."

"Thank you. You didn't think we lost them at the end?"

"Lost who, the audience? I didn't get that sense."

"I felt their interest slipping away, but sometimes you just have to accept it instead of rushing and shouting your lines as if trying to hold on to them at all costs. I refuse to go into hysterics. Is Kenny here yet?"

"He's unwinding with the director."

"They get along so well. Well, you mustn't let me monopolize you . . ."

"Oh, go ahead. Monopolize me."

"Another time, maybe. I believe this young man is trying to get your attention."

The young man, who was only a few years younger than Claudia and whom I had been making a steadfast effort to ignore, was the moonlighting Buzzy's waiter I had sent out to the store for additional ice. He was breathing hard at Claudia's side, as if he had traveled far to bring disturbing word from Sparta.

"I got the last two bags. The ice is in big solid chunks," he said. "I left the bags in the kitchen sink. After that, we're out."

In the living room, the vodka was taking effect. The director was bent double, either choking or laughing, as Kenny patted him hard on the back. I was chipping away at a bag of ice with a screwdriver when I looked past Claudia and saw several women congregrating around the entrance to the bathroom. Scratching their arms and clearing their throats lightly into their fists, they were trying to look casual and ready to take their turns, but it was obvious they were struggling to hold it in. I stopped Annette, who was framing a Polaroid shot of the makeout couple, and asked if she knew who was barricaded inside.

"That guy you were talking to earlier. He may be in there awhile."

"Why do you say that?"

"Because he took a magazine in with him. It looked like the latest issue of *The Atlantic*."

"Oh, my God."

"He definitely had the look of a man with reading to do."

"Are you two in line?" asked an older woman, dropping a handbag on the floor loaded with rocks and pipe fixtures.

"This line isn't budging," said the woman nearest the door. I recognized her as one of the stagehands. "I'm about to pound on the door with my shoe in a minute."

"Let me handle this," I said like the chief of a bomb-disposal unit, sliding between her and the door. I lowered my voice. "Gleason, what are you doing in there? I've got a line of antsy women out here."

"Isn't that what you've always wanted?"

"Seriously, how much longer do you think you'll be?"

"Let me get back to you on that."

Annette slid between me and the bathroom vigilantes. "I have an idea. Did you invite your next-door neighbor?"

"She's in the bedroom, sitting on the radiator."

"I'll ask if she'll open up her apartment and let us use her bathroom until your friend finishes. I'll tell her I really need to go."

"You'd be willing to do that?"

"Sure. Things could get ugly here."

"Then, with my blessing, go."

After a brief, urgent chat, my next-door neighbor left the bedroom with Annette. A couple of women followed them. Ten or fifteen minutes later, Gleason emerged, handing me the rolled-up *Atlantic* as if it were a college diploma.

"Did I miss anything?" he asked as the director end-rounded us and closed the bathroom door behind him.

"Only the running of the Kentucky Derby."

"Don't be horrid, as they say on *Brideshead*. It wasn't exactly fun for me, sitting there and listening to everyone's insults. You could at least put a little radio in there."

Annette handed me a stack of instant photos. "You should see your neighbor's apartment. It's like Barbie's dream house. I'd love to do a shoot there. Maybe you could play Ken."

"Before you go, could you get a couple shots of Claudia?"

"Which one is she?"

"The one all in black."

"Oh, the Tubular Woman. Let me go get my Nikon. She may be a celebrity someday."

As I said good-byes to some of the guests, I saw Annette fire off a round of shots of Claudia, who was standing in front of the only bare wall. After the fifth or sixth flash, she waved Annette off with her cigarette, as if it were a little wand, and went into the bedroom. She reemerged with her coat slung over her shoulder.

"I would have gotten that for you."

"Your cat hissed at me."

"Hi, I'm Tom Gleason. Downs here is afraid of introducing us, for fear we'll instantly ignite. Didn't I see you one summer at Williamstown?"

"You may have. Would you mind if I borrowed your drink for a minute?"

Before Gleason could think of a witty assent, Claudia took the glass from his hand and, her heels snapping against the floor, crossed over to Kenny, who was entertaining a pair of admirers in the middle of the room. As Claudia approached, Kenny smiled as if anticipating another compliment.

"Don't ever upstage me during a bow again," Claudia said, flinging Gleason's drink into Kenny's face. She turned, deposited the empty glass into Gleason's hand, and left the party without breaking stride. One of Kenny's admirers handed him a paper napkin. I apologized for the incident as Kenny wiped his face.

"Wasn't your fault," Kenny said. "Could I use your bathroom a minute?"

"Congratulations," Gleason said, punching me playfully on the shoulder as soon as Kenny was gone. "That made the party. People are going to be talking about this for days. What a pro! Most people toss a drink and spit out their explanation—'That's for hitting on my wife, you creep'—while the victim is so stunned he can't hear a word being said. Claudia let Kenny know upfront why he was getting it, let him have it, and flounced out. That woman knows how to cap a fine evening."

"I don't get it," said Annette, upset. "What did Kenny do?"

"During our bows, we're all supposed to form a single line and bow as a group. According to Gleason here, Kenny dropped Claudia's hand at the second bow and stepped forward, saluting the audience as if he were the star."

"Isn't he?"

"He and Claudia have equal parts, so what he did was kind of bad form."

"Definitely uncool," Gleason intoned, like Linc on *Mod Squad.*

"Will there be fireworks between them tomorrow night?" Annette asked?

"Maybe," I said. "I'll put you on the comp list, if you'd like to see for yourself."

"Great. I'd like to see you onstage."

"Did you get any shots of Kenny after he got splashed?" Gleason asked.

"No."

"Damn. I wanted one for my scrapbook."

"I thought it would be mean."

"Where's your killer instinct, cadet?" Gleason barked.

"Ignore him," I said. "Kenny's embarrassed enough without rubbing it in. Remember that photographer who couldn't bring himself to snap a picture of Ali in his dressing room after he'd been defeated? I always thought he did the right thing."

"Go ahead, make me look like an unfeeling brute," Gleason said.

"Do you think it's too late to take the subway?" Annette said, unplugging the flash attachment to her Nikon. "I have to head uptown."

"We could share a taxi," Gleason volunteered. "I'm going to Times Square."

"Okay, as long as we split the fare."

"Fine with me. You just stay on your side of the cab and I'll stay on mine. No funny stuff."

"Don't worry, he'll behave," I said to Annette, who was looking unsure. We shook hands, me hoping that mine wasn't too sweaty. As she was about to go, Annette's mouth made a silent "oh" and she pulled out a business card, tucking it into my jacket pocket and giving it a little pat. I gave my pocket a supplementary pat to let her know her card was safe with me. Gleason tilted the top half of his body sideways. Annette took the hint, and the two of them headed for the door.

15

I TURNED OFF THE AIR CONDITIONER and opened a screened window to air out the jazz-club funk of sweat, smoke, and alcohol. Slinky poked her head out of the closet, set her paws carefully on the floor, and shook from head to toe, getting the kinks out of her system. She hopped on the bed, sniffing my hands for vagrant odors. It was after midnight, but seemed much later. My legs ached from so much standing. As I was debating whether to call Darlene, she called me. I blurted the thing that had been at the back of my mind the entire party.

"Nicole and Pavia didn't show," I said.

"Sorry. I figured as much. It's too soon for her to be sneaking back."

"Why did you let me think they might?"

"I knew it might 'incentivize' you. How'd it go otherwise?"

"Pretty good. Everyone seemed to enjoy themselves. We had one incident involving a hurled drink, but no real damage was done."

"Did people like the decorations?"

"Oh, yeah. Got a lot of compliments on them—the inflatable alligator was a definite hit."

"Did anyone flirt with you?"

"I lit Claudia's cigarette for her with the lighter you gave me and felt quite continental. We might have gotten a cozy little exchange going if one of the hired guys hadn't barged in to bug me about ice. Also, the photographer who took the party shots turned out to be a real doll. I invited her to the play tomorrow night. Her name's Annette, and she's thinking about setting up her own shop doing actors' headshots. She gave me her business card. She hung around longer than she had to. She and Gleason shared a taxi uptown."

"You let her leave with Gleason? Are you *insane?*"

"Let's not overreact."

"Okay, but I can't believe you let some unsuspecting woman leave with that guy. That may be the last you hear of her. If her dead body turns up in an alley, it'll reflect badly on you as a host. Anyway, send me the party pictures as soon as possible and label them so I know who I'm looking at."

"Will do. Thanks for everything, Darlene. I couldn't have done it without you."

"I just wish I could have been there."

"Me too."

I hung up the phone and went into the bathroom to wash my face. Potpourri was spilled across the top of the toilet. I gathered up the stray bits and deposited them in the trash before Slinky could eat them. Sitting up in bed, still dressed, I flipped through the Polaroids Annette had taken. There was Claudia smoking, Gleason leaning on the jukebox, my next-door neighbor selecting a sandwich, a still-life study of the buffet. I slid the photos into a special envelope marked DARLENE that contained the Polaroids I had taken earlier and left it on the nightstand for next-day mailing. I rested awhile in bed and drifted off, jolting upright at the sound of a gunshot, which turned out to be Slinky popping a stray balloon with her claws. I stuck the balloon's withered skin in the nightstand drawer so that she wouldn't eat that, either. I undressed, banking the pillows to block the morning sun. Slinky settled on her corner of the bed, curling like a comma and blindfolding her eyes with her paws.

16

KENNY MANAGED TO CONTAIN HIMSELF the next night, massaging his stomach during his big monologue with doodly semicircles instead of the full abdominal rubdown. As we took our bows in front of a sparse crowd consisting mostly of other actors and a few elderly couples who prided themselves on being The Last Of The True Theatergoers, I spotted Annette in the audience with a female friend. I crinkled my nose in acknowledgment. She crinkled back, then tapped her wristwatch and shrugged, a bit of mime-work meant to signal they had to run. I shrugged to indicate I understood, wincing to convey my disappointment that we wouldn't have a chance to chat.

Backstage, Claudia thanked me for the party and apologized for any awkwardness her drink-toss had caused. "I hope you have another one soon," she said, her hand brushing mine. "I promise to behave."

The prop girl squeezed between us with a tray of glasses from the set.

"Gleason said the incident 'made' the party," I said.

"Which one was he?" Claudia asked prettily.

"He was the one who . . ." I used my hands to outline his general dimensions.

"Oh, him," Claudia said with an offhandedness that made me feel almost sorry for Gleason, who prided himself on being larger than life, like his literary heroes. As Claudia spoke, she swayed before me, not lyrically, but like someone about to tip over. I put out my hand to catch her, and she said, "I didn't eat before the performance. I guess I'm a little lightheaded. I'd better get out of these heels."

"Well, you be careful."

"I will."

A few days later, a note arrived in a demure envelope with no return address. Thinking it might be from Nicole, I nearly tore the envelope in two opening it. I unfolded the enclosed note and began to read. I had finished the note, set it aside, and poured myself an orange juice when Darlene called.

"Is this a good time for you?" she asked.

"Let me check my busy calendar. By the way, I just got this nice note from a certain female."

"Really, who?"

"I thought it might be from Nicole because it came in the same-type envelope as her stuff, but actually it's from that photographer, Annette."

"Read it to me."

"First, let me preface it by saying that I invited her to attend the play, which she did, but she wasn't able to come backstage afterward because . . ."

"What are you, Alistair Cooke? Just read it!"

"Dear John,

Just wanted to tell you how much I enjoyed the play last week. I had some problems with the play itself, but thought you were terrific, especially in the scene where everyone turns on you and you look stunned by their actual opinion of you. That sick look was very convincing! And moving. I also thought Claudia made a nice entrance.

So what did you think of the party photos?

Best, Annette B."

Darlene said: "That's a pretty nifty putdown she works in on Claudia. She sounds sharp. I don't want to burst your bubble, but keep in mind that this kid is trying to set up her own business, so flirting at the party may just be her way of buttering you up in order to network with all these other deadbeat actors you know."

"I think you're misjudging her. She struck me as sincere, although I realize that's sort of a weak-sounding word these days."

"I'm not saying don't date her. I just think you should be setting your sights higher than these downtown girls who haven't panned out in the past, which brings me to the reason I called. Let me ask you something—are you good with your hands?"

"Well, you know . . . I don't mean to brag . . ."

"I meant around the apartment. I know you think you're good with your hands when it comes to women. I'll never forget how you offered to give me 'a nice back rub' when we went on that picnic. I couldn't believe you thought I'd fall for a line like that."

"Well, you were lying on the blanket, stretched out on your stomach with the top of your halter untied, all freckly and everything. I thought I was getting an invitation. And as I recall, I didn't offer a back rub, I offered to rub some suntan lotion on you."

"We were lying in the shade!"

"Yes, I believe you pointed that out at the time."

"Anyway, I had an ulterior motive when I asked you to take Polaroids of your place before the party. It wasn't the decorations I wanted to look at. I wanted to see if your apartment had changed since my last visit. If we're going to do a makeover on you, we need to redo your apartment first. As long as you live like a bachelor, you're going to continue acting like one. Granted, you keep your cave fairly presentable, but there are definite areas for improvement."

"Since when did you become an interior decorator?"

"It doesn't take an interior decorator to spot obvious eyesores. First of all, could you at least clean up around Slinky's food bowl? There are rings of grime that look like they've been there forever. It looks like something out of World War Two, an aerial photograph of circles of bomb damage around Berlin or something. And that linoleum has got to go. If you had a wife or live-in girlfriend, it'd be the first thing she ripped up."

"What should go there instead?"

"Spanish tiles, dark blue with red accents, would look good. Or maybe something Arabic."

"I know a guy who could put them in."

"I do, too: you. Work with your hands, Johnny. Next to firemen, women flip for carpenters and contractors the most, and it's too late to turn you into a fireman. Being good with your hands means that when a woman imagines you as a husband, she won't picture you flipping through the Yellow Pages and acting ineffectual every time a knob falls off. Do you have a chef's apron?"

"I usually just tuck a dish towel under my chin."

"Get a chef's apron, a plain one with no funny messages on it. Instead of the aluminum pots and pans you have now, get a complete unit of copper ones, something that resembles a percussion set. It'll make you look like a serious cook who can improvise. You also need new dishes. You need dishes, period. A grown man doesn't dine off of paper plates even if he's eating alone. Get some earthenware dishes and, for drinking, a set of those thick pebbly glasses that are shaped like ice cubes. Everything in your kitchen should have a certain heft and conviction. Do you have a wicker tray?"

"What for?"

"So that you can bring your fiancée breakfast in bed."

"Should I get a lovely pink vase in which to place the perfect rose?"

"I realize you're being sarcastic in your painfully obvious way, but the answer is yes, you should. Did I steer you wrong about the party?"

"No."

"Then work with me here. I guarantee these investments will pay off. You've let things slide for so long there's a lot of catching up to do. I dread the very prospect, but we also need to address the bathroom. Did you ever get a small trash can for near the toilet?"

I dragged the telephone cord behind me as I entered the bathroom.

"I haven't quite gotten around to it yet."

"'Yet'! I suggested that to you over a year ago when I was there! You need one for your female guests, so that they can dispose of personal items without being self-conscious. Line the trash can with plastic and leave a few crumpled tissues inside so that they can camouflage items like tampons under them if necessary. If a woman stays overnight, empty it the next day. Believe me, she'll notice. Which leads me to another tender topic—Slinky's litterbox. Is it still next to the toilet?"

"I moved it for the party but, otherwise, yeah."

"You've got to find another spot for it."

"Why? It's convenient there."

"Because—how can I put this gently?—you don't want women picturing you and the cat sitting side by side, taking poops at the same time."

"I can't believe that image would cross anyone's mind."

"You'd be surprised. At the very least you don't want women thinking of the bathroom as *your* litter box. Describe the shower curtain to me."

"It's kind of light blue, with little spouting whales—"

"You mean you still have that same mildewed piece of flypaper that stuck to my leg when I climbed out of the tub? I'm about to faint, and I bet Nicole shuddered the first time she stayed over and showered in that *Psycho* bathroom, too. What you need to get *immediately* is a regular shower curtain with some sort of tasteful motif backed by a second one that's opaque. That way your fiancée won't fear you peeking in on her, and you can replace the opaque one whenever it gets dingy while the regular one stays clean. Describe your toiletries."

I slid open the medicine cabinet.

"Green Briar aftershave and cologne, a bottle of Scottish Kilt body shampoo, and some hotel samples from the last time I toured." I pushed some items aside. "This is odd."

Taped to the back of the medicine cabinet was a Polaroid of Annette from the party. I described the photo, and Darlene said:

"Sounds cute. Send it to me so I can check her out."

"No, I think I'll just keep this one."

"Suit yourself. As far as your toiletries are concerned, you need to find a signature scent and stick to it. Get rid of that motley assortment you have now and only stock Salty Dog aftershave and accessories."

"Salty Dog? That's what my father wore. And his father before him."

"Exactly."

"Darlene, you don't understand. This is New York. New York City. Lower Manhattan. Hipsville, baby. Salty Dog is considered corny and old-fashioned. They don't even have seafaring men anymore! They're extinct! Women up here respond to a more Euro scent, one of those unisex brands."

"Your name isn't Phillipe or Jean-Claude, and no real woman likes a

unisex anything. They only say that because they think it's sophisticated. Salty Dog will remind them of daddy, and that goes deeper than
any advertising campaign. It'll sneak right under their defenses. And
don't load up on this stuff and leave the bathroom cluttered. Look as if
you could pack and fly in a second. Women like that; it makes you seem
decisive. Do you still use disposable razors?"

"Yeah, they're easier."

"Get a real shaving kit, the kind with brush and shaving-cream bowl.
Women love to watch a man lather and shave. It reminds them of being
little girls watching their fathers spruce up."

"Darlene, it's daddy-this, daddy-that with you. A lot of women I
know feel very conflicted about their fathers. Their fathers were either
absent or doing head trips on them. I think that's what happened with
Nicole. I'm not an expert, but given some of the things she told me, he
sounds like a classic 'seductive father,' the type who . . ."

"I know what a seductive father is. I had one. It isn't the actual father
we're talking about, Johnny. It's the ideal father. Forget playground
infatuations, forget teenage romances and rock-star crushes. The first
true love in every girl's life is her father, and the second is the teacher
who reminds her of her father. No matter how horny women act in
magazines or on cable TV, *real* women want a man who's soft and
strong in all the right places, someone who doesn't judge them but
indulges and encourages them instead. So many women you meet these
days seem used up, because they weren't nurtured as children. They'll
respond to a man who can either offer them what their own father with-
held, or who can give them what their father gave them, with an extra
ingredient: sexual romance. Johnny, the thing you don't seem to understand about yourself is that you're a lousy bachelor, but would probably make *a not-bad husband.* Why fight it?"

"I don't know. Maybe I like being on my own."

"If that were true, you wouldn't have been gutted by Nicole's behavior. Personally, I think you'd like the feel of a wedding band on your
finger, the distinction it brings. Why don't you dig out a ring from
somewhere and wear it just to get used to the idea? And I'll tell you
something else, which I know you'll think is mushy, but here goes:
you'd make a great father. I've seen how kids gravitate to you. If I pick
up on that, other women do, too."

"I don't know. I had to do a lot of babysitting for my younger siblings when I was in high school and my parents were drinking. Maybe I feel as if I've done my duty. I basically spent the last two years of high school keeping the household from falling apart; I was a rock. Once I got to college, I said, that's it, no more refereeing, no more having this constant *din* in my ears. Maybe I'm not as happy as I could be, but who is?"

"Sounds like fear to me. Face it, Johnny: you tend bar, do the occasional play or commercial, fart around with Gleason, and that's about it. You almost never travel because of that cat. You hardly leave your own neighborhood unless it's work-related. You're ready for marriage but afraid to admit it because it would mean setting your sights higher than they are now and trying harder than you're trying now, and maybe failing at a deeper level than you've failed before. You probably thought you could diddle around with Nicole indefinitely."

"I'm not ruling out marriage for the foreseeable future, I'm just in no big hurry.'"

"'Not ruling out marriage for the foreseeable future' sounds like a politician talking. I don't understand why you insist on clinging to the status quo. It's not as if your status quo is so great."

"Say you're right. Even if I wanted to 'rebrand' myself as husband material, there's the matter of money. This shopping list you've handed me won't come cheap."

"You probably waste as much money on magazines and movie tickets over the course of a year as these items would cost. The other improvements only require some physical effort. That monster TV in the center of the living room, for example, could be moved into the corner and kept under wraps with a tablecloth or maybe even an opera cape. Right now the room revolves around that TV, and you don't want your fiancée thinking you're a couch potato. Make her think the TV is only for special occasions."

"I guess I could shift it out of the way," I conceded.

"Then you can start removing those neon signs and that damned jukebox. Donate them to the Salvation Army or, better yet, dump them on Gleason."

"Forget it! Those signs are collectibles, and everybody loves that jukebox. It's a seventies classic!"

"To any woman entering the apartment for the first time, they send the wrong swinging-bachelor message. Besides, that jukebox is a dust magnet. Store it in the basement for a while—I bet you won't miss it. Think of it as a booster rocket you need to cut loose before your capsule can go into orbit. That jukebox looks like something NASA built. Once you're free and clear, you'll be able to stop referring to your apartment as your 'bachelor pad.' In fact, the word 'bachelor' should be stricken from your vocabulary. From now on you're 'unmarried.'"

"What about 'single'?"

"It's not as bad as 'bachelor,' but 'single' smacks too much of 'singles' bar' and 'singles' action' and other phrases that send the wrong message. If we're going to make you into husband material, we need to modify your sense of identity. Add some depth. Volunteer work is always a good idea."

"What kind of volunteer work?"

"The kind that gets you out of the damned apartment for a change."

"I got a flyer recently, requesting reading volunteers, but I didn't follow up on it."

"Maybe you should, because everything we've done so far is you-you-you. Volunteer work will put you into contact with people worse off than yourself and help put things in perspective. Maybe you could donate some of that time you don't know what to do with to a nearby church or hospital. Church work would introduce you to quality women, women with values instead of those zombies you meet in the Village who are this far from their next overdose."

"You judge them too severely. Let me think about all this. That flyer is here somewhere."

"Better yet, why not bypass the thinking-about-it stage and actually do it? Wouldn't that be a refreshing change?"

"I hate you, Darlene."

"You love me. Is it raining up there? We've been having a lot of rain down here. A couple of people nearly drowned in their cars. Like idiots, they tried to drive through the floodwaters. When monsoon season's over, think about paying me a visit. I'd meet you at the airport and everything. It's been a while since we've seen each other."

"Are you being nice to me because you know what a sacrifice it is for me to junk my beloved jukebox?"

"Oh, Johnny," Darlene said in her most fluttery voice, "I don't *need* a reason to be nice to *you.*"

While the phone was still in my hand, I decided to give Annette a call. Even though Darlene had downplayed her friendliness, it seemed rude not to respond to her note and cute photo, especially since both showed personality. I dug out her business card and dialed the number. I was just about to hang up—six rings is my limit—when a young male grunted hello, slurring his vowels.

"Oh, hi. Is this Annette Bennett's number?" I said rather chippily.

"Not in."

"Do you know when she'll be back?"

"Maybe later."

That certainly narrowed it down. "Could I leave a message?"

"Let me get something to write with," he said. He set off on his sullen task, taking long enough to whittle his own pencil. When he was back on the line, I gave him my name and phone number, not wanting to overtax his mind and hand. As it was, I had the impression that he was only pretending to write, tracing the information in the air. "Would you mind repeating the number back to me?" I said. "Sometimes I mumble . . ."

"I heard you fine. Don't worry, she'll get the info."

He made it sound like a veiled threat, which added to my suspicion that he was probably Annette's boyfriend, one of those jealous pouters. Did they live together or was he loitering while she was out? Maybe Darlene was right, and Annette was being friendly at the party to drum up business. But that wouldn't explain the Polaroid she had left behind.

17

EVER SINCE SLINKY WAS A KITTEN barely out of the shoebox, she would knead me around bedtime at the end of a stressful day. I'm not sure what constituted a stressful day for her, but the warning signs included chasing her tail in a vicious circle and wrestling herself to the floor. As I was sitting on the sofa, she'd climb onto my lap and dip her head under whatever magazine or script I might be reading, forcing me to set it aside. She would pedal my stomach first, alternating her shoulders like a piano player doing a little boogie-woogie. Flipping back her ears, her forehead slanted like Boris Karloff's, she would proceed to my neck, entering a trance state as she conducted all of the tension out of her body. If I tried to remove her because her nails were too sharp, she'd dig in, not hard enough to penetrate the skin but enough to leave my throat red. Then, as if her entire body made a snap decision, she would hop off and groom herself. This ritual probably went back to infancy, when she massaged her mother for food.

One night shortly after the brief run of *An Oasis for Fools*, the phone rang while Slinky was pedaling. I tried to answer it without dislodging her—I didn't want her pushing off with her claws. I said a quiet hello.

Gleason said: "Am I calling at a bad time? If you're pleasuring yourself, I can call back."

"If that's what I were doing, why would I pick up the phone?"

"You tell me, sicko. Do you have the TV on? Take a gasp at Channel 34. Fuck, never mind. He's gone now."

"Who?"

"Chester Reilly. He was on *Whipsaw*, wearing a hairpiece he must have stolen when the salesman wasn't looking. It's sad when bad actors get old."

"Is that why you called?"

"No, I called to tell you Claudia Prentiss is up for a part on *Sunset Patio*. I heard they're casting her to play a society dame who bosses everybody around at the hospital where she's one of the biggest donors. There's a wing named after her late husband, blah blah blah."

"I wonder if they'll make her wear hats. Society women on soaps usually wear hats."

"They also wear fancy lingerie, which will be a step up after that ratty slip she wore in the play. Incidentally, I saw a review of *Oasis* in one of those freebie papers lying around the Laundromat, and they actually gave you a nice mention. I cut it out for you. Quick, turn on Channel 7! Major babe alert!"

Detaching Slinky, I grabbed the remote and hit 7. On the screen was an old country woman taking down laundry from a rope hung behind a wooden shack.

"Very funny, Gleason. I have to go. It's time for this gentleman to draw his bath."

"Massages, baths. No wonder you're too soft to take it."

"Take what?"

"The shit life throws at you. Speaking of flying shit, this morning Gwen and I had a discussion at the top of our lungs in which she accused me of screwing around when I was supposed to be helping her carry out a rug she's returning. I told her I forgot, one thing led to another, and I got on my high horse and said, 'Go ahead, call Downs if you don't believe me.' So if she calls, tell her I was shooting pool with you Tuesday night at that place on Elizabeth Street. She probably won't, but if she does, alibi me, OK?"

"Who were you actually with?"

"Nobody. I just didn't feel like lugging some damned rug down three flights of stairs. I went to a movie by myself and hid out for a while. I resent how so many women feel you owe them an honest explanation these days. To return the favor, I'll cover for you with Nicole some-time."

"That won't be necessary."

"Yes, I know, you're such a Dudley Do-Right, you'd never lie or cheat."

"No, it won't be necessary because Nicole and I are no longer seeing each other."

I stared at the space where my jukebox used to be. Gleason said:

"Sorry to hear that. I thought you'd been a little down lately. Want to talk about it?"

"Not really. There isn't much to tell."

The story slipped out in dribs and drabs, and within twenty minutes, I had told Gleason the entire saga, omitting Darlene and making it seem as if I had gone through it all alone.

"I don't want to play Monday-morning quarterback," Gleason said, "but maybe if you *had* made a scene when you caught her—given the other guy a shove and dragged her out of there by the wrist—she might have come around, once she got through screaming at you on the street. Women love being the center of contention. If it were up to them, men would still be having duels. I would have shown some anger, but then again, anger comes more naturally to me. Anyway, too bad. We should go out this weekend and get properly ripped."

"I don't think that would help."

"Of course, it wouldn't help, but the one good thing about a hangover is that it knocks everything else out of your head. The next morning there's just you and your ability to function. And, of course, the challenge of trying to reconstruct what happened the night before. James Dickey once sobered up with his car half-submerged in a pond, and had to wade to safety. Anyway, give me a call if you feel like howling."

18

SURROUNDED BY SPIKED IRON BARS and modeled on some-
body's idea of a Scottish castle, St. Teresa's was built in 1886, according to the tarnished plaque on the entrance wall. The stained-glass
windows of this stony fortress, capable of repelling any possible
invaders from TriBeCa or SoHo, were draped outside with sheets of
canvas that flapped like sails in the wind. It had been a gusty spring,
tropical storms carrying heavy winds north and popping windows out
of high-rises, sending them crashing to the streets below. As I crossed
the street, I recognized the lean specter of Tom Verlaine, the legendary
guitarist from Television, walking past the iron bars of the church, slipping a slim paperback into his coat pocket like a gin flask. Village lore
had it that whenever you spotted Verlaine in daylight, it was a good
omen. I knocked on the wooden door of the church and a peephole slid
open, as if someone were awaiting the password.

"My *name* is *Johnny Downs.* I have an *appointment.*"

"There's no need to shout. I'm not deaf."

"Sorry. I'm here about volunteer work."

The door opened like a sideways mouth. Standing behind it was an
elderly woman in rubber-soled shoes who looked as if she could peck
out someone's eyes. "We could use a few men around here," she said,
leading me down a checkboard corridor in her squeaky shoes. Her back
was stooped, and she had a doily attached to the back of her hair with

a bobby pin. She stopped at a side office, where an empty chair faced a vacant desk. A copying machine was going by itself, a stack of grainy pages overflowing the tray and spilling loose pages to the floor. "She shouldn't leave that unattended," the woman said. "Have a seat. I'll go hunt."

I sat, balancing my behind on a chair intended for a much smaller visitor, enjoying the buoyant sensation of finding myself in new surroundings and being able to shape myself before someone-new's eyes. I liked pretending I had just materialized in the present with no prior existence, which makes me different from most actors, who prefer working out an elaborate backstory. On the desk before me was a lumpy cup-shaped object that had been mashed together with a lot of thumbwork. Dinosaur-gray and bearing the unmistakable odor of Play-Doh, the cup was filled with paper clips. Just as I was getting acclimated to the deserted room, a woman brushed past me with smartly maneuvering hips.

"My son made that," she said, reading part of my thoughts. "It was intended as an ashtray, but then I stopped smoking."

She pressed the stop button of the runaway copy machine and picked up the copies scattered on the floor. Inserting a different document, she pressed PRINT and turned to face me. Studying her wardrobe selection, as Darlene had advised, I noted a V-necked sweater with a modest plunge, over a skirt that fit just fine. She sat down and took command of her desk.

"I'm Melanie Cole. You're interested in being a reading volunteer?"

"That's right. I'm an actor, and have had some reading experience. I helped make a recording for the blind, an audio version of letters written from the Pacific theater during World War Two. I did the voices of various soldiers."

"How did you learn about us?"

"I got this flyer that . . ."

"Have you ever done children's theater?"

"No," I said, crossing my legs in a leisurely fashion, "but I've performed in plays at children's matinees where they would bus in students on a field trip. The groups were often quite lively." Talking among themselves, throwing candy, squirming in their seats, and so on, the little cannibals.

Melanie Cole was wearing a simple gold wedding band, but gave off a more available vibe. She had a freshness about her that seemed ready to break out of the wrapping. The V of her sweater plunged lower than I would have expected in a churchwoman, but maybe I was being a prune, expecting someone like her to be wearing her eyeglasses on a chain. Keeping a line of patter going and asking follow-up questions, she seemed to have a polygraph going in her head, her eyes going from soft to hard to soft again, as if she were trying to get a true read. The copier stopped, and there was a clenched pause in the air, like the momentary suspense following the cutoff of a car alarm.

"Assuming I'm accepted, how would this work? Would I read to a single child or an entire group? Who selects the material?"

"You'll be reading to elementary–school-age children from PS 18. They're basically good kids with attention disabilities. Some are a little hyper, others a little daydreamy. Most come from homes where the parents don't or won't read, or from single-parent homes with all sorts of stresses. You'll start out with a single child and graduate to a group once you get the hang of it. It'll probably be all boys. Technically, girls are free to join, but they've expressed a preference for having their own group. I'm leading one for Sunday school, which is more religious in orientation. Right now we're reading from the lives of the saints."

"Really? As I recall from Sunday school, those saints' stories are mostly grisly tales of torture and martyrdom, being buried alive, torn apart by animals, stakes driven through hearts, that sort of thing."

"Well, the girls seem to enjoy it. So what made you decide to volunteer at St. Teresa's?"

"I'm unmarried, and although I keep busy, lately I've been feeling there's something missing from my life, a lack of involvement. I also live in the neighborhood and, for what it's worth, was raised Catholic."

"It says on the application that you're in restaurant services."

"I'm the assistant beverage manager at Buzzy's."

"Do you find the work challenging?"

"They could replace me with a robot and I'm not sure anyone would notice the difference. Acting is my real calling, at the risk of sounding vain."

"I see . . . Because you're a single man, we have to be extra careful in the selection process."

"I have a clean rap sheet, Mrs. Cole."

"I'm sure you do. Nevertheless, all of the volunteer agencies do background checks as part of the weeding-out process. Would you like to see the church while you're here?"

"Sure."

We walked down a long corridor where muted voices murmured behind closed doors. It was hard to imagine that the voices had bodies attached to them. I let Mrs. Cole get a little ahead of me, so that I could tag along behind those hips. We turned left and then it was all before us—the long red carpet, banks of ruby-red candles, the altar trimmed in gold, Jesus on the cross. The Catholic church I had attended in Maryland was on a military base, its plain chapel done in blond wood with little in the way of statues or gilding. This here was the full production. I dabbed my fingers in the holy water, genuflected in the aisle, and crossed myself. "They're cleaning the windows," Mrs. Cole whispered, pointing to the scaffolds. One of the workers waved to her with his brush. She rotated her hand, indicating they should speed up the clock, then said, "I'll walk you out."

Again, I let her lead. The inside of the church had been as dark as a movie theater. Outside, we found ourselves drenched in sunlight. With its grassy patches and mossy clumps, the churchyard seemed to be receding into the walls. A rosebush was making a last-ditch stand behind a water fountain filled with rainwater. Dipping its beak into the bowl was a huge crow, the white ripple along its folded wings resembling a customized paintjob. "You mentioned being raised Catholic," Mrs. Cole said. "Does this mean you're a lapsed Catholic?"

"I suppose, though I once saw a T-shirt that read RECOVERING CATHOLIC."

"A word to the wise," she said with a complicit smile. "Should your application be okayed, don't describe yourself that way around Father Grady. He was a military chaplain in Vietnam and later worked in VA hospitals stateside, and has little tolerance for flippant remarks. To him, faith is more than belief, it's a form of discipline. He doesn't like loose lips."

A young boy, pressing his head against the iron bars of the courtyard, stuck his tongue out at Mrs. Cole and me and began hopping up and down, scratching himself like a chimp.

"He's always doing that," Mrs. Cole said.

"Cheetah, find Boy," I called, an allusion that seemed lost on the kid but made Mrs. Cole smile. We shook hands good-bye.

19

BEFORE SUNDAY BRUNCH, I went to Shower and Tub to shop for bathroom items. Darlene had suggested I consult an attractive woman about shower rugs, but I arrived just after the store opened, and the only customers were couples pushing shopping carts like covered wagons across the West. I bought a small trash can, shower curtains, a shower rug, and a set of towels, and lugged my haul over to Wycherly's, an eatery located halfway between Shower and Tub and my apartment. I stashed the bags at my feet and paged through the *New York Post* until my eggs Benedict arrived, diverting myself by drawing death daggers and cartoon balloons on the party photos of models and restaurateurs. At a table adjacent to mine was a middle-aged man who hunched over his plate as if attempting to keep his food from wandering off. When I was done, he politely asked if he could borrow my *Post.* I handed it to him. He made no comment on my drawings. Out of the next dining room, which doubled as a party space on special occasions, strode a man in a brown leather jacket who halted in front of my table and did a double take, unsubtle even by silent-movie standards. It was the director from the Acorn beer ad.

"Hey, man, thought I recognized you!" he said.

"If you'd recognized me any harder, your head would have spun off."

"I'd stow that sarcasm if I were you. I'm somebody you might want to think about sucking up to. I'm directing a lot of TV these days."

"Oh, really, what?"

"I've done two *Code of Silences* and a segment of *Bachelor Sluts* on HBO."

The director, whose name I couldn't recall, did have the skintone of success that comes from moving up to the next level. His hair looked revitalized, too. He said: "I see you've been on a shopping spree."

"I needed to get some shower curtains and stuff for my bathroom. I'm also retiling the kitchen."

"Wow, you're a regular Suzie Homemaker!"

Wafting to his side was a cheekboned beauty with straight blond hair parted in the middle, who nestled under his arm and kissed him on the neck, her long, slender fingers cradling his chin. She was wearing a canary-yellow dress that positively sang. She must have been in the bathroom attending to her lustrous eyebrows. She turned toward me and bestowed a silent greeting, her wide-apart eyes full of amused, mild inquiry, as if wondering, Who might you be? "We have to dash," the director said, waving 'bye with one hand and hustling his date out of there as if he might have to carry her under his arm like a loaf of French bread if her feet started to drag. I suspected the reason he whisked her out was because he couldn't remember my name, either. After I got home, I called Darlene, telling her I had gotten new shower curtains but that the old rings didn't fit them, so I'd have to go back for new rings. Darlene said:

"You must be calling out of sheer loneliness. I've never heard you natter on like this before. Do you know anything about car wax?"

"Not a blessed thing."

"I'm washing my car later and I wanted to know the best brand to get. I'd call Clete but he's out fishing. It's a shame you won't be here to watch. Imagine: me in my cutoffs and skimpy top soaping up the hood and spraying the nozzle, arousing all the neighborhood boys while you're at home hanging a shower curtain."

"I know, I'm getting stir-crazy. I saw a guy at brunch today and realized that could be me in ten years. I don't want to end up being one of those guys who wears a heavy scarf even in hot weather and stuffs newspaper clippings in his pocket. To make matters worse, I ran into this director whose date was this gorgeous thing."

"And you sat there thinking, 'Why can't I get any of this golden nookie?'"

"No, I'm just eager to get back into the swim."

"Good. The question is, are you ready to go on a *real* date? Not one of those feeble charades men fob off on women these days."

"How would you define a 'real date'?"

"One that doesn't involve the VCR and ordering in food, or meeting at a neutral spot and 'maybe doin' somethin' together.' One that involves some planning and personal touches. Do you have any date prospects in mind?"

"There's this new waitress at Buzzy's who seems open to—"

"Dating coworkers is a bad idea. You can't have any mystique to someone watching you pump Diet Sprite all day."

"Don't be too sure. You've never seen me pump. Also, Gleason gave me the name and number of this friend of his girlfriend who's just broken up with somebody. He's only met her once but said she had a lot going for her."

"You don't want to get Gleason involved in your love life. Who knows what kind of damaged goods you might be dealing with? I have a better candidate in mind."

"Who?"

"That bombshell with the black hair."

"Claudia? I doubt she thinks of me as date material, much less husband material."

"But does she think of you as *man* material?"

"Well, she did lift her eyelashes when I lit her cigarette at the party and was flirty the next night. But the rest of the run she was pretty much a Popsicle. Anyway, I thought you didn't like her based on her party photo, not to mention she's an actress."

"I know she's an actress and, no, I don't trust her. That's immaterial. The point is, she must like you on some level, otherwise why did she compliment you after the party and suggest you have another one soon? Because she's polite? Most women aren't polite anymore. They don't have the patience. So she must have been at least moderately impressed by you. She also offers an opportunity for you to raise your game and tone up your act. Ask her out to dinner. The most important thing for you to do is to start structuring your dates within an overall strategy, and Claudia strikes me as someone with clear notions of what constitutes a successful night out. She isn't someone willing to hang out at a pool hall until all hours. If you can keep her amused, the women who follow should seem easy. Did you and Nicole have a favorite place?"

"We had two regular places, a diner for ordinary meals, and this French restaurant when we wanted a more romantic atmosphere."

"Good. Go for the French place. You'll know your way around and if Nicole happens to spot you there, you'll be with Claudia, which I guarantee will make her *seethe*. Claudia's the kind of woman other women hate on sight, which makes her a useful tool. Seeing her with you will make other women think you must have something going for you, especially if you show a cool command."

"I can fake that. Well, maybe I'll give her a call tomorrow."

"Don't maybe-baby me. Call her tonight. It's still early. Sunday night is when women are at their most susceptible, especially if they didn't have a Saturday night date or had one that fizzled."

"I imagine Claudia does just fine for herself on Saturday nights."

"How do you know? Maybe she's dating some rich creep, or has a married boyfriend she can only see during the week, or is between boyfriends, recovering from a breakup the way you are. If you men had any idea how many lonely women there are out there you might spend less time feeling sorry for yourselves and more time finding Miss Right. Now here's something important: When you ask Claudia out, don't phrase it in the form of a question. Phrase it as a statement. In other words, instead of saying, 'Would you like to have dinner with me sometime next week?' say, 'I want to take you to dinner.'"

"That's pretty direct."

"That's the point. In some therapy practices, that's how they get people to 'own' their desires, by phrasing them as statements. As they say in Gestalt therapy, most questions are demands with hooks hanging at the end. When someone says, 'Don't you think it's chilly?' what they really mean is, 'I'm cold—somebody do something.' So don't ask Claudia out to dinner, tell her you'd like to have dinner with her in a frank, friendly manner. And say her name a lot. Narcissists love that."

"You should write a book."

"Who says I'm not? Now, go get her, tiger."

After Darlene hung up to go buy car wax, I procrastinated on the sofa, patting the cushions and plucking cat hair off my pants. Then I placed the telephone on my lap, took a deep breath, and dialed Claudia's number. Assuming a natural aristocrat like Claudia never answered her own phone, I expected to get her service, but on the third ring she picked up.

"Hel*lo,*" she said with a deep, honeyed tone that made me wonder if she was expecting a call from someone else.

"Claudia? . . . It's Johnny Downs."

"Downs. Of course. How are you."

"Fine. Gleason sent me a favorable review of *Oasis* he cut out of one of those free papers, did you see it?"

"I never read reviews."

"Well, that's not really what I called about. Claudia, I would like to have dinner with you and was wondering if next week at Alsace Lorraine would be acceptable, assuming the soap isn't keeping you captive. Gleason told me you were up for *Sunset Patio.* Alsace Lorraine is this real nice French bistro—"

"I've heard of it, though I can't say I've ever been."

"We haven't seen each other since the play closed, Claudia, and I thought it might be nice if . . ."

"Which night?"

"How about next Thursday?"

"Thursday, Thursday, Thursday . . . ," she repeated, as if the word itself conjured up a foreign land, misty and far-off.

"Or Wednesday, maybe." Darlene's voice piped in my ear, *Pick a night and stick to it.* "But Thursday is prime for me, Claudia."

"Next Thursday. Next Thursday." Claudia seemed to close her eyes as she spoke, turning calendar pages in her mind. ". . . Thursday will be fine."

"Give me your address, so I can pick you up."

"Don't bother. I can meet you there."

"You sure?"

"I'd prefer it, actually."

I gave her the time and place with an authority of a network anchorman. "And afterward maybe we could catch *Rash Remarks.* It's supposed to be pretty good, for a commercial comedy."

"I was up for the role of Ilana. I'd be intrigued to see what Jill Donnelly does with the part. She's very much 'into' comedy."

"Unlike us serious thespians," I said with a dry chuckle. When Claudia declined to join in, I said, "So . . . I'll see you then."

"I'll call if something unforeseen happens in the interim. Thanks for asking. It should be fun. Ta."

I sat on the sofa, quietly amazed and only slightly annoyed. I phoned Darlene later that night and gave her a report.

"I swear, Johnny, these Northern women have no couth," Darlene said. "Almost any woman down here would have said 'no' nicer than Claudia said 'yes.' Mighty big of her to offer to phone first if she decides to break the date due to 'unforeseen' circumstances. But the important thing is, the little phony said 'yes.'"

"I know. Wonders will never cease."

"Don't underestimate the possibility that she may actually like you. You're a likeable guy. The trick is translating that into something more substantial. The reason so many women dismiss 'nice guys' is not because they want to ride in limos and sniff coke with rap stars, though some do, but because so many 'nice guys' seem negligible. A woman looks at a man who doesn't assert and thinks, 'In a crunch, he won't stand up for me, either.' That's why you have to stop badmouthing yourself, even in jest. It's one thing if I kid you, but you joke about yourself way too much. I've even heard you preface a joke at your own expense with a *self-deprecating chuckle.* You don't want to turn into an Uncle Joe."

"Who's Uncle Joe?"

"You know, that old fart on *Petticoat Junction.* Don't you watch Nick at Nite?"

"Not since I moved the TV set out of the middle of the living room."

"Admit it, don't you feel virtuous not having it on all the time?"

"I do feel like less of a slug."

"I'm convinced TV is the Devil. I only see Nick at Nite because Clete insists on watching it. He likes to sit and make fun of those old shows."

"Sounds like a stimulating way to spend an evening."

"Oh, like you and Nicole watching some soap opera together was so cultural. Just because Clete and I don't happen to live in New York doesn't make us a couple of dullards."

"I didn't say it did."

"Don't let this Claudia thing go to your head."

20

"HIS NAME IS GERALD," Melanie Cole said, leading me down the hall of St. Teresa's to its primary reading room. "Take care not to call him Jerry—he's sensitive about his name. He's a youngest child and resents anything that implies he's babyish."

"I shall treat him like a compadre."

"In here."

The reading room resembled a playpen with a religious theme. Pasted on a display board was a big cut-out animal alphabet, from Ant to Zebra, next to a stern NO SMOKING sign. A few stuffed animals slumped on a wooden bench with their heads hanging, as if they'd just faced a firing squad. Three small wooden chairs formed a semicircle in front of a big rocking chair with a badly eaten padded seat and arm-rests. It was all around me, the all-enveloping, half-forgotten, vaguely comforting, and somewhat suffocating compound smell of glue, stale milk, graham crackers, and wet flannel. A childhood smell that brought to mind how sticky you felt after a nap. Taking hold of the top knobs of the rocking chair, Mrs. Cole tugged it toward her, balancing a pointy shoe on one of the runners.

"Reading sessions are a half hour," she said. "Studies have shown that the attention span for readings today is about twenty-two minutes, and that's probably stretching it. The first meeting is more of an intro-ductory session so that you two can get used to each other. Ah, here's Gerald now."

Gerald, dressed like a white homey smuggling groceries in his wide-load pants, was deposited at the door by the guardian of the peephole, who then returned to her post. Gerald proceeded to perform a child's version of passive resistance, dragging his feet in a death march from the doorway to the middle of the room. He flopped in one of the small chairs as if the impact of landing had knocked the last bit of life out of him. He combed his sun-blond hair with his fingers and beat the heel of one sneaker against the rung of the rocker.

"Gerald, this is Mr. Downs. He's an actor."

"Hurray for him," he said.

"Sit up straight," Mrs. Cole said, soft but firm.

He obeyed, with just enough simmer to suggest a junior Steve McQueen. On his lap was a binder notebook and a black plastic bag.

"Have you brought a book, Gerald?"

He tapped the bag.

"Then I'll leave you two. I'll be just down the hall."

"Now what book have you brought?" I said most cordially.

Gerald handed me the entire paper bag. There were two books inside. I withdrew the first and studied the cover, which featured a train locomotive whose cars trailed behind like a conga line. The book was called *Mr. Train Conductor*, and there was a sales slip stuck in its pages like a bookmark. I thumbed through the text. Mr. Train Conductor had invited Billy, who was black, and Sally, who was pasty, to follow him from car to car as he punched tickets. On each car were passengers, taken from all walks of life and every ethnic and religious persuasion. It was a Democratic convention on wheels.

"Would you like me to read this by myself, or would you like to alternate pages?"

"You do it. I'm bushed."

"Hard day in the playground, huh? Okay, I'll read alone, as long as my voice holds out. You stop me if there are any words you don't understand, like 'choo-choo' or 'caboose.'"

Gerald gave me a sarcastic look before granting a grudging smile. I cleared my throat like an old radio announcer and began to read: "'Mr. Train Conductor had ridden many a mile on the railroad. He knew the names of every tie on the tracks, and the precise time of every stop. He had never been let down by the trusty gold watch he wore on a chain, which slept in the pocket of his vest.'"

This book was awful. I glanced over the top of the page at Gerald, who was removing something from the bottom of his sneaker. I kept reading, resisting the temptation to interject editorial opinion into the story. When I reached the point where Mr. Train Conductor introduced Billy and Sally to the engineer, a burly mama in a neckerchief named Bernice, I sounded so sappy I had to stop.

"Would you mind if I asked a question?" I said.

Gerald shrugged, as I knew he would.

"Did you pick this book yourself?"

"My mother bought it."

"No offense to your mom, but this book doesn't seem to be quite cutting it for either of us. Let's try the other one, if you don't mind."

He dug the other one out of the plastic bag. Its cover showed two boys sitting on a stoop up to their ankles in crack vials and empty bottles as a lone workman hauled a box on his back. The title, executed in graffiti lettering, was *The Summer We Were Evicted.* I flipped ahead to the last page of this slice of social realism, which had a happy ending (a less ratty apartment in an integrated neighborhood), but was illustrated with artwork so abject that the one tree on the characters' new block couldn't spare a single leaf. I was touched by the effort Gerald's mother had made. She didn't know whether to get a happy book or one that reflected our modern despair, so she bought both. Mothers really do try.

I said: "Maybe we could just leave this one for another time as well. I see you have some reading material stashed in your notebook."

"It's just a comic book."

"Really? I'm something of an expert in the field, you know."

Gerald handed me the comic, whose silver-embossed cover I opened as carefully as a classified CIA folder. The contents showed Nowhere Man, a superhero who fends off an asteroid shower with rockets from his wrist-launchers, returning from space to Earth II, an alternative-universe planet where his exploits are ridiculed on TV-screen billboards orbiting the sky like low-atmosphere satellites. Earth II is a civilization so decadent, it wants to die. An adult comic for advanced adolescents, *Nowhere Man: Exodus of Fire* featured fist-to-the-face close-ups of contorted faces dribbling with blood inserted into medium shots of rubble, corpses, and decay—the future as seen by a radioactive rat.

I said: "Very existential. Do you collect comics?"

"No, but I have an uncle in Michigan who does. He keeps them in plastic wrappers in special locked cabinets. He says he's waiting for the market to come back before he sells any and makes money. He has a Captain America from World War Two, and this comic that had Spiderman before Spiderman got his own comic."

"Do you remember who Captain America was battling on the cover?"

"Some guy who looked like a tooth."

"That probably was the Red Skull. Yeah, that would be worth something in mint condition. Does your family go to Michigan every year?"

"We used to, until my father had a fight with my uncle. He says he won't ever go back. I wish we would because we used to go fishing at my uncle's cabin, and it was just the guys, my sister had to stay home. We slept on the floor in sleeping bags, and we got to ride horses. No one gets to ride horses around here, except cops."

"You know, maybe next time I'll bring in this collection of great horse stories I have. But in the meantime, we'd better skim this book about being evicted, in case you're quizzed on it later."

Since there was a lot of foot traffic coming down the hall, along with shouts from the workmen on the scaffold, I rose to shut the door.

"You have to leave the door open," Gerald said. "It's the rule. You shut the door, and Mrs. Cole will come down here and chew your behind out."

"No, she wouldn't. She likes my behind."

"Don't say that too loud," Gerald said, pointing to the wall, where an old intercom hung over a bulletin board.

"Can they listen in?"

Gerald nodded.

"Thanks for the tip. Now let's see . . . let's start with the scene in family court . . . it looks like a real grabber . . ."

When our half hour was up, I escorted Gerald like a paroled inmate to Mrs. Cole's office. Waiting there was a woman wearing a limp blouse and smiling and frowning with different parts of her face at the same time. I assumed she was Gerald's mother. Years of conflicting emotions had given her that universal harried-mother look. "How was he?" she asked, taking Gerald's face in her hand and scrunching it.

"Enthralled."

"Yeah, right," said Gerald, who put up a weak struggle as his mother straightened his collar for him. Once they had gone, Mrs. Cole

moved her stapler an inch or so to the right, then countered by shifting her pencil box an equal length to the left. There was something
unlaced about her smile. I had the impression that she had slipped out
of her pointy shoes.

"So how did it go?" she said.

"Not bad, though that one book was el depresso."

"Well, let's see if they schedule a follow-up session. Sometimes the
mothers arrange these readings just so they'll have a free baby-sitter
service. In the meantime, there'll be a small get-together for the volunteers in a few weeks—I'll put you on the invite list. We have to coor-
dinate with all the self-help groups that use our meeting rooms, which
complicates everything."

"What kind of groups?"

"The usual. A.A. Overeaters Anonymous. Gamblers Anonymous. A
support group for smokers trying to quit. A number of women's
groups. We also have an ongoing workshop run by a trained therapist
for those unable to control their anger in spousal relationships. It's
mostly men who have been arrested on minor charges and are given a
choice between attending these meetings or doing jailtime."

"It'd be tempting to eavesdrop on one of these meetings over the
intercom. All those secrets being spilled, all that psychodrama.
Somebody could do a mystery novel about a self-help group where one
of the members is being blackmailed over the stuff he confessed at
meetings and is eventually murdered, which narrows the suspects
down to the other group members, until it turns out there was an outside party eavesdropping on the intercom, or on a webcam. A demented
nightwatchman or something."

The slap of shoe leather down the hall made Mrs. Cole straighten. I
snapped to attention as well just as a dark shape reached the doorway,
blocking the light.

"Father Grady," Mrs. Cole said, "this is John Downs, our newest
reading volunteer."

We shook hands. Father Grady put a lot into his grip. He had silver-
gray hair parted on the side that resisted being combed, as if it wanted
to go back to being a crew cut. He had a boxer's square, hunched shoulders and a sea-captain's eyes, so cold and blue they drew notice to the
red rims of his eyelids. He looked fanatically awake, the way early ris-
ers often do.

"Pleased to meet you, Father. Mrs. Cole told me you served as a military chaplain. I grew up near a military base."

"Which one?"

"It used to be called Edgewood Arsenal."

"Oh sure. They did a lot of chemical and LSD research-testing there before it became part of Aberdeen Proving Grounds. So how do you like St. Teresa's?"

"I used to be an altar boy, so this really takes me back."

I looked around as if awash in reverie.

"Have they fixed the ceiling in the conference room yet?" he asked Mrs. Cole.

"They promise it'll be done tomorrow. They're still plastering."

Father Grady's beeper sounded a triple-noted bird peep. He detached the pager from his belt, glanced at the mini green screen, and glared. His footsteps receded down the hall, followed by the sound of a door shutting.

Mrs. Cole chuckled. "'I used to be an altar boy,'" she repeated.

"I know. I got nowhere with that."

21

SLINKY ROSE ON HER HIND LEGS at the windowsill, pointlessly batting at a fly trapped between two panes of glass. It was warm out but depressingly cloudy, one of those Ingmar Bergman days. I was ironing a shirt with the phone wedged under my ear.

"I wish you were taking Claudia to a movie rather than the theater," Darlene said. "Movies are more private and romantic, plus they're easier to leave if they're lousy. What's this play you're subjecting her to?"

"A comedy I got comps for, an adaptation of a French farce set in colonial Africa, only now it's set on a Southern plantation after the Civil War. It's got a good cast."

"It better have, because it sounds awful. Before we get Claudia to the theater, though, we need to soften her up over dinner. Tip the hostess or maitre d' extra to make sure you get a choice seat, one that lets her scan the room and be noticed. Don't leave her facing a coat rack, like you did me that time. At dinner, mirror her moves. When she sips, you sip. When she tilts her head, you tilt your head. Make it seem as if you're in unconscious harmony with her."

"My God, Darlene, I'm an actor. I know what 'mirroring' is."

"And because you're an actor, you face the challenge of not opening up the old gasbag and going off on some wild-country safari about amusing incidents you're reminded of. Don't talk about your cat, either. You don't want to sound as if you dote on Slinky like some shut-in. Prompt Claudia with questions about herself, respond with nods and paraphrases of what she's just said, and ask follow-up questions. Find out about her family, especially her relationship with her father. Take in every word, and then do the Glass Test."

"What's that?"

"As the two of you are talking, discreetly slide your water glass close to hers and see what happens. If she leaves her glass in place, it means she's comfortable with your presence. But if she pulls her glass back, it means she's in a defensive posture. The beauty of this is that her response is purely instinctual—she won't even be aware of your glass moving toward hers, assuming you don't *shove* it across. It's like unconscious chess. Watch out if she lines the salt and pepper shakers and sugar bowl across the table, or bunches them as a block between you two—that's a classic warning sign. It means she's building a barricade. If that happens, wait until there's a lull or she leaves the table, and clear them off to the side. Order a martini before dinner."

"No, no, martinis hit me something fierce. The last time I had one, it was as if there were edit splices or jumpcuts in my brain. I'd say to myself, 'I think I'll reach for a peanut,' only to find the peanut already between my fingers. I'm convinced martinis do something to the time-space continuum."

"You don't have to drink the whole thing. It'll look good in your hand. Now, if she doesn't order dessert, don't you order one, either. I know that's a major sacrifice for you, but a woman doesn't respect a man who can't get by without dessert. When you leave the restaurant, support her elbow lightly with your hand at the crosswalks. Too many men up north let a woman fend for herself in traffic. I'll never forget the time you left me stranded in the middle of all those honking cars because you had already buffalo'd ahead."

"That's because you were moving too slow. Anyway, we're not going to need to cross the street. I can just hail us a taxi in front of the restaurant."

"Don't! Walk at least a couple of blocks with her before you grab a taxi, so that you can take note of which side her pocketbook is slung. The Pocketbook Test is even more revealing than the Glass Test. If Claudia strolls with her pocketbook on the side away from you, she's leaving the near side open, making her hand available for holding. That doesn't mean she wants you to take her hand, just that she is unconsciously receptive to the idea. If she slings her pocketbook over the arm closest to you, it means she's setting up a protective barrier. Don't get pouty if she does, just back off a bit."

"This all seems very clinical. Like I'm manipulating the situation."

"From what you've told me, Claudia is something of a cockteaser. I'm sure her manipulation skills dwarf anything we could come up with. All we're doing is reading her defenses so that you can gauge if she's really flirting or giving you a fake-out. She may be a woman who talks sexy but puts up guardrails most men don't notice because they're too busy imagining her being a wildcat in bed. Most sexy talk is completely counterfeit."

"Luckily, Claudia carries a pocketbook with a shoulder strap, but what do I do if I date a woman who wears one of those little designer backpacks?"

"Nothing, because you're not going to be dating no women who wear backpacks."

"That'll certainly narrow down the candidates."

"Backpackers are too young for you. You want a mature woman who takes pride in her handbags. I'd bet anything Claudia owns quite a collection. Also, arrange to have flowers delivered for her at the theater. If you bring her flowers at the restaurant, you'll feel silly holding them and she'll have to tote them the rest of the evening. Have them hold the flowers for you at the box office or manager's office, then pretend you just remembered something and pick them up and present them to her then. Imagine putting Claudia in the taxi with an armful of flowers—now that's romantic. I'd die if a man did that for me on the first date."

"Suppose she invites me back to her place or we decide to go out for coffee?"

"First of all, she probably won't ask you back after the first date. Second, you don't *want* her to—it's too soon. And if you add coffee on top of dinner and a play, it extends the evening way too long. She'll be sick of you by then, no matter how scintillating you think you've been. No, bring the evening to a distinct close. Give her flowers, put her in a taxi, and don't make the slightest hint of a sexual overture. Believe me, she'll be impressed."

"None of this comes cheap, Darlene. We're talking about a pretty expensive evening."

"You told me the theater tickets were free! You're fretting about the cost of a dinner and flowers? You're not adopting a stray from the animal shelter, Johnny, you're training to find a fiancée and future wife. Remember: Every woman, no matter how unapproachable she may act, has a best friend she regularly reports to. So even if Claudia herself doesn't respond the way you hope, you want her telling her favorite confidante, 'He took me to this very nice restaurant and then had flowers waiting for me at the theater.' Word like that gets around. Is it supposed to rain that night?"

"I don't know. Why?"

"It'd be nice if the two of you could share an umbrella, then she'd almost have to carry her pocketbook on the other side. There's no faster way for two people to get snuggly. You do have a decent, good-sized umbrella, right? Not some broken-down thing with bare spokes ready to poke out someone's eye?"

"I have a very sturdy umbrella I bought in London," I informed Darlene. "It's served me quite well over the years."

"You sound like you're talking about your penis."

"Well, I'm not. I know the difference between my penis and an umbrella."

"Whatever you say, Lancelot. Before I forget—send me some Polaroids of your new shower curtains. I want to set them next to the Polaroids of Claudia and see if I can picture her taking a shower in your apartment. Sometimes you get insights when you transpose images. Aren't you fascinated by the way my mind works?"

"Not as much as you are."

"You think you're being clever, but you know what?—you're right. You've stumbled on the truth. I love the way my mind works. I'm often amazed at my own insights. I sometimes have moments of clarity that make me feel I can fly. I'm not going to apologize for that. No matter how much progress has supposedly been made, women aren't allowed to have the pride of ownership in their brains that men are. Just the way men carry their heads on their shoulders shows you how much they prize their intellects. You should see some of the professors around here—they've already got their heads bronzed. Maybe that's why you and I suit each other so much. My brain and your heart almost add up to a complete person."

"I'm a complete person, Darlene, and so are you."

"I don't always feel like one," she said.

"I wish I were there to give you a hug," I said.

Instead of groaning or snorting with derision, Darlene surprised me by quietly agreeing. "I wish you were, too."

22

AFTER WORK, I TOOK A POWER NAP so that I would be completely fresh for my date with Claudia. I showered and dusted myself with talc. Slinky sneezed in that cute debutante way cats do. Then I brushed my teeth, putting extra elbow into it.

My clothes were laid out on the bed. My dress socks, dark-blue pleated slacks (Darlene claimed women loved running their hands along pleats), blue sports jacket, starched white shirt with a blue diamond sewn at the pocket, royal-blue tie. For me, the shirt was the key element. Gleason always advised wearing top-designer shirts on a date, because that's what women end up staring at most of the evening. You could get away with jeans and an old sports coat, as long as you had a starched shirt with a collar that cut. The white shirt brought back memories of First Communion, when my mother had laid out my new outfit on the bed.

I checked myself out in the full-length mirror from the front, turning to see how my jacket hung in the back, and decided I looked too assembled. My outfit seemed almost modular. I remembered an old trick of Fred Astaire's. When his clothes looked too stiff and new, he would ball up his jacket and throw it against the wall a few times. So I balled up my jacket and threw it against the wall Fred Astaire-style. Breaking it in felt good. It helped release some of the tension I was feeling. Slinky, sharing my anticipation, began racing around the apartment. When I put the jacket back on, it seemed more a part of me, an accomplice. I laced up my dressiest black shoes, which I had had professionally shined at a shoe shop the size of a phone booth.

Alsace Lorraine was located on Bethune Street, where the trees still had a wet polish from the rain. The name of the restaurant was painted on the front windows in ornate script. A small gaslight burned on each side of the front door. Sitting on a milk crate by the delivery door was a young man in a stained apron, having a smoke. I went inside. Although it was early, a knot of well-dressed people blocked access to the hostess who maintained the reservation book on a wooden music stand. Boisterous conversation echoed from the dining area, which was unusual. On my few visits here with Nicole, the main room had never given off anything louder than a collective murmur. The hostess recognized me from those earlier visits and smiled.

"*Bon soir.* You have a reservation?"

"Yes, for six-thirty. Downs."

"Ah, *oui.* Downs, *a deux.* We have a birthday group tonight, which has squeezed things somewhat. Will Miss Price be joining you?"

"I'm afraid not. I'm expecting someone else. Has Miss Price been in lately?"

Her eyebrows froze, as if this might be a leading question. "I just returned from vacation, so I really couldn't say. Would you like to wait for your date at the table, or would you prefer the bar?"

"I'll wait at the bar, thanks." Planting one foot on the railing like a ranch hand, I ordered a Dewars on ice, listening against my will to the litany of complaints coming from the customers at the hostess's music stand. I debated whether to order a martini at dinner, as Darlene had advised, or stick to scotch. The scotch quickly lit a cozy fire in my head, which a martini might clash with or send out of control. I checked my watch. 6:35.

I sipped slowly and engaged the bartender in some shoptalk about the bartending trade. After he supplied me with goldfish crackers, I checked my watch again. 6:49. I shrugged. Fifteen minutes wasn't so late. Claudia may have hit traffic. The hubbub behind me escalated, sounds of mutiny coming from the customers ganging up at the music stand. A couple of them flipped open cell phones and relayed trouble to those on their way. The hostess tapped me on the shoulder and said: "Mr. Downs, do you know if your date will be arriving shortly? We're having a difficult time holding tables with so many others waiting."

"I expect her any moment."

"It's just that we have a latecomers policy for holding tables at Alsace Lorraine. We only hold tables for a half-hour . . ."

"Perfectly understandable, mam'selle," I said, which must have been the scotch talking. "How about if I wait for my date at the table? That way you won't have an empty one getting everyone upset."

"Excellent. Janine, would you please seat this gentleman?"

I left the bartender a tip, swiveled off the bar stool without getting dizzy, and found myself standing before a tall woman with legs galore and a go-go girl ponytail. I followed her through the human thicket and took a seat at the table facing the dining room so that Claudia would be able to spot me easily when she arrived.

"Would you like anything to drink while you're waiting?"

"Water will be fine."

"Plain or sparkling?"

"Sparkling," I said with a little sparkle in my voice.

Filling my glass from a giant green bottle, Janine said, "I think I recognize you."

"I've done some theater, and commercial work."

"No, this was in real life. I applied for a hostess position at Buzzy's a year or so ago."

"Yes, I'm the assistant beverage manager there," I said, caressing the stem of my water glass.

"The man interviewing me said I looked as if I might be clumsy."

"That was rude. It's not as if the job requires juggling plates."

Janine smiled and departed. I scoped the room. The birthday gathering consisted of four tables pushed together to form one long medieval banquet spread. A man with flyaway hair was standing and proposing an endless series of toasts in what sounded like one of those made-up Slavic languages on *Mission: Impossible.* At the table closest to me a distinguished couple ate in such complete silence it formed a force field around them. No sooner had I vowed not to check my watch again than I flipped my wrist and saw that it was five after seven. We would have to rush through our meal if we wanted to make the first act. Yet I had to admit that I found myself more excited, more revved-up with anticipation than I had been on any of my dates with Nicole. Waiting for Claudia made the whole room seem electric. A busboy brought a

small crib of bread, which I let sit awhile, to keep the table from looking bare.

Aside from the goldfish crackers, I hadn't eaten since breakfast. My
nap had thrown me off my feeding schedule, and my stomach began to
make chemistry-set sounds. I tried to drown the minor rumbles with
sips of water, and when that no longer worked, I tore a slice of bread
free from the momma loaf. I was buttering the side of it with barber
strokes when I saw the hostess leading Claudia to the table.

I have to credit Claudia. For someone who was forty-plus minutes
late for dinner, she didn't rush her step or act flustered or offer profuse
noises of apology or otherwise wiggle or waggle. She walked as if
everyone present had been awaiting her arrival. Claudia, to my aston-
ishment, had gone Art Deco. Her black mane had been cut and shaped
so that it curved at both ends toward her mouth, and she was wearing
a black dress that might have belonged to a flapper. As she made her
way through the room, customers tracked her movement, curious to
see where she finally landed. Eyes swung my way as I stood—I felt as
if I were accepting an award. I realized that it was more ego-enhancing
to be on the receiving end of a beautiful woman's entrance than to make
the entrance with her. The silent couple at the near table glanced up at
the same beat and took notice for a full second before returning to their
seemingly bottomless soup. When the invisible line between us shortened to nothing, Claudia and I kissed on both cheeks, French-style.

"Here, you take the view," I said, offering her my seat.

Claudia angled herself into the chair as if entering a limo and swung
her legs forward, placing her tiny silver-strapped pocketbook on the
table beside the bread basket.

"You must think I'm awful," Claudia said.

"Not at all. I was just concerned . . ."

"We had a gas leak in the building and had to evacuate, which threw
me off schedule. I left the restaurant number with the super, in case he
needs to get into my apartment. I refuse to hand over a spare set. I just
don't trust him, although he seems perfectly nice. I hope you're not too
ravenous."

"No, I loaded up on crackers at the bar."

Claudia laughed, as if I were kidding. Our waitress bestowed menus
upon us and took our drink orders.

"Chardonnay," Claudia said.

"I'll have a martini."

"A martini man," Claudia said. "I never would have suspected." She rested her chin on her curled fingers, giving me a look of frank appraisal.

"You've lost weight in the face," she said. "I can see your cheek-bones."

"Cute, aren't they? What's that scent you're wearing? I can tell it isn't Vertigo."

"You have a keen nose. Most men wouldn't have noticed. It's Acclimar. Do you like it?"

"It's quite lethal."

"I didn't put on too much, did I?"

"No, I meant that as a compliment."

"Be honest now. Do you miss my long hair?"

"Me and every other man in the tri-state area. Why, Claudia, why?"

"I got tired of dragging it around. Hair that long, it was like having a tail. So I just went to my regular guy and said, Lop it off. I didn't like it short at first, I thought it was too stark. Now it feels liberating."

"It was a shock at first, but it looks great."

"The producers of *Sunset Patio* weren't too thrilled. They wanted me in long hair, so I suppose I was sabotaging myself by getting it cut. When I went in for the second reading, one of them let out a shriek. But now other parts are starting to come my way. I must admit I was surprised when you asked me out to dinner."

"Well, I just felt we didn't really get a chance to know each other, despite working together on the play. I don't know anything about you, whether you have brothers or sisters, things like that."

"I'm an only child. Can't you tell how spoiled I am?"

"You, spoiled? I'm an oldest child, myself. We oldests are supposed to be born leaders."

A burst of laughter and applause came from the birthday table. I buttered a slice of bread to quell my hunger pangs. Claudia glanced over my shoulder toward the dining room.

"What do your parents do?" I asked.

"They're retired. They live on a former plantation in Guadeloupe, not the entire plantation, just the main house. The other units are rented out."

While I was trying to think of a follow-up question to that bit of information, another explosion of laughter and applause erupted from the birthday table.

"I hope they don't intend to keep that up all night," Claudia said. "Do you think it'd be okay for me to smoke?"

"I had them seat us in the smoking section."

"That's so thoughtful! Don't worry, I won't smoke through dinner."

As Claudia tapped out a cigarette, I slipped my hand into my jacket pocket and in one seamless motion withdrew and cocked open the silver lighter Darlene had given me. Claudia bent her head and our hands met as I lit her cigarette, her fingers resting on my wrist. After returning the lighter to my jacket pocket, I took a James Bond-ish sip of my martini and set my glass down on the table directly opposite Claudia's chardonnay. It didn't take long for a result to come in from the Glass Test. Claudia withdrew her wine glass so that it was no longer parallel with my drink, took a sip, and then set it down at the edge of the table, behind the bread basket but still within view.

"I hear this play we're seeing tonight is quite funny," I said, "though I don't know how I feel about farce as a genre."

"I haven't really given it any thought."

"Really? Because I could see you in one. They love leggy women in farces."

"I did do an Ayckborn play that probably qualifies. God knows there were enough slamming doors. It was set in a rectory."

"Speaking of rectories, I've been working as a volunteer reader at St. Teresa's, the church with that beautiful Gothic bell tower."

If I were waiting for her to extol my big-heartedness, my civic spirit, etc., I could have sat there and grown a beard. Claudia mechanically nodded and exhaled smoke. By my internal clock it was now fifteen or twenty after seven, and she still hadn't cracked her menu open, so I opened mine as a not-so-subtle hint. Claudia browsed through hers, flipped it shut, and set it on the table in record time. Given her lack of deliberation, I assumed she was going to order something simple, like a house salad. I mentally whittled down my own order accordingly as our waitress approached.

Claudia said: "I'll have the salad Niçoise as a starter, house dressing on the side, filet mignon medium rare, baked potato, no butter, no skin."

I, who had planned to order the grilled chicken breast and the house salad, made a quick switch to steak frites.

"May I get you another martini?" Janine asked.

I pictured myself crawling upside down on the ceiling like Spiderman.

"Better not. Just some mineral water for the table."

So Claudia was an eater. This I hadn't anticipated. I assumed that like most actresses I knew, she was obsessed with her weight and would order something paltry to pick at. I decided not to worry about hurrying the meal along. If she preferred to get a glow-on from the chardonnay, I would go with the flow rather than shoehorn us into a taxi for a fast uptown ride to a play that was a freebie anyway.

I took a long, meaningful sip of my drink and set the glass down. Claudia nudged her glass close to mine, so close they were almost touching. Now we were getting somewhere. Our meals arrived. Perhaps it was the influence of the martini, but I found myself mes- merized watching Claudia make neat work of dinner, which she did French-style, knife and fork in constant duet.

"I've been thinking about adopting a kitten," she said. "Any sugges- tions?"

I said with the voice of experience: "Just don't make the mistake I made, kiddo. I adopted a kitten I picked out of a cardboard box she shared with her siblings. She was the only one who was all black and looked so sweet and unassuming. She turned out to be a little demon. I originally named her Crybaby, but Slinky eventually seemed more fit- ting, because she's always slinking around."

"I read somewhere that cat people tend to be more sensual than dog people, more willing to pamper themselves and others."

"I've always been more inclined to pamper others rather than myself. I like to give massages, for example, but I've never been big on getting them. I can never quite relax."

"Maybe you've never received the right pampering."

Claudia smiled, her wine glass suspended in midair.

"Maybe I haven't. What about you? Do you enjoy being pampered?"

"What woman doesn't? It's wonderful to be able to close your eyes and drift away and feel absolutely safe." She said this dreamily, as if she were already starting to drift, adding, ". . . I guess it's too late to make the play."

"Afraid so. Maybe we could bag it and do something else. The night's still young."

"If we're bagging the play, maybe we should treat ourselves to dessert."

"Maybe we could share one," I said.

"Good idea."

Claudia's hand opened like a flower to summon Janine, who re-lit a small candle at our table after she brought us the dessert menu. The candlelight softened Claudia's features, rounded them off. Through some optical trick created by the martini, the wallpaper behind Claudia momentarily loomed in the foreground, making her face look as if it were part of a floral design. Then the martini stopped playing with my mind and everything returned to its right place. As we were deliberating over the dessert menu, the maitre d' came to the table, rested a hand on the small of Janine's back, and informed Miss Prentiss she had a phone call. "Damn!" Claudia said, flustered. "I wonder who that could be. You'll have to excuse me."

"Of course." I stood as Claudia rose to answer her call. When she brushed past, she paused and caressed my wrist with a lingering fingerstroke, triggering a tingle at the back of my neck. I sat down again. With my back to the room, there wasn't much to study except Claudia's empty chair. There was no point in pondering the dessert menu until she got back. I tightened the knot in my tie, bringing up some slack from the middle, and sipped water. Moments later, a hand grazed my shoulder, and without returning to her side of the table, Claudia said:

"Johnny, I feel awful. That was the apartment manager calling—they want to get into my apartment—they think that's where the gas leak may be. They're almost sure it's on my floor. I'm afraid we'll have to call it an evening. Maybe we could have dinner again another time, my treat. Don't let my leaving stop you from ordering dessert."

"Don't be silly. Do you want me to see you home?"

"I should really dash."

"At least let me put in you a cab."

"Yeah, okay," Claudia said with a scratch of irritation. I made the universal check sign to our waitress and explained the situation, then escorted Claudia through the restaurant. I tried to take her elbow, but she was too fast for me, reaching the street and grabbing the door handle of a taxi waiting at the curb. Then, as if remembering something she had left behind, she released her death grip on the door handle and dashed back and pecked me on the cheek, apologizing with a flurry of words that included "thanks" and "sorry" (it sounded like "thorry"). She opened the cab door and swung her stockinged legs inside. I shut the door behind her. As the cab angled away from the curb, Claudia turned and waved through the window, like a member of a motorcade. I waved good-bye with a half-twist of the wrist, my hand low around my hip, a no-big-deal wave.

As I reentered Alsace Lorraine, I noticed a member of the staff standing under the archway looking at me with dead-neutral eyes. He had probably been stationed to make sure Claudia and I didn't stiff the restaurant for the meal. He kept his eyes posted to the street and his shoulders locked, ignoring me as I passed. His masters had trained him well. In the dining area, Janine deposited the bill on the table in a leather-bound folder.

"I hope there wasn't a problem," she said. "The birthday party got kind of rowdy."

"No problem, no problem at all. My date has a gas leak. Back at her building, I mean."

I pulled a credit card from my wallet and slid it into the folder, then waited in Claudia's chair, watching other people leave. Husbands helped wives into their coats and wraps. Suddenly my clothes seemed heavier on me, especially the jacket, which felt like a horse blanket. In my head echoed Claudia's slightly irritated voice saying, almost mechanically, *"Yeah, okay." "Thorry."* Janine returned with the bill and credit-card slip, standing with her hands behind her back. I signed the slip and tipped in cash, as I always do.

On my way out I stopped at one of the restaurant's old-time Parisian phone booths. I yanked the folding door shut and dialed the theater presenting the play Claudia and I were supposed to see. I asked for the ticket manager's office.

"Hi, this is Johnny Downs. I know, I wasn't able to pick up the tickets. There was a gas leak in my building. Could you hold the flowers? I'll pick them up sometime tomorrow. They are beautiful, aren't they? I know, the cellophane makes the pink roses look practically peach. You don't mind putting them in water? I can't thank you enough. And your name is . . . ? Leonard. Thank you, Leonard, I appreciate it." I hung up the phone and lingered in the booth for a minute, scratching at the metal with my fingernail.

23

"I OWE YOU AN APOLOGY," Darlene said. "I thought the reason you were having problems finding the right partner was because you were making bad choices and sabotaging yourself. I didn't realize the full extent of what you're up against. I knew New York women were high-strung, but I had no idea they were such vicious little sharks."

"Not all of them."

"Okay, just the ones you seem to know. Mind you, I've bailed out of the middle of a date before. I once walked out of a movie because my date sat with a tub of popcorn between his legs and, when not feeding himself, pointed at the screen whenever one of the characters said something funny. I excused myself to go to the ladies' room and just kept on going. But from what you told me, nothing you did justified Claudia's leaving you in the lurch like that. What she did was wicked. Don't worry, we'll fix her later. Did they have everything?"

The day before, Darlene had faxed me a shopping list of novelty-shop items, which she insisted would come in handy. The novelty shop itself, which I found on my own, was like something out of Ray Bradbury, a Depression-era hovel on the Lower East Side jammed to the darkened ceiling with clown masks, troll dolls, X-ray specs, naughty adult toys, and sun-faded board games from canceled TV series—a jumbled warehouse of carnival dreams, complete with carousel horses being resold as lawn ornaments. The owners, a married couple in their fifties or so, reminded me of Superman's adopted parents from Smallville. I handed them my shopping list and they searched for me, digging through boxes and cartons of discarded Incan treasure. They seemed pleased to have a customer who had definite wants and wasn't just browsing for something wacky.

I told Darlene:

"They had everything except the phosphorescent-ink pens. They promised to order some and call me. So what am I supposed to do with this junk?"

"See those puzzles?"

Darlene had me buy several packs of blank puzzles.

"You write a message on the puzzle, break it up into pieces, and dump them in an envelope. Picture your future fiancée. She receives an envelope in the mail. It rattles. What can it be? she wonders. She opens the envelope, and pieces spill on the table. For a brief moment she worries she's gotten a message from a psycho. Then she puts the puzzle together and sees that it's only you asking her out."

"I don't know, Darlene. It sounds pretty high-school."

"That's why it works! It makes the woman feel she's back at her homeroom desk, receiving a valentine from a secret admirer. Why do you think women make such a wave over Valentine's Day?—to relive that moment. Of course, you probably didn't get any valentines yourself back then. You probably sent valentines you thought were real funny, only no one laughed and you sat at your desk, vowing revenge. Did you get the ink pads and stamps? You can use them to embellish the envelopes. Don't let them forget about the phosphorescent pens. You can stick one up your butt."

"I have something else I can stick somewhere."

"Don't be crude. Now, do you have any business cards?"

"I have some old ones, but they're kind of faded."

"You need new ones, with your name in Art Deco type and nothing else, not even your phone number. That's what the big shots do. When you give a future fiancée your card, wait for her to say, 'But there's no number here,' then you write it out for her. It'll show her that you don't give out your number to just anyone, that only certain people qualify."

"But suppose she doesn't ask for my number after I give her the card?"

"Then she's an idiot, because all she has is a piece of stationery with your name on it, and what good is that? The point is, you want the act of writing your phone number to become a personal transaction, like lighting a woman's cigarette."

"A lot of people prefer to exchange e-mail addresses."

"E-mail is too chatty. It's too easy for creepos to misrepresent themselves in e-mail and chatrooms. Even with noncreepos, it fosters a phony intimacy. I know women in college here who have gotten all wrapped up in hot e-mail romances, which ended with them meeting the guy and finding out his postings were all a front. He was married, or living with his mother, or e-mailing other women at the same time. Some college girls engage in cybersex, only to have their escapades forwarded all over the Internet. I don't trust anyone I can't see. Do you even have an e-mail address?"

"No."

"Good. Stay low-tech. It'll set you apart."

"What color should I get for the cards?"

"Cream or ivory, with blue letters. And don't make your name too large. You want it to seem like an interesting password leading to a possible relationship."

"Darlene, no offense, but I don't know where you're coming from with this. I can't picture the men of Decatur, Georgia, handing out understated cream business cards."

"You're right, they don't. Most of the men down here introduce themselves by honking their horns at intersections. But remember, I lived for a couple of years in Charleston, South Carolina, and they had some *slick* sons-a-bitches there. I acquired quite a collection of business cards from those lawyers and real-estate developers. I must admit, I miss some of those bad boys now. They knew how to party."

"I could be bad, under the right circumstances."

"No, you couldn't. Don't lie to yourself."

"So what am I supposed to do with this Ouija board?"

"I haven't figured that out yet. I just thought you should get one."

24

I HAD JUST FINISHED WAXING the kitchen floor, having shut Slinky in the bedroom until it was safely dry, when the phone rang, something it seldom did on Saturday night anymore. I thought it might be a telemarketer, trying to catch me off-guard. My suspicions seemed confirmed when a cheery female voice said, "Is this Johnny Downs?"

"You got him," I said.

"You don't know me, we've never met, but I'm a friend of Claudia's."

"Claudia has friends?"

"My name's Amanda Baylor, and the reason I'm calling is that Claudia is staying with me while she's having her apartment painted, and has taken ill with that pesky bug she has."

"What pesky bug is that?"

"Without going into the particulars, let's just say it's a medical condition of a personal nature. Have I gotten you at a bad time?"

"I'm about to scrub the bathtub. Why?"

"You sound distracted. I called to ask a favor on Claudia's behalf, but maybe this isn't the best time, if you're busy doing chores."

"What kind of favor?"

I sounded gruff because I felt gruff. Considering that Claudia hadn't bothered to call after she breezed out at dinner or return the message I had left her the next day, I wasn't about to leap any fences for her.

"Never mind, you sound a little put off," said Claudia's friend. "I'll try elsewhere. I apologize for having interrupted your Saturday night."

Her apology wasn't the usual seizing-the-high-ground phony contrition you usually get in New York. This Amanda had the soft, coaxing Southern accent of someone with manners. I sighed, looked around the living room for no apparent reason, and said, "Okay, okay, you got me. What does Cleopatra, Queen of the Nile, want?"

"Claudia told me you were someone who might be kind enough to make a run for provisions and sit with her for a few hours, in case she has a downturn. I have a date tonight and can't look after her, and I think her being sick has brought home how shabbily she treated you. She told me all about the date you two had, when she had to run. It's been preying on her mind."

"Claudia has a conscience?" I said, as if having just received a bulletin.

"I'm not here to defend her behavior, except to say that there is a lot about her that you don't know, and she isn't feeling well, and she thought you could help. She said she thought you were a stand-up guy, and there weren't too many of those around."

"Now, now, don't lay it on too thick. What sort of provisions does she need?"

"Bottled water, Kleenex, and crackers. I'll reimburse you, of course." Amanda also mentioned a nonprescription gastrointestinal aid, which could be taken in either tablet or liquid form. She needed the extra-strength version.

"I'm beginning to get the picture," I said.

"Well, don't let on that I told you, but Claudia picked up a parasite in the Caribbean a few years ago that's been plaguing her on and off ever since. She'll probably pretend with you that this is simply a one-shot case of food poisoning, so play along. Right now, she's mostly dehydrated. What's that sound?"

"My cat. I shut her in the bedroom while I was waxing the floor."

"She's putting up quite a squawk."

"It's an incredible piece of overacting on her part."

I took down the address and changed into clean jeans and a denim shirt, liberating Slinky in the process. I rode the IRT express up to 72nd Street, then switched to the local. I stopped at a supermarket to pick up the items Amanda had requested, along with a carton of vanilla ice cream and the Sunday Times. I was carrying more goodies than a guilty divorced father when I reached the building, a prewar fortress on West End Avenue with an old dowager of a chandelier in the lobby that looked as if it belonged in a Viennese ballroom. I announced myself, and the doorman escorted me to the elevator as if every secret was safe with him. Once out, I made my way down a carpeted hall, checking apartment numbers and passing doors behind which small dogs yapped. Before I could press the correct buzzer, the door opened. "I heard the elevator," said a woman in a black dress. "I'm Amanda."

She was definitely someone. Amanda wasn't peering from behind the door, using it as a shield, but presented herself in full view, boldly framed by the jambs, her hand holding the side of the door at a high angle, as if to say, Welcome to my villa. She had cindery brownish-red hair pulled back princess-style in a velvet headband. Her eyes were a dark caramel. I nodded hello, unable to shake hands because of the bags I was carrying.

"You're like the Gentleman Caller in *The Glass Menagerie*," she said.

"A role I played in college."

"I'm not surprised. Come inside, we'll put all this on the kitchen table."

We had to traverse the living room, its walls a buttery yellow. The kitchen was a blend of classic woodwork and modern appliances, a stainless-steel refrigerator lodged amid enough walnut cabinets to feed the stablehands. Cradling a seltzer bottle, Amanda led me toward what I assumed was the guest bedroom, her heels clicking like castanets on the tiles, and called, "Johnny's here . . ." Claudia mumbled a reply. "Just a second," Amanda said, going in for a consultation.

I cased the apartment while I waited. What a layout. This was the way to live. The place was furnished in the style of a New Orleans guest house, with plenty of padded room for people to pass out on. The sofa was at least eight feet long, its corners plumped with rosy pillows. On the coffee table was a bowl filled with cashews and a small silver art-deco clock. Flanking the sofa were two dignified armchairs, fit for retired judges. The main carpet was blood-red with gold fringe. The walls brandished elaborately framed mirrors and a number of modestly framed paintings, mostly portraits of noble horses standing at attention, and crumbling mansions. Mounted over a rolltop desk was a dented bugle.

"She's napping," Amanda said, carefully closing the bedroom door behind her, as if the slightest noise might wake the baby. "But she knows you're here, so she won't be startled when she wakes up. Why don't you make yourself comfortable in the living room and read or watch TV? As long as you wouldn't mind keeping the sound low."

"Thanks, but now that I've broken myself of the habit of watching TV, I seem to have lost the urge."

"I'm hooked on some of those cooking shows on the food channel. That's my only vice."

Leaning her hand on a table, Amanda lifted a shoe to examine the heel. Her body had a hard outline, but with old-fashioned curves coming and going. Behind her modest cleavage, her breasts displayed a quality build. They said, Go ahead and compare. We've been in the business for thirty-some years, offering the utmost in service and reliability. Her skirt flared out at the bottom, making a little twirl when she moved. I had a flashback of my mother dressing for a party when I was twelve, and the excitement I suppressed and concealed when Mom fixed her stockings. I now wished I had worn something nicer than a denim shirt. Gleason was right. Always go sharp.

Amanda smoothed her hands along her sides. "Is my outfit okay?"

"Are you kidding? That outfit smokes."

"You're not just saying that?"

"No, really, it's a knockout."

"What about the earrings? They're kind of bugging me."

Her earrings were golden daggers, which dangled accordingly.

"They may be a little diverting. That dress makes such a statement, the earrings seem to be vying for attention."

"Claudia told me you paid attention to female adornments."

"Good old Claudia."

"I'll just be a moment. You sit there and amuse yourself. Have a cashew."

I could hear Amanda rustling in her bedroom. It was at the opposite end of the apartment from the guest bedroom, and seemed substantially larger. When she emerged after a brief interval, she had ditched the dagger earrings for pearl ones. I realized then that Amanda was one of those women who always seem to be inserting an earring or taking one off. She had also added a thin gold necklace, which nestled in the overpass.

"I'm attending a charity event, so I shouldn't be too late," she said. "It must be odd, baby-sitting Claudia."

"Is that what I'm doing? I see myself as more of a guardian angel summoned into action."

Amanda patted the side of my face and spun around so that I could help her on with her coat, which I did, catching a whiff of man-bait perfume. I waited by the door until she was inside the elevator.

I now had a couple of hours to kill. Like most anyone else in a stranger's apartment, I was tempted to snoop. I especially wanted to poke around Amanda's bedroom, maybe pick up some trade secrets on the life of an affluent uptown single woman. I was already well versed in the squirreling habits of downtown women, whose lack of closet space often led to tragic disarray. But on the off chance that Amanda forgot something and popped back in, I decided to make myself a dish of ice cream in the kitchen and keep to the sofa. As might be expected, Amanda had very classy spoons. The one I was using had a fancy scroll on the handle. A Russian blue cat wearing a silk-ribbon choker appeared as if summoned from the carpet and settled at my feet, giving me a blinkless stare. I reached to pet her and she ducked her head, fending off my friendly overture. Not quite ready to tackle the Sunday *Times*, I sifted through a bunch of antiques magazines stacked on the coffee table next to a heavy historical novel set in the "Age of Intrigue," whenever that was. The blades of the ceiling fan slowly rotated, lulling the entire room. I turned off the lamp closest to my head and settled into a comfortable position. I was slipping into a full-fledged nap when Claudia's voice penetrated the cloud cover, calling my name as if trying to hail a lifeboat.

Lifting my head, I had a momentary swipe of amnesia. I remembered who I was, but not where or why. I must have been truly napping. Then the mental gears began to turn and I hoisted myself up from the couch. The Russian blue accompanied me to the bedroom door, like a bedroom slipper on wheels. I knocked and said: "Claudia, it's me, Johnny."

"You can come in. I'm decent."

It was dim in the bedroom. Her black hair pressed against the pillow, Claudia lay in a four-poster bed with her bare arms resting like pipe stems over the thin blanket. The sickbed formality seemed almost Victorian. The only thing missing was a white candle burning in an Aladdin's lamp. On the nightstand were several pill bottles, the box of Kleenex I had just bought, and a stack of paper cups.

"Don't worry," Claudia said in a wan but gallant voice, "I'm not contagious. I had some bad oysters."

I nodded as if I, too, had had a run-in with them in the past. Claudia raised herself on her elbows. "Before you get comfortable, could you help lead me into the bathroom? I'm fine once I get there, it's getting there that's the problem. I'm a little shaky."

"Oh, sure."

The guest bedroom had its own adjoining bathroom, so we didn't have far to haul. I moved the netting aside as Claudia slid her legs out of bed and tucked her feet into the slippers waiting for her on the floor. She was wearing a white cotton nightie with a bluebird motif that looked as if it belonged in summer camp. She held my arm as I walked her to the bathroom, leaning against me as I switched on the light. "I'll be okay now," she said, shutting the bathroom door behind her. I heard the toilet seat lower, then, later, some sniffling.

"Johnny, can I ask a favor?" she said from behind the door.

"Sure."

"Go to the top drawer of the bureau and find me one of Amanda's T-shirts. I want to change out of this nightie."

I dug out an oversized vacation-resort T-shirt, and tapped on the door. "Thanks," Claudia said, opening it just enough for the handoff.

She was showing lots of leg when she came out of the bathroom, not that there was much time to look. She slid back into bed and tugged the sheet up to her waist, laying her arms flat after tucking her hair behind her ears. Her face was wet and cloudless, as if her fever had broken or a crisis had passed. She trembled with the shiver of a child going *brrrr*.

"Amanda said you brought ice cream. You didn't eat it all, did you?"

"No, I didn't eat it all, thank you very much. Would you like a dish?"

"Just a few swallows to coat my throat. I've been throwing up a lot, and it's a little raw. I guess I've really wrecked my mystique, letting you see me like this."

"Don't be silly. Your mystique will be up and running again in no time."

I carried my puddle of melted ice cream into the kitchen and found Claudia a clean dish. I brought her her ice cream like a butler, bending slightly at the waist. After polishing off the first serving—a few swallows my eye—Claudia asked for seconds, and I dished out what was left in the carton. When she finished, I asked her if she wanted me to leave so that she could rest.

"No, stay a minute." She extended her hand for me to hold, so I held it.

"I really owe you one," she said.

"One what?"

"Apology. It was shitty, the way I dashed off after dinner. I thought it was just going to be a friendly, low-key dinner, but when I saw the restaurant and all the trouble you went to, with the play still ahead of us, I felt that I couldn't meet your expectations of the evening. I got flustered, which seldom happens to me. I've been feeling slightly ashamed ever since. I told Amanda to call you instead of one of my other girlfriends tonight because I figured this was the best way to apologize; that you wouldn't yell at me in my weakened state, although you'd have every right to."

"I'm not a yeller. But you could have told me at the time or phoned me later."

"I should have. I'm sorry. I chickened out. I'm just not good at some things."

"Sure. Whatever. No damage done."

"Good, I'm glad." She still had hold of my hand. It was a moment that called for a kiss on the cheek, but I wasn't sure Claudia wanted contact, so I simply gave her hand an extra squeeze.

Understand, I didn't believe a word of her prepared statement. Claudia wasn't the sort of woman who fretted about a man's expectations for the evening—her own sense of entitlement was too strong. She was used to having her anticipations met and then some. And there was a crucial glitch in her behavior that night which had stuck in my mind then and since. When the waiter informed Claudia she had a phone call, she feigned surprise and said, "I wonder who that would be?"—this after she had already told me she'd left her number with the super. I suspected then that she had momentarily forgotten her cover story. Despite my suspicions, it was nice holding her hand and looking into those dark eyes. Giving my hand a farewell squeeze, Claudia rolled over on her side and smiled at me from her pillow. Her breasts pressed together beneath her T-shirt.

"What's the weather like outside?"

"Drizzly. I noticed Amanda didn't take an umbrella."

"That's because there'll be a car waiting for her and another one to whisk her home. Weather ceases to exist once you have money."

"Don't you have money?"

"Johnny, if I had money, I'd be at a hotel, not here."

She said this as if explaining that babies came from mommy's tummy, but with a sweet regret that made the remark seem directed more at her own situation rather than at my inability to grasp certain basics. With an almost audible click, Claudia changed subjects.

"How's work? Anything lined up?"

"I have a callback on this exterminator commercial. They hired another actor, but he didn't test well, so they're going to reshoot. It's a national spot, so there's real money involved. How about you?"

"Everything's on hold until I get over this food poisoning. I'm up for a small part on that HBO series, *Bachelor Sluts*, but so is every other actress in town. I won't do nudity, which probably rules me out."

"I know one of the directors on that show."

"Really? Maybe I'll drop your name, if you don't mind."

"Be sure to mention the Acorn beer ad—that'll jar his memory."

"Would you mind switching off the lamp? It's taxing my eyes."

Once I turned off the lamp, the only light came from the hallway, where the Russian blue was on sentry duty.

"That's better," Claudia said. "I'm beginning to fade. You needn't stay."

"Well, I may sack out in the living room until Amanda gets back, just in case."

"Thanks for looking after me."

"No problem. I'll close the door."

"Thanks. Good night."

"Good night."

Her eyes slowly closed as she entered repose. I pulled the door behind me, leaving it open just an inch. Before returning to the living room, I took the opportunity to check out Amanda's bedroom. The light from the living room was sufficient enough for me to scout around without knocking over a priceless vase. The bed was the main attraction. It was a large wooden sleigh with curved head- and foot-boards, sandbagged at the head with thick pillows. Normally I prefer a bed where my feet can stick out of the bottom, it's less confining, but this one looked like a magic ride where anything could happen. A large antique mirror faced the bed, opening up all sorts of scenarios.

After making use of the guest bathroom, which was painted a flatter-ing shade of peach, I helped myself to a diet soda in the refrigerator and settled back on the couch for a serious examination of the *Times*'s men's fashion special. Now that I was trying to remake myself as plausible hus-band material, I was paying more attention to men's fashion, and getting nowhere. The Russian blue slipped onto the couch, near enough to be petted but not so close as to seem pushy. Holding the magazine in one hand, I stroked the cat with the other. I had just about exhausted the many moods of men's style when I heard the key turn in the lock. The Russian blue cocked its ears but remained at my side. Amanda entered the room, dropping her keys into a seashell on the table by the door.

"Don't get up," she said as I made a move to rise. "That's how my father used to read the paper when I was a girl, returning every section to its original fold. He hated it when my mother scattered sections all out of order. How's our patient?"

"In dreamland."

"Good. She had a rough night last night. I'm sure your presence was reassuring. Would you like anything to drink?"

"No, I'll stick with this."

"I can't believe he's letting you pet him like that. He usually hides from strangers."

"I'm honored. What's his name?"

"Raja."

"Raja," I repeated.

Amanda poured herself a small bourbon and pulled up a chair next to me. "Would you mind if I took off my shoes? My feet are about to cry."

Amanda removed her shoes and massaged her stockinged feet in the carpet, flexing and wiggling her toes. Then she eased back and sipped her bourbon as if having achieved peace.

"Anything in the *Times*?" she said.

"I was just reading this world-beating article in the fashion supplement about the return of the belt. It seems that the belt is no longer used simply to hold up one's pants. I quote: 'The belt, once a neutral strip of leather, has become an information loop, like the news ticker in Times Square.'"

"Well, as my father was fond of saying, they've got to fill those pages with something. Claudia tells me you're in the restaurant business."

"An assistant beverage manager, actually, at Buzzy's, a restaurant in the West Village. Did you catch the play she and I did together?"

"I'm afraid not. I was hitting the flea markets in Paris, something I do once a year. Claudia also tells me you do volunteer reading to children."

"Yes," I said, surprised that Claudia had remembered anything I had said on our date, much less relayed the information. Women are such sneaky listeners. "I read stories once a week to a boy at St. Teresa's. It seems to be working out well so far—I know I'm enjoying it. They may give me a storytelling circle in the fall." *Ask her something about herself, dipstick.* "So how was your evening?"

"My escort developed a cough and had to leave early. I ended up making small talk with this newscaster who's in the final stages of a nuclear divorce and has this bitter way of flirting, as if he's waiting for an opportunity to snap, 'You're like all the rest!' I tried to detour him by asking if he wanted to dance, but he wanted instead to describe his recent trip to Africa, where he was made an honorary chieftain. Are you a good dancer?"

I made fiery flamenco moves with my arms and snapping fingers.

"Oh, I bet you're a better mover than that," Amanda said, smiling.

"Do you and Claudia ever hit the clubs together?"

"Claudia doesn't like to dance. The one time I saw her dance, at a wedding reception, she was surprisingly stiff. She seemed stuck to the floor."

"Maybe she assumed everyone would form a circle around her."

"Now, now."

Amanda and I traded smiles, sharing a diplomatic moment. She lightly fingered her necklace, one of those tormenting things women like to do. I mirrored her gesture, tracing my finger back and forth down the front of my shirt. There was a loose play around her mouth, a private amusement fueled by the bourbon.

"I should go," I said.

"Yes, you should," Amanda said, implying before something else happens.

We stood.

"Thank you for looking after her," Amanda said, rising on tiptoe to kiss me on the cheek. The proximity of perfume, alcohol, and female warmth was a ravishing combination I hadn't experienced since Nicole, and I felt a simultaneous spark of excitement and pang of loss as the present crossed paths with the past. Not wanting to leave, I headed for the door.

"Call me when you get back," Amanda said, "so I'll know you got home safely."

"Don't be silly. I'm a big boy."

"I can see that. Let me give you my number anyway, just in case."

Amanda went to her rolltop desk and wrote her number on the back of a business card, which had only her office listing. She flapped the card as she walked toward me to speed up the ink-dry. I slid it into my coat pocket. I wished I'd had my own card to give her, but mine were still at the printer's.

She closed the door behind me in the hall and clicked the lock. I took the elevator down to the lobby, which had a deserted-hotel hush. The doorman was sitting at a small desk, writing in a journal. From the uneven length of the lines, it appeared to be poetry.

25

"WE'RE MAKING HEADWAY," Darlene said. "It's a good sign, her giving you her phone number without prompting. See how that volunteer shit with kids paid off? It may have meant diddly to Claudia, but to a woman who wants children it signifies something. Now seize the opportunity and send Amanda a puzzle, asking her out to dinner and a movie."

"She's too sophisticated for a puzzle, Darlene. You should have seen her apartment. And what about Claudia?"

"What about Claudia?"

"Won't it bother her, me asking out her friend?"

"Let it bother her. So what? Does Claudia carry a cell phone?"

"She had one during rehearsals."

"Then why didn't she give her cell number to the super instead of the restaurant number? I'll tell you why. Because she probably has a boyfriend or married lover and didn't want to take his call with you sitting there listening. Sometimes married men don't know if they're going to be free until the last minute. She arranged it so that he'd call the restaurant and she'd leave the table to talk to him in private. She'd do it again if the situation arose, she'd leave you sitting there twiddling your thumbs. Only she'd make up another excuse. You can only get so many gas leaks."

"I wonder what tropical parasite she has."

"His name was probably Kinja. I'm sure Amanda will tell you. She's already informed you what a crummy dancer Claudia is. Translation: a stiff lay. Don't bring up Claudia again to her, and if she brings her up, chastise her if she gets too catty—show Amanda you're the man, and you don't appreciate hearing about another woman's shortcomings. That will impress her, because it means you'd show her the same consideration. Whatever you do, never let her know that Claudia's nickname is Tubular Woman. She'll be on the air with that faster than Geraldo. You should start keeping a file on Amanda."

"What do you mean?"

"Nothing fancy, just a journal where you write down how your dates went. It'll help you see patterns and remember things she told you you might otherwise forget. The names of her other friends and so on. Pay special attention to recurring phrases used in conversation. They always mean something, even the clichés."

"Claudia's birthday's coming up. Amanda told me."

"I'm sure she told you in order to tell you how old Claudia's going to be. By the way, do you know when my birthday is?"

"No, you've never told me."

"And you've never asked. I have feelings, too, you know. You shouldn't keep tabs just on the birthdays of those women you'd like to fuck."

"That's a little harsh."

"True, though, isn't it? From now on, find out the date of every woman's birthday, whether she's fiancée material or not."

"Okay, okay. So when is your birthday, Darlene?"

"Too late now. You blew it."

"Please. *Please.*"

After similar back-and-forth, Darlene gave me the date. "And I expect a nice card, not some raunchy one. I went to buy a card for my aunt Hilda last week and they had one that said, 'Feeling down about your birthday?' and when you opened it, there was a drawing of an old woman with her tits hanging at her feet."

"I'll try to find something classier than that. Or maybe I'll make you a card. Something original."

I was circling the apartment, awaiting word on the exterminator commercial, the one where I bug-bomb the wrong house, when the phone rang.

"John Kennedy Downs," I said.

"My, that's quite a mouthful."

"Well, hey, Amanda. Good to hear from you."

"Who gave you the idea for the puzzle? It was very cute."

"I'm crawling with cute ideas."

"I bet you are. It's a good thing you had your name and address on the envelope, otherwise I might have thought it was a ransom note when all those letters spilled out. Where did you find the ink stamp for the movie projector?"

"In this little novelty shop on lower Broadway."

"Well, Claudia finally moved out yesterday. She's feeling much better and said to say thank you. She may say thank you herself, then again, she may not. You know Claudia. I called to say that I'd *love* to have dinner with you, but I've already seen this particular movie. There's this French film playing near me that's supposed to be good."

"And if it isn't, we can always flee."

"Don't you feel guilty leaving a movie before it's over?"

"No, my attitude is: Why suffer? But I would only want to leave if we were both miserable."

As we spoke, it occurred to me that Amanda's mentioning that the movie was playing nearby might be a way of laying the groundwork for us returning to her place afterward for a nightcap, everything being within a nice walking distance. We agreed to catch an early show, which would leave the rest of the evening free, an easily made decision, which bolstered that scenario. I hung up the phone a happy man. I had the notion of taking Slinky into my arms and waltzing her around the apartment, but she didn't like to be disturbed when she was in the closet. I did a few waltz steps by myself, nothing fancy, and looked across the courtyard at the music school whose entrance was on the southern side of our block. In the window a violin student was studying a score on a sheet-music holder. She lifted the violin to her chin and cocked her elbow.

From my journal:

Friday, July 3rd. Picked Amanda up at her place. Beaded black dress with a diving plunge, camouflaged with a gypsy shawl, which she drew back like a curtain at opportune moments. During dinner I did the Glass Test, probing the front line with my water glass; she nudged hers forward until they were almost

head to head. Almost by default we were the best dressed couple at
the French film, nearly everybody else looking like they had been
flushed out of their apartments by a fire drill. After the awful
movie I did the Pocketbook Test on the walk home and A. swung
her bag over arm, freeing the one near me. Two Go signs in one
night. Decided not to press my luck, made no effort to get myself
invited into her apartment.

Wednesday, July 8. Progress with A. Had dinner at Mexican
restaurant, the red and yellow decor putting an added glow in
her eyes. We ordered margaritas but o/wise behaved ourselves.
Went to a gallery opening where e/one faced away from the
paintings, as if framing their profiles against them. A. intro'd me
to man who I thought might be old b-friend. He brimmed as if he
knew something I didn't but was o/wise nice.

"You sound perky," said Darlene, checking in.

"I just found out I got this insect-control commercial I'd auditioned for a couple of times. We shoot it next week in New Jersey."

"You'll have to send me a tape. You know how closely I follow your career."

"Ha ha."

"How are things proceeding with fancy pants?"

"If by 'fancy pants' you mean Amanda, we seem to be on track. We made out at the movies the other night, got pretty frisky in the taxi, and have had some pretty good phone conversations. We have our first Saturday-night date next Saturday, which may stretch into Sunday brunch, if I get lucky."

"Luck has nothing to do with it. I had no idea things were moving so fast. If you land Amanda in bed this weekend, you have to promise me you won't have sex with her. Or rather, that you won't have intercourse with her. You know what intercourse is. That's when you stick your—"

"I know what intercourse is, Darlene. It hasn't been that long."

"Exactly. It hasn't been that long. And waiting a little longer will only make it more intoxicating. You're going to outfox her expectations by doing something to Amanda no man's ever done to her before; something she's wanted to have done to her and didn't even know she wanted done; and once she has it done, she will never ever forget. You do this right, and she'll dissolve into pudding. God, I'm getting excited myself, just thinking about it. I almost wish I could be there to supervise, to guide you on your merry way."

"I don't think I could handle a threesome."

"You're not ready to handle a twosome yet. But if you do what I tell you, you'll have Amanda staring up at the ceiling in a dreamy daze wondering why no woman has snapped up a man as masterful as you, even if you are a mere lowly actor. She'll want to tell her girlfriends and yet keep this secret treasure all to herself."

"This isn't something kinky, is it? I mean, this isn't one of those sex-tease techniques guaranteed to drive a woman crazy? You know, like inserting only the first couple of inches until she's begging for more. Because I tried that once after reading an article in some magazine and the girlfriend I was with at the time said, 'What are you waiting for, can't you get it in?—*push.*' She thought I had a 'fold-on,' which is when . . ."

"God, give me strength," Darlene said.

"That's one of my grandmother's favorite phrases."

"I'm not surprised. And for your information, they're not 'fold-*on*'s, they're either 'soft-on's or 'fold-*in*'s."

"Let's not argue over semantics."

"Will you stop goofing around and listen? This is important. Don't be so sure this will be the weekend Amanda lets you waltz her into bed. You dated a friend of hers, after all, even if the date did peter out. For all you know, Claudia told her, 'There's this guy I met, he isn't right for me, but the two of you might click.' Whatever the case, Amanda will want to establish that you're interested in her, not simply making do because you couldn't bop Claudia. So she'll probably put you through a series of border checks first. Once she allows you entree into bed, we have to make sure that you don't make love like every other man around—a bit of foreplay, some titty twiddle, then the inevitable thud."

"I think I bring a little more to it than that."

"*Hah.* Here's what you do. First, don't take her to bed at her place. You want her on your turf so that you can set the mood and make breakfast-in-bed preparations. Set the usual romantic atmosphere: candles, soft music, lowered blinds. When you light the candles, let your hand shake with the match. Don't be afraid of looking nervous. It'll make her suspicious if you come on too slick. Do a lot of making out on the sofa. Draw it out as long you can. Then tug her gently and draw her into the bedroom. Slowly undress her. Draw back the covers. Usher her into bed. Tell her to lie back and let you take care of her. That's a key phrase, 'take care,' because it has lots of nonsexual, reassuring, husbandly connotations. Take off all of your clothes except your boxers and lie next to her. Next to her, not on top. Kiss her all over, and not just in the usual places. Kiss her tummy more than you kiss her breasts. Kiss the palms of her hands and the instep of her foot. Don't make the kisses wet and sloppy. Don't lick. This isn't a tongue bath. Purse your lips. Imagine you're the lover in one of those old French films, paying homage to the female form. Pay special attention to any parts of her body that she seems self-conscious about. Ask her to roll over on her stomach and cover the other side of her with kisses. Take about ten minutes on the flip side, then roll her over on her back again, and really kiss her breasts. Lift her chin, and concentrate on her mouth, making lots of eye contact. Say as few words as possible. Murmur instead. Kiss her from head to toe, stem to stern, for at least forty or fifty minutes."

"That's a lot of foreplay."

"You're so lazy. Anyway, it's not foreplay, it's something better. Because after you've given her the all-over, you're going to plant almost ceremonial kisses on the corners of her lips and eyelids and then one last big gentle one on the lips. At which point you whisper good night, that it's time you both went sleepy-bye, then roll over to your side of the bed. It'll take her a moment to realize what's happened, and she won't believe it. She'll be in shock."

"I'm in shock now. Do all of that and then *stop*? I thought you were going to recommend mutual self-pleasuring or one of those things teenagers practice. 'Outercourse,' or whatever it's called."

"This isn't about you, Studly Dickmore. Any man can be a sticker-inner. This is for her. If you go to bed with Amanda knowing ahead of time that you're going to stop short of actual penetration, you'll be able to practice restraint. Mind over matter. Think of yourself as a sculptor, working with soft material. Once Amanda gets over her surprise, she'll feel completely cradled. She won't believe what self-restraint you have, especially when she remembers reaching into your boxers to make sure you were hard and not because of impotence, *which she will do.* The fact that you had it and didn't use it will make her quiver. When you bring her breakfast on the wicker tray—which is why we bought it, bub—she'll feel as if she's at a spa. She'll want to test your resistance and show her appreciation. She'll lavish some loving on you the likes of which you've never seen. You may not get out alive. Can you do it, Johnny? Can you put a cap on that thing for the night?"

"I'll try, but in the heat of the moment things can happen."

"Trying's not good enough. Do it. We've come too far to let your peeny screw things up now. And don't have sex with Amanda and lie to me about it afterward, because for an actor you are one lousy liar."

"Why are you getting angry?"

"I'm not angry, I just *sound* angry. I'm frustrated because I sense we're this close to a breakthrough, and I'm afraid you might wuss out on me and, worse, wuss out on yourself."

"Suppose she laughs at all this body-kissing stuff?"

"She may giggle, but she won't laugh. Johnny, if a woman stretched you out on the bed and kissed you from head to toe, nuzzling you in all the right places, running the full length of her body along yours, tenderly tracing her fingers across every . . ."

"Stop, I'm beginning to get turned on."

"*Exactly.* The biggest turn-on of all is learning how to stop at the brink. Because then, when you do go over the brink, it's momentous. You'll think you're in love even if you aren't."

26

AMANDA MET ME UNDER THE AWNING of her building. As my cab pulled up to the curb, she was inspecting the tips of her shoes. She had wheeled out the full artillery, this time without a scarf to serve as curtain and veil. The straps of her dress were thin as shoelaces, the entire dress a marvel of engineering. After a cheek kiss and a mutual look-over, I held the cab door open for Amanda as she squeezed in. I climbed in after, and, as usual, there was so little sardine room in the back seat our knees were practically propping up our chins. The taxi took off, veering in and out of traffic like a stunt car and trying to beat the lights. I was about to tap on the plastic divider and ask the driver to cool it when I caught a glimpse of Amanda in his rear-view mirror. Her eyes looked amused, slightly wowed. She was enjoying this thrill ride. We arrived intact at a new downtown restaurant located in a converted firehouse adjacent to a warehouse that had been converted into luxury lofts. The block, once a sore tooth in the area, was now lit at night like a movie set. Money seemed to be flying out of everyone's mouth. As we waited in line for the frantic host to lead us to our table, Amanda kept up a steady streak of nervous banter. "I wonder if they'll slide down the pole to take our orders. Does my dress look okay in the back? The springs in that cab were so busted that—"

"It looks fine. But it looks even better from the front."

"Oh, stop."

"If you insist. But my eyes have their own ideas."

I placed my hand near the small of her back as we maneuvered through the madness of the main dining room to a table at the quieter rear. Men glanced at Amanda as she passed, the women with them glancing even harder, running various calculations through their heads. The host seated us at a cozy table where our knees couldn't help but meet. Upstairs, where the firefighters used to bunk, a finicky jazz trio provided their idea of "atmosphere." The waitress who brought our drinks complimented me on my tie clasp before launching into a recital of the specials that night, half-closing her eyes to remember all of the entrees. Amanda asked how one of the dishes was prepared and the waitress said she would have to consult the kitchen. While we awaited her report on the pork-chop filling, I fiddled with the napkin on my lap and Amanda, her eyes bright, made a conscious effort to relax. The band upstairs, invisibly raising their instruments, segued into a jaunty Dixieland number, which sounded a little anemic without a horn section.

"Have you ever been to New Orleans?" Amanda asked.

"Once."

"You don't sound too enthused."

"It was like being in a malaria ward."

"Really? It's one of the few cities in America with any personality. I have to swing by there soon on one of my antiquing trips, and can't wait to hit my favorite spots. You're the first person I've met who hasn't been entranced by New Orleans."

"The fault was probably mine," I said, swiftly backtracking as if to receive a punt. "I visited during the off-season, and couldn't see what all the fuss was about. A guy threw up on me in the elevator when I checked in, which pretty much set the tone."

"He was probably a tourist. You didn't see the real New Orleans. You need me to be your guide."

As Amanda described her favorite hot spots, I nudged my drink glass a whisper away from hers. I listened to her New Orleans stories with both eyes, matching her sip for sip. Amanda played with her earring, always a good sign. We compared notes about our favorite cities through dinner, our real interests running on a separate track underneath the conversation. This, we both knew, would be the night. After ordering coffee, Amanda said: "I need to use the ladies' room. Back in a jif."

As I waited, I studied the sliding pole in a nearby mirror. It was wrapped with red and blue stripes in preparation for the Fourth of July. I tried to imagine the dining room as a painting, everyone's mouth open in jolly uproar, like those antique prints of Bowery saloons. Suddenly everything went dark as a pair of hands clamped across my eyes.

"Guess who?"

"I'd recognize those soft hands anywhere."

"Flatterer," Amanda said, releasing my eyes. I took one of her wrists, kissing the palm of her hand. A daring move, but one she didn't seem to mind.

We walked to the movies, which gave me the opportunity to do a pocketbook check. The result was positive. Amanda wore her pocketbook on her far arm, leaving her near arm free. The movie itself, *Hidden Lake*, was one of those ensemble numbers about four female friends who used to share a summer bunkhouse and have now grown up to be variously miserable: one married to a cheat, the other divorced, etc. During the film's sexiest sequence, where the divorced mom lures a neighbor kid upstairs so that she can model outfits for him, her white lacy bra and panties bursting with plenty, Amanda began to drag her fingernails lightly across my bare wrist. As the woman on screen stood before the mirror preening herself, the teenage boy on the bed in the foreground, Amanda stroked the inside of my wrist with her fingertips. On screen the woman asked the neighborhood boy to do up this tricky clasp for her. He breathed on the back of her neck. At that moment I ran my finger down the back of Amanda's neck and she rested her hand on my knee. She squeezed my knee as the divorcee turned and pressed the neighborhood boy's head between her breasts.

As we left the theater, I said: "Why don't we go back to my place for a nightcap?"

"I'd like that," she said softly.

I cupped Amanda's elbow and steered her past the stragglers in line for the next show. We didn't talk much during the walk back to my place, reserving our words for our thoughts. It was a cloudless night, the moon was so yellow and bright, you could see its pockmarks. We shared the elevator of my building with a Chinese delivery man who had a look of deep uncertainty. After we dropped him off, we continued to my floor. I opened the door to my apartment. Slinky, hearing or sniffing unfamiliar company, was nowhere in sight, probably holing up in the closet. I switched on the light, and the lilies in the vase seemed to burst into color. Amanda looked around, marveling at how neat everything was, how perfectly placed.

"You sound surprised," I said.

"With bachelor apartments you never know what might be waiting for you on the other side of the door. I remember walking into a studio where the man had empty pizza boxes stacked six or seven high in a corner for recycling. Claudia told me you had a jukebox."

"I got rid of it and replaced it with that side table."

"Why?"

"I just felt I had outgrown it."

"Did you dance in front of it with all your girlfriends?"

"No, I boogied alone."

As Amanda admired the lilies, I poured her and myself each a small glass of Frangelico. We sat on the couch, rolling the contents of our glasses between sips. Knowing Amanda's thing for jazz, I had preset the radio to the proper FM station, which was grooving away softly in the background. Placing each paw down slowly and carefully, as if crossing a mine field, Slinky entered the living room on a reconnaissance mission. Sniffing the air, she stopped at the front of the sofa, hissed at Amanda, then spun and swatted at her tail before dashing into the bedroom to make her customary dive into the closet. "She's jealous," I whispered to Amanda. "Pay her no mind." Amanda nodded abstractly and touched my hair as if seeing it for the first time. We were sipping in sync, as if our arms were attached to the same lever. I felt none of the hurry or lurking doubt I usually experienced the first time I brought someone new back to the apartment. This was partly the result of Darlene's prep work, partly the Frangelico, but mostly Amanda. I wanted to spoon her right out of her dress. When she finished her drink, I took her snifter, set it on the coffee table, and gave her a kiss that said, *Let's begin.*

We kissed long and slow on the sofa, pausing only when Slinky reentered the living room on her way to the kitchen. After taking several laps of water from her bowl, the cat padded through the living room, then suddenly accelerated, tearing into the bedoom. Her finger playing with my earlobe, Amanda said, "Maybe you should get a rug for that part of the floor, before it gets too scratched up. The right Indian rug would do wonders."

"The floor does look a little bare."

"Does she scratch the furniture?"

"Sometimes. She has a scratching post, but doesn't always use it."

"Have you ever thought about having her declawed?"

"No. I hear it can be demoralizing for the animal, because it leaves them defenseless."

"I had Raja declawed, and I haven't noticed any particular moping."

This didn't seem the right moment to debate the pros and cons of cat declawing, or the relative psyches of Raja and Slinky. To steer us back onto the love track, to quote the great Barry White, I slipped my hand through her hair, tracing the arc of her ear. We kissed. I kept my hands away from her body, touching only her face and hair, pressing my thumb lightly on her lower lip as my mouth met hers. Her mouth swallowed the tip of my thumb, as if to suck it, then scraped her teeth along the top. It sent a tingle through me all the way down to the stock exchange. Amanda slowly detached her face from mine, kicked off her shoes, then clasped my head in her hands, twisting her body and drawing it to me. Her skirt hiked up, baring a flash of white skin. Everything was moving faster than I anticipated, but also in slow motion, as if what was happening was playing on twin screens at different speeds. At one point Amanda lay her hands on my head and pressed me downward. I thought she might press until my head was between her legs but she stopped at her cleavage. Her head was thrown back, as if she were a romance heroine welcoming ravishment. I worked my lips up her throat back to her mouth and then whispered in her ear. I stood, taking her wrist and raising her from the sofa before leading her into the bedroom.

Ignoring Slinky's front paws, which were lurking from under the bed, I lit candles as Amanda removed her jewelry and put it on the night table. For reasons I can't explain, watching a woman remove her jewelry excites the hell out of me. I intended to undress her, but when I turned after lighting a stick of incense, I saw that she had already found a wooden hanger and stored her dress in the closet. The efficiency of women never fails to amaze me. Amanda then posed by the side of the bed in black strapless bra and panties, garter belt and stockings. "Would you like me to leave these on?" she asked, thumbing the clasp on one of her garters.

"Take them off," I said. I didn't know if I could do the All-Over with her wearing stockings. She raised a leg, rested a foot on the corner of the bed, and rolled down her stocking.

Stripped to bra and panties, Amanda slowly took hold of me. The Frangelico and kissing had given her lower lip a life of its own. "Not fair," she said. "You're still dressed."

Gently encircling her wrists, I removed her hands and undid my shirt buttons. As I cast the shirt aside, she pressed against me and made expert use of her fingernails, drawing little circles on my chest. At that moment I almost abandoned the idea of doing the All-Over. It seemed unnatural, when Amanda and I were so poised to ravish each other. I could hear myself breathing as Amanda lowered her mouth to my nipple and began to suck. I unlatched her bra, its former occupants popping free and crowding against me. My hands welcomed them into the new world. Massaging the outside of my silk boxers, Amanda said, "My, my, what have we here? It looks as if it wants to come out and play."

Amanda was alluding to the movie we had seen, mimicking the manner with which the divorcee seduced her teenage neighbor. She even pursed her lips together, like that actress. I would never impress Amanda as a man if I let her treat my penis as a boy toy and our first time together as a movie fantasy. I intercepted Amanda's hand as it reached inside my boxers and brought it to my mouth, kissing the inside of her wrist.

"That can wait," I said.

"Are you sure? It seems raring to go."

"I'm sure. You lie back and let me set the table."

"If you insist."

Amanda lay in the middle of the bed, resting slightly on her elbows, allowing me room to maneuver on both sides. "Close your eyes," I whispered, tipping her shoulders flat against the bed. By candlelight the contours of her skin unfolded like a landscape seen from a plane at night. I felt like a pilot crossing Nova Scotia on an Atlantic run, the only one awake in a sleeping world. Even Amanda seemed to be dreaming. The candle burned down to a drop of flame.

27

IT WASN'T UNTIL LATE SUNDAY AFTERNOON that I report-
ed to Darlene. I stretched my legs across the coffee table as I punched
in her number. An adjacent building blocked the sun, rendering the sky
Tiffany-blue.

"Darlene? It's me, Johnny."

"Johnny who?"

"You know Johnny who."

"It sounds like Johnny Downs, but not the Johnny I know. This
voice carries a note of manly assurance I've never heard before."

"Perhaps a new spirit has taken hold of me, Darlene."

"Oh, God, what have I created? Tell me everything."

"Isn't much to tell, really. I performed a little miracle called the All-
Over."

"My hero! How did she like it?"

"Well, when I said, 'That's enough for now,' her eyes popped open
and she said, 'You're joking, right?'"

"I bet that's when she reached into your boxers to try the doorknob."

"No, her hand had been there for some time. I assured her I was serious and pulled the sheet over both of us and lay on my back. She turned
and swung her leg over me, wrinkling her nose to show she was suspicious of my motives. Then, it being so late, her hand just sort of went
soft, and she began whistling through her nose. That's when I knew
she had fallen asleep."

"So did you slip away to the bathroom and beat off?"

"No, but thanks for asking. Actually, I felt completely at peace. I felt a sense of accomplishment. Part of it was knowing that you would be proud of me. I know that sounds weird."

"I don't see why. We're in this together, after all. So did you make her breakfast next morning?"

I did. I served yogurt and orange juice on the wicker tray covered with a linen napkin I bought at Shower and Tub. I didn't want to prepare too much since we planned to go to brunch. When I brought in the tray, with its single rose in a vase, Amanda was standing at the bedroom window wearing the big fluffy robe I had left for her. Her arms were folded, so I knew I was in for one of those we-have-to-talk talks. She had slept like an angel, she said. I said I had, too, once I had dropped off. Then she said that although she appreciated what I had done the night before, she was concerned. She had read an article in the *New York Magazine* about men avenging themselves on women by refusing to have sex with them. It's this passive-aggressive thing where they lead the woman on and act like, to use the article's own phrase, cunt-teasers. It's apparently their way of hurting and punishing women for what's been done to them in the past. This has happened to friends of mine, Amanda said, and I hope you're not playing that kind of game with me. I set the tray down on the bed and went over to Amanda and stroked her arm. "You shouldn't believe the trash you read in magazines," I said. "They try to inflate every crummy incident into a national trend." She didn't seem quite convinced, so I slipped off her robe, and allayed her concerns the best way I knew how. I told most of this to Darlene.

"Not to be a nag, but I wish you had waited a bit longer," she said. "Given her more time to think about you and let the curiosity build— that would have made the payoff even bigger. She'd have come at you like a tidal wave. So how was it?"

"Well, I don't mean to brag . . ."

"Never mind you, how was it for *her*, doofus? Did she say anything to indicate nobody had ever done anything like this for her before?"

"Not in so many words. She kept asking me what I was thinking."

"That's good. She was probably wondering if what had happened meant as much to you as it meant to her. I hope you didn't try to be too ride-'em-cowboy in bed. We don't like it when men try to make us keep rotating positions like gymnasts—it spoils our concentration. I should have mentioned that earlier, except I couldn't picture you being that mobile anyhow. Now here's what I want you to do. Don't phone Amanda tonight. Give her some time to get all gooey thinking about what happened, then send her flowers tomorrow, along with a very gentlemanly note. The next time you see her, it'll take a crowbar to pry you apart. She'll wonder what you have in store *next*, you big strapping man, you."

"Darlene, how did you know this would work?"

"Because a man did it to me once. Took me to a motel, kissed me from head to toe, then withdrew to his side of the bed. The next morning, he drove me back to my place, let me out of the car, gave me a passionate kiss, and said, 'Thank you.' Never even said if we'd ever see each other again."

"It sounds pretty mind-gamey."

"Yeah, but it *worked.* I was ready to walk naked in the rain to see him. When he didn't call the next day, I called him the day after that, breaking my own rule. The next time we met, well, we didn't have intercourse then, either, but we did everything but, and I nearly floated out of my body and joined the clouds. I don't know if it's because of all those porno movies, but most men today try to *pulverize* you with their dicks, like they're trying to leave you battered senseless. So don't let this success with Amanda go to your head and start acting like a dumb stud. In the interests of science, you need to practice the All-Over on a variety of women, see which ones it works on. I mean, I have no idea how this'll play out on your average Prozac gal. They may slip into a coma and never come out."

"I'm just started up with Amanda. I don't think I should be out there practicing on Prozac women."

"Just don't get too attached too soon. Right now you need to fool around some and find out more about yourself, make some useful mistakes. For all you know, Amanda may still have an old boyfriend or two stashed away in the pantry. Do you really think a woman with her looks and money runs around New Orleans just for antiques and Cajun cuisine? I'm not saying you should be a fuck-around, I'm just saying don't form a couple just yet. You latched onto Nicole without doing any kind of background check and got blindsided. Pace yourself."

"I've been pacing myself all my life."

"No, you were just waiting for *me* to come along. Now, unless you have any other tawdry details to relate, I'm going to hang up so I can catch some rays. It's the only foolproof way I have of getting some peace from all the needy people in my life."

Darlene claimed she sunbathed topless on the slanted rooftop of the house she shared down in Decatur, Georgia. I say "claimed," because whenever I saw her, her skin was always the same protected white, and I couldn't picture Darlene submitting to any higher power, even the sun.

28

DURING INTERMISSION, appalled ticket holders shuffled around in the lobby, saying things like "Jesus, Mary, and Joseph" and "I need a drink." Others stared with disbelief at the blown-up rave reviews mounted on easels, lip-reading highlighted phrases such as "a corncob attack on colonialism" and "*Jungle Fever* freshened with mint juleps." The play was *Rash Remarks,* the farce I had intended to take Claudia to until her convenient gas leak. Seeing the play was Amanda's idea. She'd heard from a friend that the play was funny, so I wheeled another pair of comps, and we snuggled into our seats as if something wonderful were about to unfold. Fifteen minutes later, a single sentence formed in my head: Never trust somebody else's friends. It was one of those over-wrought farces where every surprise gave the cast a round of whiplash. The sole redeeming element for the girl-watchers in the audience (a dying breed) was the presence of Lara McNair, one of those dancer-turned-actress sprites, who traipsed around in crisp white undies and threw herself at the mansion's black retainer, who seemed to have cornered the market on rippling muscles. At one point she ordered him to play horsey. As he got down on all fours and she climbed on his back, I could hear the director urging them in rehearsal, "Have fun with it." She rode him around the room until some old coot fainted on cue.

At the lobby bar, Amanda and I sipped sparkling water and tried to recover. I said, "We don't have to stay for the second act."

"Are you sure?"

"Why torture ourselves?"

"I was hoping we could leave, but I didn't want to seem ungrateful."

"We should be grateful just to be alive after what we've just been through."

"The strange thing, the audience seemed to enjoy it. The couple next to us was in hysterics."

"Yeah. I don't know what's worse, the play or their *hollow laughter.*"

Once we were in the open air, the play began to shrink in my mind to the scale of a puppet show, a lot of jerky action on a tiny stage. For some reason, leaving a show at intermission always creates this sort of tunnel vision. As we turned the corner and reached Grove Street, almost giddy with freedom, Amanda dipped her head into my shoulder and asked, "Did you think she was sexy?"

"Who?"

"You know who. The girl in white lingerie, McNair."

"Oh. Her."

"You didn't find her attractive?"

"I can't say she lit up my life. She's awfully unformed, emotionally unformed, I mean. She's not quite a person yet. Or an actress, for that matter."

"You have to admit she has a fabulous figure. Nothing unformed about that. I suppose a lot of men would find her overbite sexy."

There followed a pause just long enough for me to realize that this was a question, not a statement. I said:

"An overbite is useful if you're peeling an apple, but personally I think a person's teeth should remain behind their lips, where they belong. She also doesn't know how to open a parasol, something you think they would have rehearsed. I should have known this would be a stinker when I heard it was based on a French farce."

"Johnny, you're not one of those people who hates the French, are you?"

"Nah. I've never even gone to Paris to get insulted. I've always wanted to go, but I'm afraid of getting stuck in some chilly hotel room, unable to order room service because my French is so nonexistent. It's embarrassing, having to point at the menu."

"I speak French well enough to keep us fed."

"I could have hopped over to Paris when I was in London years ago, but I didn't want to go alone."

"It's my favorite foreign city. I love it even in August, when every-one's away."

"Have you ever been to London?"

"Of course I've been to London, silly."

"Well, you know, a lot of people haven't."

Our walk took us toward St. Teresa's. As we approached, a door opened, spilling light onto the sidewalk. A group of men emerged, forming a loose circle on the sidewalk. They looked like strikebreakers, standing with their hands jammed in their jeans pockets, but as one separated from the others, he was given a round of good-bye hugs. I couldn't make out their faces once the door behind them closed—the streetlight cast them in shadow. But as Amanda and I slipped between them, one man nodded at me. It was a succinct nod, one guy to anoth-er. I nodded back. When we'd passed St. Teresa's, Amanda said, "Who was that?"

"A member of one of the self-help groups, I guess." I wondered if the men belonged to a twelve-step group or if they were members of the men's-anger workshop Mrs. Cole had told me about.

"He seemed to recognize you," Amanda said.

"He's probably seen me around during my volunteer work."

"For some reason, those guys gave me the creeps. Even their hugs looked sinister."

"I'm sure they're harmless. Anybody'd look sinister in that light."

I didn't quite believe what I had just said, but I didn't want Amanda thinking I volunteered at a church that administered to thugs. After a cab ride uptown, she and I had dinner at a Swiss fondue restaurant in her neighborhood. She seemed subdued, but I decided not to try to jolly her out of it by making fun of the play. Everybody's entitled to their moods. She sipped decaf in silent thought, as if weighing a decision. As she avoided eye contact, I pretended to contemplate the mountaineer-ing prints and maps on the wall next to us. Amanda and I had gotten to the point where my staying overnight at her place after a date was assumed rather than discussed, but I wondered if this might be a night when she announced a headache and sent me home.

Out on the street, however, she took my arm and walked with her usual sway. It was nice, having so much womanhood leaning into me. Looming ahead of us was a convenience store called Speedy's.

"Let's pop in," I said. "I need to pick up some necessities."

"I have plenty of soda in the fridge."

"That's not what I had in mind. Let's just say I could use a new set of shower caps, unless you've got some stocked at home."

"No. We're all out."

A chain store, Speedy's was twice as bright as any regular local one, with that lunar glare that turns everyone's face into a latex mask. The magazine section reminded me of a Maryland 7-Eleven or Wawa: a library consisting of a dozen or so different biker magazines, four tattoo titles (including a crossover item, *Biker Tattoo*), three crossword puzzle magazines, six bodybuilding publications, and the latest *June Bride*, which I had already read and discussed with Darlene. Amanda waited by the cashier's while I skimmed the aisles.

I lingered at the snack section, in case I might like to have a little bite before church the next morning. I tried to attend regularly now, making mass three Sundays out of four. Attending mass hadn't brought me in closer to God or grace, as much as I could tell, but it gave my life a kind of order that made everything seem less drifty. I felt I was on a more secure guidepath than before. Amanda said she had qualms about organized religion (like who hasn't), so I went alone, though I often chatted with other parishioners afterward, including Mrs. Cole and her son, who was quite an adept conversation-interrupter for such a young lad. Standing in front of the snack-food rack, I mentally seesawed between the chocolate cupcakes with vanilla squiggles on top and the vanilla cupcakes with chocolate squiggles on top, finally opting for the chocolate ones. I also picked up a bottle of Diet Dr Pepper and a large bottle of Perrier.

Amanda's arms were crossed when I reached the cash register. Worrying that I had kept her waiting too long, I clunked the bottles on the counter.

"What's that in your hand?" she said.

"Cupcakes, baby."

"I know what they are. But what are they doing in your hand?"

"Not much. They're inanimate."

"That's not funny. Johnny, do you know what's in them?"

"Sure. It says on the label, 'Fat Free!'"

"It also says on the label, in much smaller print, that they're loaded with chemicals and preservatives. I can't believe you'd want junk food after the nice fondue we've just had."

As any comedy writer can tell you, "fondue" is one of those intrinsically funny words, like "kumquat" and "rotunda." The cashier and his teenage assistant laughed, and I had to bite my lip not to join them. Amanda failed to share our mirth. Her face formed a solid plate. With the cashier and his smirking teenage assistant witnessing this little scene, I knew I would look like a whipped dog if I returned the cupcakes to the snack rack, and it was hardly worth explaining that I was saving them for the next day. Then again, my pride, not to mention my digestive system, would easily survive the loss of a pack of cupcakes.

"Oh, go ahead and get them, if you have to," Amanda said. "It's just so adolescent, this craving for sweets. But maybe it was the way you were brought up."

She had forced my hand. I slid the cupcakes across the counter, along with the beverages.

"Anything else, my friend?" the cashier asked.

"I could use some condoms." The condoms were kept behind the counter.

"What kind?"

"Eureka."

"Smooth or ribbed?"

"Ribbed."

"Dry or lubricated?"

"Lubricated."

"With Eureka Plus, you get two extra to a box."

"Well, you've sold me."

As the cashier totaled up the items, I tossed in a double pack of Dentyne. Behind me Amanda impersonated an iron mummy.

We left Speedy's with a tense strip of space hanging between us. I carried the goodies in my left arm, leaving my right hand free, but Amanda successfully blocked it by slinging her pocketbook over on that side. She wouldn't allow me to cup her elbow as we crossed the street. Her held-back fury was like a thunderstorm about to burst. When we reached her awning, I expected her to tell me she had had quite enough for one evening, but although she didn't invite me in, she didn't order me to stay out, either, so I followed her into the building with my clanking bag. I said an extra-friendly hello to the doorman, as if we had just returned from someplace fun.

Once we were in her apartment, Amanda tossed her keys on the kitchen table and unscrewed the top of a seltzer bottle as if it were my head. I put my bag on the table and drew out the cupcakes, deliberately rattling the plastic wrapper, hoping to kid her out of her annoyance. She poured the seltzer into a glass—Upper West Siders love seltzer— as I stowed the soda and Perrier in the refrigerator. She waited until I had closed the refrigerator door, then opened the door again herself to put away her own bottle, segregating it as far away from mine as possible. Then she stood in the kitchen with her glass, taking every sip as if it were abhorrent to her.

"*Something* wrong?" I asked mildly.

"I cannot be*lieve* you did that. I have to walk past that place every day, and you embarrass me . . ."

"Amanda, aren't you a wee bit exaggerating? I hardly think they're going to come out from behind the counter and point at you as you walk by. Grown men have bought cupcakes before."

"It's not the cupcakes, and you know it. You must think you were awfully cute buying those condoms. 'Well, you've sold me.' Well, you won't need to be cracking any of them open tonight, Mr. Comedian. And don't think it was lost on me that you specifically asked for lubricated ones, as if you needed all the moist help you could get to service this dried-up scold trying to deny you your precious snackcakes."

"Sweetie, I hardly think they were computing all that in their heads. Besides, I always buy lubricated. Nonlubricated can cause irritation."

"That's not the only thing that can cause irritation, and don't 'sweetie' me. It's like that time in that Italian restaurant when you ordered a Coke with dinner. You're not supposed to wash down a meal like that with soda. You and your sweet tooth! God only knows how you'd behave in Paris, although I noticed that when I brought up Paris, you immediately diverted the subject, the same way you did when I brought up New Orleans before."

So that's what was bothering her. By shrugging off her offer of showing me New Orleans or Paris, I had planted doubt in her mind whether or not the two of us had even a short-to-middle-term future. I started to soften and tell her I understood, I'll toss the cupcakes in the trash, when I noticed how large her pupils were. Her whole body was intent on defying me, but her eyes and nostrils were wide open, her lips parted. It was exciting her, ripping into me.

"I guess I can be selfish sometimes," I said, "a little crude."

"You like being crude."

"No, I don't. I just don't know any better."

"I don't have the time to teach you."

"You don't? But you're such a good teacher, Miss Amanda, and I'm such an eager pupil," I said, edging nearer.

"You're not going to talk your way out of this one, buster."

"I'm not?"

"You're not going to fuck your way out of it, either."

"You seem sure about that."

"It's probably that little actress you want to fuck."

"You can send her over when I'm done with you," I said, slipping my arms under Amanda's and sliding my hands down her hips as her hands crept up against my chest, her fingers loose and curled, offering token resistance. I stole a kiss from her, hard at first, then soft. The kisses then came in a flurry as we mashed against each other like forbidden lovers. Working my hands over her dress, I squeezed Amanda every which way, then released her and stepped back to give our bodies breathing room. She kicked off her shoes and reached back to undo her zipper. Her eyes were ready to ride. It was one of the rare times in my life I really felt I had a woman in my power.

Amanda had trouble opening the clasp. I spun her around and unzipped her dress in one slow pull, nuzzling her neck and kissing her shoulders as the dress fell to her feet. I palmed her breasts and she reached behind and fondled me. I took her by the wrist and led her into the bedroom, where she perched on edge of the sleigh bed, undid my belt, unzipped my fly, and opened the condom wrapper with her fingernails.

"I'm not giving you head first," she said, "because you don't deserve it."

Moments later, we were bouncing in bed like stagecoach passengers, her heels beating against my hips, her arms wrapped around me as if she were holding on to a barrel going over the falls. Feeling I needed to throw something special into this, I flipped Amanda over on her stomach, something I couldn't have done if she hadn't cooperated, then wiggled into her from behind. Leaning forward to take some of the strain off my lower back, I whispered, "This is how they hump in all those blues records you like." She called me a name but scooted backward, smooth against me. We watched ourselves in the mirror facing the bed. I smacked her bottom. The stagecoach started rocking faster, rocking until I grabbed the back of her hair and Amanda swiveled her head to look at me, one eye wild, and I went over the brink, paisley nebulae instantly born and detonating in my head, as she plunged her head into the pillow to muffle her scream. It was a double kaboom, as if we had both just smothered the same hand grenade. We laughed at the sound of our own labored breathing.

After we slowly disentangled and sorted out our body parts, I blew on Amanda's damp back, where my stomach had pressed. We needed to shower, but our funkiness had a certain animal-kingdom splendor. Raja sat at the foot of the bed like a tiny dignitary, completing the picture.

". . . Johnny," Amanda said, indulging herself with a rare cigarette, ". . . you can have those cupcakes if you want."

"That's okay, I'm saving them for breakfast."

"You know, they're really not good for you, fat free or not. But I'm sorry, though, about what I said about your upbringing. I guess I was trying to bait you."

"I'll have you know I was a very promising baby. Do you want me to get you anything?"

"No. Don't move."

Since I didn't really want to move, it was easy to comply.

"God, that was good, wasn't it?" Amanda said.

"You'll get no argument here."

"How would you rate me as a lover?"

"Up there with the hall-of-famers."

"No, really."

"It's like cashing the biggest check in the world."

"I wasn't too loud, was I? I've never screamed like that before."

"Was that you? I thought maybe I had stepped on the cat."

"I had a boyfriend who used to complain I was too vocal in bed."

"Sounds like a Republican."

"No, not really. He just found it overwhelming when I seemed to lose control. He said he couldn't concentrate."

"Excuses, excuses."

"You're feeling awfully cocky, aren't you? You know, when you flipped me over, I thought you might be going in another way."

"I would never attempt that without proper authorization," I said, trying to sound like Gregory Peck. I had acted once with his daughter Cecilia.

"Have you ever taken a woman there?" Amanda asked.

"Nope."

"You must have wanted to. I hear a lot of men are into it."

"I wouldn't know, the subject's never come up at the country club. It seems like a lot of work and discomfort—I suspect it's one of those sex things that's sexier to imagine than actually do, like S&M or orgies. Being into S&M is like having a second job with those sweaty leather outfits, all these unofficial rules you're supposed to follow, not to mention all the gear you have to lug around unless you're rich enough to have your own dungeon. Normal sex can be wild enough. No need to go to extremes. Maybe I'm too conventional."

"Not at all. If I thought you were into that stuff, I would have said hi—good-bye the first time we met. Claudia dated a man who asked her to wear long black gloves and drip hot wax on his nipples."

"For some reason, it's the nipples part that's the most disgusting. So did she?"

"She says she didn't, but that's not what I'm getting at. Johnny, to be serious for a moment, as much as I enjoyed what just happened, I hope you don't think everything can be resolved sexually. Sometimes things have to be talked through. You're not Stanley Kowalski, you know."

"I'm aware of that, believe me. I just felt that the moment called for something dramatic."

"I enjoyed being in your grip," Amanda said. "I did. It just scared me a little, seeing the look on your face in the mirror. It was a look of pure, heaving lust."

I refrained from telling Amanda that her face in the mirror might have frightened children, too. That would have only made her defensive. Instead, I stroked her arm and told her again that I understood. Amanda stubbed out her cigarette, setting the ashtray on the night table. A street-cleaning truck went by outside, its rotating brush sounding like huge, wet whiskers. Amanda turned on her side, tracing a figure eight on my stomach with her finger.

"I have to make my annual Southern swing next week," she said.

"Where?"

"There's an antiques fair in New Orleans, and from there I'm heading to Savannah and Charleston. I hope we'll be able to see each other before I leave. You can give me a proper sendoff."

"When are you leaving?"

"Thursday."

"Wednesday night you'll probably want to pack, so why don't we say Tuesday?"

"It's a date. Can I bring you back anything?"

"Just yourself," I said, then, thinking it might sound corny, asked for a bottle of New Orleans holy water, which was rumored to possess magical powers. The red bottles themselves were beautiful and would look nice on the mantle. Amanda said she knew exactly where she could buy them, then rolled over and reached for the clock, holding its round head in her hand.

"What time do you want me to set the alarm?"

"Around ten. I need to get home and feed Slinky before noon mass."

"Since you've been such a good boy tonight, maybe I'll give you my own special wakeup call in the morning."

"I thought I had misbehaved."

"You had. But you redeemed yourself. Would you mind if we switched pillows? The one you're on is my favorite."

29

ON THE SUNDAY AFTERNOON following the Saturday night with Amanda, I was napping like a lion under a shady tree on the savannah when my mother rang.

"Son, you know I hate to bother you," she said.

"I wasn't aware of that."

"Your grandmother is in intensive care. Her emphysema has finally caught up with her—this may be your last chance to see her."

"It's that serious?"

"I'm afraid so. She's becoming disoriented on the medications they have her on and keeps asking for the phone to call her dead sister Irene. Her heart's also in bad shape. She refused to go to the doctor for her tests, and a UPS man found her slumped in the living room. So if you could see your way to . . ."

"I can't leave until I shoot this TV commercial in New Jersey—I really need the dough. But I'll come down later this week after I get someone to cover my shift. I'll also need to line up a catsitter. She'll last out the week, won't she? She's a pretty tough bird."

"The doctor I talked to didn't want to put a time frame on anything. It's probably better they don't. Remember when they told us your grandfather would be out of the hospital in a week and he died the next day? I've never gotten over that. Your father's staying up in the attic, but you could stay in your brother's room, if you don't want to pay for a motel."

The brother my mother meant was my youngest brother, Jim, who had returned the previous winter after two hazy years in Wyoming and taken up residence in the basement, which he had converted into bachelor quarters, complete with water bed, cable TV, minibar, and shag carpeting. He hadn't been entirely successful in ridding the basement of laundry-room smell or the occasional pipe-drip, but otherwise he was living the life. Sharing the basement probably meant rolling out the old sleeping bag.

"Let me think about that," I said.

After my mother hung up, I called Gleason. I was leaving a message asking if he could sub for me at Buzzy's when I heard a call-waiting click. I completed the message, then switched over.

"Well, you kept me hanging long enough," Darlene said. "Where *were* you all weekend?"

I recapped the cupcake incident with Amanda and told her how the situation had been happily resolved. Darlene said:

"So let me see if I understand this. First, Amanda tells you that she wants it understood that sex isn't the all-purpose way to solve personal differences, then she rewards you with a b.j. the next morning? I think that's what's known as a mixed message. Anyway, you managed to squeak by on this one, though she does have a point about your sweet tooth. You are very oral. It's a sign of some sort of neediness. Maybe your mother didn't breastfeed you enough—why don't you ask her while you're down there?"

"Yes, I'll be sure to ask her that."

"Maybe once you have a wife, you won't be such a snack fiend. It's hard to eat all them Tastykakes with someone else watching. But she shouldn't have started steaming at the checkout counter. She should have kept you wondering what she was upset about the entire walk home and then unloaded on you back at her place. That's what I would have done."

"Do you and Clete fight?"

"I pick an argument every now and then, just to stay in condition. He says I'm such a brat, one of these days he's going to spank me."

"I used to be into spanking—on a fantasy level, I mean—but lately it doesn't do anything for me. I guess I've matured."

"If Amanda asked you to spank her, you'd be on her butt like Ricky Ricardo. The reason I called was to ask if you could hit the flea market this weekend and find me a particular type of lampshade. I'll fax you a photo."

"I can't this week. I just got some bad news about my grandmother and have to head down to Maryland. I need to line up a catsitter before I go."

"What about Amanda?"

"She's out of town for a couple weeks, antiquing. I'm going to post some notices on the church bulletin board and at the restaurant, see what happens."

"I have an idea. A friend of mine is driving north and needs a place to crash. She doesn't mind burning up gasoline, but can't afford to stay in a New York hotel. If you stocked the refrigerator, I'm sure she'd cat-sit for you while you're gone. I don't think she'd do your apartment too much damage and you'd finally get to meet her."

"Meet who?"

"Caroline Dupree."

It was at Caroline's house in Athens, Georgia, that I had first met Darlene, sitting on an abandoned hearse parked on the lawn. I never did meet Caroline, who had been detained upstate for speeding violations and resisting arrest.

"In fact, if you left some theater tickets, she'd probably clean your apartment, no charge. Do you want me to call her? I'll tell her you'll reimburse her for some of the gas money."

"Whoa, baby, this trip alone is costing me. I'm darn near broke."

"Well, you're the one who insists on being the last of the gentlemen actors. Maybe it's time we found you a real job, something appropriate to your station in life, you know, like handing out towels in a tanning salon or something. Unless, of course, you plan to marry Amanda and live off her money."

"She'd have me on a strict allowance."

"She'd have you on a nookie allowance, too."

"I don't know about that. We gave each other quite a bon voyage. We took a bubble bath together."

"As I recall, Nicole gave you quite a sendoff, too, the last time you left for Maryland, and look what happened when you got back. I think it's highly suspicious that Amanda sprung this New Orleans trip on you only after some hot lovin'. 'Bam—bam—bam . . . oh, baby! . . . and, oh, before I forget, I have a little antiquing I need to do over the next couple weeks . . .' Did you check out which underwear she packed for the trip? I wonder if she packed any of the sexy stuff, because normally you don't need a lot of lingerie to sort through furniture. Too bad you couldn't put a bug in her Wonderbra and track her movements."

"I don't think that's necessary. Or appropriate."

"If you think relationships are based on trust, you've got a lot to learn. Women spend so much time lying to themselves that lying to men comes easy."

"I'll try to remember that."

"Please do. Let me off the phone so I can call Caroline."

Though I kept my tone light, I was thrown by this conversation. What rattled me wasn't Darlene's distrust of Amanda in particular and women in general, which I dismissed as a bum rap, but the scorn and impatience in her voice, as if she were prosecuting a case any idiot could see. I heard that sneer before, but never directed at me. Later that night, while I was down in the basement retrieving laundry from the dryer, Darlene left a message on my machine.

"Spoke to Caroline. Everything's cool. She says she may want to stay a couple extra days, so that she doesn't feel as if she's making a long U-turn. Let her crash on your sofa after you get back, she'll stay out of your hair. She said to leave instructions stuck to the refrigerator listing all the cat's special needs, the vet's number, where trash should be dumped, etc. She'll be arriving Friday morning. I hope your grandmother pulls through. I know she was rough on you when you were a kid, but it's always hard to lose a relative. And forget what I said about Amanda—I'm sure she's behaving herself. Call me if you need anything."

I was relieved. Darlene's voice didn't have that nicky edge it had before. I told myself to remember that women are often funny about other women, even women they've never met. Darlene herself had said so more than once.

30

I PACKED THURSDAY NIGHT and set my alarm clock early so that I could have breakfast before I left. It was one of those life-is-good mornings, birds chirping, the streets creamy with sunlight. The one trouble spot was that Caroline hadn't shown. She was at least two hours overdue. I began to get agitated, leg-restless. Why should it be so hard to find a reliable catsitter? As I considered last-ditch alternatives, the phone rang. The first thing I heard was a Radio Shack crackle of static, like bad reception on a walkie-talkie.

"Johnny, it's me, Caroline. How are yew?"

Caroline had one of those Southern voices that reminded me of lemon meringue. Before I could reply, she said: "Try not to freak. I had a little car trouble."

"Where are you?"

"At a picnic area at the Walt Whitman Rest Stop on the Jersey turnpike. One of my tires blew, and a nice trucker is putting on the spare as we speak. I should be on the road shortly. Leave the keys with the super and let me handle the rest."

"I could catch a later train."

"Don't on my account. I'm only a couple of hours from Manhattan. Your kitty won't starve. My guy is waving to me, got to run, bye!"

I said my own good-bye to Slinky, who seemed grumpy now that I was leaving, though this time she didn't crawl into the travel bag and try to stow away, as she had in the past. I took a cab to Penn Station and grabbed a window seat on the Amtrak. The aisle seat was soon occupied by a woman with uncommonly shiny brunette hair who was bulging with leather bags. She was still unharnessing herself when the train pulled out of the station. As part of my matrimonial research, I flipped open the latest issue of *Wedding Bells*, landing on an article about bachelorette party dos and don'ts. Unable to contain herself, my seatmate said: "Excuse me, but I've never seen a man reading a bridal magazine before."

"I'm a recent convert."

"As it happens, I'm heading down for my sister's wedding in Annapolis. They're going to pick me up in Baltimore. She's my younger sister, so everyone's going to be waiting to see how I 'handle it.' Then they're off on a honeymoon cruise."

"My brother and his wife went to Disney World for their honeymoon and came back complaining about how long they had to stand in line. I'm Johnny, by the way."

"Miranda."

She looked like a Miranda, too, one of life's English majors. We continued chatting, and by the time the train pulled into Baltimore I knew enough about her life to produce a documentary. Wreathed in luggage, Miranda tidied her hair as she rose on the escalator, then flew into her sister's arms beneath the station's restored clock. I had intended to leave them to it, but Miranda waved me over to meet her sister, Janey, who was so lit up with happiness and expectation that commuters were glancing at her and cueing up their eyes, trying to place her. Her happiness was like a small flame of fame.

"Janey," I said, "Miranda's been raving about you the entire trip."

"Oh, stop."

"I'm afraid I have to rush—I have annoying relatives waiting. Best wishes on your wedding." I gave Janey's elbow a slight squeeze, a farewell squeeze with a hopeful note for the future in it, and gave Miranda a speed hug.

The reason I had to cut it short was that I saw my brother Donny slouching at the door, jiggling his car keys as if I were the only thing keeping him from the open road. He must have stood in the driveway like that waiting for his wife a thousand times. Donny is a middle child, with all that that entails.

"I saw you hugging that woman," he said.

"I saw you playing with your keys. Where'd you get that shirt, off a dead hunter?"

"At least I can afford a belt."

"This is the new look."

"The car's over here."

Outside the station, sunlight bounced off the sunroofs of cars as if they were Roman shields. In the parking lot, I spotted my nine-year-old nephew Mark dropping wrappers out the window. Donny said:

"Before we get in the car, I want to tell you something. Mom's talking about starting to hit the bottle again. She may have actually already started."

"What about Dad?"

"No, he's straight."

Unlike my father in his drinking days, my mother never touched hard liquor, but she could polish off a six-pack of beer without leaving the sofa. I nodded, indicating I'd say something to her about it. Even though there were no longer children in the house, we didn't need that starting up again. When we reached the car, I asked Donny to open the trunk so that I could load my carry-on bags inside rather than pile them on my lap. He pressed the release button as if it took his last ebb of energy. "Wait a sec," I said, after closing the trunk just hard enough to make the car bounce. Then I picked up the candy wrappers his son had dropped and disposed of them in the trash. "Everyone has to do his part," I said.

"Just get in the car," Donny said.

I slid into the scorching backseat, trying to find a place to plant my feet amid all the returnable cans.

"Give Mommy's lap a rest," Bev said, as my nephew climbed into the back seat with me. I secured his seat belt. "Hello, Johnny," Bev said, without turning her head.

"Whud you bring me?" Mark said.

"It'd better not be another flashlight," Bev said. "He about drove us crazy shining it in our faces every night. He said you told him to make sure Mommy and Daddy were asleep."

I chuckled at my own craftiness.

"No, it's not a flashlight," I said. "It's a pack of powdered doughnuts that I bought on the train, which makes them even more special."

"You can eat them when we get home," Donny told Mark.

"Why can't I eat them *now*?" Mark wailed.

"Because they're in my travel bag, locked in the trunk," I said.

Mark swung his head from side to side in an infinity-shaped Stevie Wonder loop, as if we were all playing with his mind.

We roared out of the parking lot. My sister-in-law gripped the dashboard, then checked the rearview mirror to make sure Mark hadn't shot backward into space. Once we hit traffic, Donny asked if I wanted to go straight to the hospital or stop by the motel.

"The hospital. How is she?"

"You'll see."

Donny was never big on description.

We made Route 40, heading north, passing the blackened ruins of a bar that had burned to the ground and now stood out like a cavity. Otherwise, Route 40 was its usual photocollage of motels, gas stations, go-go bars, and billboards touting local TV news teams who looked as if they had been thrown together at the last minute. Looping off the highway, we passed shopping malls that used to be horse farms, industrial storage facilities where grain silos used to be. Now there were only strips of green and scraggly trees functioning as borders. Hill upon hill had been shaved to clear space for instant communities called Avalon Acres and Cedar Forest, the signs at their entrances promising all the latest in amenities—sundecks, playgrounds, indoor whirlpools. The streets we passed had fake gaslight fixtures and ceramic lawn ornaments of cute animals. I tried not to cop a New York attitude. If I had stayed in Maryland and become a teacher, as my parents wanted, I would probably be living in a suburban bachelor condo with a sundeck and a hot tub. But when I was growing up, all those trees added a depth of field. They were full of places to hide, they had secrets. I had assumed they'd always be there.

The hospital, set on a mild incline, had a few trees posted around it for a nice picture effect. My nephew, who wanted to wait in the car and play with the radio, had to be dragged through the seeing-eye doors into the waiting room. Inside, it was hushed. Suburban hospitals don't have the searing drama of New York hospitals—there were no junkies twitching on stretchers, no women giving birth to the miracle of life in the lobby. Mark was the only one creating a spectacle. Now that we were indoors, my brother seemed sheepish in his oil-streaked work clothes.

"Stand up straight or I'll leave you behind in the ward with the other babies," Donny told his son.

"That's right, scare him," Bev said. "He won't be crawling into *your* bed with nightmares."

"Come on, Mark, let's get your uncle Johnny a soda. I'm parched." Mark followed me to a visitors' lounge. I handed him a bunch of quarters and hoisted him up so that he could insert them into the vending machine. After considerable thought, he punched in his selection. As we walked back, I said: "So Mommy and Daddy are sleeping in separate beds?"

"Thank *good*ness. They were making so much noise before, I couldn't get to sleep. Fight, fight, fight. And they get mad when I fight."

"I know, it's so unfair. So where's Daddy sleeping?"

"On the pull-out sofa. He says it's lumpy in the middle and hurts his back. I'm getting a walkie-talkie set for my birthday so I can talk to him from my room without having to yell downstairs."

I tousled his hair and we rejoined Donny and Bev in the reception area. They were sitting in plastic bucket seats with their knees stuck out hard. When Donny married Bev, he was about twice her weight, but over the years she had reached parity. They now looked like a matched set, and none too happy about it. My brother stood when a nurse appeared, and replaced his blank frustration with a troubled look, sliding his hands down his work pants. I left Mark with Bev, who said, "It's you boys she wants to see."

We followed the nurse down the hall, listening to the sounds of small moans, mild consultations, and paging beepers. The nurse paused at a door. The first pair of feet I saw belonged not to my grandmother but to her older roommate, who looked like something left up in the attic. On the other side of the dividing curtain, my grandmother's bed was empty. In the crisp sheets was a slight indent her body had left behind. Sitting in a chair by the window was my father, who was reading a newspaper and fidgeting with the sports section as if trying to get it into focus. He must have left his glasses at home.

"Hey, bud," he said. He rose and shook my hand hard, squeezing some life into me. I was struck, and not for the first time, by the realization that over the years my parents had become more real to me over the phone than in person. Their disembodied voices superseded any picture of them I carried in my mind. Each time I returned to

Maryland, there was an awkward moment of reentry, a mental stutter-step on my part, as we got reacquainted on the physical plane. Sometimes the stutter-step was more severe, when they seemed to have aged suddenly after years of staying on the same visible plateau.

My brother slumped in a chair in front of the bed and leaned his head against the wall, directly under the TV mounted overhead. After a loud flush, the bathroom door opened and my grandmother tottered out, supported by my mother, who was so taken aback to see me that she nearly let my grandmother drop. Two-thirds of the woman she was last time I saw her, my grandmother shuffled forward, concentrating on pushing her slippers across the floor. It took both my parents to fold her back into bed.

"They took her off the tubes yesterday," my mother said.

"Is that good or bad?"

Bad, said my mother's expression. Finally recognizing me, my grandmother seized my hand, and patted it. Her veins looked bigger than her bones. Her skin felt crackly. She and I hadn't gotten along since my college years—she had always been so negative about me pursuing acting, telling me with The Voice Of Experience before I left for New York, "You'll be back," as if my failure had already been posted on the scoreboard—but seeing her in this condition erased all that. "You're wearing your grandfather's watch," she said.

"I put a new watchband on it."

"He bought that watch with his first horse winnings. He taught you to play pinball when you were Marky's age. Where is Marky?"

"I remember. He put a stack of nickels on the pinball machine and stood me on a beer crate. Mark's down in reception with his mother. We can fetch them later."

"I need to talk to John alone," my grandmother said.

"Do you want us to wait outside?" my mother said.

"No. Just go."

"Great. I drive all the way over here . . ." Donny said.

A nurse appeared at the curtain, balancing a water pitcher on a tray. "My, aren't we popular?" she said, as they were all getting ready to leave. She set the tray on the night stand and rattled the paper cup full of pills. My mother and father took turns trying to hug my grandmother without hurting her, and Donny hauled himself up as if to say, Well, hell, I might as well go out and mow the lawn.

It took a lot of gulping before my grandmother was able to swallow her pills. Before leaving, the nurse pressed her thumb to a wall unit, lowering the headrest to a comfortable angle. I started to say something suitable for the situation, but my grandmother cut me off. "Let me talk, before these pills put me out. I need to talk to you about my will. Don't wave me off. Telling me I'm going to be all right isn't going to change anything. I wish you'd sit down. It makes me nervous, your standing up."

"Okay."

I pulled a chair close to the bed. My grandmother said:

"Your mother and father don't know what's in my will because I kept it from them for a reason. I can't trust them to manage the estate. They may not drink anymore, but they still piddle everything away. They are going to get the house—your father and Mick can fix it up. But the money your grandfather left me, I'm leaving to you. I'm entrusting you to invest at least half of it in college funds for your nephews and niece. I don't want their parents getting their hands on the money and spending it on any goddamn boats or giant TVs." Donny had once written a bad check to buy a motorboat that was later repossessed at the marina. It was one for the annals.

"How much money are we talking about?"

"We're talking a good amount. Your grandfather established a stock portfolio that he let sit, and it has been reinvesting dividends for over forty years. We're talking about three quarters of a million, though there'll be taxes to pay, of course. John, you have to understand, your grandfather didn't just play the horses, he ran numbers out of the barbershop. By the time you were growing up, he was only betting on the side. His big money was made before and socked away. The point is, everyone's going to be upset when the holdings revert to you. They're going to want you to divvy up the money then and there. They've always resented the fact that you were your grandfather's favorite."

Not that I deserved to be. I can remember ignoring him once when I was with friends of mine walking down the street after football practice. I was a lineman. It was after six, he had just closed up the barber shop. I was afraid they'd laugh at his red vest, his pinkie ring, and talcum smell. I was a teenager then, with all the fierce, stupid pride that throbs through those years. So I pretended not to see him even though I knew he saw me. I just kept walking and yapping away with my friends. I can't even recall which friends. I know he was hurt. He never mentioned it, but I knew. Over the years I kept the incident to myself. It was one of those things that you can never undo, no one teaches you how. He died when I was in college, of heart failure hastened by his excess weight. He was dead by the time I reached the hospital.

The sun emerged from a barrage of clouds. I lowered the blinds to spare my grandmother's eyes. The woman in the next bed was sobbing with her head turned to the side.

"That woman has had a sad life," my grandmother said.

"Do you ever get scared?" I asked. "I heard you were trying to—"

"They had me on medication that had me doing all kinds of crazy things. Right now I'm in too much discomfort to be scared. I just want to stop aching all over. I can't blow my nose without giving myself a seizure. Before you go, could you ask the nurse to change the water in my denture glass?"

"I'll do it. Do you need anything else?"

"No, that's it. How's your cat? Don't you have a cat?"

"She's great, though she's been looking a little wan lately."

"You've had her a long time."

I nodded. She made a weary sigh. It was time to go. I left a clean tissue in her hand and refilled her water pitcher. A black man about my age entered the room as I was leaving, saying to the woman in the other bed, "Now, now, now, what's all this crying?"

31

I FOUND MY WAY BACK to the reception area, following a man in a wheelchair being pushed to the departure desk. My mother was the only one waiting. She was trying to peel open a pack of sugarless gum with her bitten nails. Ever since she had given up drinking, she chewed three or four packs a day. "Your father is down the hall talking to the doctor who did his gallbladder operation last year," she said.

"Reminiscing, eh?"

"So how did you find your grandmother?"

"Better than I expected. Frail, but hanging in there."

"Hanging on out of pure spite."

"That's not a very nice thing to say, especially since you and Dad will be getting the house."

"I don't want that old pile of toothpicks. Your father and I intend to sell the property once we get rid of the termites in the basement."

"I just did a commercial for an exterminating company. Maybe they have a local outlet."

"We've already picked out a condo at Raven Court we want to buy once we get the proceeds. It's an adult community with tennis courts and its own church. Your father and I like new things, and everything there would be right out of the box. Son, while your father's down the hall gabbing away I wanted to ask you something."

"Shoot."

"You would tell me if anything was wrong, wouldn't you?"

"Uh, no."

"That's what I thought. You've always been like that. I'll never forget the time you were six years old and you were hit in the head with a rock and you hid under a neighbor's porch until dark rather than come home. We had the whole neighborhood looking for you. If your father hadn't noticed that cat staring under the porch, you might have been there until morning."

I can't remember who threw the rock, but I remember crouching in the dirt, looking out through the honeycomb trellis, hoping I wouldn't bleed too much and die. I thought I would be punished for getting into a fight. A neighborhood cat sat on the lawn, staring back at the trellis, as if watching over me. By the time I came out from under the porch, the blood on my forehead had dried. My mother wiped my face that night with a warm cloth.

"What makes you think I'm hiding anything?" I said.

"It's just that you've lost weight since we saw you last, and you have dark circles under your eyes. You seem somewhat down. Your father and I can accept whatever lifestyle you've chosen. You're still a young man, and I would hate it if . . ."

"Mother, I barely have a life, much less a 'lifestyle.' I'm looking beat because I never sleep well before a trip and I was worried this morning when my catsitter didn't show. And while we're on the subject of health, what's this I hear about you backsliding?"

"Backsliding how?"

"You know how. I'm talking about going off your Oprah diet."

"You've been talking to Donny. He ought to keep his trap shut. He knows the only beer I drink is nonalcoholic. I'm well aware of what alcohol would do to my liver. Sometimes I talk about going back to the bottle, but it's only to stir the pot. You get to be my age, that's about the only fun left."

"Stir the pot some other way and stay off the booze, okay? I realize you're under a lot of strain, but still. Between you and Grandmom, I can't afford two caskets."

"I prefer to be cremated, anyway. I've given it a lot of thought."

"Well, tough. You're going in a box."

"Did you notice how much weight Bev has packed on? She's become a snack machine."

"Well, Donny's no ballerina. Where is he, anyway? I thought he was driving me to the motel."

"No, he decided to go shopping. Dad and I will drop you off at the motel, then Donny will pick you up later, after he drops Mark off at his cousin's house. He's been driving Bev's car since his was repossessed."

"Transportation in Maryland is always so complicated. So where's dad?"

We finally had to go look for him. He was discussing catfish with the doctor who had removed his gallbladder, across the bed of a patient who was also joining in the conversation. They were so engrossed, I hated to break up their little party.

When we arrived at my brother Mick's house, the lawn sprinkler was twirling a weak lariat of water over the patchy lawn. In the middle of the yard trooped a happy family of ceramic ducks, one of them missing a head and part of a tail. There were two cars in the driveway and one in the garage, which left room for ours at the broken curb. In a last-minute change of plans, my father had picked me up at the motel. After he turned off the motor, he said: "The thing I don't like about this Raven Court is that they don't allow pets."

"You don't have any."

"Not now, but I've been thinking about getting a French bulldog. Your uncle Milt had one, remember? I always got a kick out of that dog. That's the next thing I'm going to spring on your mother."

We looked toward the house. My father's hands gripped the steering wheel, as if not wanting to let go. He glanced up at the rearview mirror, then faced ahead. "So how's it going in New York? They still treating you all right?"

My father asked me this every time I was home, and after all these years I still didn't know who he meant by "they." But instead of giving some smart response, I said, "Things have been going okay."

"That's good. I hope Mick's wife didn't make meat loaf. I can't stand her meat loaf. She doesn't season it enough and it comes out bland."

"Well, let's be brave . . ."

As we pushed open the front door, a bowling ball came thumping down the stairs, which were booby-trapped with toys. Water was running in the upstairs bathroom, possibly overflowing. The TV was blaring. It was like a council estate in a BBC crime drama, every room piled with twice as much furniture as necessary. In the kitchen my mother, Bev, and Mick's wife, May, took turns opening the oven and poking what was in there. As my father suspected, it was meat loaf, though in my experience meat loaf didn't require that much poking. Leaning against the kitchen sink and being absolutely no help whatsoever was Donny, who had changed pants. Planted at the table was my brother Mick, the next oldest to me, who had grown a mountain-man beard since I last saw him, a real twig-collector.

"Phone the *Sun*. I can't believe Number One honors us with his presence." Mick shielded his eyes with his big hands as if flash bulbs were going off at a Hollywood premiere. "By the way, down here we wear belts to hold up our pants."

"It's the new look."

Mick was flanked by his sons Kit and Kyle, who were leaning over the kitchen table, rummaging through a shoebox.

"Oh no," I said, "not the shoebox."

It was where all the old family photos were kept that didn't qualify for pasting in a scrapbook or displaying in Lucite cubes in the living room.

"Say hello to your uncle Johnny, boys. Boys, would you like to see what Johnny and your father looked like when we were around your age?"

They shifted their shoulders and made noncommittal noises.

"Well, tough." Mick fished out a black-and-white photo with scalloped edges, taken the summer I was six, the same summer I hid under the neighbor's porch, but earlier in the season. It showed me and my brother, both perfectly blond, on tricycles. Seated between us on another trike was a girl our age who was even blonder. We were all laughing at the camera.

"Who was that girl?" I asked.

"Susan Cominsky," said my brother, the official captain's log of the family. "She transferred to another school after first grade and we both cried for about two days. Her father was a pharmacist, which we thought was so cool."

"Where's Jim?" I asked.

"He's working late at the country club," my mother said. "He's running the buffet for a going-away party. He might be by later."

The adults sat down at the dining room table, the assorted nephews taking their meals on TV trays in the living room. It struck me as we sat how overscaled we all looked hunkered around the table. Just as Donny leaned forward with an ice-cream scoop to make a major land-grab on the mashed potatoes, my mother cleared her throat. Everyone put down their utensils.

"Sons, your father and I seldom have all you boys together under the same roof, even on holidays. Since we started to attend mass again, we like to begin every meal with a blessing. Would any of you boys like to lead?"

It took about two seconds for me to look at Mick, Mick to look at me, both of us to look at Donny, Donny to look back at me, and me to look blank. We were passing each other looks faster than the Harlem Globetrotters. I said: "Maybe Dad should do it. After all, he is the head of the family, chortle, chortle."

"That's enough of that. Ted . . ."

"Heavenly Father," my father began . . .

If you eliminated the nephews' screaming and muffled Donny and Bev's bickering, this informal family get-together was on the tranquil side. Mom asked me if I planned to be in any more commercials. Donny discussed his truck. Mick stroked his beard. This dinner had none of the danger and drama of the old days when Dad would slam the refrig-erator door when he was out of beer and peel out of the driveway, with Donny left behind bawling and me and Mick wondering if we should call Mom at the American Legion and warn her Dad was on a tear. In my parents' absence, I often had to heat something up or send the youngest brother out to McDonald's. The fights at night, when they came rolling in, were the worst. It wasn't so bad if they rolled in together, but if one was waiting home for the other to return, it was like a bomb went off when the other one walked through the door. To this day, I'm hypersensitive to noise, particularly of the yelling variety.

There were some funny moments, though. I remember being home during college vacation once when Mom for some reason decided to pound on Mick's car with a ball-peen hammer. We both had to carry her twisting and writhing from the front lawn. It was summer, so there were neighbors out in their striped beach chairs to witness this natu-ralistic slice of life. We finally barricaded Mom inside and stationed ourselves at the front and back doors to cut off her escape routes. Once she'd conked out, Mick turned to me and asked in a professional announcer's voice: "So, Johnny, how come you never bring any of your school chums by to meet the folks?"

During dinner I noticed how no one made eye contact except my mother. Everyone else wore an invisible helmet. After dessert, my father solemnly rose from the table as if every bone was predicting rain and said, "Mick will drive you back to the motel."

"I thought I was supposed to drive him back," Donny said.

Mick put a heavy hand on Donny's shoulder. "No, Don, your place is here with your wife."

"Can we go?" Kit or Kyle called from the living room.

"No, you stay here and watch that scary video Daddy brought upstairs. Johnny and I need to have an adult talk. That's why your uncle Donny isn't going, either."

Seeing an opening to practice husband-material skills, I said: "I shouldn't leave just yet. Bev, May, let me help you with the clean-up. It's the least I can do. Would you like me to wash or dry?"

Stunned by my offer, Bev stood motionless at the kitchen sink.

"All you have to do is load the dishes into the damned washer," Donny said. "It has an automatic dryer."

"Well, Mr. Wizard, if you'll move your tree-trunk legs out of the way, we'll do just that. And I insist on staying and helping put the dishes away."

As we passed the ceramic ducks, a car making a turn honked at Mick, who waved an acknowledgment.

"Who's that?" I said.

"I don't know. Some idiot."

Mick opened the driver's door of his faded blue 1992 Tekla and unlatched the passenger door. I tried not to crush any of the cassette tapes littered in the leg area of the front seat. Mick sashed his safety belt, which reminded me of the belts the school's safety patrol used to wear, complete with Dragnetlike badges.

"Don't worry, you and I don't need to have a talk," Mick said. "I just wanted to get out of the house before a migraine kicked in. They're probably having a bicker-fest right now, Bev saying, 'Your brother helped with the dishes, why can't you?' and Donny saying, 'I'd help, too, if we had a dishwasher,' and Bev saying, 'We'd have a dishwasher if you hadn't bought that awful entertainment center.' And the terrible thing is, they're thinking about having another."

"Another child?"

"No, another raccoon. Jeez, don't they teach you anything in New York?"

"I hear Donny and Bev are now in separate beds, so they're going to have to make an appointment to procreate, if you can imagine anything that sordid."

"After you've been married a few years, you can imagine anything. What they'll probably do is get smashed one night and tumble into the sack accidentally on purpose, the way most people down here do. For a while, Donny was actually sleeping in the van. I know for a fact he still has a roll-up mattress in there. I thought about going over there one night and scaring the piss out of him, you know, putting on a ski mask and then popping up at the window. But I waited too long. That's my problem, I don't seize opportunities when they're ripe. Now he's gone and created his own little bachelor pad in the rec room. He didn't show it to you?"

"No, but I heard about Jim's."

"He's trying to outdo Jim's. Donny moved the sports memorabilia in there, all our old Baltimore Colts pennants and stuff. He has his own minifridge, stocked with sodas and the little bottles of liquor you get on airplanes. It's as if he thinks this would be a neat place to impress junior-college chicks. He just sits down there by himself in his own little hideaway. It's like he's married and single both at the same time."

We drove past the local library, where I used to sit with a periodical and think about Nancy Lockheart, who was in my English class. I used to guess which day of the week she would wear her yellow sweater. She would cup her hands over her mouth when she laughed, something no one does anymore, I've noticed. Even the name "Nancy" seems to have fallen out of favor. As we passed a defunct Dairy Queen, I said: "Isn't this our turn?"

"I thought we'd take the scenic route."

We drove past our old high school, past the goal posts and bleachers. There was one car parked in the driveway in front of the school. "I wonder if it's the same night janitor," Mick said. "I always felt sorry for that guy. There's Dale's old house."

Dale was my best friend before high school. Summers we would camp out at his place and play 45s and dance on the tiles in our socks. His sister was a tomboy who burned Dale in his sleep with lit cigarettes and liked to get me in a headlock. Good dancer, though. Their mother had run off with a married man, leaving them with their father. Unlike ours, their father wasn't just a yeller but a hitter, too, so everyone stayed out of his way when he gave off liquor fumes. Fortunately, he was often out of town for weeks at a time (he was a plumbing-supply salesman who, we suspected, had another family tucked somewhere up the highway). While he was gone, we would drag the sleeping bags out of the sliding closet and spend the night in the backyard, checking out constellations. The town wasn't so developed then. Cars, shopping malls, and residential spreads didn't drain away as much of the dark.

"I need to make a pit stop," I said, as the cheap extravagance of a minimart beckoned at the intersection. Mick flipped on his turn signal. Inside, the night manager and a customer were comparing near-misses in the state lottery. Along with my own stuff, I bought Mick a small bucket of soda with crushed ice. Instead of leaving with our goodies, Mick kicked back and began to drink his soda in the car. He seemed in no hurry to get home.

"They put enough syrup in for a change. Want a sip?"

"No, but you might want to use a bigger straw."

"I am straining a bit here. I think a piece of ice may have blocked the hole." He withdrew the straw and tapped it against the top of the plastic lid. "Much better. So how are you doing?"

"Okay. Things are on a slight upswing. I got dumped by this one woman and now I'm dating someone else. That's about all there is to tell."

"Well, whatever happened has made you easier to take. When you used to come down, you were so full of yourself it was repulsive. 'Well, I'm waiting for a callback on . . .' We didn't even know what a callback was, but were afraid to ask because we knew you'd give us one of your sniffling looks. You're acting like a normal person this time, though helping with the dishes was a bit much. So did Gran'ma discuss the will? Are my boys going to be able to afford college, any college? Because the second they turn eighteen, I'm hitting the EJECT button, whether they have any place to land or not. The wife and I have earned our peace."

"They'll be taken care of."

"What about the house?"

"Mom and Dad are getting the house."

"I was thinking of maybe buying the house from Mom and Dad and getting myself a good deal, since they don't want it. It's bigger than the one we have, and it holds a lot of memories."

"You like memories, don't you?"

"I've never been able to blank everything out, like you. Besides, I have serious plans for that place. I want to convert the attic into a study, and set up a computer system there, one that has everything, the works. Pick up live feeds from NASA, stuff like that. The garage out back will have to go, and I was thinking about putting in a pool. Don't worry, I won't tell Mother Dear about the will. You know how she is. I'll tell her just enough to make her think I grilled you."

"How are your ulcers?"

"On and off. May's also been having stomach upsets. There's a lot of anxiety floating around. It all relates to money. Didn't you think Donny's pants were too much?"

"They're not even pants."

"I know, they're like a sack with legs sewn on. He says they enable his stomach to breathe."

My room at the Rest Stoppe was on the second tier, overlooking the swimming pool. A lone life-preserver shaped like a sea horse floated motionless at the shallow end. Beneath the floodlights of the hill rising to the intersection I could see rabbits racing around playing tag in the sparse grass. They were fuzzy-white in the light, linty. I filled the ice bucket and switched on the TV with the remote that was bolted to the side table, muting the sound. Half-watching a beach volleyball game between two teams of bikinied contestants, I phoned Darlene and got her machine. Then I phoned my own number, and got my machine, which had a new message:

"Hi, this is Caroline Dupree. I'll be catsitting for Mr. Downs while he's away on an important trip. If you'd like to leave a message for either of us, please do so after the beep. If this is Carl, I'll be at the Chocolate Bar until ten. And if this is Mr. Downs, don't worry, the cat's fine. Your agent Marjorie called, said it was urgent."

I wondered what could be so urgent. Marjorie tended to be one of those raspy Dorothy Parker types who spoke as if she had seen the rise and fall of empires from the eagle's nest of her Broadway office. She was one of those people impossible to imagine ever having been young. Even good news she delivered with a sardonic twist, as if it would all end in folly. Sitting in the room's one reading chair, I listened to ice settle in the bucket in minute glacial shifts. Headlights swept the blinds as a big truck or trailer swung into the parking lot. I thought about what Mrs. Cole had told me about the men's group that met at St. Teresa and the men on the sidewalk after my date with Amanda, wondering if the two were one and the same. I doodled some notes on the motel stationery, diagramming relationships within a squad of such men, trying to imagine what would make them turn on the women they knew, what would incite them. I did cartoon sketches on a separate pad, based on the body language of the men on the sidewalk. The strange thing was that the faces I found myself mentally pasting over those shadowy bulks belonged to my brothers, Gleason, and me. Was my imagination telling me we harbored that kind of anger, or was this just a way of gluing familiar faces on unknown forces? I fiddled with this Wild Bunch, as I now thought of them, while someone ran gurgling bathwater in the next room.

32

"WHAT'S THAT RACKET? I CAN BARELY HEAR YOU."

"It's a lawnmower."

"A *lawnmower*? Where are you, anyway?"

"I'm in Maryland, visiting the old plantation. You left a message?"

My agent, Marjorie, said: "I have good news for a change. A small part has opened up on a soap, and it's pretty much yours unless you're planning to stay down in Merry-land."

"Are we talking a recurring—?"

"No, it's only for five shooting days. You'd be playing a bartender on *The Last Ray of Hope*. They cast another actor for the part and had to can him when he insisted his character mix fruit spritzers instead of fake booze. Claims he didn't realize until he saw the script that he'd actually be serving *drinks* to characters who'd proceed to get *drunk*. He also had other suggestions to broaden the scope of the role."

"I'm sure they loved hearing those."

"He seemed to think he was part of a creative collaboration and was quite taken aback when they sent his ass flying. The casting director remembered you from *Rough Waves*, and I assured her you had no scruples about serving drinks on camera, that in fact you had done beer ads."

"When am I supposed to start?"

"Wednesday."

This being Monday, I said, "That's awfully short notice." From my motel window I could see the riding lawnmower dip down the hill.

"That's why they'll be especially grateful," Marjorie said. "Don't worry, the first day you won't have any lines. They just want to establish you in the background, pouring drinks and such. The other days you have lines. In fact, you not only get to speak, you have three scenes with Phil Green and one with what's-her-puss playing his wife. So can I call them back and tell them it's a go?"

"Definitely." Philip Green was an actual actor, with theatrical credits stretching back to the days when Broadway meant something.

"You haven't grown a beard or mustache lately, have you?" Marjorie said.

"No, why?"

"Because one of the leading men has it in his contract that he's the only one on the show allowed to have facial hair. I told them that if you had a mustache, you'd be more than happy to lose it. Which reminds me, you need to get some new headshots. The ones I have look historic."

"I'll take care of it when I get back. Thanks, Marjorie."

"Only doing my job, doll. Phil Green can be testy, so be sure to humble yourself."

"What about the one playing his wife?"

"Oh, don't worry about her. She won't even know you exist."

33

As I ENTERED THE APARTMENT, something tinkled overhead. In my absence chimes had been hung from the ceiling to catch the top of the door. When the door closed they tinkled again, like geishas giggling behind a paper screen. Slinky sat on her haunches in the bedroom, underwhelmed to see me, to judge by her modest yawn. Then she trotted toward me, and I petted her head. In the bedroom a red flag was draped over the bookcase. The punched-in pillows indicated the bed had been slept in, but there was also a sleeping bag crumpled across the living-room sofa.

"Anybody home?" I called.

"In here." The voice came from the kitchen.

Standing at the sink, filling the ice-cube tray, was a woman in a Dutch boy's haircut whom I semirecognized from a photo I had seen pinned to a bulletin board at her house in Athens, Georgia. Caroline had packed on a few since then. She was wearing a terry-cloth bathrobe loosely sashed around her waist and flip-flops suitable for the beach. Since it was two o'clock in the afternoon, it was fair to say Caroline began her days on the lateish side. She removed a set of Walkman earphones from her head and let them hang around her neck as we exchanged "hey's."

"So how was your trip?"

"Fine, but I'm glad to be back. There's only so much family togetherness one can take until the walls begin to close in."

"I bet they were glad to see you, though. I like your tiles."

"I put them in myself."

"I know, Darlene told me."

Caroline slid the ice-cube tray gingerly into the freezer, between two bottles of vodka. She dried her palms on a towel and fixed herself an ice tea with the couple of cubes she had salvaged. She turned and formally introduced herself. Her face was a place setting for the clearest pair of blue eyes I had ever seen. They belonged to a child, the clear forehead, too, a forehead that reminded me of Nicole's, without the computer hum. Caroline said: "I hope you don't mind what we did in the bedroom. Are you up on feng shui? It stresses the use of power colors, so we hung a red banner over the bookcase and painted the bedroom door. Red conducts energy and the apartment seemed energy-depleted, based on how poorly your plants were doing. We probably should have checked with you first, but Darlene said it was okay."

Caroline set her ice tea on a coaster and rolled the sleeping bag into an informal ball to clear a spot on the sofa. As she curled her feet beneath her, Slinky leapt to her side and tried to duck her head into the bathrobe pocket. "I've been giving her vitamin E for her coat. It was looking a little nubby."

"I couldn't help noticing someone slept in the bed last night while somebody else took the sofa."

"I let Kris take the bed. Did Darlene tell you Kris was making the drive with me?"

"No."

"You'll like her. She's very sweet. We're driving up to Cambridge to see her mother and she wanted to do some job interviews while we're here in New York. She's had it with Athens. Darlene said you wouldn't mind."

Darlene seemed to have green-lighted a lot of projects while I was away.

"I'm sure she's delightful. How long are you two planning to stay?"

"You can boot us out any time—we can both find other places to crash. It's just that it's so *nice* here, especially with the afternoon light." Caroline took a sip of ice tea. "Your mail, by the way, is on the desk."

The mail had been sorted into subscription magazines, bills, junk mail, and personal letters (of which there was a grand total of one). All of the pencils in my old college mug had been sharpened, and the desktop smelled lemony.

Caroline said: "As for your phone messages—you had a call from a guy named Gleason who said, and I quote, 'You dog,' and one from Amanda, whom Darlene gave me the lowdown on. She sounded quite snippy until I explained I was merely your catsitter and that you hadn't returned yet. That seemed to placate her. She left a New Orleans number."

The downstairs buzzer buzzed.

"I'll get that," I said, sheer formality on my part, since Caroline showed no signs of budging. Minutes later, the chimes tinkled again. Standing in the doorway was a young woman with car-paint red hair cut in the style of a Japanese comic-book heroine. Her wardrobe was a thrift-shop hodge-podge—a baseball jersey unbuttoned to the middle, jeans with a hole in the right knee big enough to fit your hand, striped socks, hightop sneakers with orange soles—yet somehow it all cohered. I had the impression that poured through her ragtag outfit was skin of unparalleled smoothness. Ah, youth. Slinky waited at her feet, then wove between her legs.

"Hi, I'm Kris! You must be Johnny!"

I was so used to jadedness that her enthusiasm threw me.

"I guess I must be," I said. "What's in the bag?"

"Guess! Candles. We used up the last one you had. These thick ones are slow burners. We could hold a seance! Caroline and I are going to a movie this afternoon, so we'll be out of your hair in case you need to unwind, unless of course you'd like to come with us."

"Which movie?"

"We haven't decided yet. Caroline, did you study the papers?"

"Darling, I'm just now having my first iced tea of the day. Pick anything. I'm not particular. Johnny, do you have any suggestions?"

"Just don't go see that one about the psycho professor and the coed. It's pretty gruesome."

"I love gruesome movies!"

"Well, even so, I'd hesitate to recommend it."

"Don't worry," Caroline said to Kris, "we'll find something to keep you diverted."

The scented candles lasted the first couple of days of Caroline and Kris's stay. Caroline bought an inflatable cushion and spread the sleeping bag over it on the living-room floor. She and Kris alternated between it and the sofa. I offered to take the sofa and let one or both of them have the bed, but Caroline was firm on this score: "No," she said, "the master of the house gets to sleep in his own bed."

Master of the house was a new concept for me.

With Caroline and Kris on the premises, my days acquired an orderly routine. Two cold apples and a glass of orange juice for breakfast; yoga stretches on the padded mat in the bedroom, then a quick go-over of my script pages, followed by a subway ride up to Lincoln Center, within walking distance of the studio for *The Last Ray of Hope.* I would get into wardrobe, do my scene, hang around to watch a few other scenes being taped, then take the next day's script home to study. I liked having women waiting for me at the end of the day. It was like having two wives, or a pair of devoted daughters. It got so I knew which one was home from hearing their footsteps in the hallway as they followed Slinky to the door. They usually went out for the evening, toting their pocketbooks like gun holsters. After they returned from whatever bar or club they had hit, they'd light the candles and smoke pot and play music on the radio real low. If the hour wasn't too late, I'd join them in the living room in my robe, sitting in the living-room's official chair with a smidgen of scotch, listening to them recount their exploits as Slinky bagged it on the arm of the sofa, her eyelids at half-mast, like some beatnik cat.

Before they began their revels one night, Kris put on a little fashion show for us, modeling a couple of different job-interview outfits, trying to find a skirt length that showed enough leg to get her noticed but not enough to send the wrong message. Kris looked different in business attire, her postmodern hair suitable for an Internet startup and her eyes trained on some attainable goal. She would pivot on her high heels in front of us, so that we could see how her jacket hung from different angles. Then she would shed the jacket, to show us how the outfit looked without it.

"The pimping I do for you . . ." Darlene said.

"Don't think I don't appreciate it. But, of course, it's all strictly platonic."

"Yeah, I know: She played and I drank tonic. You've told me that old Moms Mabley joke a million times. Is Amanda wise to this setup?"

"No, she's still in New Orleans. I'm not sure when she's returning. I talked to her the other night and she said something about tracking down an antebellum loom at an estate sale."

"They sure got a lot of old shit in Louisiana. But are you sure antiquing is all she's doing? Why don't you have flowers sent to her hotel? That way, if she's fooling around, you can at least make her feel guilty. So where are the girls tonight?"

"They're going to a lesbian bar to see how they compare to the ones down South."

"Caroline's been known to be into other women when she's drinking, but Kris is strictly boy-girl. So what are you going to do?"

"Stay home. I have lines to learn."

"Well, don't putter around too much while Amanda's out of town. Take the girls to a comedy club or something. See how other guys try to pick them up and learn from their amateur mistakes. I'm worried that all this Catholic stuff you've been doing is going to turn into a crutch. Besides, Caroline told me Kris has taken a liking to you."

"Really?"

"She has a thing for actors. She'd be a good one to lay the All-Over on."

"I've begun to think of her almost as a kid sister."

"The layers of your insincerity . . ."

"She's very cute, but I wouldn't want to take advantage."

"If she gets a good job in New York, she might have a future you could be part of. She acts spacy but she's got brains. Her mother's a Harvard professor. About the time she hits her late twenties, she'll really kick into gear. You've got to take the long view, Johnny, and not get bogged down with the first woman who'll have you."

"How's Clete?"

"You don't care how Clete is."

"That's true. I was doing what's known as Changing the Subject."

Around midnight, I took a plain bath, holding my elbows straight to keep the script pages from getting soaked. I took two capsules of Valerian, an herbal sleep aid, left a night-light on in the hall, and went to bed. I lay in the dark awhile, visualizing the scene I had to do the next day until my eyelids began to close. When I rolled on my back some time later, I was dimly aware of another presence in the room. At first I thought it was an intruder, or an intruder-dream, which I have every so often. Valerian deepens the R.E.M. state for me, giving dreams a depth and duration they normally don't have, pulling me deeper under. I lifted my sunken head and saw Slinky sitting on the corner of the bed, ears perked. This wasn't a dream. There was a shadow next to the window.

"Johnny? . . . I can't sleep."

It was Kris, wearing some kind of T-shirt or tanktop.

"What's wrong?"

"It's Caroline. She's snoring up a storm."

"Did you try turning her on her stomach?"

"She is on her stomach. Can I camp here just for tonight?"

"Sure. No problem." I couldn't hear anything myself, but snorers sometimes lull you into a false sense of security before launching into a full-fledged aria.

The shadow departed. I heard the sleeping bag being gathered up in the living room and quiet whispering. Kris's bare feet slapped across the floor. As she spread her sleeping bag at the foot of the bed, I made a mental note not to step on her in the morning. Slinky remained on her haunches until the novelty wore off, then returned to the fetal position.

"How was the lesbian bar?" I whispered.

"We looked in the window, but didn't go in. It was a rougher-looking crowd than we expected. Too many leather vests. We wanted to go to one of those places where they're all wearing business suits."

"There's one Wall Street bar where a lot of them go. It's not a great place to get cabs from late at night, though."

"So then we went to CBGB's, but Patti Smith was having a poetry reading, and it was too crowded to get in. While we were hanging around we heard about a neat bar on Avenue C. Maybe we could all go tomorrow night, if you're not too beat. It's called The Coffin. Have you ever been there? The bar is laid out like an altar, and supposedly they have actual coffins you can set your drinks on in the lounge area. I'm not into Goth, but it might be fun. Caroline said Avenue C will probably be spookier than the bar itself."

"A lot of Avenue C has gotten gentrified, like every other neighborhood in New York. Anyway, I'd be there to protect you."

"You wouldn't run away and leave us there?"

"You have my solemn oath."

"Well, good night."

"You, too."

I couldn't go back to sleep. I wasn't tormented by thought or any-thing. I just lay there, plopped. I heard Kris open the flap of her sleep-ing bag and raise herself with a sigh to a seated position. I could see the back of her head and the stem of her neck. She seemed almost crea-turely in the dark. I closed my eyes and heard her sleeping bag rustle. The next morning, I didn't need to worry about stepping on Kris. She was already up and padding around barefoot.

"Downs, it's Gleason. Where you been?"

"I did a commercial shoot in New Jersey, then had to go to Maryland to see my grandmother who's not doing well. My catsitter told me you called."

"Then why didn't you call me back, suckwad?"

"I've been working on a soap. I'm playing a bartender on *The Last Ray of Hope.*"

"What great casting—because you already know how to mix drinks!"

"You're being even more obnoxious than usual. What's up?"

"Kate and I were wondering if you'd like to bowl with us tonight."

"Kate who, that bartender?"

"Exactly. I managed to work my voodoo on her, and we've started going out."

"What happened to Gwen?"

"Gwen and I are a thing of the past, as of yesterday afternoon. It's for the best."

"I'm sure it is where she's concerned. I'm afraid I can't bowl tonight, though, I have to hit the script."

I wasn't about to tell Gleason I had two women staying with me and that we had our own plans for the night. He would want us all to get together, and the last thing I needed was for him to meet Amanda someday and make sly insinuations about my "catsitters," playing up the plural. I could just hear him: "I couldn't quite get why Johnny felt he needed two catsitters for one cat." Or, "Johnny's the only one I know who has his catsitters work as a tag-team." So I asked for a raincheck and told him to say hello to Kate.

That night, Caroline, Kris, and I had one drink at The Coffin, which turned out to be an ordinary dive, and took a cab across town to The Blue Parrot, where we played darts with some Danish backpackers. Bewitched by her red sundress, one of the Danes kept buying Caroline beers. Kris was wearing a bare-midriff outfit that excited everyone else when she wiggled at the white line before taking her shot. She didn't bother asking if she could sleep in my room once we got home. She promptly unrolled the sleeping bag flat on the floor, doing yoga stretches from a seated position. After she lay down we chatted like overnight campers in a tent, occasionally pausing to monitor the noise from the living room. Kris hadn't been kidding. Caroline snored. Her loudest numbers sometimes snapped off in mid-ascent, creating a cliffhanger silence, as if she had stopped breathing. I wondered if she had apnea, which I've always worried about having myself. Then there would be a snort or some other respiratory sound, and Kris and I would resume our midnight chat.

"Do you believe in ghosts?" Kris asked. "Last night I thought I saw a shadow or something flutter past."

"It was probably the spirit of one of my former girlfriends wanting her self-respect back."

Kris laughed. "You weren't *that* bad a boyfriend, were you?"

"No, I like to exaggerate. How did your job interview go today?"

"The man who interviewed me stared out the window most of the time. He got all friendly and enthusiastic at the end, though. I didn't know how to interpret that. Luckily, it's a tight market. Everybody's looking for candidates they don't need to enroll in remedial English or teach basic math."

"What's your field again?"

"Medical-resource management."

"Hmm," I said, as if well acquainted with this burgeoning field.

"I seem to have a crick in my neck," Kris said, flexing her head.

"It's probably from sleeping on the floor. That sleeping bag doesn't provide much support."

"It's not that bad."

"Don't be stoic. Sleeping on a mattress will be much easier on your neck. If you'd like to share the bed, I promise to stay on my side, scout's honor."

"You sure?"

"I'm sure. I feel funny, making a guest sleep on the floor."

"Okay, I'll take the side by the window."

Kris slid into bed, lying at first on her back, then turning on her side to face me, so that we could talk better. At one point I reached over and touched her chin but the self-protective way she tugged down on her T-shirt told me not to proceed any further on this expedition. She told me more about her life in Cambridge before we agreed to call it a night. We rolled on our sides, our backs facing each other. Our bottoms bumped together, as if introducing themselves, before inching apart. Slinky, deprived of her customary spot at the foot of the bed, inserted herself between us, stretching out like a dividing strip.

I awoke earlier than usual the next morning, but not earlier than Kris, who had already vacated the bed. I ran my hand over her side of the sheet, which was still warm. I had to get cracking. Using the salary from my brief stint on *The Last Ray of Hope*, I was going to quiet my agent's pleas and get new publicity photos done. Now that I had lost weight again, I no longer looked like a cheerful knucklehead. I thought about calling Annette, who I knew did headshots, but I didn't want to deal with her gruff roommate or boyfriend, so I booked my usual photographer. I fed Slinky, who looked spindly in the morning light reflecting off the shined floor. If the kitchen had been any brighter, I would have been able to X-ray her bones. She showed little interest in her breakfast, but she often turned up her nose at a meal, only to return to it later. I took a GI shower (two minutes) and was combing my hair like a high-school greaser when I heard a soft rap at the bathroom door.

"It's me," Kris said. "You busy?"

"I'm about to shave."

"Can I watch?"

"Sure. I'll try not to cut myself."

Kris peeked in and sat herself on the toilet-seat cover, carrying her coffee mug. She was still wearing what she wore to bed, a droopy T-shirt that fell to her thighs and a pair of white socks. She fluffed her lopsided hair with her free hand. "Where's Caroline?" I said.

"She went to the green market."

"The one on Union Square?"

"I guess."

I had a towel wrapped around my waist, and another towel wrapped around my neck. The bathroom was still steamy from my shower. I whipped up a batch of foam with my shaving brush and lathered evenly. Then I used the brush to dab some foam on Kris's nose. "My father used to do that," she said, smiling. She wiped her nose with the back of her wrist.

I began to shave, puffing up my cheeks to smooth out the blade action. I was careful around the mustache area, where I often draw blood. I didn't want any minor cuts the day I was having my picture taken. I rinsed off the blade and wiped my face with the towel, then applied a splash of aftershave. Kris rose and stood behind me, resting her chin on my shoulder for an instant. Then she kissed the spot where her chin had rested. Her eyes didn't close when she kissed, but studied the action and the reaction in the mirror. The angle of her body told me she was on tiptoe. I suspected she was braless under her T-shirt when she came in, and now I knew for sure.

"Johnny, you can be so sweet when you want to be."

"Sometimes I'm so sweet, I could just eat myself. How's N'Orlins?"

"Hot enough for fainting spells. I must have been out of my mind to come this time of year. But then I returned to the hotel after a long tedious dinner and here are these lovely flowers waiting for me. I wish you were here. The bed has a canopy and big sturdy posts I could tie you to. Are you behaving yourself?"

"But of course. When are you heading back?"

"Thursday, maybe Friday. I have to make another side trip to Baton Rouge to attend a plantation sale. I can't wait to show you the thimble collection I bought. Who's that?"

"Who's what?"

"I thought I heard someone."

"Oh, that's the catsitter."

"What's she still doing there?"

"Gathering up some things she left behind."

Caroline, who had been humming to herself as she misted a geranium, put a finger to her lips, admonishing herself to be quiet.

"I was hoping it was a cleaning lady," Amanda said. "I wanted to tell her not to miss that clump of dust behind the toilet."

"I'll be sure to direct that to her attention. Take care."

"You too, honeybun."

Honeybun hung up the phone, feeling more like a honeybum.

"I assume that was Amanda," Caroline said. She was now flopped on the sofa. "When is madame due back?"

"Thursday night, Friday morning. It was supposed to be earlier, but she fell in love with an ottoman or something."

"Good, that gives me and Kris a couple extra days if you don't mind. Let us make dinner for you to pay you back for your hospitality. Though I understand Kris is already paying you back in her own special way."

"I'm sure I don't know what you mean."

"It's like *The Blue Lagoon* in there. Don't worry, I'm not jealous, though I sometimes wish I was in on the joke. You two were really yucking it up last night."

"I love the way she holds her stomach when she laughs. Most women only laugh with their mouths."

"That's because most of the time we're just humoring you guys. Are those your new headshots?"

I dug them out of the manila folder I was pretending to clutch protectively and fanned them across Caroline's lap. Each picture was more silvery than the last. When she got to the bottom of the pile, I said: "That one was a gag shot. The photographer thought it would be funny to shoot me with lipstick on my collar. His lovely assistant Germaine did the honor of applying the lipstick kiss. You'll notice I put a little extra twinkle into my eye when the picture was taken."

"Could I keep it as a souvenir of the trip?"

"Sure. Just don't let it fall into enemy hands."

"Would you autograph it for me and Kris?"

"Just give me a moment to think of something roguish to write. What do you think of the others?"

"They're nice, but this one makes you look like Bobby Darin."

"I accept that as a compliment, being the Bobby Darin fan that I am. I used to have a couple of his 45s in my jukebox. 'Dream Lover,' 'Sea of Love.'"

"You had a jukebox? What happened to it?"

"I outgrew it. It was time to move on."

To go with my lounge-singer smile, I wrote across the photograph in dashing letters *Keep kool, kittens!—Johnny D.*

34

AT THE COUNTRY-CLUB BAR on the set of *The Last Ray of Hope*, the veteran actor Philip Green and I waited while a light adjustment was made. This was our big scene together. His character Lloyd Fairwell—once a pillar of the community, now the town skunk--was due to barrel into the bar, desperate for another drink. I, Mitch Hogan, bartender and confidant, recognizing how far gone he is, refuse to serve him and offer to phone his wife. The script called for us to wrestle with the breakaway bottle of scotch at the bar until I get the better of him. With the director in the control booth, we practiced doing it a less clichéd way. Instead of wrestling with the bottle, I would whisk it away when Lloyd reached for it, and his eyes would follow it as it disappeared behind the counter. Then, after a beat, he would lunge at *me* for denying him the thing in life he wanted most.

"Another couple minutes, chaps," the director said from the control booth. "Sorry for the delay."

Phil Green said: "Drake, we'd like to try it a different way. It won't alter the shot."

"Let's do it the way we rehearsed it, to be on the safe side. We're behind schedule as it is."

"Could we at least demonstrate it for you?" Green said. "I really think it would be dramatically stronger."

We then demonstrated how it would be done. After a pause, the director said: "I see how it would play, but let's stick to the original blocking. Good, good, we've lost the glare."

The two-man lighting crew folded their ladder and left. The stage manager held up two fingers. Green twisted his tie to the side and said to me, "Follow my lead." I nodded. He went to his place behind the door. The director called for quiet. All chatting ceased. The stage manager held up one finger, then gave us the sign.

The door swung open. Lloyd Fairwell, managing a glassy smile, entered the bar, trying to appear in control. He steadied himself, but his clothes looked slept-in, and every time he reached out to touch something, he missed by an inch or two. He hoisted himself onto the bar stool with an effort that tokened pain.

"Mr. Fairwell," I said. "We're just about to close."

"You can leave the bar open for me, Mitch."

"You know I can't. The boss would have my hide."

"I can buy and sell your boss. Pour me a drink."

"The usual, sir?"

"As if you need to ask. Only this time lose the ice. I hate ice!"

I poured a modest amount of colored fluid into a glass, sandwiching a look of concern between two obsequious smiles. Lloyd took what seemed to him a well-deserved swig, then closed his eyes in blessing.

"Mitch," he asked, "do you happen to have a wife?"

"I have a girlfriend."

"Anyone I know?"

"I doubt it, sir," I said, Lloyd and I being from different sides of the proverbial tracks.

"Tell me when the wedding is, assuming couples your age still marry, and I'll buy you and the missus a present. You know what wedding gift I wish I had gotten lo those many years ago? A shotgun. That way I could have blown out my brains at the wedding reception and saved myself years of torment."

"You don't mean that, sir."

"You don't have to 'sir' me, Mitch. And damn it, I do mean it. Have you ever met my wife? That woman is the most scheming bitch in Crescent Bay. When I was a young buck, I had my pick of bad women, but I made the mistake of marrying the most evil one of all. And you know why? Because she was also the most beautiful one of all. Still is. I look at Marissa sometimes when she's taking off her jewelry at night and I'm still stunned. But then she opens her vicious trap and I can't decide which one of us deserves to die more. And don't mention divorce to me. She'd get everything, especially now that she knows about—" He waved his hand in the air, alluding to something I had no inkling of.

"Pour me another," Lloyd said. "And keep on pouring."

I freshened his drink, strategically moving the bottle farther from his reach. I wiped a glass as Lloyd resumed his monologue.

"You should have seen Crescent Bay thirty years ago. It wasn't gussied up, like it is now, it didn't have nightclubs and coffee bars, but everyone knew each other and took the time to talk. Now look. I'm the wealthiest man in town, yet I have no one to talk to, just my daughter and you. My daughter refuses to speak to me until I stop drinking and you probably think . . ."

Long pause, as Lloyd reflects, so that a flashback to be inserted later during edit. Then, with a snap of his head, he jerked awake as if from a dream.

"Well, I've wasted enough of your time. You probably want to get back to your fiancée. Here's a little something for the both of you." Lloyd began to take large bills out of his wallet.

"That's much too generous."

". . . I'll just take the rest of the bottle with me."

"I'm afraid I can't let you do that."

"Of course you can. Here's another twenty."

"It's past closing time, Mr. Fairwell. Let me call you a cab."

"I don't need a cab. I have my own driver waiting for me. Just give me the bottle!"

"You know I can't do that. It's closing time."

"I know it's closing time! For me every waking moment is closing time!"

I set the bottle under the bar. Lloyd trailed it with his eyes, then gave me a glassy look, sinking inward. I let my guard drop and he lunged, tearing like a drowning man at the lapels of my vest before recognizing defeat. His rage was no match for my size and, what was even harder on his pride, he'd embarrassed himself, wrecked his dignity. His hands slid back down to the bar and he lowered his head, banging his fists against his eyes, something he hadn't rehearsed. Then he bolted from the bar stool and through the flapping doors. After Lloyd left, I picked up a telephone and pretended to dial.

"Cut," came the director's voice.

Under my clothes, I was covered with sweat. My throat was closed tight. Despite everything, we had made something real out of the scene. While Green waited in the corner, adjusting the angles of his herringbone jacket, the studio crew resumed their headphone consultations. There was rustling in the control booth. Finally, the director said: "Could we just do the last bit one more time? The way we planned it. Take it from the line 'I don't need a cab.'"

Green stood at the bar and looked at me. He lowered his voice and addressed the control booth.

"Was the first take okay?"

"Perfectly fine. But—"

"Any technical flubs or pauses?"

"No, it all tracked."

"Then I don't think we'll be needing this." And with that, he took hold of the neck of the prop bottle, smashed it against the bar, tossed the surviving neck behind the bar, and walked off the set. Stagehands stood aside to let him pass. I looked up at the control booth, where there was much conferring into headsets. The director leaned into the mike and said: ". . . Let's clean the bar of debris. First we'll do an insert of the clock. Downs, I want to do an insert of you picking up and talking into the phone. Then we can break."

After pantomiming Mitch the Bartender alerting an unspecified someone that Lloyd Fairwell was on another toot, I changed in the dressing room reserved for bit players and regular extras and swabbed myself with Breezettes, since my temporary status didn't grant me access to a shower. Someone from the crew patted me on the shoulder.

"That was some dedicated shit, man."

"You mean when Phil smashed the bottle?"

"No, the scene itself. It looked intense on the monitor. His eyes were *scary*."

"They sure scared me, I just wasn't sure if the camera picked it up."

"Whoosh," he said. "Why else do you think the director let him walk? He knew he had the scene bagged. Hell, they have other breakable bottles. They let Phil have his moment. Gotta let the old guys have their moment now and then."

As I was leaving, Green and I congratulated each other at the row of vending machines by exchanging profound nods. He pumped his arm as if he had just bowled a game-winning strike, and I answered with an arm pump of my own. He bought gum and offered me a stick, which I accepted. Never refuse anything from a senior actor. Green had changed into an elegant pair of slacks and a blue shirt that screamed luxury vacation. His face had a classic actor's tan, with white knife-cut creases around the mouth and eyes.

"You leaving?" he said.

"Yup."

"I gave myself a damned headache hitting myself in the head. Had to take some aspirin. Let's go out the side door to avoid the fans."

As we neared the side door, Green fastened his sunglasses on like a jet pilot about to cross the Tarmac. He was better prepared than I was. After the dark corridors of the studio, the sunlight struck like a scimitar. I was shielding my eyes, when an elderly woman wearing wool socks and every knitted sweater she owned waddled up and thrust an autograph book in front of Green.

"Haven't I given you one before?" he asked.

"It got wet."

"Well," he said, signing, "keep this one under your pillow."

"I will. I wanted to ask you if—?"

"I'm not at liberty to discuss any future storylines, you know better than that, Dot."

Before the autograph hound could ask the same unasked question a different way, Green picked up his pace just enough not to be rude and left the woman behind on the sidewalk.

"You don't see her type around much anymore," I said.

"Not in daylight, anyway. I wanted to thank you for giving me something in that scene at the bar today. I usually have to manufacture everything myself. You can't believe some of the test products I have to work with. Heading downtown?"

"Yes."

"Wait with me. We'll ride the bus together."

My eyes adjusted to the light as we waited. A downtown 102 screeched to a stop like the dying German war machine. We sat in the back. A woman across the aisle recognized Green and tenderly patted him on the arm, like a reassuring nurse. He responded with a grave nod of gratitude that made no other communication necessary. After she got off at the next stop, he said: "That's happening more and more.

They spot me on the street and think I'm the one battling alcoholism. I get these pitying looks and little gentle waves. I've learned to bear it admirably."

"That was quite a nod."

"Pure Gielgud. So you have one more scene?"

"Tomorrow I do a brief one where Marissa comes into the bar searching for you. 'So this is where my ex-husband-to-be ruins his liver.' Which is quite a mouthful. What happens to Lloyd after that?"

"After his next series of blackouts, he wakes up in a sanitarium, a virtual prisoner of Marissa, who controls the staff with puppet strings, bribing them to do her evil bidding. I'll be doing a lot of bug-out scenes. But they're also going to do some AA-type meetings in the sanitarium, which'll look improvised but won't be. It'll at least allow us to use some real actors for a change. Maybe you should let them know you're interested. It'd be a twist, a bartender in AA."

The bus stopped to let a wheelchair person on board. A few passengers sighed as the hydraulic lift lowered while others checked their watches. Nobody cuts anybody any slack anymore.

"That AA thing reminds me of an idea I had recently," I said as we waited. "They have a group at this church where I do volunteer work, for guys who have problems managing their anger. Apparently, they not only discuss their attitudes but act them out, with some of the men playing women's parts. 'Now, Darryl, you pretend you're in the kitchen making dinner for Mike and he comes home cranky,' etc. There have been other group-session plays, but none that have used gender-switching to that degree. I'm trying to decide whether to sit down and write the piece full-out—something I've never done before—or get some guys together and flesh it out through improvs, which would require a lot of man-hours. And you know how most actors are in improvs, especially the men."

"They go ape."

"Exactly. I can picture so much of this in my mind that maybe I'll storyboard it and worry about dialogue later."

"Have you told anyone else about it?"

"I mentioned something to Tom Gleason."

"I know Tom. Good actor, but he always seems to lead himself astray. I wouldn't tell him too much about it until you're further along."

"So you think it's worth pursuing?"

"Oh, sure. It sounds like something that could have some pop to it. Let's face it, actors have to write their own projects. No one else is going to do anything for us."

After a mighty heave, the bus resumed motion. Talking somewhat out of the side of his mouth, Green said: "Just between us, Downs, they're phasing me out of *Last Ray* as part of their permanent youth movement. The new writers don't care about Lloyd or Marissa or any of the other longstanding characters. They started dropping hints months ago about me darkening my hair or considering a facelift, but the fact is, nothing I do is going to subtract twenty years. They're hoping Lloyd's alcoholic breakdown will win me a daytime Emmy, which will enable them to ease me out of the show with a clean conscience. 'A fitting cap to a fine career,' and all that. So I'm looking to line up something that might be challenging for a change. I don't need the money. My wife and I have a nice place in Connecticut, so I don't need to worry about being in a 'hit.'" He made the last word sound like something that crawled.

"I'd be happy just getting this off the ground," I said.

"Think about an older character who functions as a sort of den father to these guys. A former priest, perhaps, or a former con. This is my stop. Get off with me. Keep an old man company."

"You're not old."

"I feel old in this light. Each summer seems to get brighter."

Green fitted his sunglasses into jet-pilot position and took hold of the railing. The bus shook as it came to a halt.

35

WHEN THE ELEVATOR DOOR OPENED, I was met by the smell of home cooking wafting through the hall. It was as if a portion of the South had taken up residence. Inside the apartment, my fold-up card table was covered with a checkered cloth. Kris was shining silverware and setting the table as Caroline beat potatoes in a bowl. Slinky sat on one of the chairs, peering over the table and testing the reach of her right paw. Bottles of Coke, beer, and mineral water were jammed into a bucket of ice. Caroline said:

"We figured we'd give you a real Southern fried-chicken dinner, like the kind mother used to make when she bothered to cook. How'd the shooting go?"

As if at the touch of a button, I found myself giving a full report of the taping session, including my chat with Phil Green afterward. Over her shoulder, Kris said, "You didn't tell us you were working on a play."

"Well, it's not a play yet. It's still in the mental stage."

"Is there a part in it for someone based on someone like me? That'd be cool."

"No, I'm afraid the characters are all screwed-up men."

"Some of them better be good-looking, because a lot of men together can look loggy."

"No kidding. You should see me and my brothers standing around doing nothing."

"The chicken should be ready shortly," Caroline said, husking corn. "Anything I can do to help?"

"Just keep Slinky off the table. She's been into everything."

I held Slinky on my lap—not easy given her wrestling abilities—and watched Kris finish setting the table. She bent to light a candle, a night-before-Christmas look on her face. I noticed she was wearing high heels without stockings. I wanted to pat her behind as she passed, but had my hands full with Slinky. "I'm going to lock you in the bedroom," I said to Slinky, shaking her playfully.

"We already tried that," Kris said. "She scratched at the door and yowled until we let her out."

Extending her elbows out like a true hostess, Caroline, using one of my old T-shirts as an apron, bore a steaming dish of corn on the cob to the table. Kris followed with a bowl of garlic mashed potatoes. Then Caroline brought in the fried chicken, whose crunchy aroma now probably pervaded the whole building. We all sat, smoothing the napkins on our laps and commenting on how good everything looked. Caroline peeled the skin off her chicken before eating. Kris and I dug right in. On the floor Slinky attacked her own dish of sliced chicken.

"That's good," Caroline said. "She barely touched her breakfast."

"She barely touched it yesterday," I said. "Maybe it's the heat. Pass the gravy?"

A half-hour later, we were all sitting back contentedly in our chairs, like the citizens of Mayberry after a church social. Kris patted my knee. Since the womenfolk had labored all afternoon over dinner, I volunteered to do the dishes. "Leave them for later," Caroline said. "Stack 'em in the sink and let them soak."

"Caroline," Kris said, drawing out the syllables of Caroline's name, "don't you think this is a good time for the *unveiling*?"

"What unveiling?"

"I almost forgot!" Caroline said. "Let me mix some cocktails so that we can make a proper toast."

"What unveiling?"

In the kitchen she mixed a batch of cocktails she called Hickory Switches, serving them in the special Durabar glasses that I had ordered from one of Buzzy's suppliers. These glasses sat in your hand with the heft of service revolvers. When I had mine, I started to take a sip. "No, wait," Caroline said. "Close your eyes first."

I closed my eyes and heard a mild rustling.

"Open."

On the mantel of my nonworking fireplace was a squarish object covered in black cloth that looked like a mourning veil.

"Shall I do the honors?" Caroline said.

"Let's both do them," Kris said.

Flanking the fireplace and nabbing the bottom corners of the cloth like magician's assistants, they whisked off the covering with a snap of their wrists as Kris cried, "Ta-da!"

Beaming from the mantel was the now-framed headshot of me with lipstick on my collar. And what a frame—silver Art Nouveau, slightly tarnished, with mane-strewn nymphs stretching from every corner. Inside the silver frame, the photograph seemed almost camp. Ideally, it should have been set on a piano top, so that I could croon love tunes to myself. "Isn't it hideous?" Caroline said. "When I saw the frame in a thrift-shop window, I just knew it was the perfect match."

"I feel clammy all over."

"I think it's cute!" Kris said. "And now that you're going to be a big soap-opera star, it seems quite appropriate."

Between sips of Caroline's special cocktail, we debated the finer points of the picture, discussing if there was a better place in the apartment for it to call repulsive attention to itself. The Hickory Switch was brown in color and brown in taste, like something brewed in a tree hollow. My eyes began to liquefy. Bodies began to soften. As Kris and Caroline flopped on the sofa, I sat in my high-backed chair, imagining myself on a rocker on a front porch in the South. The phone rang. I picked it up as languidly as was humanly possible and said hello. I had to repeat myself since Kris and Caroline were talking in the background and I wasn't sure my first greeting had been heard. After the second hello, there was a click at the other end.

"Wrong number," I said. Caroline switched on the radio, which was still set to the mellow-jazz station. As a lone tenor sax toodled away against what sounded like the tide coming in, Kris mimed a face-splitting yawn.

"Now, now, it's Johnny's apartment," Caroline said. "He's allowed to listen to whatever boring music he wants."

"Ladies, ladies," I said, rising from the chair with the dignity of a frontier judge who kept a volume of Shakespeare next to his Bible. "Put on whatever station you want. Just make sure Slinky doesn't go after the chicken bones."

I locked the bathroom door, one of those unnecessary precautions one takes in life. I did my business, taking more careful aim than usual, a little unsteady from the cocktail I had just had. I washed my hands and splashed cold water on my face. When I returned to the living room, my houseguests were lodged on the sofa acting abnormally still, like kids about to pull a prank. As I lowered myself into the rocking chair, they exploded into convulsions, gripping the sides of the sofa for support, their legs crossing over each other. Kris pretended to hold up a stopwatch, which made them laugh all the more.

I said: "Let me in on the joke."

"You are the joke," Kris said.

"No offense, Johnny," Caroline said, "but that may be the longest pee on record. Darlene told me you were a long peer, especially in the mornings, but I thought that was just another one of her exaggerations. You hung a rope there, daddy."

"Did you want to be a fireman when you were growing up?" Kris asked.

"'Only you can prevent forest fires.'"

Rising above their ridicule, I said, "I can only wonder what other legends Darlene passed on."

"Don't worry, it's all in your folder," Caroline said.

"Doesn't matter. My life's an open book."

"And we all might get to read it someday."

"What do you mean?"

"Oh, nothing."

With that, Caroline returned to the kitchen and began cracking ice for a second round of cocktails. Like a bloodhound, Slinky sniffed the top of the table for additional chicken bits, then, coming up dry, retired to the bedroom. She walked with a hitch in her step and seemed for the first time to be showing her age. It was an animal version of an old person's walk. Maybe I'd better schedule a visit to the vet's, I told myself. It's been a while since her last one.

Caroline set the drink tray on the card table, lit the remaining candles in the living room, and switched off the overheads. The candles cast *Citizen Kane* shadows against the wall. With the framed portrait on the mantle, my apartment looked like a shrine, a shrine dedicated to me.

"I'd like to propose a second toast," Caroline said. "To Johnny, for letting us overrun his life and being such a sporting host. And to Darlene Ryder, for somehow bringing us all together. Now sip this very, very slowly. I added something extra to this round that'll sneak up on you. See if you can taste it."

We sipped slowly, appreciatively. The cocktails now had a rummy undertow, with just a hint of a hidden depth charge. The candlelight flickered and the apartment became a cave with sagas on the walls.

"I'm a little hot," Kris said, unbuttoning the top two buttons of her blouse, which left only three holding down the fort.

"I could turn on the A/C," I said.

"Don't," Caroline said. "It's healthier to sweat alcohol through your pores."

"I like sweating," Kris said. "It feels good afterward and I'm not afraid of being a little stinky. Let's put some real music on and dance. I know a lot of people like it, but jazz just sort of sits there for me."

"I only had it on as mood music. Put on what you want."

Kris fiddled with the radio knob until she found a retro disco station at the high end of the dial, which played only medleys of seventies hits. She hit the sweet spot of station reception and hiked the volume. Still in her heels, she began to move in the middle of the room by herself, not so much bumping to the beat as weaving around it with her eyes closed and her arms making S-shaped patterns. Before long she was cupping the sides of her head and raking her fingers through her hair as her hips joined the beat. She opened her eyes from another dimension and Caroline set her drink on the floor to join her. They began dancing in the middle of the living room, separately but somehow linked. Each twirl of their bodies tickled the candle flames, which threw fitful shadows on the walls. Extending a hand, Kris invited me to dance. I would have preferred to sit in my chair like a sultan and watch the two of them, but I knew I couldn't refuse. The next song was more midtempo, so Kris and I did a little jitterbug, me being just tall enough for her to comfortably twirl. After that number, she stopped and took off her heels, cranking up the volume another notch. When we had danced a few more numbers, I excused myself to the bathroom, to pat my face with a cool cloth. It really was like being in the South again.

While I was wringing out the cloth, the phone rang. I heard Caroline pick it up and say over the music, "John Down's residence . . . hello?"

"Should I turn down the radio?" Kris said.

"Hello?" Caroline said again, louder.

"Tell whoever it is he's *indisposed*," Kris said.

"Whoever it is hung up," Caroline said.

Second one tonight, I thought. I dried my face, feeling much fresher, and rejoined my catsitters. All danced-out, Kris and Caroline were sharing another joint on the couch. The candle flames were flickering more regularly now, with no ruffles of air to disturb them. It was only a little after eleven, but it seemed much later, nearer the hour of the wolf. I began picking up glasses until Caroline said: "Don't start tidying up now. It'll make me feel I have to help, and I'm too inert. Leave it 'til tomorrow. Are you sure you don't want to share a joint?"

"No, thanks. What I could do is wheel out the TV and tape today's episode of *Last Ray*. I don't have any lines, but it's the first one that shows me tending bar in the background."

"Could we watch it with the sound low? I get sensitive to sound when I'm this totaled. Is that okay with you, Kristin?"

"Do what you want," Kris said. "I'm *completely* out of it. If aliens land, they can *have* me."

I sat on the sofa between Kris and Caroline. Kris lay her head on my shoulder. As we watched in a semidaze, I kissed her on the corner of her lips, which brought her momentarily back to life. Although Caroline was on the other side of me, she was out of the frame, so to speak. Kris and I necked very quietly. I stroked her bare legs. I had forgotten how much fun making out after a party can be, maybe because I hadn't done it since college. During a commercial break, Kris tried to stand, then stumbled as if she had hit her head on an invisible ledge. She braced her left hand on the sofa arm, knocking an ashtray to the floor. After she stopped teetering and was fully upright, Caroline said: "You'd better put her to bed before she injures herself."

I walked Kris into the bedroom and started to unzip the back of her dress, but she keeled over on her side into bed, tucking her bare legs under her and making a little fist under her chin.

It was time to call it a wrap. I muted the TV and switched the radio back to the jazz station, whose moody atmospherics would help the evening taper off. Having drunk more than usual, I was trying to guide my system to a soft landing. As if through telepathy, Caroline and I began retrieving stray glasses and bottles in the living room despite our earlier agreement to let everything sit until morning. We worked quietly, not wanting to disturb Kris, who seemed to have fallen instantly asleep. I was about to fetch a whisk broom for the ashes she had spilled, when the buzzer rang. The noise was so unexpectedly loud, it gave me a jolt, a sci-fi zap. I thought it might be a random entry (sometimes residents who have forgotten their keys buzz other apartments until someone lets them in), or a delivery man who had pressed the wrong button. I hit the talk button and said: "Who is it?"

"*Amanda.*"

"Who?" I said, thinking I must have misheard.

"Amanda."

I paused, then pressed the entry buzzer. I didn't know what else to do.

"Did I hear right?" Caroline said.

"I'm afraid so. Amanda's coming up."

I started to pick up the remaining glasses scattered in front of the sofa.

"Leave them be," Caroline said. "It's too late now to make everything magically disappear."

36

THERE STOOD AMANDA, wearing a blue cocktail dress and high heels. She was clutching the tiniest of handbags, the kind small and stylish enough to hide a derringer. Her eyes were already trained down the entryway as I held open the door. I leaned forward to kiss her but she took two tart little steps and paraded past me. Technically, it takes more than one person to make a parade, but Amanda proved otherwise. She strode to the invisible spot in the hallway where the lanes from the bedroom and the bathroom intersected with the opening of the living room, and stopped. I stood behind her, following her gaze as her neck swiveled, like RoboCop casing a crime scene: shadowy living room—coffee table covered with beer bottles, soda cans, dirty ashtrays—couch strewn with stray items of clothing—Kris's shoes lying sideways on the floor—candles burning near the bottom of their wax—a silent TV throwing spastic prisms of color against the wall. Amanda clicked her head just far enough to the right to nail the bedroom, where Kris's legs lay angled on the bed, the bottoms of her bare feet pointed in our direction. If Amanda had been wearing white gloves, she would have removed one of them at that moment and slapped it lightly against the inside of her wrist.

"I see you had yourself quite a party," Amanda said, with a voice that took the high road, leaving us peons below. "I wonder why I wasn't invited. I enjoy parties. You even have the radio tuned to my favorite station."

"Actually, it was my party," Caroline said, coming in from the kitchen. "I'm Caroline, Johnny's catsitter. And you must be Amanda. Johnny has spoken so much about you. Won't you take a seat?"

"I prefer to stand."

"Johnny's missed you something fierce. He says you were antiquing in New Orleans. Did you eat at Castellano's? Aren't their cocktails divine? He told me all about how the two of you met, and about your actress friend Claudia. You've got yourself a loyal Mountie here, Amanda."

"It doesn't appear that way."

"Well, it's really my fault. I asked Johnny if I could have a little party before I left town and he said yes. He'd forgotten how much Southerners like to party. But he's such a gentleman, he let us have our fun as long as we kept curfew. He has to get up early for that soap he's in."

"Where were you were planning to sleep tonight?" Amanda asked. "Given that you need your rest. The reason I ask is that your bed already seems to be taken."

From the angle of the doorway, Kris looked like a casualty slumped where she was. If she came to, I would really be in deep quicksand.

Caroline said: "That's Kris. She overdid it, I'm afraid, and I had to tuck her in. Johnny was kind enough to offer to take the sofa tonight while we shared the bed."

"So you're the catsitter," Amanda said, sounding mildly placated. "What do you think of Johnny's cat?"

"Hey, let's not go there," I said, wagging my hands as if to ward off a divisive debate. "Would anyone like mineral water? We've got tons."

"None for me, thanks," Amanda said. "You're probably wondering why I'm here."

"You did catch me a little off-guard."

"I can see that. I was unpacking when I received a phone call from a friend of yours, Johnny, a certain Darlene, who thought you might be at my place. She sounded nervous, as if she had said something she shouldn't. Then she asked about an armoire her aunt had, if it might be valuable or not, because she had seen a similar one on *Antiques Road Show* and you had told her I dealt in antiques. She was overexplaining things until I thought I was going to scream. I then phoned you to see what was up, and a woman answered. I could hear music in the background and another woman laughing about you being 'indisposed'—so what was I to think? I could have stayed home and fretted about it all night, but I decided to check for myself. How long are you staying in New York . . . ?"

"It's Caroline. I'm going to help Johnny clean up the debris, then I'm packing up tomorrow morning before heading back to Athens, Gee-ay."

"And what about Sleeping Beauty in there?"

"I'm driving her to Penn Station so she can catch a train to Boston before I turn the car south. I know things look sloppy, but we've got everything organized."

Humming softly to herself, Amanda took a couple of curious steps into the living room. "What's this?" she said, catching sight of the framed photo of me with lipstick on my collar, which was flanked by votive candles. She read the inscription aloud. "*Keep kool, kittens!*—how cute."

Coming to the rescue, Caroline said, "I stole that shot out of the pile of new publicity stills Johnny had made and got it framed as a gag gift. It is cute, isn't it? Did Johnny tell you about how well things are going on *Last Ray?*"

"No. I guess we have a lot of catching up to do."

"I'll walk you to a taxi," I said. Since Amanda didn't say no, I took her nonresponse as a grudging yes. As we waited for the elevator, Amanda made a point of standing sharply sideways next to me, like a commuter on a subway platform. Her body language said that she was fencing herself off from further contact until she collected her thoughts, so I kept quiet while we waited, not that I had anything of value to say. Once out of the building, we walked toward the nearest avenue heading uptown. She seemed to unclench somewhat as her legs went into motion, so I decided to venture a safe comment before the silence between us became a hard surface.

"Nice dress," I said. "Is it new?"

"No, but you've never seen me in it. I was hoping to surprise you, and I guess I did."

"I know things looked funky back there, but I'm glad we got everything straightened out."

We waited at the corner for a taxi. Amanda glanced at my face in the glare of the street light, then turned toward the direction of traffic. She tucked her little handbag under her arm. I could smell the last wisp of her perfume.

"Maybe we can take in a play this weekend," I said. "I can get free-bies. Did you ever find that butter churner you were—?"

Amanda spun and slapped me hard across the face. Half of my vision went black from the shock while in the other half street lights and car lights grew comet's tails. As the functioning part of my brain tried to reestablish communication with the other half, Amanda said, "How *could* you, Johnny? Like a fool, I *trusted* you. You must think I'm *stupid*! I was suspicious the moment I heard your 'catsitter' rustling around the apartment when I called from New Orleans. I didn't want to believe you were playing around behind my back, but the guilty, chickenshit look on your face when I entered the apartment told me everything I needed to know and that was before I spotted that girl passed out in your bed. And then you think you can make everything right by offer-ing *freebies*? You jerk, I thought we *had* something together!"

"We do."

Amanda's face was raw now, fury and injury joined at the jaws. She slapped me again, harder, a real tooth-rattler that spun my head forty-five degrees. Behind me I heard a woman comment, "He must of deserved it." I understood her attitude, because that's what I usually think when I see a woman strike a man on the street, that he probably deserved it. I did deserve it, too, but even so, I wanted to put a stop to this before we drew a crowd. As I tried to think of the right thing to say, knowing there was no right thing to say, Amanda strode to the curb and flashed two fingers to flag a cab. When one stopped, she reached into her pocketbook, and for a split second I thought she might have a gun. She hurled a small object, which shattered on the sidewalk, splattering liquid at my feet. It was the bottle of holy water she brought me from New Orleans. She swung her legs inside the cab, slammed the door, and faced forward, toward a future that didn't include the likes of me. The cab was moving before the light turned green.

37

IT WAS A SHORT DISTANCE HOME, but it seemed like the last mile. Dazed as I was from drinking and getting clocked on the street, one thing kept rolling over in my mind: Amanda's saying she had gotten a call from "a certain Darlene." Why would Darlene call Amanda's number, then get nervous when I wasn't there? Never in my life had I heard Darlene come across as nervous or unsure. I even found myself wondering if that first hangup call was from Darlene, checking to make sure I was home. I wouldn't have suspected Darlene if it hadn't been for the other surprise call she made, the one as 'Suzanne' during my summit meeting with Nicole. Darlene wielded a wicked telephone.

When I got back to the apartment, the TV was still chucking light against the wall, creating silent hysteria. I ejected the tape from the VCR and turned off the set. Now it was truly dark. The bedroom door was shut. In the kitchen Caroline piled dishes into the sink. I began clearing bottles off the coffee table, going through the motions. When Caroline saw me attempting to do something constructive, she blurted with laughter. "Stand still," she said. She lifted a flickering candle that had been sitting in a dish and held it near my face, taking care not to spill hot wax.

"She clipped you pretty good. Be glad she wasn't wearing a ring."

"I know. The second shot would have sliced me open."

"She slapped you *twice*? She was ticked off."

"I made the mistake of asking about a butter churner."

"Oh, well, such is life. This sort of thing happens down in Athens all the time. Catch your boyfriend with another girl, kick both their asses, drive off in a huff, laugh it off a few days later."

"I don't think anyone's going to be laughing this one off."

"No, I can see that. I'm making chamomile tea, it'll help us unwind. Kris stirred while you were gone, then sunk back into a coma."

"Lucky her. I'm going to go wash my face. I feel like I've got clown makeup on."

I left the bathroom door open so that I wouldn't have to flip on the switch. I didn't want to see myself under bright light this particular evening. In the living room, Caroline had set the tea on the coffee table. I repositioned a chair so that it faced her directly. Caroline poured and passed me a cup.

"Did you shut the bedroom door?"

"Kris must have. I heard her stumbling around while I was putting stuff away."

"How good a friend are you of Darlene's?" I said.

"Why do you ask?"

"Because I want to discuss a few things that I don't want getting back to her. I'm relying on you not to rat me out."

"Go ahead, shoot."

I gave Caroline the full lowdown on the meeting Darlene stage-managed between me and Nicole, how she had surprised me by ringing up pretending to be someone named Suzanne. "Darlene suggested I leave an ashtray full of lipsticked cigarettes around for Nicole to see when she arrived as evidence I already had someone else. When I refused, she pretended it was a joke. But maybe when I said no, she decided to go to Plan B, the Suzanne call."

"What excuse did she give for not tipping you off ahead of time?"

"She said she wanted my reaction to sound spontaneous."

"Jeez, Johnny, you're an actor. I'm sure you could have faked a little spontaneity. I have to tell you, if I was sitting here having a talk with my boyfriend and he started being cutesy with some other woman on the phone, I'd be thinking, 'He sure works fast. We're not even official-ly broken up and he's already sweet-talking somebody else.' Keep in mind also that if you and Nicole had met at a restaurant, as you origi-nally intended, Darlene wouldn't have been able to interrupt unless they brought the phone to the table, like in those old nightclub movies."

"And tonight—she knew the three of us were having dinner together. She knew I wouldn't be over at Amanda's unless I went over after dinner. It's as if she intentionally tipped Amanda off."

"She may have just wanted to make mischief. After all, suppose you had picked up the phone when Amanda called instead of me. You still would have had music blaring in the background, us yammering, a lot of explaining to do. Darlene may have just wanted to get you in the doghouse with Amanda to see how you'd bail yourself out. She probably didn't figure things getting so out of hand."

"But why would she *want* to make trouble between me and Amanda?"

"To have her way. To stay Number One and maintain her hold on you. You and Darlene drifted apart when you were dating Nicole, and it was the breakup that brought you two back together. Now Nicole's gone, and Darlene's in the catbird seat. Divide and conquer. You have to understand, it's more interesting for Darlene having you messing around with a lot of different women. It allows her to conduct more experiments. It was Darlene who talked you up to Kris in order to spice things up a little. She figured you'd take the bait. Even if Amanda had never found out, Darlene would have had something incriminating on you, something to put in her folder."

"You keep talking as if she's really keeping actual records."

"She is! She has a filing cabinet full of dossiers. She takes tons of classes, reads all the clinical psychology books, and conducts behavioral tests on people she knows to see how they'll react in different situations, where their stress points are. She's taken detective courses in how to conduct interrogations and do voice-stress analysis. It all feeds into the psychology project she's working on for her master's, a series of case studies on self-sabotaging mating behavior. She told me she wants to subtitle it 'Losers in the Game of Love,' maybe package it as a book. I'm sure she's keeping a file on you. I know she has one on me, because she showed it to me once. Didn't let me read it, just flipped the pages in front of me."

"That must have been creepy."

"It was and it wasn't. It's sort of flattering, being an object of someone else's scrutiny. It means you're intrinsically interesting, because Lord knows, Darlene wouldn't waste her time on bores. And then, of course, there's the curiosity factor—what does she see in me that I don't see in myself? Does my behavior fall into a destructive pattern? It gives her a sense of power, keeping charts on people. Darlene's father was a chart technician, a financial stochastics expert and a complete control freak. He used to grade his kids at night at dinner for their conversational skills. If you got a C or lower, you had to spend the rest of the night without television. That's why today Darlene can talk the twists out of a pretzel. I'm going to light up a cigarette, if you don't mind. It helps me think."

"Go right ahead."

Caroline set her tea cup and dish on the coffee table and dug a pack from her pocketbook. Her lit cigarette looked like a red dot on a stereo console.

"So what do you really make of Darlene?" I said.

"As a person, or a phenomenon?"

When Caroline threw the question back at me, I realized that for the last few months Darlene had so deeply invaded my brain that she now existed for me primarily as an energy force, a form of electricity. I said:

"As a person."

"Darlene has a sort of cracked genius, but she's never been able to apply it to anything for any decent spell. That's why I wonder if she'll ever finish her master's. As focused as she is, there's something basically shaky about her whole life, a wayward quality. She's one of those people who takes diet pills to cram for an exam and then flunks because she's so keyed up, she can't concentrate on the page in front of her. There are a lot of people like her in the South, especially in college towns. Brilliant people with pockets of expertise who never quite got it together."

"She's still young."

"Sure, but most women feel time is running out faster for them than it is for men. Men can fart around longer, soak things up. One of the reasons Darlene likes you is because you're so malleable. That was her exact word."

"Makes me sound like a sponge."

"She didn't mean it as a putdown. As an actor you're much more receptive to trying new things, breaking old habits. I think on some level Darlene sincerely wants you to succeed. But on another level, it's better for you to fail, because once you link up with someone, you won't need her anymore. And if you succeeded in getting married, you'd really be one up on her."

"I don't know, she and Clete seem to be on the right track."

"Clete . . ." Caroline drawled. "Are you sure it's not Clem?"

"What do you mean?"

"Johnny, there's no Clete."

"What do you mean? She's always talking about going away on trips with this guy who owns his own garage and restores old cars."

"Clete is just the latest in a long line of made-up boyfriends. For some reason, she always gives them one-syllable names. Clem. Clete. Clint. Boyd. Jake. She told me she had a boyfriend named Bic. 'Bic, like the pen!' Like an idiot, I believed her. It's all a con. For years she's been running around with the same guy, Ben Mountain. Everybody calls him Bud."

"Come to think about it, she has been dodgy about this guy. They always seem to be going off together to parts unknown. She told me once she was going to fax me a picture of him so I could see how handsome he was, but she never did."

"She didn't want you to see the wedding band. Bud's married. He's been stringing Darlene along for years promising to divorce his wife and marry her, asking her to be patient. This is probably the only area of her life where Darlene has been patient, but I don't think it's going to work. Why should he leave? He's got it made. He's got a wife who puts up with his philandering, two kids he adores, and a girlfriend on the side. He doesn't want to pay alimony, and he sure doesn't want a scandal. He's the head librarian for the county school system. He and Darlene are always running off to 'conferences' together, forcing her to make up all sorts of stories to cover her whereabouts. If she were in a beauty pageant, her talent portion would be 'Lying to Cover Her Ass.' The last time she visited Athens, she gave out my number to various people and had me screen her calls with a different fake-out for each one. 'If it's my mother, tell her—' 'If it's my brother, tell him—' I finally had her type out a list so that I could spit out the correct response. She told people she was staying with me, see, but she was actually at a motel with Bud. Each day she'd drive by my house to pick up her messages."

I lay my head back, visualizing wheels whirring within wheels.

"Do you want me to stop?" Caroline said. "I know I'm dropping a lot on you."

"It's a lot to take in," I said, "but it's good to know. It's filling in a lot of gray areas for me."

I massaged my scalp, trying to get some blood circulating, then took a sip of tea. Caroline lit another cigarette and stretched out her legs, crossing her ankles.

"How many people know about Darlene and Bud?" I said.

"Quite a few. It isn't so much that they *know* as that they've suspected for so long that after a while you accept your suspicions as fact. Darlene's just trying to sow enough confusion to give herself room to maneuver."

"Do you think her lying will level off at some point?" I said. "Maybe it's a manic phase that'll pass."

"It's manic, all right. She and Bud can't really spend time together except on weekends, and she's frantic when they're apart. I've ridden with her and seen her pull into a gas station in the middle of nowhere to place a credit-card call to him. And I mean, *swerve* that car, sending things flying off the dashboard. And they had spoken only an hour earlier! I got to hate going out to eat with her. She couldn't sit still for two minutes before she'd start squirming and excusing herself to make a call. Once we were in a diner where the phone was broken and she began to have the shakes, the literal shakes, like a junkie trying to kick. The telephone cord hooks right into her vein."

"Why doesn't she use a cell?"

"Bud doesn't want her to have one—he knows he wouldn't get any peace. Darlene would be calling him every time her foot itched."

"She told me I shouldn't have a cell phone. That being less accessible would add mystery."

"There might be some truth to that, but believe me, if Bud wanted her to have one, she'd be packing one in a holster."

"He seems to have quite a spell on her."

"All I know is, for some demented reason, Bud is her idea of what a man should be. In Athens, we could always tell when some guy was getting the Bud Treatment. All of a sudden, men who had never drunk anything except Rolling Rock were ordering martinis and splashing on Salty Dog cologne. She had some of them wearing penny loafers. Bud is behind everything she says and does. They're joined at the brain. He's whispering into her ear as she's whispering into yours."

"How old is he, anyway?"

"A few years older than Darlene. But he married young, so he seems more rooted than most men his age. He always speaks in a very soothing voice, as if he's talking to a child. Darlene says he loves to read to his children before bedtime. One of his jobs as county librarian is supervising the read-aloud programs."

It was now sinking into place: the emphasis on Daddy, the marching orders she delivered, the image she had in mind. Darlene was trying to mold me out of her own desires to win a married man, projecting his attributes onto me. I was Bud II, the New York edition. I said to Caroline: "What would happen if Bud did get a divorce? I can't see Darlene being a stepmother. In fact, it sounds like the basis for a horror film."

"She'd most likely be less interested in raising his kids than in starting a family of their own, and his wife would probably get custody anyhow. Which means Bud has to ask himself: Do I want Darlene enough to give up living under the same roof with my children and going through the whole business of being a father again? It's not an easy choice, especially with Darlene getting antsy and wanting you to make a decision."

"Has Darlene met his kids?"

"She baby-sat them!" Caroline said. "Bud told his wife he found her name on a flyer. Bud's wife must have sensed something fishy, because she hired her own sitter after Darlene'd done it a couple times."

"Bud sounds like a sickie. I mean, arranging to have the woman you're having an affair with to baby-sit your children under your wife's nose!"

"Maybe it was an experiment. Maybe Bud wanted to see how his kids related to Darlene, whether they'd ever accept her as a possible stepmom. Or maybe Darlene talked him into it."

"Either way, I don't want to get sucked into some psychodrama," I said, yawning. "I feel like I'm getting tangled up in barbed wire as it is. After tonight I'm going to start distancing myself from Darlene."

"Good luck!" Caroline said with a sharp laugh, as if she were wishing me bon-voyage. "Darlene's a great person to have on your side because she's whip-smart about people and plays situations like a pool hustler, anticipating every angle. But keep in mind, Johnny, *control freaks don't like to be crossed.* For them, there's no nice middle ground. The thing is, I like Darlene, even if she is demento."

"I do, too. I love Darlene. Not *love* love, but you know what I mean."

My left ear began to ring, a delayed reaction to the two slaps I had gotten. I flexed my jaw, trying to make it stop, and the pitched whine scrambled into white noise, which was easier to take. In all the talk about Darlene, we had neglected the most important party.

"What do you think Amanda is doing right now?" I said.

"Sleeping. But she had herself a good cry first. She's going to have a lot of good cries, so leave her alone for a while. She doesn't want to hear your voice any time soon."

"The irony is that technically I didn't actually cheat on Amanda. Kris and I never really . . ."

"'The irony is . . .' Jesus, Johnny, it's a little late to cite technicalities. Face it, buddy, you fucked the dog."

"I know, I know."

I took the last sip of tea. It was nearly dawn. Gray light was mousing across the window blinds. Slinky came up to where I was sitting and curled up on the crook of my arm, something she almost never did.

I said: "Has she seemed a little off to you lately?"

"She's been a little subdued the last couple days. I thought I heard her throwing up in the bedroom while you were out with Amanda. I checked, but couldn't find anything. I'm wrecked. Have you ever been so tired, your eyeballs burned like charcoal?"

"No, but my hair feels heavy all of a sudden. Fortunately, I have a late call tomorrow."

Caroline settled into the sofa as I lowered the blinds, then dragged myself to the bedroom. Kris was sprawled on her back, wearing one of her T-shirts over a pair of my boxer shorts. I turned her over on her side, away from the morning light, undressed, and slid into bed. As my body pressed into the mattress, Kris rolled back over and lay her head on my shoulder, curling her fingers on my chest. Without opening her eyes, she said: "I'm wearing your shorts."

"They look cute on you."

"I thought I heard someone come in."

"We had a mystery guest. She didn't stay long."

"Could we go to the flea market Saturday? I want to buy some tassels."

"Sure, if you want."

Kris murmured something as she dug her head into the pillow. We kissed, and she rolled over to her side. I lay my arm over her stomach and secured her to me, smelling the smoke in her hair.

38

AFTER THE AMANDA FIASCO, my personal life went on temporary hiatus. With my catsitters gone, the apartment seemed sedated,
giving me plenty of quiet space to reflect on how breathtakingly I had
blown it with Amanda. The persistent pang I felt was not so much for
the end of our relationship, but for the hurt I had caused, a hurt that
reflected badly on me. When Amanda smacked me sideways, it was as
if her worst suspicions had been confirmed: men were pigs, and I was a
worse pig, because I had pretended to be better. I also had to consider
Darlene's role in this debacle, her hidden hand.

This was a hazy area to enter. Caroline and I could theorize all we
wanted, but there was no evidence Darlene made that first hangup
call. As for Amanda's call, if I had had a functioning brain instead of
a sponge, I would have let the machine answer it or hushed the girls
before answering myself. If I hadn't been half-sloshed, in other words,
this whole mess might have been avoided. This wasn't an isolated
incident. I had done a fair amount of drinking lately with Amanda,
Caroline, and Kris, being Mr. Conviviality. I'm not someone who
believes alcoholism is a genetic curse, but given my family history, I
needed to keep better tabs on myself. I wouldn't torture myself about
the occasional scotch or beer, but from now on the second drink
would be my cut-off point. And if I couldn't keep to that, I would
enter a twelve-step program. I just wouldn't join one at St. Teresa's,

where too many people knew me. I didn't want to become that familiar a face.

A week after Caroline and Kris departed, I was mulling over an apology I had written to Amanda, reading it aloud to myself for false notes.
As I read, Slinky came into the living room after her afternoon nap.
Usually she strolled in like a gunslinger entering a saloon, but this time
the hitch in her stride was more pronounced, like an injured quarterback limping off the field after a late hit. Caroline hadn't heard wrong:
Slinky had been sick that night, throwing up the chicken she had for
dinner. She hadn't thrown up since, but her appetite was spotty. She sat
on her haunches, and I could see that one eye was duller than the other,
clouded. Combined with her loss of appetite (the night before she
wouldn't even try the baby food I tempted her with), the clouded eye
made me phone the vet. She had a checkup scheduled for next week, but
this looked like it shouldn't wait. They were able to take me that afternoon.

When it came time to put Slinky in her carrier, she offered token
resistance, forgoing her usual rotary-limbed struggle and softly bending in the middle as I lifted her. In the past I had to hold her head down
and zip fast; this time I was able to press it slightly, like a cop easing a
perp into the squad car. The vet's office was located in the basement of
a building on Morton Street. I filled out a card and took her into the
examining room, comforting her during the checkup to prevent a
replay of our previous visit, when she broke loose and they sealed off
the immediate area to foil her escape. Because of her cloudy eye, they
asked me to leave Slinky overnight for additional tests.

It was the first night she'd spent outside of the apartment since I had
adopted her. Now the apartment really seemed bereft.

"Mr. Downs, would you mind taking a seat? Dr. Crowley will be with
you in a moment."

I dropped anchor on a wooden bench. Opposite me was a young man
with a military crew cut, leashed to a German shepherd with front
paws bandaged like a prizefighter's. Sharing my bench was a prema-
turely gray-haired woman rocking a cat carrier on her knees. The carrier had a clear roof, enabling the cat to see and be seen. When it made
a feeble mew, the woman told the cat, "This is what you get." To me,

she said, "She ate the fingers off one of my wool gloves, and now I think the wool's clogging her digestive tract."

A butterball turkey with fur, her cat did look a little backed up. Its entire face compressed with each blink.

"Mine chews photographs," I said. "I have to tuck them in a drawer."

"Napoleon likes photos too, don't you, Napoleon?"

A receptionist wearing a traffic-controller's headset called the woman's name, and Napoleon's owner lugged the carrier down the corridor, one arm hanging low, as if she were dragging herself through customs. The German shepherd stretched its bandaged paws and rested its chin on the floor, sensing that whatever was happening here was going to take a while. I heard my name called.

Dr. Crowley, holding her clipboard like a square discus, was wearing raspberry slacks, which no amount of white coat could cover. I stood, lifting the empty carrier by the handle.

"You can leave that here at the reception desk for the time being," she said. "Let's go to my office before we look in on Slinky."

The hallway echoed with the cries and moans of a miniature zoo. We passed an examining room where an intern was shining a penlight into a rabbit's ear. Dr. Crowley's office was one of those obstructed-window rear offices where the view is always dire. On her desk was a framed photo of her hugging a black Labrador in a green field. As Dr. Crowley's white coat swept around me, her hand patted my shoulder with a note of consolation. Seating herself, she laced her fingers together in front of her with a formality straight out of a counseling guidebook.

"According to our records, Slinky is seventeen years old," she said.

"Really? I've lost track. I thought she was fifteen, but I tend to cut off everyone's age at a certain point."

"So she's had a good long life."

The air between us suddenly took on freight.

"I'm afraid the blood tests and the CAT scan disclosed bad news," she said. "Slinky has a form of cancer called lymphoma. We don't know how far the cancer has progressed, which is why we'd like to authorize another CAT scan for her chest. Once we know how far it's spread, there are several options, none of them, I'm afraid, magic bullets. Would you like me to cover them now or wait for more conclusive results?"

"Now, I guess," I said, feeling as if everything in the last few months had led me to this room.

"First of all, her clouded eye will have to be removed. We're not equipped to perform such surgery, but we would refer you to Manhattan Animal Hospital, should you decide to go ahead with the operation. You may decide not to, for reasons I'll explain. The cancer can be treated with chemotherapy, but chemo won't cure the cancer or spur remission—it may, however, prolong the animal's life. As with humans, it also has upsetting side effects and, frankly, Mr. Downs, I'm not sure Slinky's temperament is suited for regular treatment. This morning, for instance, she tore out her catheter. We might consider steroids, which would stimulate her appetite. Otherwise, she might just wither away from the lymphoma."

"I've never heard of steroids for cats."

"They wouldn't affect her personality, the way they do with athletes or professional wrestlers. We're talking minute dosages."

Dr. Crowley brought her hands, which she had been using to illustrate her points, together again in a clasp.

"The last option is the most difficult one," she said. "If the cancer has metastasized, you need to consider euthanasia. Some people refuse to put their pet to sleep, finding it comforting to provide companionship to the animal in its dying stages; others simply refuse to face reality, hoping the animal will rally. Both responses are understandable, but I must caution you of the danger in trying to get as much time as possible with the animal at the end. In the late stages of disease, Slinky could become incontinent, suffer from dementia, become as cut off from her former associations as someone with Alzheimer's. Seeing her transformed before your eyes can distort your memories of her and the past you've shared. I'm not *recommending* termination, just saying don't let sentiment determine your decision. We must be realistic and think of her first. An animal deserves a dignified death as much as we do. Maybe even more."

"I understand. If we were to put her on steroids or just let nature take its course, how long would she have at the outside?"

"That's difficult to say, but . . . probably six months, tops. We'll know more after further tests, and even then we won't be able to say how many of her remaining months would be *good* months. I realize that this wasn't the conversation you were expecting when you came in this afternoon."

"Can I see her?"

"Of course. In fact, while you're here, would you mind helping us administer her oral antibiotic? We were unable to this morning, she was being so feisty. Your presence should help calm her. Angela?"

A young woman holding a grooming brush leaned into the door.

"We're going to pill #17," Dr. Crowley told her.

"Y'sure?"

"Mr. Downs, Slinky's owner, will assist us. Tell Ramon to bring a clean towel and prepare to act standby, just in case."

I followed Dr. Crowley down a different hall. The noise multiplied as we approached the holding compound, accompanied by a captive odor of pee, dank fur, and moldy straw, though there was no straw to be seen. I was led to a cage where "Slinky Downs" was typed on an index card inserted into a filing-cabinet slot. Taped above the name card and written in ink was the word "Careful!" with small lightning bolts shooting from it. Slinky's cage was the only one with a warning label. I called her name. One ear twitched. Dr. Crowley unlatched the door. As it squeaked open, Slinky, slumped so far against the back of the cage that only her one vivid eye was visible, let out a high, thin, drawn-out cry of abandonment. It was such a self-pitying note, it might have been funny under different circumstances. I floated my hands low toward her, letting her sniff my fingers, then eased one hand beneath her stomach and with the other reached for her scruff. As I lifted her out of the cage, a claw caught on the bar. I carefully unhooked it, calming her by softly telling her what a good cat she was being. Her fur felt like black ash against my arms, as if she were already gone.

Slinky began to wriggle as I carried her into the examining room, where Angela and Ramon were waiting. I set her down tenderly on the silvery examination table. Under the bright overhead light, Slinky splayed her legs, trying to get purchase on the stainless-steel surface. Angela handed Dr. Crowley an oblong pill. I transferred my hold on Slinky to Angela, who grabbed the hinge of the cat's neck. Her mouth snapped open, revealing the upper ridges inside. Her back legs scrambled as she lifted the front ones like a horse pawing the air. Angela got a firmer grip. Pill in hand, Dr. Crowley leaned forward, guiding it toward the cat's mouth. With a quick right paw, Slinky swatted it aside, nearly knocking it out of her hand.

"There, there," the vet said.

Angela tugged at Slinky's head, enlarging the mouth cavity. It looked red as hell inside, inflamed. As Dr. Crowley bent to administer the pill, Slinky jabbed with a right-left combination and snapped at Angela's wrist with her teeth, her rear claws skittering across the exam table. "We're going to have to restrain her," Dr. Crowley said. "Watch closely, you have to do this at home to get her pills down. Ramon, a clean towel."

Angela lifted Slinky by the scruff until her stomach stretched and with two quick twirls Ramon whipped the towel around her midsection, straightjacketing her front legs. The top half of her body bound, Slinky's rear paws skidded against the table and her good eye went white, epileptic. A surge of electricity shot through her, every muscle turned into copper wire, and her thrashing body ascended toward the overhead light, dragging the two pair of hands upward with her, like a swaddled infant levitating in a cone of light. This seven-pound cat seemed stronger than the both of them. I had never seen an animal in such a fury. Then Ramon and Angela wrested Slinky from this tractor beam and subdued her against the table. Ramon twisted the towel tighter as Angela tugged the back of her neck and opened the mouth portal with a snap that indicated they'd all had just about enough of this nonsense. As if sinking a small basket, Dr. Crowley popped the pill into Slinky's mouth.

"Nice shot," Ramon said. "Nothing but net."

We watched and waited, Ramon and Angela relaxing their grips as Slinky's throat showed her swallowing mechanism at work. Her nose made minor sneezing sounds, nasal hisses. Then, like a film strip running backward, the throat movements reversed and Slinky spat and the pill, wet, chalky, and virtually unrecognizable, dribbled onto the examination table. It lay there in a mushed puddle, making its own little statement.

"This isn't going quite as I had hoped," Dr. Crowley said.

"Do you want to tranq her?" Angela asked.

"Maybe I could hold her," I said.

"Are you sure?"

"Just tell me when to tug."

Everyone shifted into position. I pressed my nose against the back of Slinky's head, between her ears. She snapped back at me, trying to bite, but I continued babytalking her as Dr. Crowley shook another pill out of the bottle. She tried to conceal the pill in her palm, but Slinky wasn't fooled. For the next few minutes it was like trying to prevent a falcon from taking off.

Afterward, they told me to wash my hands in the staff's bathroom and apply antiseptic to the wrist where Slinky had sliced me with her claws. The fresh spots of blood on the cuffs of my white shirt looked like hollyberries. Ramon, scrubbing his hands alongside me, said, "That's some feline you have."

"Sorry. She's not used to strangers handling her."

"No kidding. We had a cone on her earlier, for our own protection, and she batted me in the head as I was carrying her back to her cage. It was like getting hit with a giant Dixie cup. I was lucky the edge didn't cut my eye. You're going to have to crush the antibiotics up in her food once you get her home. Either that, or call Siegfried and Roy."

Before I returned to the reception desk to sign the forms okaying further tests, I stopped by Slinky's cage to say good-bye. They had put the cone back on her. Curled up asleep, she looked small behind bars, as if she were reverting to kitten size. I unlatched the cage and stroked her gently as the iguana in the next cage gave me an immortal gaze. The water in Slinky's bowl had a few black hairs floating on the still surface, as if stuck there. I filled her bowl with fresh water and latched the cage.

39

IT WAS RAINING OUTSIDE, one of those dark, all-day rains that blacken the sidewalks. I used the bar phone to call the animal hospital where Slinky's surgery was performed, and was told that the eye operation had gone as expected. She would be kept overnight for observation; I could pick her up the next morning. That night on my way home from work I bought several bunches of flowers from the local deli. I wanted to brighten up the apartment for Slinky's return, partly for her benefit, but mostly to lift my own dragging morale. The apartment was such a cell, I was beginning to feel like the Birdman of Alcatraz without the birds. I was arranging one of the bunches in a vase when the phone rang. I answered in an uptempo voice, not wanting to sound like a moper. It was Darlene.

"Someone sounds chirpy."

"Believe me, it's all an act."

In the background, a TV set was blasting loud enough to leave a hole in the wall. Darlene's next few words were lost in the maelstrom.

"Darlene," I said, "if we're going to talk, you need to turn that monster down. I can barely hear you, and I hate shouting."

"Okay, okay, okay." She disappeared into a roaring mouth of stadium noise. She cut down the volume, and I heard footsteps as she returned and picked up the phone.

"Clete acts like he's deaf sometimes. He can't live without his sports."

"Clete's there?"

"Yeah, waiting for pizza to arrive. We're in this highway motel because everything nearer civilization was booked. *Somebody* forgot to make reservations. What are you so coiled-up about? First, you answer the phone all sweetness and light, then you're complaining about the noise like an old lady."

"My nerves are on edge. I took Slinky to the vet's because her appetite was off, and the tests say she's got lymphoma. They may be able to keep her going with chemo or steroids, but it depends on how far the cancer has spread. I feel guilty for not taking her to the vet for checkups the last couple of years. Maybe they could have caught the cancer earlier if I hadn't let things slide."

"Guilt gets you nowhere. You're being too hard on yourself. How old is that cat?"

"Seventeen, according to the vet's records."

"Well, that's too bad," she said. "It's never easy losing a pet, but you can't hold on to her forever. She's had a good run. Something was bound to catch up with her sooner or later. I know how devoted you are to her, but maybe it'd be better for all concerned if you just did the right thing and had her put to sleep. That way, she won't suffer and you can get on with your life. That cat's been holding you back from going out and meeting people for years. Never mind Nicole and the others, *she*'s been your one true love."

"I wouldn't go that far."

"I'll never forget the time right after we met when I heard you use the word 'slinky' over the phone so tenderly I thought you were talking to some girlfriend hanging around the apartment. 'C'mere, slinky . . .' I thought, Johnny must be dating some skinny actress. Turned out you were talking to the cat! It was sort of endearing, the way you babied her, but she also became your all-purpose excuse for getting out of everything you wanted to get out of. You're the only man I know who let himself get pussy-whipped *by an actual cat.*"

"Gleason thinks I'm pussy-whipped by you."

"He's just jealous."

"I know I've doted on Slinky, but I want to do what's best for her. If it's hopeless, I'll put her to sleep. But if the vet says she has a few good months left—"

"You'll what, play Florence Nightingale? What's the point of dragging this out? It won't change the end result. I think maybe you like the idea of being a martyr. 'Oh, there's Johnny, nobly sacrificing himself for his cat.' That's the Catholic side you insist on cultivating. Listen, she's your cat, your responsibility, you do what you gotta do. Let me get to why I called, since this is costing me money. My mother's been giving me a lot of static lately about Clete, and instead of telling her we were going to the NASCAR races together, I told her I was heading north to stay with you for a week. I gave her your number so she'd think everything was on the up and up. On the off-chance she calls to check up on me, reassure her I'm up there having a great time, et cetera, et cetera."

"What do I do if she asks me to put you on the phone?"

"Tell her I went to a Broadway show or something."

"Which show? We should have that straight in case she asks you later."

"I don't know. You're the theater expert—pick one. She won't know one show from another. Just give her your best reassuring guidance-counselor voice and tell her I'll be driving back Monday night and should be back in Decatur on Tuesday. Tell her I'll bring her back a souvenir. I still have a *Jekyll and Hyde* poster from my last trip, so I'll just dig that out when I get home."

"I don't know about this."

"What's the problem?"

"I'm not comfortable lying to your mother, Darlene. I feel funny lying to people I've never met, especially people's mothers."

"Don't think of it as lying, think of it as spreading a little ground fog, if that makes your precious conscience feel any better. What's with this sudden attack of virtue? You've lied your own ass off pretty good lately. You wouldn't have gotten laid otherwise."

"At least give me your motel number, so that I can let you know if your mother calls and throws me a trick question. You know how mothers are."

"You don't need to call me. I'll call you. You're making this more complicated than it is."

"Are you and what's-his-name planning to—?"

"His name happens to be Clete."

"'Happens to be' is right."

"What?"

"Nothing. Forget it."

"What, you think I have some other man here? I don't fuck around, unlike Nicole or some of your other playmates. You realize Kris has a boyfriend in Athens she was cheating on when she wrapped those pretty legs around you? She's a very sweet kid, but kind of a slut."

"I don't like hearing her talked about that way."

"Too bad."

"I guess that's why you encouraged her to stay with me even though you knew I was dating someone else. You think we're all patsies."

"Kris was driving up with Caroline anyway. I didn't stick her in the car! I didn't hand her top-secret instructions! It's true I didn't give you advance notice she'd be arriving with Caroline. I thought it'd be a nice surprise. Don't blame me because you couldn't keep it zipped while your girlfriend was out of town. You wanted to stray. Amanda was too bossy, and you know it. She was fluffing you up for the kill. Didn't you tell me the first thing she talked about in your apartment was having your cat declawed? If you can't figure out the symbolic message in that, I'll make a drawing and fax it to you."

"It was still early in the relationship for us," I said. "We might have gotten somewhere if you hadn't thrown a monkey wrench into the works. What were you doing calling her about some cockamamie antique? Since when have you been so interested in that stuff?"

"Since I inherited this ugly armoire from my aunt. I wanted to find out if it might be worth something, or if it was a hunk of junk. And I admit, I was curious to hear what she sounded like on the phone, get my own take on her when you weren't around. How was I supposed to know she'd call you as soon as she got off the phone with me and Caroline would pick up? I certainly didn't tell her to grab a cab downtown and bust in on your little dance party! The fact is, you could have sent Caroline and Kris packing before she returned and spared yourself all this angst, but, no, you were feeling cocky, having those two flounce around. You were the one playing Hugh Hefner."

"I don't claim to be a saint."

"No, but you pretend to be a nice guy, which is worse. You act like you've got a big heart attached to your dick. But the truth is, you never sounded in love with Amanda, the way you did with Nicole."

"Maybe I'd still be with Nicole if I had followed my own instincts. I now think we should have met at a restaurant or over coffee instead of in my apartment. It might not have made a difference, but your calling out of the blue didn't help."

"Nicole? We're still talking about Nicole?" Darlene said. "I thought you were over her. So maybe we made some tactical mistakes, so what? If it'd been up to you, you'd have been on the phone, begging and pleading. You didn't even have the balls to be angry with her. You beat up on yourself instead. At least this way things ended in a draw and you were able to preserve some dignity. For what, I don't know."

The motel television went back on, as loud as before, maybe louder.

Raising my voice to be heard over the din, I told Darlene: "Maybe some of what you've said is true—"

"Some?"

"—but the point is, I feel guilty about the way I've behaved. All this conniving seems cheesy, and I don't want it to become second nature."

"The way it is with me?"

"I didn't say that."

"You didn't have to! Fuck, you act as if all I do is think up lies! As if it's my whole career! The advice I gave you, the pep talks, they weren't all lies. I didn't lie when I said you had potential, though maybe I was lying to myself. If it weren't for me, you'd still be a Baby Huey."

"You know, I'm tired of you taking shots at me. I used to think your insults were a form of affection, like rough-housing, but now I think you really do believe I'm this piece of Silly Putty you can bounce around. I'm not putting up with that anymore, Darlene. I appreciate your being in my corner when it counted . . ."

"Gee, thanks. You 'appreciate' me. That's something you say to some-one you're showing out the door, and if anyone shows anyone the door, it'll be me. I'm not the one in pathetic need of companionship. Unlike you, I have someone in my life, someone who's more man than you'll ever be."

"Oh, yes, the legendary Clete."

"What's that supposed to mean?"

"Why don't you put him on the phone? I'd love a chance to talk to the man behind the legend."

After a micro thought-processing delay, Darlene said: "Clete has better things to do than waste his time talking to a half-man like you. Considering how much I've done for you over the last few months, con-sidering how I single-handedly dragged you out of depression and put you back on your feet and instilled some confidence in your sorry self, it seems to me the *least* you could do is head off my mother if she calls and not be a prig about it. But if you won't, you won't. I'll call my moth-er myself and tell her something, that way you won't have to tell anoth-er lie and feel oh so cheap inside. Tell you another thing, next time I see Caroline, I'm going to whip her fat ass, because I know she's the one who's been feeding you this crap."

"Oh, give it a rest."

"I need a rest. From you."

"It's not about me. When we first met, you were fun, you were interested in all kinds of things, you weren't taking potshots every five minutes. Now all I hear is how strung-out you are from all the manipulation and plotting and last-minute changes of plans. The best thing that could happen 'for all concerned' would be if Bud—yes, Bud, *like the beer*—dragged himself away from the TV, put on his penny loafers, and went home to his family, where he belongs. Then you wouldn't have to lie anymore and be on the lam like a couple of grifters." My saying the unsayable—Bud's name—shocked Darlene into almost unprecedented silence. Then she said:

"I'm going to nail Caroline to a cross."

"No, you're not," I said, laughing. "You talk tough, but deep down you're no tougher than I am."

"That's what you think."

"No, here's what I think. I'd miss you if we stopped being friends. You're not honest enough to admit you'd miss me."

"Before we start missing each other, there's something I'd like to say."

Darlene set down the phone and muted the motel TV. To this day I wonder if I would have stood up to her if it hadn't been for that set blasting in the next room, upping the anxiety level. I heard the return of Darlene's footsteps. She picked up the phone. In a level voice that called attention to its own control, Darlene said:

"I just want to mention that I once chided you for not knowing my birthday and you insisted on writing down the date. Well, my birthday was this week, and did I get a card or call from you? No. No, I did not. So the next time you're feeling like applying for sainthood, you might want to ask yourself how much you truly care about the people you say you care about, and how conscientious you are when it counts. And since you dredged up his name, I have news for you. Bud isn't going back to his family. He's going to divorce his wife and marry me. And on that note, fuck you, forget you ever knew me, and good-bye."

There was a click on the line, followed by a flatline hum. I hung up the phone. I had been gripping it so hard there was a red bar across my palm. I shook out my wrist and stood. The ear that had been pressed to the phone popped open like a submarine portal, letting in a flood of sound from the outside world.

40

I BROUGHT SLINKY HOME from the hospital. She seemed lost at first, wobbling from room to room, her protective cone banging against the walls like a beggar's cup. She made several attempts to leap on top of the kitchen counter and misjudged the distance, landing on the floor with a muffled thud. In frustration she began scraping her neck against the door frame, trying to pop the cone off of her head. I would gently pull her away and talk to her as if reasoning with a child. There was nothing else I could do. The cone had to stay on for at least two weeks so that the cat couldn't reach the eye stitches with her scratching paws and risk infection. After the third or fourth try, she gave up on getting the cone off, and sunk like a shadow to the floor. She barely ate, though she swallowed her antibiotics without much trouble, and slept for hours lying on her side as if forsaken. I cashed in one of my mutual funds to pay for her medical expenses, wondering if it was worth running up any more bills. I stayed home at night, fleshing out my play and listening to the radio, waiting to see if there were any signs of improvement. Kris invited me to visit her in Cambridge, but I didn't want to leave town until the situation was resolved. That fall and winter, I was mostly catsitting.

Once Slinky's cone came off, she continued to list to one side, hugging the wall like Lee Marvin in *Cat Ballou*. But her jumps improved as her vision adjusted. One afternoon I came home after tending bar and

she met me at the door for the first time since she had returned from
the hospital. She followed me into the kitchen, where I rewarded her
with a special treat, feeding her bits of fresh chicken that she snatched
from my fingers with her jaws, both paws clapped around my wrists.
Her appetite returned as if it had a lot of catching up to do. There was
a spark of greed in her good eye, the sewn one as black as a pirate's
patch. "Not so fast," I said, as her head snapped at my fingers. As I
wrapped the remainder of the chicken in silver foil, she bent over her
water bowl, refilling like a supertanker. When she was done I carried
her to the sofa and set her on my lap, breaking open a vitamin E capsule and dabbing the oil on my fingers. I massaged it into her fur to
nutrify her coat, which was still wispy, and then brushed her fur, something she had never let me do in the past. As I drew the brush back
between her ears, Slinky lifted her chin and bared her teeth, grinning
like a small crocodile.

41

AFTER DEMONSTRATING the smooth action of his new cross-country ski machine, Gleason stepped off and pretended to pat copious sweat from his brow. He was in his workout socks, having removed his shoes Japanese-style upon entering. He made me do likewise, saying he just had the rug shampooed. It looked as if Mary Poppins had taken a magic whisk broom to his apartment. Ancient scuffmarks had been erased from the walls, piles of clutter banished, the windows scrubbed clean. Sunlight, normally a stranger in these parts, cascaded in. My former jukebox, polished and stocked with fresh oldies, occupied a corner spot, almost gleaming with pride. On Gleason's coffee table were a matched set of new coasters replacing the corked assortment of yore taken from various places where he had tended bar. Our bottles of beer were resting on them now. But the biggest change was with Gleason himself.

He had dyed his hair. It was now as black as an oil slick, glistening when he turned his head and catching the light like the hood of a new BMW. Not knowing how sensitive he was on the subject, I didn't make any wisecracks or let my jaw drop in shock-horror when I came through the door. I wondered if he was wondering if I noticed.

"I've only been doing this cross-country crap for about a week, but I can already feel it through here," Gleason said, running his hands under his Mets sweatshirt along the region of his stomach where his lats were submerged.

"So what made you spring for it?"

"I was rehearsing this thing a few weeks ago that required me to get up from the couch to answer a doorbell. It was a real low-slung couch—I had to exert a ton of pressure on my heels just to uproot my ass. After the fifth or sixth run-through, I was so winded the director had to call a break. It was embarrassing. So I decided it was time to get myself in gear, before I completely fall apart. Would you like some pretzels? I can't eat them—too much salt—but there's no reason you should starve."

Gleason, who lived in an apartment building jutting over Times Square, which rented mostly to Broadway actors, dancers, and other mad dreamers, had invited me over to watch *Catwalk*, a show we had kept religious tabs on as roommates. It featured the latest footage of models slivering down the fashion runways of New York, London, Paris, and Milan, and together we used to critique the models and fashions in intricate, utterly uninformed detail. I was surprised when Gleason invited me over to watch it with him, since it had been years since we had even mentioned the show to each other. Unfortunately, *Catwalk* was being preempted this afternoon by some standoff in the Mideast involving a hijacked plane. Gleason kept the TV on mute in case CNN returned to its scheduled programming, which didn't seem likely, given that their cameras had been trained on the same strip of Tarmac since I had arrived. Meanwhile, the two of us sat there in our socks and waited for something to unfold.

"This reminds me of an idea Hector Franks once had," Gleason said. "He was watching riot footage from the West Bank where protesters were throwing rocks at the police. Suppose, he thought, one of those teenagers had a wicked arm that could knock off an Israeli soldier's helmet at fifty paces. Cut to this baseball scout down on his luck watching riot footage in his ratty motel room. An electric fan blowing in the background, flipped-open pizza carton on the table, the usual. The geezer grabs the next flight to Tel Aviv, hunts the kid down, and brings him to America to teach him how to pitch and use that arm to make money on the mound rather than throw rocks at people who shoot back. The kid becomes a sensation, and the scout wins the respect not only of his sneering peers but the daughter he abandoned as a child."

"Somehow I can't see Hollywood making a movie about a Palestinian pitching prospect . . ."

"Yeah, but here's the hook: *The scout is Jewish.* Teaching the kid base-ball becomes a way to break down the barriers of distrust between Arabs and Jews. So now it's not just a movie about sports, it's got the brotherhood of man going for it. That's the kind of bullshit those cyn-ical Hollywood idealists can't resist. All excited, Franks went off and bought a book on screenplay writing, loaded up on drugs, and whipped off the whole thing in about three weeks."

"Did he ever sell it?"

"I guess not, otherwise we never would have heard the end of it. 'Hi, guys—guess what?—I just fucked Paramount.' He does have his own website, though, where he posts publicity stills, stage credits, fan let-ters, his future itinerary . . ."

"He posts *fan letters* on his *website?*"

"He probably writes them himself, hoping others will chime in."

"At the risk of being lumped in with Hector, I'm progressing pretty well with this thing I've been working on."

"You're writing a get-rich-quick screenplay?" Gleason said, turning his head fractionally my way.

"No, it's for the stage."

"Don't tell me you're writing a *play?*"

"It's not really a play. It's more of a theater piece, about a group of guys in a self-help group."

"You realize the group thing's been done. There was *The Connection*—of course, that's going back a ways, and that thing with . . ."

"I know it's been done. Everything's been 'done.' But this is a group of men trying to manage their anger. They do a lot of role-playing, and through the role-playing, where they pretend to be both sexes, we learn that at the bottom of their anger is a fear of women. At least I think that's where it's going. I've been spending most of my nights working on this, using color-coded index cards for each char-acter and diagramming the conflicts between the men almost like football plays. I've got the sequence down now. I just need to fine-tune the dialogue."

"You should hear yourself. You're on the verge of becoming preten-tious."

"I appreciate your support." I set the beer on the coaster.

"Don't get sensitive on me. So what are you going to do when you're finished, put on a little puppet show?"

"For your information, Phil Green is interested in the older-guy group-leader role. He and I hit it off last time we worked. I'm meeting with him next week to go over the first draft. He wants to do something that offers a change of pace, especially now that he's being phased out of *Last Ray*."

"If Phil's interested, this thing might actually come to something. Is there a part for me? Want another beer? I'll even pour it for you."

"No, thanks. One's my limit. Anyway, it's far from done at this point. I've got a lot of tinkering to do."

"Well, get with it. None of us are getting any younger. I assume you're writing yourself a part."

"I'm going to play a guy who's been told all his life that he needs to express his anger, and the first time he does he gets arrested."

"That is so you. If you have enough spare time to be this creative, it must mean things have slowed down in the romance department."

I told Gleason about the breakup in rough-sketch form, leaving out some of the more embarrassing details, such as the framed portrait on the mantel with the lipstick collar.

"As it happens, I heard something about this from an interested party," Gleason said. "Incidentally, this is the second girlfriend who gave you the boot before I got a chance to meet her. What gets me is, here you were with these *Hee-Haw* honeys lounging around the apartment and you never once invited me over. I guess you were just too selfish to share. So what's Darlene say about all this?"

"She and I aren't really speaking. We had a slight falling-out."

"Whoa," Gleason said, extending his hands as if halting traffic. "I need to absorb this. This is better than the Mideast. You got *dumped* by your latest girlfriend, you're tending to a sick cat, *and* you had a falling-out with Darlene? You're on a roll! If your luck gets any worse, you can become a blues singer. You and Darlene were too tight for it to be 'a slight falling-out.' It must have been more like a midair collision. I want a complete blow-by-blow."

Before I could answer, I heard a key turning in the lock of the apartment door.

"That's probably Kate," Gleason said.

The door pushed open and in popped Kate, the bartender I had met before, hauling a heavy shopping bag. She kicked the door shut behind her, then set the bag on the floor. I stood, and seeing me stand, Gleason followed suit. She slipped off her shoes and set them next to ours. Kate was dressed much girlier than when we had first met.

"Kate, you remember Johnny," Gleason said.

"Need any help with the groceries?" I asked.

"Go ahead, make me look bad," Gleason said. "I would have offered to help."

"That'd have been a first. No, thanks. You two just sit and watch your supermodels. Why do you have the sound off?"

"Because there's some half-assed crisis in the Mideast that's preempting regular programming," Gleason said. "You'd think nobody'd ever seen a hijacked plane before. By the way, I saved you a beer, lambkins."

"Did you do your twenty minutes on the CC Flex?"

"No. I did about twelve, okay, ten, and then Downs here interrupted me just as I was getting into a groove."

"Maybe you could do another ten minutes tonight to stay on track. You don't want to start backsliding. Johnny, don't you think Tom's already looking better?"

"Yes, and no wonder. You should have seen him pedaling away."

I imitated Gleason on the cross-country machine, blinking hard and braving the lashing snow.

"I know you're teasing," Kate said, "but I really think he's making progress."

"Oh, I agree. His rosy vitality was the first thing I noticed, aside from how clean the rug looked for a change."

"I just had it shampooed. Tom, I bought more bananas."

"Oh, great. Super. Wow. Groovy."

"Bananas are good for you. You know you need more potassium."

"Potassium," Gleason repeated in a mutter, as if this was what it had all come to.

Kate went into the kitchen. Not only did she have her own key to Gleason's apartment, but she was now storing away the groceries with the swift hands of someone who had arranged the shelves to her liking. It was also clear that the cross-country machine wasn't Gleason's purchase or idea, but a message gift from her. She was moving in a chunk at a time, which would also explain the new adobe-orange Santa Fe-style bedspread in the bedroom (Gleason usually hibernated under a down comforter). In another month or two, his things and her things would be one big family.

Kate plunked on the couch and kissed Gleason on the cheek, curling her stockinged feet on the edge of the coffee table. His remote control at the ready, Gleason switched to a bowling tournament, where a bowler was blowing on his fingers like a safecracker before gripping the ball. Kate said:

"Tom, how come you're not wearing your slippers?"

"I used one of them to kill a bug. Before you barged in, babe, Downs was telling me about this exciting 'piece' he's working on."

"I didn't know you were a writer," she said, with just a hint of wonderment.

"He hasn't quite come to fruition," Gleason said. "Downs, did I tell you I saw Mistress Claudia at Actors' Study recently?"

"No. How was she?"

"Who's Claudia?" Kate asked. Ignoring her, Gleason said:

"She was in a German one-acter that dates from around when Fassbinder was directing plays, I'd guess. It had that grubby feel, like being in limbo with the dregs of the welfare state. The characters had to share a couple of ratty-looking cots. Claudia was better than okay, for her. More real and unguarded than before. It was a shock seeing her without her long hair. It suggests some element of self-hate, her cutting her hair. I mean, why would you subtract your greatest asset? It'd be like a dancer saying, 'I think I'll go in for stumps.' Well, it's not an exact analogy, but you know what I mean."

"Did you talk to her?" I said.

"Oh, sure. Afterwards, I waited to tell her how good she had been. Since she actually was good, it meant I didn't have to lie, which is always a relief. I mentioned that I might tell you about the workshop so that you could catch it, and she snapped her eyes away and said, 'Don't bother.' When I asked why, she said, 'He fucked my friend Amanda over. I thought he was better than that.' I assured her you weren't. At any rate, the woman detests you. Congratulations."

"I guess she can join that long line of people who are fed up with me. Did Claudia say anything else about what she's doing acting-wise?"

"Acting-wise, no. But I found out, get this, that she's now working as a personal shopping assistant at Bergdorf's."

"Men's or women's?"

"Men's. Maybe she's meeting rich businessmen and running a one-woman call-girl racket out of Bergdorf's. You never know." In a lurid announcer's voice, Gleason intoned: *"Shopgirl by Day, Call Girl by Night: The Claudia Prentiss Story."*

"Phil Green has a personal shopper," I said. "She's going to help me pick out a sports jacket."

"I'm sick of hearing about Phil Green," Gleason said. "What is he, your father?"

"Never mind that," Kate said to Gleason. "Tell me about your play. What's it about?"

"It's not a play, it's a 'suite for voices,'" Gleason said with a fruity lilt.

I gave Kate the same summary I had given Gleason, but with more particulars about the individual characters, since she actually seemed interested.

"Are there any women in the cast?" she asked.

"No, but I have role-playing scenes in which the men play women."

"That may not be enough. Because, you know, without a woman in the group, women in the audience are going to feel there isn't anyone on stage representing their interests. Let's face it, it isn't going to be easy getting women to sit and listen to the problems of a bunch of angry men."

"I see your point. My friend Kris said something similar. Well, as I say . . ."

"Yeah, we know, it's still in the dicking-around stage," Gleason interrupted. "Quit putting doubts in his head, Kate. Right now Downs needs encouragement, otherwise he'll never get this damned thing finished. He may look like a load, but he's sensitive, like me."

"Johnny doesn't look like a load, and neither do you. Another month on the bike, and you'll be able to fit into those new jeans you just bought."

Having scored a direct hit, Kate stood, gathering the empty bottles from the coffee table. On TV, one of the bowlers missed an easy split. The bottles clinked as she put them in the recycling bag. When she emerged from the kitchen, I could tell she was about to initiate a tonal shift. "I was wondering if I could get you to do us a favor—take a picture of Tom and me on the patio. The little camera I have has a self-timer, but we don't have a level place to rest it out there with that wind. Would you take a shot or two of us?"

"Sure."

Kate retrieved a camera from the bedroom, a small Olympus point-

and-shoot that made my fingers seem big and bumbly. She opened a sliding door and moved a round metal table aside, positioning herself at the corner of the terrace. The popcorn-kernel clouds above us looked like the aftermath of a spectacular air-and-sea battle. Kate motioned with her hand for Gleason to join her. He shambled over and rested his arm on the railing behind her. I crouched a little to frame the clouds into the background, which I knew would look impressive on film. As I was about to click, Kate said: "Not yet. Tom, put your arm around me."

He draped one arm around her, his hand hanging over her shoulder like a bear paw. I peered through the viewfinder and pressed the shutter. Gleason's smile only took up half of his mouth, but when Kate smiled, her entire face snapped open. I shot the rest of the roll, trying different angles and arm placements and taking a couple of shots of Kate standing alone. She liked posing. Her eyes connected with the lens. The camera whined as the film rewound.

We went back inside, closing the patio door.

"Do you want anything from the fridge when I get back?" Kate said, implying a visit to the bathroom.

"No, we're fine."

She walked away, adding a comic wiggle to her walk. Gleason crossed his legs at the ankles and resettled on the couch, crushing a throw pillow.

"So how does it look?" he said.

"How does what look?"

"My hair."

"Looks good. It takes a little getting used to. Does Kate know?"

"'Does Kate know?' Women know everything. Who do you think's dyeing it? I don't think the eyebrows quite match yet, though."

"They'll require further experimentation."

"Oh, shut up. I'm sorry I invited you over."

"Kate's not."

"What do you mean?"

Sounding to my own ears like Darlene in full throttle, I said: "Don't play dumb. You invited me over here knowing she was going to pop in. To Kate, that means you're letting other people know you're a real couple. Why do you think she wanted pictures taken? She's building a scrapbook of your life together. You should have seen her face when I took the pictures of you two—she was *beaming*. You, my friend, looked like one of those big marlins Hemingway used to pose with at the dock. Face it, Tom, you're hooked. Next thing you know, she'll be proposing that the two of you and me and somebody go on a double date."

"Don't be too sure. From what I told her, she thinks you're a bad influence on me."

We both had a hearty alehouse laugh over that one.

"So do you think it's love?" I said, keeping my voice low.

"That's a word I have no faith in," Gleason said. "What's it to you, anyway?"

"I just don't want to see you blow a good thing."

"Oh, like your record with women is so stellar."

The toilet detonated with an explosive flush and we reverted to TV-staring mode. Entering the kitchen and half-opening a cupboard door, Kate said, "Should I make us some popcorn?"

"No need," Gleason said. "Downs is just about to leave."

"Really?"

"Yes, I really should be going. I have to tend bar at a private party tonight, so I need to go home and shower. Let me know how the pictures come out."

"I'll get a second set made. Tom, see Johnny to the door."

"He knows where the door is."

"*Tom.*"

"Oh, all right."

I retrieved my shoes and sat in a small chair by the door, tying the laces. I stood and put on my jacket. I took one last look around and said, "I can't get over how much cleaner the carpet looks."

"Believe me," Kate said, "it was some operation. Tom, would you mind going out with Johnny and stopping at the deli? I forgot to get saffron for the rice tonight. They sell it near the front in those little plastic tubes. Ask for it if you don't see it."

"I know where they sell it," Gleason said, grabbing his jacket by the neck.

42

I TENDED BAR NEW YEAR'S EVE, and nearly went home with a waitress catering the party, until I realized she was on a coke high, her babble making less and less sense as her gestures became more and more emphatic. Another waitress offered to look after her, and the three of us ended up having coffee at an all-night diner as drunken revellers threw up in trash cans to the cheers of their friends. Weeks passed until one afternoon when the wind shook, I wound a scarf around my neck, pulled on a stocking cap, and batted a pair of mittens together, preparing for my expedition to The Copy Café, where I was going to drop off the first draft of *Learn to Duck*, the working title of my play. Because someone was moving into an apartment on a higher floor, the elevator was in constant use. I took the stairs down to the lobby and passed through the bare aluminum bones of the awning, the canopy-cover having been torn off during a previous storm. That storm also brought cold, pelting rain. This was a dry invasion. Leaning into the cold blasts, pedestrians pressed forward on the flat sidewalk as if they were straining uphill. I was blinking away tears when I spotted The Copy Café, whose stenciled windows were steamed, giving a false illusion of old Vienna. Inside, the place appeared devoid of human life, a deserted outpost with all the machines on standby alert.

Wiping my eyes with the heel of my mitten, I spotted a familiar figure at one of the copying machines. Her back was to me, but the pixie haircut was the property of Annette Bennett, who seemed stymied, judging by the set of her shoulders. She retrieved a printed sheet from the landing tray and balled it up in her hand, lobbing it into a trash can which contained a heap of rejects. She pressed a couple of glowing icons on the control board, crossed her arms, and waited for the next copy. I could see her faint reflection in the unsteamed part of the mirror, her downturned eyes with their upturned lashes, her thoughtful brow. Where most people dressed for the bitter cold in drab, bulky shells, some of them resembling walking igloos, Annette looked trim and put-together in a padded red Chinese jacket and matching mukluks. I snuck around from behind, carrying the manuscript box in both hands. When I was close enough to peek over her shoulder, I lifted the manuscript chest-level high, and, altering my voice, said: "Miss, would you mind if I cut ahead of you? This won't take long."

Annette turned, glimpsed the size of the manuscript I was holding, and swung her head full around to determine what form of fool she was dealing with. Then her face half lit up and she said: "Oh, it's you. You almost scared me! I thought you might be some creepo."

"Sorry about that. Speaking of creepos, I tried calling you a few months ago, and this real sweetheart answered. I thought he might be your boyfriend, so I didn't call back, not wanting to rile up a possible pyscho. I guess he didn't pass on my message."

"No, that was my roommate's boyfriend. She's since moved out, thank God. I was wondering why I hadn't heard from you."

"I'm glad we ran into each other then. It's good to see you."

We brushed cheeks within an awkward embrace, my L. L. Bean coat capable of housing two.

"Don't you have a copy place closer to home?"

"This is near the place I buy my darkroom supplies. I like to do everything in one go-round."

"You seem to be at a standstill here," I said.

"I can't quite get the shading I want."

Annette retrieved a fresh copy from the tray. The image on the page was of two vivacious actors (one male, one female) grinning like contest winners, their cheekbones about to pop. Under their faces, in big letters, were the words PUT YOUR BEST FACE FORWARD! and a block of smaller text I couldn't quite read. We chatted as the copier hummed and a line of green light crawled lengthwise under the protective cover.

"I'm sorry. I'm sure this is probably boring for you," she said.

"Not at all."

"You sure? You looked a little spaced out."

"Thinking has that effect on me. I was considering maybe getting some headshots done myself. I don't need any actor ones, but maybe I should have some done for the program when they stage this thing I've been working on. A playwright's photo—you know, one that makes me look like I possess inner stature."

"You've written a play? When did this happen?"

"You make it sound as if scientists have discovered a new moon. It's not that incredible an event."

"Sorry," Annette said, smiling. "You just don't look like the type who agonizes over words."

"You're so wrong, and the masterpiece I hold in my arms proves it."

At the next copying machine, a flannel-shirted employee crouched by an open panel, trying to yank a wad of paper jammed between the rollers.

"To be honest," Annette said, "I guess I thought you might be one of those people who dabble at something without ever finishing. You know, a dilettante."

"Actually, I've been spending the last few months looking after my cat, Slinky, who's got lymphoma. With all that time on my hands, I had no excuse *not* to finish. Right now it's just a one-act, so it's not like I embarked on some epic saga."

"So what's it called?"

"Learn to Duck."

"Is it a comedy?"

Annette turned her eyes toward me. They were green and spirited, the eyes of a Jane Austen heroine who prides herself on being amenable in polite society but undeceived. Her eyelashes, long and piquant, added a playful air. She brushed a strand of hair behind her ear, putting it in its place.

"Well, there are some funny moments, but it gets pretty intense toward the end."

"I'd love to read it. I wouldn't offer a critique or anything, unless you *wanted* one. It'd be fun to see what you've concocted."

"I could use the female point of view, I guess."

"I can only give you my point of view, John. You know, not all women think alike."

Momentarily distracted by how nice it was to hear Annette pronounce the shortened version of my name, I forgot my place in the conversation. Fortunately, at that moment the copy machine stopped. After Annette gathered her stack of flyers, we went to the front desk, where the front-desk man was discussing the pros and cons of buying versus renting with a man stocking up on bubblewrap. She paid for her copies, which the front-desk man evened into a neat pile and placed in a carton. I set my manuscript box on the counter and ordered three sets, to be billed to Phil Green. After we both conducted our business, there was a pause. Neither one of us seemed eager to go.

"Would you like to have coffee?" I said. "Or hot chocolate?"

"Sure! That'd be great. I just can't stay too long. I have to shoot an engagement party tonight."

"Because they have a coffee shop right through here . . ."

"Johnny, I already said yes."

"I know, I just thought I'd complicate things."

We crossed through the ribboned curtain leading to the cafe section of The Copy Café, pausing on the other side and taking a quick survey. In the corner was a kid reading Kerouac. There's always a kid in the corner reading Kerouac, but this one looked as if he had been marooned on the same page for hours. The only other customer was a man circling personal ads in the *New York Press.* Standing guard behind a slanted display case of sliced cakes and big round cookies was a waitress scratching her throat and looking as if she wanted more from life. She observed us standing in the doorway and leaned on the counter as if to challenge us into declaring our intentions. *In or out?* her posture said. "Let's scram," I said.

"You sure?"

"Let's try Highland Fling. It's not far."

Outside, windows shuddered as the wind cracked a thin branch loose from a scrawny tree, flinging it like a stick across the street. Across the street a woman slipped and fell.

"Is it much further?"

"No. I can see it just ahead."

Lacking sled dogs, we struggled arm in arm, double-teaming the wind. Once we made it to Highland Fling, we stowed our caps, scarves, and gloves in our pockets, and handed our coats over to a tiny coatcheck girl wearing a tam. As we entered the tea room, a pair of spinsters who looked as if they had a lot of bones to pick with the world were vacating a spot near the fireplace. We pounced before anyone else could claim dibs. In the fireplace fat logs burned and crackled with royal abandon. From above the fireplace protruded the head of an antlered stag, its head wrapped in a tartan. We ordered tea, which seemed the civilized thing to do. Drawing back her bangs with both hands as if giving her brain an opportunity to breathe, Annette said: "It's like being in another world in here."

"I know. There's nothing like a fireplace. I wonder where they get those logs from. They're *huge*."

"Well, I'm sure you could ask someone if you really need to know."

"No, no, that was just me thinking aloud. Have you ever been to Scotland?"

"No."

"Me neither. But I intend to go someday, check out those moors. I'm half Scottish, on my mother's side."

Annette took a reflective look at the fire, then turned full toward me. She had something on her mind other than moors. The waitress arrived, bearing a teapot covered in a tartan cozy, and poured us each a cup. Annette took a test sip, then blew on its surface. A man from a nearby table rose and stood before the fire, ostentatiously warming himself, putting his hands out flat and rubbing them together as if to restore vital circulation. Then he turned and presented his fanny to the fire, rocking back and forth on his heels like a country squire. Annette and I stared at him with mutual fascination mingled with mock-horror and bordering on admiration. When his rear end was sufficiently toasted, the man reversed himself and warmed his hands again before toddling off to his table of loved ones.

"He reminds me of one of my uncles," Annette said. "When he mixed drinks at parties, he'd do this little rumba as he shook the cocktail shaker, as if he were in one of those musicals set in South America. It mortified the rest of the family, though we kids thought it was hilarious. Or, as we used to say, hilaire."

"They don't make uncles like that anymore."

"It's true. He died a few years ago, Uncle Milt."

"I have an Uncle Milt! He's still alive and has a French bulldog, which has put ideas into my father's head. Is your father still around?"

Our second pot of tea arrived shortly thereafter, as Annette was telling me about fishing trips her father used to take her on, before his Parkinson's.

43

IN FEBRUARY, I HAD A WORKING LUNCH with Phil Green in which we went over the play. Incorporating some of his suggestions and diplomatically ignoring others, I revised *Learn to Duck* and we began to round up actors for what's called a "cold reading." Since the play was set in a church basement, I prevailed upon Father Grady to let us use one of St. Teresa's meeting rooms so that everyone could get a feel for the atmosphere. The night of the reading Father Grady greeted us at the church gates, rubbing his hands together for warmth as he led us down the dim hall, most of the lights having been turned off to save money on electricity. Inside his office, which was as cloaked in shadow as a mafia don's greeting room, he and Phil ceremonially shook hands and traded comments on each other's vintage watches. Father Grady removed his to show Phil the inscription on the back, which had been dictated by Cardinal O'Connor.

"I have to apologize for the boiler going down," he said. "We have a man coming tomorrow to bang on it, but until then I put a space heater in the meeting room, which should keep it from getting too cold. I've never seen the soap you're on, but I remember seeing you on stage in the late seventies in a revival . . ."

"It was probably *A Drink Without Remorse.*"

"That's it. I remember the actors staring straight ahead as they spoke their lines instead of looking at each other."

"That's one of the awful conventions directors insist on in memory plays. That, and keeping the stage half-dark. Somebody turns on a light in an Eugene O'Neill play, it's like a major scientific advance."

"And then with that fog in the second act . . ."

"Well, actually, it was supposed to be smoke from the nearby burning fields, but a lot of the audience mistook it for fog. I'm surprised you were able to catch the play—we didn't have much of a run after the *Times* killed us."

"I had just arrived in New York and was up for everything after being overseas for two years. Art exhibits, concerts in the park, you name it. These days, any time I attend something cultural, I dread what might be in store. I don't mind the shock effects as much as I resent the notion that they're *for my own good*, to roust me out of my moral slumber. One thing I learned from my work as a military chaplain is that in real life, shocks numb people, and the worse the shock, the deeper the numbness. After a while, your response system shuts down."

"A few years ago a producer called to ask if they could make a mold of my head for a movie about a serial killer who kept his victims' heads in a freezer," Phil said. "He said he wanted to use mine because it was so 'distinguished.' I asked to see the script, which annoyed them, since they wanted a quick yes. And no wonder. Turned out it was for a scene where the serial killer tried to force one of his female victims to kiss my severed head on the mouth. I decided I didn't want that to be part of my legacy. I have grandchildren to think about."

I wanted to ask Green whose head they eventually did use as a prop, but didn't want to interrupt him and Father Grady. They were standing with their arms crossed, rocking back on their heels, like two umpires chatting between innings.

"I'm pleased that you're letting us use the room for the first couple readings," Green said. "You're not afraid the groups here will feel their privacy's been invaded if they find out we're basing a theater piece on them?"

"Aside from my assistant, Mrs. Cole, whom Downs here can vouch for, no one knows you're using the room tonight. If word leaked out, the only ones who might mind would be the men in the original anger workshop, and they disbanded about a month ago because of some factional dispute. There's no privacy concern as long as Downs here isn't planning to degrade us all with some scathing exposé."

"I'm blowing the lid off this place!" I said.

"So what was Joel Geller like to work with?" Father Grady asked Green.

The heavy clomp of shoes down the hall indicated new arrivals. When we were assembled, Father Grady herded us into a different meeting room than the one where I did my readings. The coils of the space heater glowed orange, warming the immediate air, but the floor seemed cold despite our bundled feet. "I'll be in the chapel if you need me," Father Grady said. "Do you want the door open or shut?"

"Shut," I said. "And no listening in on the intercom."

I intended it as a joke, but Father Grady gave me a football-coach stare and said, "Call me if you need anything."

There were six of us in the room—Green, Gleason, Steve Mullin, Ron Fairlow, Gregory Watson, and me. Mullin and Fairlow were part of the AA group from *The Last Ray of Hope*; Watson, a black actor sporting cool-nerd eyeglasses, was invited by Gleason, who had met him at the Apollo barber school near St. Marks Place, where he was an apprentice clipper. Except for Green, who was wearing a pullover sweater and cuffed slacks, everybody was dressed like undercover cops, in blue jeans, sweatshirts, and layers of T-shirts or longjohns. We were a thick band of men.

We each pulled a plastic chair from the stack in the corner and formed a semicircle. I remained standing behind my chair with an armful of scripts as everyone got settled. I was feeling an onset of stage fright, a tightening in the throat at the prospect of hearing my words read aloud for the first time. Gleason, who had brought a thermos and some extra cups in his backpack, was pouring coffee for the others. Taking a silver flask out of his pocket, he proceeded to pour whisky into his own. He wiggled the bottle for the benefit of anyone else who was interested in a taste, then screwed the cap back on and tucked the whisky in his coat pocket, patting it affectionately. I had never seen Gleason do this at a reading or rehearsal before. I looked at him, and he winked at me.

When I had everyone's attention, I said, "Before I distribute the piece, I'd like to make a few comments."

There were a couple of muted groans.

"Learn to Duck," I continued, "is about a men's group that meets once a week to discuss and deal with managing their anger. Some of them

are compelled to attend as part of a plea bargain—it was either this or jail time—and others have come on their own or been referred by a shrink. So it's a mixture of your average hotheads and hardcore cases. In the piece itself, there'll be a coffee machine at right rear, and I may decide to incorporate the space heater—the orange glow on a dark stage might make a neat effect before bringing up the lights. Since this is a piece that will require us to reveal ourselves and unload a lot of personal baggage, I thought that before we begin we might go around the room individually and talk about ourselves a bit, about something private we wouldn't normally share, an adolescent rite of passage, perhaps. I was thinking maybe as an icebreaker we could all describe the first time we masturbated, and whether or not we felt shame."

Several chairs squeaked as the actors shifted position. Phil Green ran a concerned finger under his chin. The brief silence was broken by Gleason, who said:

"Just hand out the goddamn scripts, Downs. I need to get home by ten."

"Me too," Watson said. "I have a late date."

"Okay," I said, passing out the scripts, "if that's the way you feel about it. Maybe another time."

"The ink on my copy's a little faint," Mullin said. "It's hard to read."

"Here, take mine."

Since it was a cold reading, the actors read as neutrally as they could, as if they were doing the farm report on the radio. About fifteen minutes into it, Gleason freshened his coffee with another nip of whisky, and began looking even softer around the edges. Given that Gleason had the storage capacity that went with a big frame, I could only assume he had been drinking before the reading, since this amount alone wouldn't have been enough to affect him so fast. He tucked the flask into his coat pocket, its small neck protruding. We got to the part where he and Watson role-play Watson's tantrum at a restaurant when he finds they've lost his reservation for his anniversary dinner with his wife. In the role-play Watson will be the snooty maitre d' and Gleason the customer, so that Watson can see what anger looks like from the other side.

The two read their role-play dialogue straight until Gleason started to do his in black dialect, sounding like George Jefferson and ad libbing, "Weezy! This honky here done lost our reservations! He ain't no maitre d', he's a maitre don't!"

"Who you callin' a honky, Negro?"

"'Negro'! I'll put a knee to your gro'!"

This choice bit of repartee got everyone chortling, even Green, whose face normally resisted humor except for the occasional pinched smile. I chuckled a bit myself so as not to seem like a killjoy, but it privately bugged me, not only because Gleason and Watson broke protocol by cutting up during a cold reading, but because this exchange revealed that they were more than acquaintances, they were buddies, and buddies are allies, and allies are trouble. They clearly thought they were the jokers in this deck. As Gleason was reading his lines, there came an apologetic knock at the door.

"Come in," I said.

Father Grady entered, carrying another space heater wrapped in a black electrical cord.

"Sorry to interrupt, but we had this one in the choir room and I thought it would help. It can get like a meat locker in here."

Father Grady set the heater on the floor, unwound the cord, and plugged it into the wall. Now we had two heaters going, like twin speakers. Father Grady stood as the second heater began to warm up. Soon its coils glowed orange too, encompassing us with warmth.

"Thanks, pops," Gleason said. "Now how about bringing in some snacks?"

Father Grady began to smile until the rest of his face decided against it. He stepped toward Gleason, leaned into his face, and said, "Son, you're a guest in this church. You mock me again and I'll bounce your ass out of here so fast you'll develop rhythm."

Then Father Grady reached forward and tucked the top of Gleason's flask into Gleason's coat pocket until it completely disappeared. With that he left, leaving the door open behind him rather than slamming it for extra-dramatic effect. Gleason, who along with the rest of us had jumped inside his skin when Father Grady leaned forward, put a drawl into his voice and said: "Well, I guess he told me."

"I guess he did."

"I wouldn't gloat, Downs. It's not as if you would've stood up to him. And what are you snickering about, Watson?"

"Nothing I need burden you with now," Watson said, leaning back satisfied.

"I've seen you pussy out before," Gleason said.

Fairlow burped and banged a fist against his chest, which triggered another round of commentary.

"Maybe we should get back to the reading, which is why we're here," Green said. "The dry air in here is bad for my throat, and I have a scene to shoot tomorrow morning."

Suitably chastened, we resumed the reading and got to the end of the play without further incident, although there were a couple of stifled giggles along the way from the two soul brothers, and one of the space heaters died on us.

"At this point," I said, "we hear a rap at the door, which tentatively opens. It's a pregnant woman, who says that her group has the room next. As the guys shuffle out, she hangs up her coat, that's when we see how pregnant she is, and begins shifting the arrangement of the chairs somewhat. She erases the blackboard, and as she begins writing new letters, the stage lights dim."

"Why is she pregnant? Is that meant to be symbolic or something?"

"That's just how I picture it."

"He's tapping into his unconscious," Gleason said. "'It came to me in a dream.'"

"Well, that's the piece, and I welcome suggestions, though maybe we should meet another time to exchange notes. I can always add lines later. Or cut. Whatever."

"Don't be so diffident," Green said, standing. "There's solid meat here, Downs. The role-play scenes take the piece in all sorts of interesting directions."

"Thanks."

"I'm impressed," Watson said. "At the beginning, I thought—but by the end—"

"Thanks . . ."

Gleason said: "You might want to tweak that part early on where the one guy says, 'Is he dead?' and the other guy says, 'No, he's deaf,' because 'dead' and 'deaf' are such soundalikes the audience could get confused. But, yeah, otherwise, you did good. Having established that, could we please clear out of here posthaste and shift our asses to a respectable bar? These space heaters have me hypnotized."

"I have to get uptown," Phil Green said. "But you guys go."

A look crossed Gleason's face that said Thanks for your permission, gramps, but for once his lips didn't move. We put on our coats and roped our scarves around our necks. I unplugged both space heaters, having read too many stories about their bad habit of bursting into flames. I went to Father Grady's office and thanked him for the use of the church, apologizing for Gleason's behavior, which he shrugged off as no big deal. I guess he had dealt with a lot worse in his time. As I crossed the courtyard of St. Teresa's, the city lights beyond the fence gave the impression of being fixed in place forever. Through the gates I spotted the gang, huddled on the sidewalk in a broken circle, presumably trying to decide which neighborhood bar to hit.

"Hey, Downs," Mullin said. "We were debating whether or not you really expected us to share our first jerk-off experience back there."

"No, I was mimicking the kind of director we all hate, who wants us to open up and 'share.' I thought you'd realize I was kidding—I had no idea I'd be so convincing."

"Yeah, you had us going there for a minute. We're heading over to Petey's, maybe shoot some pool, check out the new waitresses."

"No, thanks. I want to go home and jot down some notes before I forget."

I had been uncomfortable during the reading, trying to concentrate on how the play tracked while keeping tabs on my own character's lines. If this play were to actually happen, I might have to excuse myself from the cast and watch from the sidelines. The part I had written for myself fit a little too easily; it lacked muscle tone. Another actor might bring something new to it, something I could bump up in the rewrite stage. It was something I wanted to mull over.

"You're not mad about us goofing around before, are you?" Watson said.

"No, I just want to get home."

"If he doesn't want to go, he doesn't want to go," Gleason said. He turned, and the others fell in behind him, forming an unsolid block.

44

SLINKY DIED IN THE EARLY SPRING. I got home late one night after tending bar at a private party held in a new hotel in SoHo. I was tired and jangly, my ears buzzing from the technopop music blasted from the loudspeakers flanking the bar. In the elevator, I tugged on the front of my white shirt to air myself out, looking forward to a nice hot bath. When I turned on the light in my apartment, I saw a black shape on the floor. It was Slinky, slumped in the hallway. At first I thought she might be sleeping, but when I called her name, neither ear twitched in response. Her good eye stared blankly ahead. She was gone. From the way she was lying, one leg outstretched, she must have been waiting for me to come home. I knelt beside her and stroked her stomach fur, kissing her one last time on the top of the head. I wrapped her body in her favorite blanket and set it inside her carrier, zipping her inside. I drew myself a bath, feeling old as I lowered myself into the steaming water. The next morning I called the vet.

As New York law requires, Slinky was cremated. A few days later I picked up her ashes after work from the vet's. They were sealed in a brown ceramic jug with a cork plug. Around the bottleneck was a pink ribbon bearing Slinky's name.

"Think of it this way," Dr. Crowley said. "You had some good months with her at the end. She held on about as long as we could have hoped. She was a very resilient cat."

"I know. I just wish I hadn't been out so late. That way I might have been with her at the end."

"She may have needed you to leave so that she could let go. She may have been hanging on for you. That's not uncommon among pets. We sponsor a support group here for those bereaved by the loss of an animal companion, if you're interested. It might help you through the grieving process."

"That's okay. I can do my own grieving."

"Let me give you an information sheet anyway. Ramon also wanted to extend his condolences."

"Tell him I said thanks."

I signed the remaining paperwork on Slinky at the reception desk, using a credit card to pay for her cremation.

A few days later, I received a flower bouquet with a condolence card signed by Mrs. Cole and other staffers at St. Teresa's. In a separate envelope was a card from Father Grady expressing no sentiments of his own. Instead, above his scratchy signature, was a passage copied from Ecclesiastes. The passage read:

> *I said in my heart with regard to human beings that God is testing them to show that they are but animals. For the fate of humans and the fate of animals is the same; as one dies, so dies the other. They all have the same breath, and humans have no advantage over the animals; for all is vanity.*

I wondered if Father Grady had that passage handy for all of his parishioners who lost pets, or if it had popped into his head about me in particular. I suppose it didn't matter. The words went home either way. I rested the card on the mantlepiece against the jug containing Slinky's remains and set the flowers where they would catch the best light.

45

THE LOFT WHERE ANNETTE RENTED her photo studio was in a thin, exposed building shelved like a library book between two parking garages in the flower district. Each parking garage had its own sentry box, where mustard light festered behind a wire-meshed window. At night, after the flower shops had closed, the neighborhood was taken over by drug dealers, their customers, and staggering representatives of the undead. On a winter weekend afternoon like this, however, the sidewalks were bare. The few people on the street looked as if they had wandered in the wrong direction.

In the lobby of Annette's building, painted an enchanting shade of blah, I pressed the chipped UP button, setting giant pulleys into motion. A freight elevator clanked to the first floor. I levered open the door, pressed 3, and the elevator ascended, doors and floors passing vertically across my eyes like a giant film strip. Annette was waiting, leaning against the door as if it held some tantalizing secret. As I reached for the elevator handle, she said: "Wait, I have to unlock the gate first. I see you got a haircut."

"Well, I was looking at the playwrights' photos in various *Playbills* and most of the male playwrights looked like they had spent the winter holed up in a cabin. So I thought I'd shoot for something less scruffy."

Once I was let out of the cage, Annette continued inventorying me with photographic interest, one hand fingering a demure string of pearls. She was wearing a pink T-shirt under a V-neck cashmere sweater and dancer leggings, a collegiate look I've always liked, despite the fact that none of the women I knew in college ever dressed that way. Having completed her survey of my upper slopes, Annette asked if I wanted coffee.

"No, I'm jittery enough."

"You get nervous having your picture taken? I thought you ate it up."

"I do. I must be jittery for other reasons."

"I'll be gentle," Annette said, laying a hand on my forearm and giving me the benefit of her eyelashes. As she crossed the warm gold of the wooden floor, her walk carried a note of elevation, as if she could rise any moment on tiptoe. Unlike most photo studios, this one was more than a blank slate. The floor was covered with overlapping rugs, which took some of the chill out of your classic loft space. Lining the sills facing south were bonzai plants that looked more like symbolic bits of nature than actual green life. Against one wall was a leather Freud couch whose elevated end was covered with a silk shawl decorated with the signs of the zodiac. Near the rear wall of the studio, the only wall that was windowless, a wooden stool sat on a white sheet that ran from a secured hanger above and behind the stool and curled up a few feet in front of it, creating a flowing ski slope.

"I'm ready if you are," Annette said. "Why don't you take a seat?"

She adjusted the wooden stool, moving it an invisible degree. I edged myself onto it, thinking of all the photographs of celebrities from the fifties and sixties I had seen posing on wooden stools for album covers and publicity stills, how they braced their legs for support while still managing to look as if they were ready to jive. Annette looked into the viewer of a Hasselblad mounted on a tripod, then drew a scrim across the part of the window getting the biggest load of sunlight. Then she took a meter reading off my face. From where I was perched I could see the blue neon sign of a fur store. After subduing even more of the afternoon light, Annette took another light reading, her knuckle grazing my cheek. She looked at the numbers, but remained where she was.

"Would you mind if I patted down your forehead? It's a little shiny." Annette fielded a hand above her eyes, as if warding off a blinding Spanish sun.

"Okay," I said, "I think you've made your point."

She opened a makeup case banked on the floor and I sat like a ventriloquist's dummy, silent and still, as she powdered my forehead. I noticed her fragrance but didn't want to ask its name just yet. She combed my hair, smoothing it back along the sides and neatening the part. Then she took one last look and returned to her camera. She peered into the viewfinder, adjusting the manual focus, then looked up at me.

"Since your play has both comedy and drama, I thought what we'd do is take some serious shots and some looser ones as well so that you could go either way, depending on how you want to promote it. For the first few rolls, don't force a smile. Be as serious as you want, just try not to scowl."

Using a Polaroid back, Annette fired off a shot, a light flashing from a single white umbrella. She tore off the foil and we waited as the instant film developed.

"Do you want to see?" she teased.

"No, that's okay."

"I thought all actors liked looking at themselves."

"No, that's a myth. An accurate myth, as it happens, but . . ."

"You look good," Annette said, looking at the developed Polaroid. "Very handsome, in fact. Give me a sec to attach the film back."

When all was in readiness, I raised my chin. Light flashed from the white umbrella, spotting my eyes. We paused as I placed one foot on the lowest rung of the stool, letting my other leg support my weight. I made a series of body shifts and chin adjustments as Annette shot the rest of the roll.

"If I had an assistant, he or she could just hand me reloads. Unfortunately, I have to do it myself, so you'll have to hang tight. We have to finish by five, anyway, so don't worry, I won't keep you all day."

"Hot date?"

Never ask a woman her Saturday night plans! Darlene's voice rang in my head.

"Dinner with friends. They're one of those awful married couples, if you know what I mean."

"Not really. All my awful friends are still single."

"Rita and Jay are always telling you things you already know, things everybody knows, as if they've just made an exclusive discovery." Putting her thumb to her chin, Annette said: "'Ironically, Europeans appreciate the indigenous art form of jazz much more than we do here in the States.' And then there's . . . 'The French, of course, consider us utterly puritanical and hypocritical when it comes to sex. Over there, Monica Lewinsky wouldn't have raised an eyebrow.'"

"Well, the French can have her, and we'll throw in a free beret. So how'd you get trapped into dinner with these two?"

"Rita's a sorority sister of mine from Penn. She and her husband caught me off-guard by calling and saying they were in town and wanted to get together. When people call you from out of town to tell you they're coming in, you can beg off by talking about all the work you've got to do, maybe we could all meet for a quick drink instead, all that. But when they're already *here*, it's hard to say no because you feel as if they can see into your apartment and know you're not doing anything. I'm just not up for a big night out. What would you do in my situation?"

"I'd probably go and pretend to have a good time while studying their marital behavior from behind the menu. Now that I'm a self-styled playwright, that's what I do, observe life. I just wish there was something worthwhile to observe."

Scrolling past that comment, Annette took a moment's silence and said: "Let me pat down your forehead—it's gleaming again. Then we'll rip through another roll. Would you mind if I played some music?"

"No, go ahead."

Annette turned on a radio with big white knobs tuned to a station that played mostly Sinatra, Tony Bennett, Peggy Lee, and Nat King Cole. "This is the music my father listened to when I was growing up," she said. "It gave me this mental picture of what Manhattan was like, which I didn't know then was already ancient history. I really thought New York was going to be *sophisticated*. Cultured. Instead, it's all about money. That's what I get for being naive."

"I was naive when I first came to New York."

"How long did it take for all your illusions to be stripped away?"

"Oh, about a week."

Annette's eyes switched to another topic. "Would you mind if I slicked your hair back?" she said. "I want to see how it looks."

"Sure."

Annette wet a comb under the running water in the sink and, as I sat on the stool, she reparted my hair and combed it back. I inhaled her smell, now a mixture of citrus scent and honest labor. She was so reachable that I had to will my hands to remain at my sides. She removed the camera from its tripod, holding it waist-level and balancing herself with a slight bend to knees. She motioned for me to move the bench out of the frame. The radio station went into a Chet Baker medley, his frail, romantic vocals creating an intimacy that shuttered the outside world as Annette hovered around me, taking sideways cha-cha steps as her camera clicked to the inflections of the music and the white umbrella flashed.

"Wait till your female fans see these photos," Annette said.

"I appreciate the compliment, but it raises the question, 'What female fans?'"

"The ones you're going to have after you become a studly playwright, all those actresses who'll be chasing after you."

"I've had actresses running after me before, some of them waving knives."

"No, you haven't."

"Okay, I haven't. But, believe me, I'm also not staying up nights fantasizing about being the toast of Broadway, or off-Broadway, or however far down you want to go in the *Village Voice* listings. Like most projects, this play could easily bomb or never get staged."

"Don't talk that way. Remember, I've read it. I know how much it has going for it. The thing I can't quite figure is how you can write so well about men's anger without being an angry person yourself. I really can't imagine you losing your temper."

"I don't let myself get angry. Some people have said that by not letting myself get angry I'm just storing it up inside until one day I'll EXPLODE. But I've had plenty of opportunities to explode like an oil tanker and I never have, except this one stupid time in college. I'm just not an angry guy, and the next person who says I am is going to get creamed. By the way, I've been meaning to tell you since I got here—that's a terrific cashmere sweater you have on."

"You like it?"

"Definitely."

Annette lifted her head from the viewfinder and said, "I thought you would."

After the shoot, I waited at the elevator as she switched off the lights one by one. It was like watching someone strike a set. We rode down in the elevator together, standing close but honoring each other's personal no-fly zone. When the elevator reached bottom and stopped, I asked Annette if I could fix her collar, which was uneven in the back. "Thanks," she said when I was done. It wasn't her conversational voice, more like a voice overheard, a single word making a soft landing.

As we were walking to the desolate corner, I told her about Slinky.

"I'm sorry to hear that," she said, laying a hand on my arm. "Your friend Gleason told me in the cab that you and your cat were inseparable."

"He probably told you that to make me sound like some old maid."

"Well, if he did, it didn't work. You must miss her."

"It was hard at first. I still can't quite get used to the hush in the apartment now. I've had very consoling dreams about her lately, which I guess is part of letting go. She could be such a demon when she was alive, and in these dreams she's practically a little saint. I know it's ridiculous, romanticizing a cat that way."

"I grew up around horses. I remember some of them better than I do my best friends from back then. Did you have a happy childhood?"

"It had its ups and downs."

"Maybe Slinky represented some childhood longing that wasn't satisfied until she came along. Then again, I had a happy childhood, and I still dream about my first horse. So there goes that theory."

"Not necessarily. Annette, would you like to have dinner next week? I was thinking of The Blue Danube near Lincoln Center. A lot of the after-ballet crowd goes there, especially now with the dance companies doing their spring seasons."

"Are you a ballet fan?"

"I used to go when I first came to the city, but I could hardly get anyone to go with me, and the few who did found it silly, or the female dancers too anorectic, or the atmosphere too 'rarified.' I even had a subscription for a while, but let it lapse years ago and haven't been back much since."

"I have to confess: I've never been to the ballet in New York. I keep meaning to, but . . . ."

"Really? You carry yourself like such a dancer that I assumed you were part of the scene. I just thought you might be more into modern stuff."

"I took dance lessons as a child, but I don't think they had the lasting effect my parents did. They drummed into us kids the importance of good posture."

"Gee, mine never did. They drummed a lot of other things into us, but not that. So would you like to go?"

"I'd love to."

"Great. I'll get us tickets for New York City Ballet, and we'll have dinner at the Danube afterwards. Be sure to wear your chinchilla. Are you taking a cab home now?"

"No, I'm going to catch the bus."

"Maybe I should wait with you."

"Aren't you going downtown?"

"Yeah, but still."

"You don't need to be concerned. I'll be fine."

"I know, but I'd feel better knowing you got on the bus safely. This area gets a little creepy after dark."

The bus stop was nothing to sing about either, with its bent girders and a diamond spill of shattered glass. Annette slipped her arm through mine and leaned into me, answering with a physical *okay*. Specks of rain began to fall. There was only one other person waiting at the stop, but the first bus that pulled up took itself out of service due to a problem with the wheel alignment, forcing its passengers to deboard. Twenty or so weary travelers set their shopping bags down like suitcases and periodically craned their necks down the street with a growing sense of injustice. Some gave up hope and tried to flag down a scarce cab, only to return to the refugee camp scowling. Numerous cell phone conversations went on simultaneously, some of the callers cupping a hand to their other ear and repeating what they had just said in a louder voice. A terrier being carried in a designer totebag began to bark.

"And you were worried about me being stranded alone . . ." Annette said in a gently teasing voice.

Across the street came the thunderous rattle of an Indian shopkeeper lowering his shutters.

46

PHIL GREEN DECIDED TO THROW A PARTY for the first public reading of *Learn to Duck*. His rationale was that most readings were humdrum affairs, and the prospect of a party afterwards—an added treat—would make the audience more receptive to the play. He rented the upstairs room at Calliope, an elegant snake pit in the West Village whose upstairs windows were usually lined with men and women holding stemmed glasses and miming laughter. The upstairs walls were painted a tawny yellow so that big shots could bask in their own glow. Springing for the party was a generous gesture on Phil's part, but it wasn't entirely selfless. This was his first project since being put out to pasture on *The Last Ray of Hope*—I think he wanted to prove that he still had some juice left. He even invited some of the younger stars from *Last Ray* to the reading, perhaps to show those pretty faces what he was capable of doing on stage. He said they would help gloss up the party afterward with their dopey sex appeal, something everyone appreciates.

The expense-account aura of Calliope was quite a contrast to the theater we booked for *Learn to Duck*, a former labor hall named in honor of John Reed, which seemed musty with old arguments that history had rendered moot. The hall's chief attraction was its raked seating, which drew the audience's attention deeper into the action through sheer force of gravity, if nothing else. On the night of the reading I arrived early, pacing the lobby to walk off nervous energy. One by one, the other actors arrived like poker players for their weekly game, nodding to me as if further words were unnecessary. Only Phil Green, dressed like a defrocked priest down to his scuffed black shoes, looked as if he weren't there to move a piano. He made a point of establishing strong eye contact as he shook my hand and told me everything was going to go gangbusters. Gleason, carrying a Starbucks bag, offered me a cup of coffee, which I declined. In the antsy state I was in, the last thing I needed was a burst of caffeine. I was saying my hellos in the lobby because I had decided to make myself absent backstage. Since bowing out of the cast, I felt like something of an intruder, and I knew from my own experience that the last thing an actor needs is the author hanging around backstage like a hospital visitor, spreading worry. Instead, I watched the audience arrive, including a fresh posse from *The Last Ray of Hope*, who didn't seem to know what to do with their hands without adoring fans to wave to. Behind them a town car slid to a perfect stop. Wearing a silver lamé minidress that reflected light like a disco ball, Claudia Prentiss appeared on the arm of a Hugo Boss-type who looked like an inside trader who hadn't gotten caught yet. Claudia bowed her head like royalty and wished me luck. I nodded to Kenny from *An Oasis for Fools*, who gave me a big thumbs-up as his date took a swig from a bottle of Evian water he was carrying in case of sudden drought. Unraveling his scarf, Father Grady entered the lobby and approached me without preamble. "Is it assigned seating?" he said.

"No, sit anywhere you want."

"Good. I always prefer an aisle seat in case there's a fire. Now if this is a success tonight, I hope it won't so go to your head that you'll stop volunteering at St. Teresa's. Don't go Hollywood on us, okay?"

"Don't worry, I won't."

I greeted a couple of coworkers from Buzzy's and spotted a few producers and casting directors I knew mixed in with the civilians. I received a mild shock when my agent Marj arrived, clutching the arm of her husband Harold, whom no one had ever heard speak. "Where are the restrooms?" she said. "Harold needs to wash his hands." After I sent Harold in the right direction, I entered the theater to take a seat by myself in the back row. Annette and I agreed beforehand to sit apart, since I knew I was going to be a quivering mass and didn't want to inflict that on her. I also wanted to be able to watch the play without being influenced by anyone around me. From my vantage point, the theater looked less than half full, not bad for a first reading, especially since the front rows were packed. I could see the back of Kate's head as she doodled on her program, a four-page flyer that had an artfully blurred cover shot of St. Teresa's taken by Annette, along with stamp-sized inside shots of Phil Green, a group shot of the cast, and a separate one of myself. For these pictures, Annette received a photo credit that could easily be read under a magnifying glass. Annette herself was nowhere in sight.

The stage was bare except for six folding chairs and a space heater placed dead center. A dark green curtain hung across the rear of the stage, hiding a concrete wall. Members of the audience popped cough lozenges and candy mints into their mouths while others checked their watches or made vital entries into their Palm Pilots. A vague restlessness filled the air. The plan was that we would allot an extra five minutes for latecomers; at 7:05 Green would take the stage and make a few introductory remarks. They waited until 7:07. With a studied modesty it takes a lifetime to achieve, Phil Green entered from the side of the stage as some couples in the audience continued their conversations. He said: "Since I'm not miked, I would like to say a few words without having to *shout.*"

Claudia's date closed the clamshell on his cell phone.

"I want to welcome everyone here for the first reading of John Kennedy Downs's *Learn to Duck.* As many of you know, Downs is an actor who's been in a number of plays and commercials and this is his first effort. We met on the set of *Last Ray,* where he played the bartender trying to keep me from drinking myself to death. He managed to get on my good side, which, as many of you know, isn't easy. Since Mike Felton, whom many of you will recognize from his recurring role on *Sesame Street,* joined the cast late, he'll be reading from the script for practically the first time, so, I trust, you'll make some allowance. Believe me, what he'll be doing tonight is quite a departure!"

As Green spoke, a silhouette appeared at the top of the stairs, then entered the light. It was Annette, wearing a smart blue beaded dress and a short haircut, shorter than before and parted wet to one side. I knew I'd be glad to see her—what I didn't expect was to feel a thrill. She saw me in the back row, seated almost parallel to where she was standing, and gave me the AOK sign, followed by a thumbs-up. A few heads swung in her direction, causing Green himself to pause and take notice. Somewhat sheepishly, she slipped into an aisle seat a few rows down, right behind Father Grady, who was tapping his knee with a rolled-up program.

Green concluded his remarks and left the stage as the first two actors entered. One of them turned on the space heater. The stage lights slowly brightened. The reading began. The characters were still exchanging pleasantries when there was a tremendous crash backstage, followed by a smaller receding clatter, like a loose hubcap rolling to the side of the road. The audience laughed, but I could see Fairlow flinch. Felton, the actor replacing me, said, "Uh, actually, that's not part of the play. I don't know *what* that was."

The audience laughed again, more tentatively. Once he had their undivided attention again, Felton held the script flat in front of him, but was unable to find his place. Claudia's date snickered. Fairlow pointed to the line where they had left off. They started again, faltering over the next few lines.

I could hardly bear to watch. The men on stage didn't seem like flesh-and-blood creations but transistorized broadcasts of what I had imagined in my head. Their voices sounded tinny and unconvincing to me. When you're in a play, you're tense backstage, but you know you have some control of the situation once you're under the lights. Now I was just a glorified bystander. I had handed the car over for others to drive. I found myself squinting at the stage between my drawn-up knees, ready to shut my eyes at any moment, the way I used to brace myself for the gory parts in horror films.

Gleason entered, his burly manner drawing a few chuckles as he lowered himself on his folding chair as if offended by such dinky seating. I have to say this: he had authority. The power dynamics on stage shifted as soon as he dropped anchor. But after that anxiety spike I had gotten from the crash backstage, I was too agitated to sit still. As discreetly as possible, I unwedged myself from my seat and stood at the back wall of the theater, dropping my head so that I could listen to the play and hear the words in their pure form, without visual distraction, disembodied. As the actors became attuned to the theater's acoustics, their voices got more conversational, just loud enough to make the audience complicit. The thing began to knit into shape. They got to the part where Green drafts Fairlow and Felton to perform a role-play as husband and wife, Felton being the wife. He has them face each other sitting down and begin each sentence with the words "It hurts me when you . . ."—"It hurts me when you make fun of my ties."—"It hurts me when you comment on other women."—"It hurts me when you stay out late without calling." The hurt statements escalate until the two are accusing each other of every crime in the book and leap to their feet, nearly crushing Green as he tries to separate them. The actors really made the scene work. They smacked their lines clean and hard, like baseballs out of the batting cage. But when I trained my eyes on the stage I realized there was still something off, something missing.

I edged away from the wall and stood in the stairway, where I couldn't see or be seen. Now I could only hear laughter and other word-less responses as the dialogue sounded like a radio playing in a distant room. The laughter came with greater frequency, tapering off into quiet as the last role-play ends with a confession that leaves the others speechless. There was a brief pool of silence, followed by an isolated clap (probably from my agent), which was answered by others and then mul-tiplied into genuine applause. I took one last glance at the stage and saw the cast lining up to take a bow. I could still hear the applause when I reached the lobby, which I took to be a good sign. If it had been dying-quail applause, the kind that poops out in midair, it would have been over by then. I hurried to the bathroom to splash cold water on my face so that I could look refreshed when I met my public. Marj's husband Harold was already there, patting his face with a paper towel.

Annette wasn't waiting in the lobby but on the steps of the meeting hall, where she was twisting a rolled flyer in her hands. She gave me a hug that had a lot of lift to it and kissed me on the cheek. "You play-wright you," she said. "It was great!"

"Really? There were a couple sections, though, where I thought—"

"Why's your shirt collar damp?"

"I splashed some cold water on my face afterward and kind of over-did it. Would you mind if we walked to the restaurant? It'll give my shirt time to dry, and I need to get the blood recirculating. I was stand-ing so stiff, my knees seem to have locked. By the way, don't think I haven't noticed how stunning you look tonight."

"I wanted to look good with all those actresses swarming around."

"What actresses?"

"Please. I saw Claudia leaving in her silver lamé dress."

"Oh, that old thing."

The brightly lit upper room of Calliope came into view, with all its balloons. Before we went in, Annette paused on the sidewalk and turned, blocking my steps.

"Can I say something to you before we go inside?" she said.

"Sure."

Annette lay her fingers lightly on my chest.

"You're going to get a lot of compliments tonight on the play," she said quietly. "Don't shrug them off or crack jokes the way you usually do, okay? People don't *want* their compliments swatted aside. Now that things have gone well tonight, stand up for yourself. Accept your due. That doesn't mean you can flirt with those soap-opera actresses, especially that redhead with the nasty cleavage. I saw her staring at you in the lobby."

"I'm afraid I'm not familiar with her. You'll have to point her out to me. Anyway, I wouldn't count on me getting swamped with congratulations. Once some of these people have had a few drinks, they'll feel free to dish out advice. The theater's full of Mr. Fix-its."

What I didn't say to Annette was that for some reason I had more stomach-butterflies over the party than I did over the reading itself. I really wanted to turn around and call it a night. Sensing something, Annette squeezed the top of my arm, signaling everything was going to be all right. I nodded, and we resumed our walk to Calliope, whose front door was being held open for us by a princely young man who said, "Welcome."

47

THE CATER-WAITERS WORKING THE PARTY seemed to circuit the room on grooves cut into the floor, like carved figures in a German clock. When Annette and I made our entrance, Phil Green led a round of applause for me, and those whose hands weren't full joined in. Instead of motioning for them to stop, which was my first impulse, I heeded Annette's advice and acknowledged them with a suitably abashed nod I borrowed from somewhere in the memory banks before introducing her to Green and a couple of actors who remembered me from *Last Ray*. As others came to offer congratulations, Annette excused herself. Pulling a compact camera from her pocketbook, she went on safari around the room, snapping pictures. She said she wanted to have a permanent record of the event, something for the old scrapbook. I maintained visual surveillance as I yammered away, wanting her to know she hadn't left my mind in case she looked my way. As I sipped champagne, I heard the unmistakable hoofbeat of Gleason trudging up the stairs, the remaining cast members trailing behind.

Met with a round of applause, Gleason saluted and dipped his head, as if it were intended solely for him. He separated from the others and presented himself to me.

"Congratulations, Bard of Avon," he said, clasping my hand.

"Oh, knock it off."

"We gave you up for dead. You know, it doesn't do much for the cast's confidence to see the author take a powder fifteen minutes into the reading."

"That crash backstage put the fear of God into me. It seemed like a bad omen. What was it, anyway?"

"The lighting guy, none too steady on his feet I might add, knocked over a ladder, which hit an empty paint can. I thought Green was going to have a heart attack. Have you seen Kate?"

"She's here somewhere. Why didn't you walk over together?"

"We did, but I had her nip in ahead of me so that I could make an entrance with the guys. You know, showmanship doesn't stop at the end of the stage. So where's your date? It took her forever to find a seat."

"How do you know?"

"I was peeking from the wings. She's looking quite delectable tonight. I don't remember her being that leggy at your party. Of course, then I was staring down at her and this time I was staring up. The angle of view was different."

"You were checking out women from the *wings*?"

"No, she just happened to arrive while Green was gassing away and we were all waiting to go on. Watson was the one who pointed her out to me. 'Check that out,' I believe were his exact words. So how is she?"

"What do you mean?"

"What do you mean what do I mean? Since when do you and I need a translator? You know what I mean. In the saddle."

"We haven't really got to that point yet. We're pacing ourselves," I said, uneasy at being questioned so directly and possibly being overheard.

"Wait, you haven't struck gold yet?" Gleason said. "How long have you two been dating? I don't recall you ever 'pacing' yourself before. Maybe you need to go in for a checkup. They have a lot of new drugs on the market that might help."

"Do they have a drug to make you go away?"

"This is the thanks I get for busting my hump out there tonight to bring your precious words to life. 'The bigger they are, the harder they fall on me.' When did you come up with that winner?"

"Busting your hump? You barely had to move! You came out, sat down, read your part, then stood and took a bow. It's not like you were writhing in agony like Antonin Artaud up there."

"Believe me, I was writhing in agony inside," Gleason said, giving his chest a good thump. "You just couldn't see it, because you were hiding in the hallway."

As I was trying to think of a good comeback, an academic gentleman in a white turtleneck approached and introduced himself as Leonard Mitchelson, a producer and board member of the Manhattan Theater Guild. Assisted by a bald head, he was one of those men who professionally beam. "Congratulations seem to be in order to both of you," he said, rocking on his heels.

"Thanks," I said.

"Yeah, thanks," Gleason seconded.

"So is *Learn to Duck* your first effort?"

"It sure is."

"I enjoyed the way the characters deconstructed each other's narratives."

"Yeah, me too!" I said, and Mitchelson laughed.

"Kate looks as if she needs rescuing," Gleason said abruptly. "You two try not to lather each other up."

After an awkward pause, Mitchelson and I traded a few more cordial pleasantries and exchanged business cards. He paid me another compliment on the play before leaving to say hello-goodbye to Phil. As if to the sound of trumpets, Claudia walked in with her date, who ran a finger in a quick zip under his nose lest there be any doubt he had done a line of coke in the limo. With a tap of her hand she dispatched him to the bar. Ignoring everyone else, she made straight for me, which I found shamefully flattering, and gave me an enthusiastic cheek press, which would have represented a kiss to most bystanders. I complimented Claudia on her outfit.

"You don't think it's too much?"

"I have spots dancing before my eyes, but they'll go away."

"We have another party to go to tonight, so I decided to err on the side of extravagance. But I wanted to tell you two things before I dip into the champagne. One, I really liked your play. It had so much more *texture* than I expected. It didn't sound like TV, the way most things do these days. The other is, that although she couldn't make it tonight, Amanda wanted me to tell you she appreciated the apology note you sent. She still thinks you behaved badly, but at least you owned up to it."

"How is she?"

"She's dating an older man she met antiquing. I think they may even get married, though it would mean moving to Virginia. He has a horse farm there."

"That sounds like it would suit her. Claudia, can I spring something on you? Don't say yes or no right now, just hear me out."

Finding herself the object of a proposal, Claudia flashed a look of Venetian intrigue and stepped away from the gaggle of people standing near her. When no one else was in listening range, I said: "Tonight I realized, when I saw all those guys on stage, that what I had been resisting all along is true—we need a woman on stage. Otherwise the play is going to look like a Teamsters meeting. What I'm considering doing, and admittedly I'm thinking aloud, is rewriting Green's part for *you*, making you the group leader, a shrink maybe. It would give the piece a whole different dynamic and would change the chemistry of the cast. Men want to impress you, Claudia. They're also intimidated by you. I want that."

"Will Green go along with losing the 'padre' role?"

"It'll take some sweet-talking on my part, but he's been complaining that I've made his character too namby-pamby, too much of a referee. I'll make him one of the angries, and you could be the play's resident dominatrix. Come on, you know that's what you've always wanted!"

"Down, boy. Well, let me think about it. Dorian and I are going away for a few weeks, so we'll talk when we get back. You know, I'm now a personal shopper at Bergdorf's. It's good money, decent hours, I don't have to work in rat traps, and I'm just not sure how committed I am to acting anymore. When you're away from it awhile, it seems all the more absurd. Then again, I've never had anyone write anything specifically for me before. It's kind of exciting. But I better not get too excited—we don't want to make your girlfriend jealous."

"I don't think she's the jealous type."

"Johnny, you fool, any woman interested in a man is the jealous type. You should have seen the look she gave me when I swanned in. If you don't mind, I want to go say hello to Phil Green."

"Compliment his performance and tell him how much you'd love the opportunity to work with him. Plant the seed in his mind."

"You're getting so cunning."

"You have to be, in this racket. Listen, he'd much rather rehearse with you than listen to Gleason and Watson swap lies all day. That silver lamé dress alone should persuade him. I can't believe you're dating someone named Dorian. It's too perfect."

"Now, now. Off I go. We'll talk soon." Claudia raised her hand to my chin and planted a kiss on my cheek, a slow kiss that seemed to have a torrid history behind it that had cooled into fond regret. Then she met her date as he approached her with drinks in both hands, and steered him toward Phil Green and his fan club. The fan club parted to grant Claudia admittance. I withdrew a handkerchief and wiped the lipstick from my cheek, not that there was much to wipe. Under a grape-bunch of balloons, Annette pressed the button that retracted the lens of her compact camera, tucked it into her pocketbook, and grabbed a glass of champagne from the nearest tray. She came up to me with some iron in her step and said: "Any other shots you want taken?"

"No, my angel."

"Don't 'angel' me. I saw you and witchy-woman."

"We were talking business, believe it or not. Besides, it's your fault for abandoning me for so long. I blame you."

"I didn't want to intrude. After all, this is your big night."

"It's *our* big night," I said.

Annette tilted her head to take me in, running various calculations on her internal computer. "Is it?" she asked.

Some questions supply their own answers. We moved from the center of the room to one of the windows, where we talked about everything but how and where the evening would end. When Annette finished her champagne, I took the glass from her and left it on the sill next to mine and led her by the hand away from the window toward the stairs. Along the way I said a swift good-bye to Green, thanking him again for the party, waved to Gleason and Kate, who appeared to be on the verge of a quarrel, shook hands with Watson and Mullin, and scattered a few other good-byes. We stopped at the coatcheck for Annette's wrap. Behind us, a couple discussed their recent trip to Brussels, where it had been overcast.

After the coatcheck girl presented Annette with her wrap, I said: "I believe Miss Bennett has something else to claim."

"I only brought a wrap," Annette said.

From behind her half-door, the coatcheck girl smiled and brought forth something in green tissue paper. It was a single long-stemmed white rose I'd picked out at the florist. Darlene had always recommended ordering a dozen and a half, but I thought that big a bunch would be awkward for Annette to carry. I opted for simplicity.

"This is for you," I said, offering it to her.

As I tipped the coatcheck girl, Annette parted the wrapping and put her nose to the soft petals. "It's beautiful," she said. "I've never had any-one do anything this—"

"Romantic?"

"I was going to say 'thoughtful.' But in this case both words mean the same."

Once we were outside and on to the street, the night air seemed charged and alive, carrying secret waves of crosstown messages. We reached the curb. The passing cars were like moving sounds. Everything seemed larger, the buildings, the sky. Although we had kissed before, I felt as if this was the first one that carried consequences, and I wanted to get it right. I lay my hand on the side of her head, bringing her mouth to mine for a long, submerged kiss, followed by two short ones, our faces separating with a silent wow. When the lights changed and it was okay to cross, I shifted around to Annette's other side, putting myself between her and possible traffic. She didn't need my protection, but it seemed the appropriate thing to do. As we crossed, I said, "So what did you think of the party tonight?"

"It was okay, but not as much fun as the one you threw, the one where you and I first met. That was the first thing I found attractive about you, how concerned you were that everything go well. You real-ly put your heart into being a good host."

"Maybe I was showing off, knowing you were watching."

"No, you weren't thinking about me that night. You had someone else on your mind. I could tell."

Rather than claim otherwise, I said to Annette, "She's history now."

The restored awning of my apartment building jutted into view. Just a few more steps, and we'd be there.

48

ONCE CLAUDIA ACCEPTED the group-leader role, everything snapped into place. She brought a sexy friction to the play that had been lacking when it was just the guys locking antlers. Lounging on the sofa with a yellow legal pad to sketch out my ideas, I had a bolt of inspiration that nearly made my head launch from my neck, an idea that must have been bubbling in my unconscious all along. I would write Claudia's role in the voice of Darlene. I would meld them together into one unforgettable monster. I pictured Darlene, petite in size, big in bravado, riding roughshod over the anger-management group, listening to their war stories with barely a nod of patience or empathy, topping their searing confessions with, "Aw, man, that's nothing. I had a client once who . . ." Just as Darlene maintained files on her friends, Claudia/Darlene would have a dossier on every man in the group, a manila folder with his name on it. A bad report, and they could end up behind bars. That way, each time she scribbled notes during a session, she might be sealing someone's fate. Once I started channeling Darlene, my pencil was whizzing across the page. Claudia's dialogue crackled, as if she were thinking at twice the speed of everyone else. To complete the identity switch, I even named her character Darlene.

At first, Phil Green was dubious and reluctant about surrendering the group-leader role, but he relented once he saw what a lifelong reprobate I had made of his new character. Without any prompting from me, Claudia paid a personal call on him in which she said she never even would have *considered* my offer if she thought it would upset him in any way, an actor for whom she had such respect and high esteem.

"I hope you didn't lay it on too thick," I said.

"Johnny, please. I studied at Juilliard. I laid it on *just right.*"

Word circulated about Claudia's involvement, creating a buzz for the second reading at Actors Arena, which went over with a blaze, if I do say so myself. This time, I didn't have to assume the fetal position in my seat—I was able to kick back and enjoy the show like everybody else. Claudia's wicked critiques of the role-plays—the two guys stranded on their feet as she dissects their performance—were like Darlene's Greatest Hits. They turned the play into theater-within-theater, which the audience of mostly actors appreciated like mad. After the reading, I got to talking with the *Code of Silence* producer I had run into at brunch. After teasing me about the bug-exterminator ad I had done, he asked if I might be interested in doing a script on spec for a new police series that would be shooting in New York. When I told him I didn't know how to write for TV, he said, "Nobody does. Don't think of it as TV. Look at *NYPD Blue.* Take away that jittery camera, and it's essentially a play set in a precinct house. You can pick up the cop lingo in about five minutes, and what you can't pick up, you make up. Do you think real Baltimore cops riff like the guys on *Homicide*?"

"Actually, I grew up near Baltimore, and I don't recall hearing any of the troopers discussing karma at great length."

"Well, there you go."

"Just once," I said, "I'd like to see an interrogation scene in a cop show where the detectives didn't browbeat, yell, and manhandle the perps. Where the interrogator was all sweet and seductive, but sneaky underneath, instead of the usual 'You stick to that story, crabface, and you'll be cleaning toilets at Rikers with your sister's blouse!' Maybe make him gay. That would be a nice twist."

"Write me something like that. These guys in your play could easily translate into cops. I just wish I could steal that woman from you."

"You mean Claudia, or the character she plays?"

"The character, Darlene. She's got a real, hard coat of shellac. She's like a hot-rod girl with an education. But the truth is, she wouldn't translate to TV unless we could see her vulnerabilities emerge over time, those sad moments when she's all alone, nursing a private hurt. And that becomes such a bore."

"True. And besides, Darlene's mine, you can't have her. Don't you think Gleason would make a good TV cop?"

"Actually, I'd like to talk to him about a perp role he might be interested in reading for, a suspected pedophile who works as a janitor in a Catholic school."

That sounded like something up Gleason's alley. I could almost see him wringing dirty water out of a mop into a pail and giving students the fishy eye.

"Then let me introduce you two," I said. "I wouldn't want this opportunity to get away."

49

ONE AUTUMN AFTERNOON Annette and I were comparing and contrasting blue splotches on my living-room wall. Taped next to the splotches were paintstore chips identifying the colors.

"I like that shade on the far upper right," I said, stroking Annette's back. She was wearing cut-off jeans, one of my old shirts, and a headband to keep her bangs out of her eyes.

"That's Duck Egg Blue," Annette said. "It's calming, but I think I like the Baby's Breath better."

To me, they all looked like different pieces of the same sky, but I nodded as if the Baby's Breath had a distinction I could now appreciate.

"Once we paint these walls it'll make such a difference," Annette said. "And we can repaint if we're not happy with it."

I embraced her from behind and we stared at the blue patches together. A crow cawed from the bell tower of St. Teresa's. It had been raining earlier, but had stopped. "Have you given any thoughts to what color curtains?" Annette asked.

Curtains. Paint chips. Fabric swatches. Words to strike fear into any bachelor's heart. But I guess I was no longer a bachelor at heart because all I said was, "Gold might go well with that blue."

"Gold might be nice," she said with a teaspoon of doubt. "But I think we'll stick with white. That was my original conception."

"If your mind was set on white, then why did you ask me which color I preferred?"

"Because I *value* your opinion," Annette said, patting my chest as if humoring a mental invalid. "The real question is how long we want the curtains to hang. To the floor, or pooling on the floor."

"I'll let you and your crack team of scientists handle that one."

"White curtains against that blue will make the room seem suspended in air."

"Great, we can float by and wave to one another."

The phone rang. I thought it might be the *Code of Silence* director, getting back to me on the script I had submitted. It wasn't. I didn't recognize the voice at first.

"Hey, Johnny, it's me."

"Me who?"

"Darlene. I know it's been a spell."

My face and posture must have acquired instant *gravitas*, because Annette, using sign language, asked if she should leave the room and give me privacy. I shrugged no, but she left anyway, retiring to the bathroom to wash paint from her hands, judging from the amount of water gushing.

"So what's up?" I said. I didn't know what tone to take with Darlene. I wasn't overjoyed to hear from her, given the ugly snarl of our last conversation, but I also no longer held a grudge. I'm not good at staying mad at people, and I had made my peace with Darlene when I popped her into the play, putting the genie in a different bottle. Darlene's voice sounded shaky, but I couldn't tell if it was genuine nerves or something exaggerated for effect, to gain sympathy and/or get me to drop my guard. I decided to reserve judgment and just listen, like the guidance counselor she had always encouraged me to emulate.

"As you know, it's not easy for me to admit when I've been wrong, since I almost never am, but I figure I owe you one. An apology, I mean."

"What for?"

"When I got back from my trip after that last phone call, I found the birthday card from you waiting in the mailbox. You know, the one with the bats on it. I realized you hadn't forgotten my birthday after all, but by then I was so spitting mad at you for busting me about Bud that no way was I going to call and backtrack. So that's basically why I called, to put that right. It's been bugging me."

"Don't tell me you've got a conscience?"

"I must have, because it's been working overtime. I was also curious about how you've been doing. Caroline told me Slinky died. I was sorry to hear it, after all the flak I gave you."

"She had a peaceful death," I said, closing that topic. Lowering my voice so Annette wouldn't overhear, I said, "I do have one bit of news about someone we used to know. Nicole got married."

"How'd you find out? Did she tell you?"

"No, I saw the announcement in the *Times*. She married someone in her firm. You should have seen the photo. Instead of having them with their heads side by side, they were posed on top of each other, her chin resting on his head. They looked like a nightclub act."

"Just think: that could have been you! Anyway, she's doing better than I am. Maybe Caroline told you already, but Bud and I broke up a while ago. He went back to his wife. It was an ugly breakup, which I managed to make even more memorable when I got arrested for driving my car onto his front yard and trying to ram his porch. The charges were dropped, but I sort of lost it afterward, and moved back home with my mother. I even put on a little weight, which, of course, did wonders for my self-esteem.

"I recently met this guy I really like a lot but nothing seems to be gelling. I can't get a handle on him. I kept wanting to call you, get your feed on the male side of the equation, since you know exactly what another guy would be thinking in most situations. I can't tell if I'm wasting time with this boyfriend or not. I don't want my heart broken again. Besides, next time I go crazy and try to drive my car into somebody's house I'll lose my license for good. They only suspended it this time, and I had to walk to the damned Seven-Eleven every day for Mom's cigarettes and lottery tickets for three months. I never want to go through *that* again. How's your grandmother?"

"Pushing an air tank around and making everyone's life difficult. Darlene, no offense, but I haven't heard from you in ages. How do I know this isn't a trap? How do I know you won't take down everything I say and stick it into one of your dossiers? For all I know, Bud may be there with you this very moment, flicking a toothpick in his mouth."

"He's not here. Whatever you may think of my character or lack thereof, you know I had to swallow a helluva lot of pride to call you and ask for help. For all I knew, you could've hung up on me in a huff, or yelled, or made fun of me for getting dumped. I took a chance calling you, and all I'm asking is that you take a similar chance on me. *I know you have a new girlfriend and don't need me anymore. I can hear the water running in the next room. You're not the one who's alone now."*

The bathroom water stopped. Annette leaned against the hallway entrance, drying her hands in my presence and trying not to look overly inquisitive.

"I can't really talk right now," I said. "—I'm in the middle of decorating. But why don't I call you tonight and we'll try to figure out whether or not this guy is worthy of you?"

"She's standing there, isn't she?"

"Yes, she is."

"It's that photographer, isn't it?"

"Yes, it is."

"Is it serious?"

"Uh-hum."

"I guess all my coaching actually finally paid off."

Stealing a look at Annette, I said, "I like to think that I won her over with my charm, confidence, and rugged good looks. Communication, that's the key."

And at that, all three of us started laughing.